Magical Midlife Love

Also by K.F. Breene

LEVELING UP
Magical Midlife Madness
Magical Midlife Dating
Magical Midlife Invasion
Magical Midlife Love
Magical Midlife Meeting (coming soon)

DEMIGODS OF SAN FRANCISCO
Sin & Chocolate
Sin & Magic
Sin & Salvation
Sin & Spirit
Sin & Lightning
Sin & Surrender

DEMON DAYS VAMPIRE NIGHTS WORLD
Born in Fire
Raised in Fire
Fused in Fire
Natural Witch
Natural Mage
Natural Dual-Mage
Warrior Fae Trapped
Warrior Fae Princess
Revealed in Fire (coming soon)

FINDING PARADISE SERIES
Fate of Perfection
Fate of Devotion

MAGICAL MIDLIFE LOVE

BY K.F. BREENE

Contact info:
www.kfbreene.com
books@kfbreene.com

CHAPTER 1

W HO WAS COMING to stab me?

I stood stock-still next to the newly closed winery tasting room at the end of the town's main street, wrapping my gargoyle magic around me like Jasper had taught me, trying to blend into the building. Hard-eyed men and women walked down the sidewalk on the other side of the street, their movements full of lethal grace. It didn't take a genius to know they were part of Austin's budding pack.

Was one of them wielding the knife?

An older woman walked down the sidewalk my way, and I controlled my breathing and sucked in my gut, pushing against the wall. Neither of those things were necessary for the gargoyle magic to kick in, but given I couldn't get the hang of disappearing, I figured it wouldn't hurt.

The strap of her purse slung across her full breasts and rested on the side of her soft stomach. Each relaxed hand was empty. No weapons were strapped to her thighs or her back. Not like that was a normal thing in the middle of town, but still...

Out of shape, older, no weapons—she didn't look dangerous. Which made her exactly the sort of person Jasper would hand a knife to and set on my trail. The rules I'd created for this particular training exercise were brutal. If whomever Jasper had set on me found me, I'd have to just stand there like an idiot while they jabbed me in a spot my magic could heal. I'd had Jasper pick the assailant so I wouldn't be able to cheat and hide if I saw them coming.

The two people he'd chosen for the previous weeks had found me, and their apologies hadn't meant much when the knife was going in. This was my third attempt.

I would do it this time, I could feel it!

The woman paused two buildings down. I concentrated a little harder on blending into my surroundings. My stomach churned.

Jasper had said I'd get a feeling in my gut—was this it? Or was I just anxious about getting stabbed?

She bent to a half wine barrel filled with blooming zinnias, marigolds, and morning glories; bright pops of color. Spring was moving into O'Briens, soft and sweet and lovely. Spring break was next week, and my son was coming to stay.

I hadn't seen Jimmy in person in over six months. A

wave of excitement rolled through me, but I squashed it down, trying to focus.

"Well, well, well…"

I snapped my head away from the woman, only to see my nemesis approaching.

Sasquatch, whose real name I had forgotten in favor of the name I'd given him, had shaggy, greasy hair sticking out at all angles, a scraggly beard reaching down past his neck, and clothes covered in stains. He stopped near me, and the smell of feet wafted up from his well-worn black boots.

We'd been at odds since my first night in town— he'd made a disparaging comment to me at the bar, and Austin had punched him clear off his stool. The pattern had repeated itself plenty of times since.

I narrowed my eyes at him. "Get out of here. I'm busy."

"Busy with what? Standing around looking useless? You do that all the time; why is now any different?" His eyes darted to the older woman down the way, just straightening up.

Was Sasquatch in the know? Jasper usually picked my opponents from the bar, which was Sasquatch's second home. Since no one willingly talked to him, he listened in on everyone else's conversations. Maybe he'd heard Jasper hire the woman…

Regardless, I clearly needed to find a new place and try again. If this idiot could see me, the whole town could.

I stepped away from the wall. "Get out of my way."

He stepped with me, a smug grin on his face.

My world drained of color as he reached around to his rear jeans pocket. His muscles loosened and then contracted, a pocketknife coming around in his stubby fingers. He pulled out the blade.

"Oh no," I breathed, freezing. "No…"

I could magically blast him like a bug. I could unravel his skin from his bones and let his blood leak down onto the sidewalk. I'd been afraid of him once, but now that I'd mastered (most of) my Ivy House magic, he was nothing more than a nuisance.

Still, there were rules. I couldn't retaliate.

A jack-o'-lantern grin slid across his face. "Oh yes. *Yes.*"

His knuckles whitened on the hilt.

"Why'd he pick you?" I asked through numb lips, looking between that knife, the blade a bit dirty and rusted, and his awful smile.

"Right place at the right time." His eyes twinkled with malice.

"You'll pay for this," I seethed.

"No I won't. I accepted an approved job."

The older woman passed us by, her pleasant smile turning to a look of alarm when she noticed the knife. I'd picked a terrible location to fail at my magic. With any luck she was magical, and the only person she'd tattle to was Austin. I didn't feel like lying to the police. Again.

"If you hit back, it'll be against town law, and the alpha will have to put you in your place. He's made it very clear he doesn't play favorites. He won't ruin his reputation by ignoring an attack on one of his people..." Sasquatch's smile was triumphant. "Not even for you."

I gritted my teeth. With hard work, plus help from Austin and Edgar—gardener, vampire, amateur doily maker, and interpreter of Ivy House's magical books—I had turned the tide in my magical ability. Austin and I were now about even in power. If he tried to cow me for knocking this dirty butthead around, it would be a well-matched battle.

I didn't want to put Austin in that position, though. His pack was barely contained chaos right now. Or so Niamh had told me. He had said he needed space from our friendship, which kept skirting the line of something more, and although we trained together every day, we hadn't had a conversation that wasn't directly related to training in a month and a half. Niamh, on the other hand, still visited his bar nearly every night, and she kept me up to date on the latest goings-on. Everyone had heard rumors of the great Austin Steele, the fierce polar bear shifter alpha, and shifters were flocking to O'Briens from all over the U.S. and Canada—some even came from other continents. They came to bask in his power, to (hopefully) share in his prestige. And some of them simply came to satisfy their curiosity, wondering if the rumors were true. Wondering if he couldn't be beaten.

Whenever someone challenged Austin Steele, that curiosity was quickly sated.

His primary objective in securing this territory was to protect me. He was building a castle around my keep. I would not spit in his face by going against the laws that he needed to uphold to run this town. He was my alpha here, just as I was his alpha on Ivy House soil.

"You may not pay for this now, but you *will* pay for it," I ground out, fisting my hands, bracing myself. "I'll find a way that doesn't violate the town law."

"Yeah, right. Whatever."

Terror constricted my chest as he shifted his weight and poised. His muscles bunched and that knife sped toward me, choking me up. The point pierced my side, a momentary flare of bright white pain before I snubbed out the feeling with magic. The blade squelched as he drove it all the way in, the hilt bumping against the circle of crimson quickly expanding on my white shirt.

There he paused, his glinting eyes connecting with mine. I distantly felt Austin drawing nearer, walking up the street, but the usual fluttering of my stomach was absent. Because I had a blade embedded it.

"Well?" I asked quietly, anger flowering in my middle. "Do you plan to pull it out, or are you trying to give me rust poisoning?"

"That's not even a thing for magical people, *Jane*." He let go of the hilt and pulled his hand back, joy soaking into his features even as blood soaked my shirt. He clearly didn't intend on pulling the knife out himself.

I didn't feel the blade, and I was already working on damage control with my healing magic, but that didn't stop the primal part of me from cringing in dread. A deep part of me still connected a stabbing with a grave. My mind edged into survival mode, each second that dangerous weapon stayed lodged in my flesh pumping out another wave of adrenaline.

I could easily pull it out, sure. I wouldn't feel it. But half the time it didn't hurt to work out splinters, either, and digging those out with a sewing needle had always been beyond me.

"Pull it out," I said through clenched teeth, my

hands shaking, not daring to look down at it again. "There's nothing in the rules about you getting to leave the knife in."

"Exactly. There's nothing in the rules about leaving the knife in…or pulling it out, either." Sasquatch just looked at me with that awful smile, enjoying my turmoil.

"The game is over." Austin's deep, rich baritone washed over me. I'd lost track of his approach.

Sasquatch jolted as though struck, his spine snapping ramrod straight, his beer belly popping out. He hadn't noticed Austin coming at all. A moment later, he bent like a dying reed, drooping over and reaching for the knife.

"No, no!" I slapped his hand away, my reflexes faster than they'd ever been. My body stronger, too. Austin wasn't just training me in magic. "Careful!"

Sasquatch staggered to the side before lunging back at me. "Alpha said the thing is done. Give me my knife!"

"Don't grab like that. You'll make it worse." I slapped his hand away again and sent a tiny blast of magic to shove him back.

He flew off his feet and sailed ass over end toward the building, his back hitting first, his head pointed toward the ground. My power kept growing, and every time I thought I had a handle on my range, I went and blasted someone across the room. Or down the sidewalk, as the case may be. Oh well. It probably wasn't the first time he'd been dropped on his head.

"Oops. Too much power," I said.

Sasquatch struggled to his feet, hand to his cranium. He pointed a finger at me. "You saw her, alpha. She assaulted me. Aggressively! She broke the law. Punish her."

Austin stepped back into the gutter. Power throbbed off his robust body. Hard eyes surveyed us from a harder face. This was Austin the alpha, not my friend and trainer. He was hearing a complaint from someone in his territory and discerning its merit before he reached a verdict. He was police, judge, and jury in this town, and he couldn't afford to let someone upset the extremely precarious balance right now.

But then...I wasn't in the habit of letting people beat me up, either.

This might be bad.

CHAPTER 2

"**S**HE HAS A knife sticking out of her body and she worried you'd do further damage by carelessly yanking it out." Austin's eyes sparked with danger. "Every magical person in town is aware of her power situation. You should've known how your fumbling would be received. This matter is over."

The commanding tone had Sasquatch stepping back, uncertainty and fear on his face. "Okay, but…"

Austin looked down on him, unblinking. His power throbbed once, twice, daring Sasquatch to push back. Darkness bubbled just under the surface of his eyes.

"It's just…" Sasquatch pointed at the knife lamely, reminding me it was still there. Reminding me that a *knife* was lodged in my *stomach* and blood was seeping down my side. "I need my knife back."

"Possession is nine-tenths of the law, and currently it's in her possession," Austin replied.

"Finders keepers," I muttered miserably, looking at the hilt with my hands spread to the sides. My mind swam. I wasn't sure if it was from blood loss or the prolonged dumping of adrenaline into my blood, or maybe my mind was convincing my body that it should be in shock.

"Go," Austin growled, and Sasquatch took off running, grabbing the waist of his pants as he did so, apparently worried they'd slip down and show his cheeks.

"Except I still have a knife sticking out of me." I swayed.

Austin quickly stepped closer, and his warm hand grasped my shoulder.

"It's okay," he crooned, his tone soft and comforting, a complete one-eighty from a moment ago. "I got it."

I met his eyes, soaking in that beautiful cobalt blue.

"I didn't mean to retaliate against him," I said, holding his shoulders for stability. It was like gripping two large boulders. "I was trying to get him to step back."

"You seem to forget that I've been on the other end of that sort of accident a few times."

"It's just…I know you're under a lot of pressure to keep everyone from killing each other here. I didn't mean to add to that."

His gaze dipped to my tongue sliding across my lower lip. "Jess, you don't have to apologize. I know exactly what happened. I watched the whole thing. I was at the other end of the street when he first caught sight of you. If I weren't officially alpha now, I would've told him to get lost. Being the alpha, I had to at least appear to weigh both sides."

"I thought you didn't play favorites."

"I don't. But I also don't listen to whiners who delight in stabbing beautiful women."

I smiled at him, my heart warming.

"Does it hurt?" he asked softly, his hand near the knife, getting ready to pull it out.

I squeezed my eyes shut so I wouldn't accidentally look down and see. Unlike with a splinter, you couldn't just leave the knife in until it worked itself out.

"No. I think I've mastered my healing magic. It's just..." I blew out a breath. "My brain is bleating in panic every time I think about it. I have a knife sticking in me, man! For forty years I've lived with the idea that being stabbed is a potentially life-threatening situation. It's hard to ignore that just because I don't feel the wound. It's hard to get used to. People in shock don't feel things either. Shock means something very bad has happened to you. I can't—"

"I'll handle it, okay?" His breath dusted my face, spearmint and something sweet.

"Did you eat cake? I could use a slice of cake. I haven't had cake in…" I trailed away, wondering what the hell was taking him so long. Just yank it out, already!

I flinched at the thought.

"Listen," he said, his voice still so soft, so comforting. "I wanted to talk to you about the winery."

As in the winery he'd asked me to buy and run with him. The arrangements had already been made, but what if he'd changed his mind? Did he think it was a bad idea for us to work together?

A wave of worry washed through me, and I blinked my eyes open to see his expression.

His hand moved so fast that I didn't register it. He grabbed the hilt and yanked.

I cried out, bending in anticipation of a pain I didn't feel.

A gush of warmth soaked my shirt and then dribbled onto the lip of my jeans. Deep crimson coated the blade in Austin's hand before he dropped it to the ground and pressed his palm against my wound, bracing his other hand against my back, using pressure to stanch the blood flow. Shifters healed fast, and I healed faster—when I was on my game—but for a handful of heartbeats, magical people bled like anyone else.

"Sorry, I just mentioned the winery for distraction purposes." Austin grimaced at me, and his smell permeated my world, clean cotton and sweet spice.

"I'm good." I touched the corded muscle of his bare forearm. "The worst is over." I glanced down at the knife. "Do you really tell people about my magic?"

"Absolutely. Everyone is warned. I make it very clear that I can't control you any more than you can control yourself. People are instructed to leave you alone, and if they don't, they must take what comes. They also know that your property is not part of my territory, and if they trespass, I cannot help them."

I widened my eyes at him, back to gripping his flaring shoulders while he pressed against my wound. "But Sasquatch said…"

"Ryan just doesn't seem to learn his lesson."

I tapped his hands. "I'm good now. Thank you."

He slowly pulled his hands away, not seeming to notice the flare of crimson staining his palm. "I don't like this game, by the way," he said, a growl working into his words. "I don't like you placidly allowing people to hurt you. If they hit wrong, they could kill you before you could do damage control."

"I have Jasper pick people because he's a good judge of character. He usually picks more trustworthy people, though. He either didn't know that Sasquatch and me—"

"He knew. He's trying to push you, I think."

"Ah." I frowned down the street, noticing Jasper

lounging against the wall, easily blending into the building behind him, utterly invisible to everyone except for me because I could see through a gargoyle's glamor-like magic. Magic I could not figure out how to apply to myself.

"It's not working." Austin turned before gently placing his hand on the small of my back, guiding me down the street. He scooped up the knife as we went. "I know I said I'd defer to your judgment of what you can handle, but with all due respect, just because you can handle it, doesn't mean you should."

I sighed with frustration. "I keep hoping it'll work."

A man walked toward us with effortless grace and hard gray eyes. Shifter. "Alpha," he said as he approached, stepping into the street and offering a slight bow. "Miss."

"Damn that Mr. Tom," I grumbled, Austin ignoring the man completely. It was apparently an alpha custom to ignore greetings from townspeople and pack members. "He keeps convincing people to call me miss instead of just letting them call me by my name."

"He wants you to have some semblance of a title. It isn't a terrible idea."

"Don't you start. Turning this town into a big shifter pack is your thing. You need the title; I don't. I'm just a home owner."

"The owner of the most powerful magical home in the world, with the ability to create your own army if you so choose."

"Okay, okay, let's settle down. No more reading up on the history of Ivy House and its heirs. This is modern times—if I created an army, I'd have the government swooping in, thinking I was a terrorist. Besides, I'm not trying to form some magical empire. I just want to defend my home." I smoothed my hair back, lowering my brows at him. We slowed to a stop on the corner. "You know what I meant, though. No more asking Edgar about the history of the house. It's giving you crazy ideas."

He looked away. "I ask Edgar because I need to know the ins and outs of what I am guarding."

"You don't. *I* do." I looked off toward the house crouching in its wood, not visible from the town's hub. "There's a list of vulnerabilities I don't understand and don't have the knowledge or magic to work out."

"No sign of anyone to fill that summons?"

I'd sent out a magical summons, asking for a mage who could help me. Over a dozen had shown up, trickling in with their swagger and egos. One practice session, though, and each and every one of them had been fired or quit. None of them had been powerful enough to work with me.

Most of the mages had assumed (wrongly) that I would know some of the basics of spell casting, based on my age alone. I'd changed their perception quickly.

I'd nearly blown off a mansplainer's head by accident. He'd stopped 'splaining real quick and got the hell out of there. I'd almost killed another, thankfully able to patch him up before all of his blood leaked out. He'd accused me of tricking him…while sobbing. A woman had admitted she wasn't the right fit after losing half of her robe to a spell gone wrong.

My power blindsided them, one and all. My complete lack of knowledge widened their eyes. My haywire spells sent them running.

I'd had to devise a test to weed out the duds.

I'd rigged up a spell to send applicants to Agnes's shop. Once there, she'd instruct them on how to create the spell capable of hiding them from Ivy House's detection. The challenge was to ingest the spell, mosey onto my property, and knock on the door. Simple as that.

Many had tried. All had failed.

"Nope," I said, dabbing at the garnet stain ruining my shirt. I probably should've worn black today. I'd really thought I'd get it this time, though. I'd hoped to show everyone my clean white shirt with a triumphant smile. "Five came last week. I doubt they're even from the summons anymore. I think word has gotten out that there's an open mage position and people are just showing up to apply. Three of them were able to make the potion, but not well enough to mask their heat signatures from Ivy House. She booted them off the property with the new trap Edgar installed."

Austin shook his head slightly. "You guys and that house…"

"We're not normal, I know."

"No, you are not. Effective, but not normal." He paused for a moment. "Yes, it's probably word of mouth at this point, which is why only the lesser mages are coming to apply. More established mages might've ignored the summons entirely, if they're happy where they are." Austin's upper body tightened up, his pecs popping through his shirt as his biceps strained the white cotton, flexing so as to prevent himself from releasing tension through a physical tic, like running his fingers through his hair. He'd had to make some changes since assuming the alpha role.

"What did you want to do that you can't do any-more?" I teased.

His gaze zipped to me and then away. His lips quirked, but he gritted his teeth again, his face in hard lines that somehow didn't detract from his handsome-ness. "It's not that I can't anymore. It's that you loosen me up too much and I forget my place."

"Your place... At the top?"

His gaze connected with mine, this time digging in, primal and dominant. A zip of excitement tore through me, and I felt loose and tight at the same time. A feeling, I fully realized, that was not the way a person was supposed to feel with a *friend*.

"Yes," he said.

"And why can't you smile and...tuck your fingers into your belt?"

"I wasn't going to tuck my fingers into my belt, and it's because I have a reputation to uphold."

"The reputation of a grumpy guy who wants to...scratch his chest?"

"The reputation of a hardass who won't stand for anyone stepping out of line. If you show weakness as a dominant figure, someone will prey on it. And no, I did not want to scratch my chest."

"How is smiling or...running your fingers through your hair...?"

His eyes crinkled. "Caught me."

I laughed. "How is that a sign of weakness? I don't get it. People who allow themselves to feel and show emotion are not weak. They're stronger, actually."

"Honestly, I don't know why, but when an alpha is too nice, too easy, too expressive...he or she gets an increased number of challenges. People see me loosening up as a green light for them to do the same, and for violent people, that often takes the form of challenges and rowdy behavior."

"It means more work for you, basically."

"Exactly, yes."

"So you'll never smile again?"

Even though he must've known I was teasing, his expression turned uncomfortable and he shifted his body weight away from me. Looking toward the opposite side of the street, he said, "There are a few exceptions."

"Like...?" I rolled my hand in the air, not sure why he was forcing me to drag information out of him today. Of course, it had been a month and a half since we'd had a normal conversation, minus the rest of my demented Ivy House crew. Clearly he'd forgotten how.

He shifted his weight again, antsy to go. "Like when he's in private with those closest to him."

"But not in public?"

He paused for a beat. "In public, people only give exception to an alpha when he's with his mate or his offspring."

"Well, at least that's something. It would be hard to date if you couldn't laugh at your date's jokes."

"No." His tone was hard. "Not a date, a *mate*. It's a

magical bond that manifests physically, similar to the magical link we have from Ivy House but much deeper. More primal. It changes a man. It makes him less reasonable. Less logical." The full weight of his focus came back to me, punching through my humor and lightness like a steel mace. "People forgive an alpha for smiling with his mate or offspring because they know if they do anything that might harm them, even indirectly, the alpha will lose his mind and end the threat with unspeakable force. He will protect his own with everything in him. The smallest slight can turn into a bloodbath. It is safest for all to give an alpha leeway when he is with his mate or children."

I blinked, my eyes wide, his tone and bearing hostile and haunted.

"That woman from your past…she was your mate?"

"No. I thought she would be, at one time. The reason I acted out back then was because I was young and dumb and full of…" He stopped himself. "Even without that bond, though, I was a menace to society. Even without it, I put people in the hospital and nearly killed my brother. What do you think might've happened if she'd been my mate?"

I nodded slowly, watching him, aching for him. I could feel his pain through the magical link we shared. I tended to unblock it these days when talking to him, needing to feel his emotions to gauge what was behind that hard, expressionless mask.

"Gotcha," I said softly. "I'll be careful not to badger you into smiling in public. I assume it's fine on Ivy House soil, since that's not your territory?"

He watched me silently for a beat. His emotions flicked from one to the next so fast that they were just a jumble of *uncomfortable*. He finally nodded.

"Well, there you go, then. You just have to stay for a moment after training one of these days. I'll get Mr. Tom to tell you some jokes. He's got a few zingers. Of course, he doesn't realize they are jokes. Since he's the punch line and all."

He swore under his breath and looked away. "It's a lesson in self-restraint speaking with you. Anyway, listen, no biggie, but—" His muscles popped again and his jaw clenched.

I laughed and pointed at him accusingly. "Thumbs in belt loops!"

"Hands in pockets. I did actually want to talk to you about the winery. Mr. Tom sent through the check. He said you'd approved the expense. You still need to actually sign the paperwork. My lawyer is putting that together now. We'll be partners, fifty-fifty. Is that still good?"

I swallowed. "Yeah, good. Sounds good. My son is

coming for a couple days, but outside of that, I'm free…"

While I was glad he hadn't decided to back out after all, and supremely excited about Jimmy's visit, I felt weighed down by the memory of the house financial ledger splayed in front of me in the office. I'd never seen such large numbers in my life, and I was the one responsible for the estate. Which was fine—*beyond* fine—except the generous gift came with an unexpected commitment, something no one had thought to mention to me when they'd explained about the whole magic thing.

I'd finished mastering the first spell book Ivy House had provided for my training, and although we still had a ways to go in Book Two, it was time for me to claim the full gamut of my magic, apparently. But before that final burst of power was unleashed, I needed to give a blood oath—a blood oath!—to protect the house and the people in my circle. To officially become their protector and provider. To become a leader, like Austin was for his pack.

Once I made that oath, I'd be stuck in this position forever. *Forever.* There would be no divorce court to get me out of this one. No do-overs. I would literally be the heir of Ivy House until I died, and it would almost certainly be a bloody death.

Because one of the supposed upsides of the blood oath was that I (and my crew) would get to live forever. Given I was one of many heirs, it wasn't a leap in logic to realize my predecessors had all been killed, and that the same bloody fate was in store for me one day.

If I took the oath.

CHAPTER 3

"**H**OW'D YOU GET your son to come?" Austin asked, back to facing me again, bent a little to study my face.

I closed down the link between us so he wouldn't feel my churning emotions. He might want to talk about things. I most certainly did not.

"Easter break is coming up. He broke up with his girlfriend, so he's free." I rolled my eyes, but a grin broke through. I missed the little goblin terribly. Horribly! "I also think he got some pressure from his dad to come home. He's not really excited about meeting the new stepmom."

"Oh. Did your ex get remarried?"

I pulled up my shirt to check my blood-crusted skin. A small pink spot of crinkled skin was all that was left of the stab wound.

"No, but you know what I mean. The girlfriend. They're living together, so it's probably only a matter of time."

"Does that…hurt you?"

I furrowed my brow, looking at him, then scoffed at his expressionless face. "Do you think it should? This stoic thing you've got going on is annoying. I can't read you anymore." I tapped into the magical link again, feeling more confusion. Laughter burbled out of me. "No, it doesn't hurt me. Honestly, I don't really care one way or the other. I want him to be happy, and I hope he wants me to be happy. He and I didn't work out, and that's okay. I sincerely hope she's cool, because my son will be the one who suffers if not."

Austin nodded. "It's just that a lot of divorces end badly. There are hard feelings on one side or the other."

"I mean, we're not friends or anything. But I don't see the point in being bitter. I wouldn't change my past, and I'm happy where I've ended up. Mostly. Except for some…official house issues." I pushed away thoughts of that damned office and what was expected of me. "It took some hard times and some heartbreak, but that's life. The hard times make us appreciate the good times."

His focus was intense, his eyes rooted to mine, his body frozen.

"What?" I asked, suddenly uncomfortable. "Have I turned into one of those annoying *life is sublime* people or something? Too chirpy?"

A small smile flirted with his lips, and for once, he

didn't dampen it. "I continually look up to you, Jacinta. It feels like I never really learned the rules of being an adult, and you're teaching them to me, one by one."

"Good Lord, Austin, you're in trouble if you're getting life tips from me."

I gestured in the direction of Ivy House, silently asking if he would walk with me. For a moment, I thought he was going to say no—he glanced in the direction of the bar, indecision on his face—but finally he stepped forward.

"I'm a mess," I said, falling in step with him. "You *know* I'm a mess. You're the one that always builds me up when I'm wallowing."

He shook his head, glancing to his left, where Jasper shadowed us on the other side of the street.

"You can smell him from way over there?" I asked.

"Just barely. I can…sense him. That gargoyle can inflict some serious damage. I don't need to see or smell him to know he's there."

"Like a sixth sense? Women's intuition type of thing?"

"Exactly, yes. All animals and people have the innate, primal ability to sense danger. It's built into us. Women have to listen to it more than men because you are so often prey. Shifters are more in touch with their primal sides in general, so we pay attention to it. The best of us have cultivated the sense into a defensive measure."

"I don't need to ask if you rank yourself as one of the best."

"No, you don't. You already know that I am."

I shook my head. He wasn't putting on airs—he was stating a fact.

Something occurred to me. "Damn it. I bet Sasquatch smelled or felt me. That's how he knew I was there."

"No, he saw you. The whole street saw you."

"No one on the other side of the street looked at me," I argued. "Usually your people acknowledge my presence."

"They knew you were playing the game, though I really can't have people stabbing you in public, Jess. More magical people have moved into the area, but there are still a lot of Dicks and Janes. That's not something they should see. Please remember that in future. But anyway, my people were giving you space. It's not polite to point out someone's failures."

"Well." I huffed. "Maybe they could have acknowledged me so I'd know my magic wasn't working."

"That'd be cheating."

"You're quickly becoming my least favorite person."

He barked out a laugh before wrestling his features

back into submission.

I smiled as I watched. "You're going to have to beat up, like, five people after that outburst."

His lips tweaked before settling. "Probably."

I sighed, taking in the lovely late March day, the sun warm on my face and a cool, floral-scented breeze tickling my skin. "I'm out of my mind excited for my son to get here, but I'm trying to calm down. Just because of how it went with my parents, you know?"

"Are you going to tell him you're magical?"

"Yes. As soon as I get up my nerve. I won't be able to hide it, so I might as well... just hope he accepts it. I'm not allowing myself to worry that he'll..." I shook my head, not even voicing the thought. "He's always been a good kid and a mama's boy. Let's hope that's enough to keep him from..." I shook my head again, fear worming through me before I could shove it away.

"It'll go well." Austin rubbed my back as we walked. "Your parents were a tough situation, and that ended up just fine, even if they did assume you were the head of a cult."

I chuckled, comforted by the warmth seeping through his touch.

"When's he supposed to get here?" Austin asked, his hand slipping down to the small of my back.

"Tomorrow. That's why I canceled training. I'll

probably be sitting in the front room, pretending I'm not anxiously looking out the window every second."

"Well…" Austin stopped near the No Outlet sign at the corner of my street. "If you need anything, call me."

"Are we…" I pointed at him as he made to turn back. "Are we back to being friends, then?"

He didn't smile at my teasing. "You're one of the most important people in my life, Jess. We'll always be friends. I'll make sure nothing gets in the way of that."

"You need to lighten up."

"I'm the alpha. I don't lighten up." He winked at me, which I appreciated all the more because I knew it couldn't be on the approved list of social interactions.

"Can I ask a favor?" he said.

"Sure."

"I'll need to run some training exercises with the new pack members, see what I'm working with, and I wondered if I could use the Ivy House woods. I can feel people on the grounds better now, and it would be helpful to—"

"Of course. Just make sure to enter the grounds before the others so she knows not to harm them. And don't allow any stragglers. Ivy House is very moody lately, and she often acts before I can defuse the situation."

"How do you defuse the situation?"

"By taking control of the arsenal. It's like grabbing a plastic sword out of a child's hand so the kid doesn't thwap someone."

"I didn't know that was possible."

"It is once the heir has enough power and control."

Something glinted in his eyes, and I found myself tapping into our connection. His pride beamed through it, making my face heat. "Any idea how much power you have yet to…inherit?"

"I don't know how much is eventually coming, no. Edgar thinks I'm over halfway there because we've made it through the first book."

Austin's eyes crinkled, and that feeling of pride almost overwhelmed me. "I'll have to work hard to create a castle that is worthy of your keep."

I shrugged, my embarrassment flaring higher, although I wasn't sure why. "I need more instruction, though. The books only have so much. The instructions are literal, and there's not much room for reinterpretation or tweaking. I need a powerful teacher who can help me with nuances."

"It'll happen." He nodded to me. "You sent out that summons. The right mage will come." He took a step back, and his muscles popped once again. He gritted his teeth. "Hands in pockets," he murmured, taking another step back. "I have to get going. Text me when your son is around. I'd like to meet him. See if he's as crazy as his mother."

He gave me a brief smile before turning, clearly willing to beat up a few more people to give me a proper goodbye.

"He's conflicted about—"

Sensing another presence, I cut myself off and spun around, ballooning my magic around me even as I sent out a wave of power with a "Hah," chopping my hand through the empty air for emphasis. Once that would've been a ridiculous karate chop; now it was an unnecessary flourish.

Austin turned just in time to see Jasper go sailing, up over the stop sign and into the trees, catching halfway up before tumbling down, hitting a dozen or so branches before he splatted onto the dirt.

"Oh my God, are you okay?" I rushed to Jasper as Austin kept going, probably figuring it was just another day when dealing with me. He was right.

Jasper lay with his hands spread out to the sides, wheezing. "Sorry!" I said, sending a prod of magic to make sure nothing was broken or punctured. Finding he was just bruised, I quickly repaired the damage. "Are you okay?"

"You've taken away the pain. I am okay. Just…dazed."

"Okay." I rested my forearms on my knees as I looked down at him. He didn't make a move to rise. "Do you…" I bit my lip. "Should I help you up, or…"

He struggled to his side before pushing up onto his knees. "Was that punishment for using the hairy shifter in your training?"

I grabbed his arm and hauled him to his feet. "No. I was just distracted and didn't hear you creeping closer."

"Why use ears? You can feel me."

"Oh no—I could've sworn I told you, sorry. I usually block the links to give us all some privacy."

He braced his hands on his lower back and arched back, trying to stretch it out even though he couldn't feel the pain anymore. It gave me a little validation for my reaction to the stab wound.

"You've said you block it, yes." He nodded, dropping his arms. "But since it has never been blocked, I assumed I was still on trial."

I blinked at him for a moment. "What do you mean it isn't blocked? I'm blocking it right now. You shouldn't be able to feel my presence or emotions or anything. I can't feel yours…"

His dark eyebrows drew in. "I can still feel your presence and…confusion."

I blinked at him. He stared at me.

I pulled the block away, his confusion and wariness

immediately rushing in. "Is that any different?" I asked.

"Is what any different?"

Frustration boiled within me, and his wariness grew.

"You feel my emotions all the time?" I demanded.

He stiffened, and I could sense his anxiety through the link. He was stopping himself from stepping backward in the face of my anger. "Yes."

"Do you always feel it at the same strength? The feelings through the link never dim or anything?"

"I can't feel emotions when you're sleep, just your location or proximity. When you startle awake, it wakes me."

The heat drained from my face. "What about when…" I cleared my throat. "What about after I go to bed, but before I actually go to sleep. Like…late at night…"

"When you pleasure yourself? Yes, I feel that."

I could do nothing but stare. In mute horror.

Whatever he felt through the link got the words flowing.

"At first that confused me," he said, "since you did not express interest in bedding me. Then I thought maybe you were trying to pleasure me through the link. Only, it was just the feeling of pleasure and not actual pleasure, if that makes sense?" My expression clearly insinuated that it didn't. "I could sense *you* were feeling pleasure, but it wasn't directly manifesting into *my* pleasure. So I finally realized the link was like a two-way radio, and each person controlled the volume from their side."

This was the most he'd ever talked in my presence. He rarely said a couple of sentences jammed together, let alone a whole paragraph. This wasn't the subject I'd have chosen for him to find his voice.

"Please tell me you started turning the radio down during those times?" I whispered.

Wariness crowded the link now, so heavy that I felt like I was drowning in it.

"I didn't know I should," he responded. "Gargoyles are sexual beings. We share it freely. I thought…"

His words ceased at the shaking of my head, at the continued horror that was surely on my face. Not that he'd need the cue. He could apparently feel it.

I turned and headed for the house, my mind whirring.

"Do you know if it's the same with Ulric?" I asked.

"I have not asked," he said, falling in behind me.

It occurred to me that one or the other, Jasper or Ulric, was always out in the halls whenever I got up from a nightmare, a frequent occurrence lately. Almost as if they knew what was happening. And then there was Mr. Tom, who was always one step ahead of me when it came to getting up in the morning, either waiting by my bed or getting coffee ready to bring up. He could accurately predict my hunger and had a sixth sense about what I needed before I asked for it.

Because he'd been feeling my emotions the whole time.

We neared Ivy House, its massive shape cloaked in dark shadows that matched my mood. Niamh sat on her porch across the street, a rock in hand. She was watching a man who'd stalled in front of Ivy House. He reached into the satchel hanging at his side, probably to grab a newly created potion. Given she hadn't thrown the rock yet, she knew he wasn't a tourist. Now she was watching to see if he'd become my next professor.

I had my mind on other things. Mainly, the fact that Mr. Tom and the gargoyles were not the only people who'd been lying to me.

Austin had been able to feel me all this time as well. He'd randomly called when I was upset for some reason or other, or in danger, to check in. The "coincidence" had always been welcomed. But now I realized those calls hadn't been random. He'd been responding to my distress.

He hadn't turned the volume down on his side. At least, he didn't all the time.

In this time of peace, did he still feel everything I felt even though I was giving him the privacy I thought he wanted?

My gut pinched in anger and I started forward again, Jasper shadowing me, back to silence. He hadn't apologized, and why should he? He hadn't known any better.

Austin did.

The man in front of Ivy House upended a bottle of yellow potion into his mouth before putting it away.

"Not enough power," I murmured. The color was wrong for that potion, which meant the creation wasn't powerful enough to mask him from Ivy House.

I quickly crossed the street onto the sidewalk, passing in front of Niamh's house, Jasper following suit.

The mage stepped onto the walkway leading to my front door. One hesitant step, two... Picking up the pace now, four steps, five...

He reached the magical panel Edgar had installed in the sidewalk. I'd covered it with a simple masking spell, blending its look and characteristics with the landscape around it. A good mage should have been able to recognize the spell—fuzzy edges and a slight sheen gave it away.

The panel popped up with a loud *snap*.

The man didn't have time to swear. The vial flew

out of his hand. His body soared up into the air, the spelled and spring-loaded panel flinging him in an arch.

He windmilled his arms as he rotated. "Whoooooooaaaaaaa."

He smacked down onto the pavement in the street, his arms splaying out and his satchel half under him.

Niamh cackled, leaning back in her rocking chair and holding her stomach with one hand.

"What the…" The man flailed like a turtle on its back. "Why…"

"Here ye go, a participation medal." Niamh pushed to her feet and hurtled a rock at the man. It pelted his chest.

"Hey!" The man jerked, flailing harder now.

Niamh doubled over, guffawing. She loved that new ejection cord, as she called it. She also loved sending the failed candidates running.

She scooped up another rock and threw it, cracking him in the side of the head. "Have'ta be stronger than ye are. Now off ye get." She threw another. "No time to waste."

The man cried out, finally making it onto his feet. The satchel dragged at him as he stood, anger tightening his limbs. He faced Niamh down, his power surely building, probably readying a spell.

I hurried forward to intercept, but I needn't have

bothered.

"Oh, so ye want to play cops 'n' dinguses, do ye?" Niamh stripped out of her clothes like a woman on speed, her movements that of someone half her age, her deftness and strength compliments of Ivy House. (The magic would have made us all young too, but I'd accepted only some of the perks. I'd earned my age, and I wasn't ashamed of it.)

The man lifted his hands to fire off a spell, but she'd already changed into her nightmare alicorn form, with ink-black scales and a flaring golden mane, her golden hooves drumming against the ground as she charged at him. She lowered her head, pointing her crystalline horn at his chest.

"Holy—" He fired off the spell, the blast going wide, before scrambling out of the way. "A puca?" he choked out, panic riding his words.

Niamh ran past him, narrowly missing an impaling strike. The man would have no way of knowing she'd aimed badly on purpose. She wasn't on Ivy House soil— she knew better than to kill someone, unprovoked, in Austin's territory. She had a very, *very* short list of things she feared, and he was high on that list.

I ignored her antics, my mood souring further. Yet another mage had failed the tests, and I had to wonder if anyone appropriate would show up. I walked past the mock battle in the street and magically reaffixed the trap panel before pushing into Ivy House a moment later.

Mr. Tom was walking down the hall toward me, his tuxedo wrinkle-free in opposition to his lined face. His wings looked like a cape, brushing the backs of his legs. A sandwich waited atop a silver tray next to brown liquid in a crystal glass. Iced tea, no doubt.

"Good afternoon, miss," he said, his voice stuffy. "Would you be taking lunch in…your room, perhaps? Maybe overlooking the gardens?"

That spot always calmed me. He knew that. Given what he could sense through the link, he knew I needed it.

I clenched and unclenched my fists. "Why didn't you tell me it doesn't do squat on your end when I block my magical link to you?"

Mr. Tom stooped in front of me, and his snobby butler's facade slipped. "Ah. You clued in to the real nature of the link, I see."

My anger burned brighter. "Yes, I did. You've all been keeping a very important piece of information from me."

"It's been a collective effort of sorts, yes, miss. We had sound reasoning to do it."

"That right?" I glanced back at Jasper. "You may

go." Those words made it sound like he was a servant, which I didn't love, but it was the nicest way I'd found to politely tell people to get lost. Otherwise there would be a four-letter word involved.

"Of course, miss," Jasper mumbled, and regret curled through the link. He'd realized, belatedly, that the others had been purposefully keeping the link thing a secret.

"And what sort of sound reasoning would that be, Mr. Tom? What sort of sound reasoning would excuse anyone—*everyone*—for refusing to give me the same privacy I've given all of you?"

Niamh let herself into the house, having clearly scared off the mage.

"Let's sit and talk about it, miss." Mr. Tom gestured toward the front sitting room.

"I don't want to sit and talk about it, Mr. Tom. I want to hear your very sound reasoning, and then I want to...do something horrible. Do you have CDs? I kind of want to scratch all your CDs."

"Your honesty is refreshing, miss." Mr. Tom sniffed. "But no, I have moved into the modern times digitally. You'll have to find something else to ruin, I'm afraid."

"What's goin' on?" Niamh asked.

Mr. Tom set the tray down on the side table further in the entryway, pushing aside an antique vase crawling with mustard leaves and tangerine thorns. "Miss has recently learned that she can only block her side of the magical link."

"Ah." Niamh backed up and leaned against the wall.

"Why didn't anyone tell me?" I demanded, magic roiling within me. "*Why*? I look like an absolute fool! Jasper thought I was trying to pleasure him through the link, of all things. Can you even fathom how embarrassing that is?"

"No. What sort of *eejit* would think you'd give someone like him the time of day?" Niamh said, grossly missing the point.

Edgar opened the front door and popped his head in. "Is everything okay?"

I rounded on him. Before I could get a word out, his eyes widened and he ducked back out, slamming the door on himself to get away. Clearly he'd felt my anger.

I barely stopped myself from magically ripping the door open and dragging him back in with invisible hands just so I could yell at him, too. I was that mad. No, it wasn't just anger. I felt embarrassed, *betrayed*. I'd been lied to this entire time by people I trusted. People I cared about. They'd collectively kept something big from me, and here I stood on the outside looking in, vulnerable.

"You've uncovered a grave error on my part, miss."

Mr. Tom bowed his head solemnly. "I did not take the new recruits—Jasper and Ulric—aside and explain how and when to deaden the link. They can set it up so the link automatically muffles when you're engaged in certain activities, such as...*personal* time..." My face heated. I knew what he meant. "Locations can also deaden the link, like the bathroom. Ulric did mention that he'd figured out how to quiet the link for a little peace of mind. I can easily train them in ways to increase your privacy. You see? It isn't as bad as you thought."

Anger blistered and power boiled.

"It's not up to you to decide when you peek on me and when you don't need to," I ground out. "I will not tolerate having no control over my privacy. I don't want Jasper listening in when I'm...otherwise occupied. And what if I start dating? It'll be like having a bunch of voyeurs."

"In fairness, we haven't any privacy either," Niamh said, unconcerned with my anger. "You control when to use the link and when not to."

"I keep it blocked unless it's an emergency," I replied.

"As do we. Well...most of us, anyway." She side-eyed Mr. Tom. "*Some* of us are like mother hens."

"My job is to look after her," he said. "The link helps

me do that. Which is why there is a link in the first place."

"Did you tell Austin how and when to deaden the link?" I asked.

Mr. Tom pursed his lips. "No, I did not. An oversight I will happily remedy—"

"He knows how," Niamh cut in. "Maybe not automatically, which he'll be happy to learn, I imagine, but he knows how to deaden it when he wants to. Doubt he does very often—he can't be around, so he has to keep an eye on ye in other ways, Jessie. It's his job. It's all of our jobs. This is what we signed on fer. Ye have to let us watch over you."

"I let you watch over me," I said. "I let you tag along, barge into my room, keep tabs on my location— I've been pretty lenient with all this. In return, *you lied* to me. Don't you see? It isn't just that I am incredibly embarrassed that my...private time was spied on, or guilty that every time I wake up and wander around the house, all of you wake up, too. It isn't even my frustration that I can't have a moment alone—totally alone— to miss my son or feel sorry for myself in other ways. It's all of that *plus* the deception. Austin made a big deal about wanting out of this magic—about wanting privacy—and I gave that to him, only to find out he's been emotionally watching me. That sucks."

"He didn't at first," Niamh said. "He started to pay it heed with the first wave of danger. He wasn't doing it to spy. None of us are doing it to spy, and if you're feeling sorry for yerself, we just tune ye out, so we do. We got our own problems; we don't need yours, like. But ye're smart, so ye are, and we knew ye might find a way to cut us off if ye knew the truth. And if ye find yerself in a spot of trouble and the danger seems great enough, ye might try to hide yerself to protect us. We couldn't take that chance. Ye're too damn nice, girl. Ye know ya are. So we deceived ye, as ye say, to help protect you."

What she said made sense, but it still stung. They should've been more open with me. Maybe not right in the beginning, but we'd been through a few battles by now, and I could see the value in what she was saying. At the same time, they were the original crew of this place, deeply entrenched in their positions and their ways, and I could forgive the misstep. I would also acknowledge that the Jasper and Ulric situation had been an oversight on Mr. Tom's part. Fine. People make mistakes.

But Austin…

That guy had made a big deal about privacy. A *big* deal. He knew I didn't tap into the magical link unless I needed emotional cues to interpret his new expressionlessness. If he'd decided to keep his side open, he should've said something. I had trusted him from day one. Why didn't *he* trust *me*? If he'd explained that he was keeping the link open to ensure I stayed safe, protecting my privacy as much as possible, I would've been okay with that. I would've understood.

But he'd said nothing. Not a peep. Nor had he hinted that the others could tell every time I was sad or anxious or moping. No, he'd helped ensure that everyone in the crew could open me like a book to be read at their leisure. That Ulric and Jasper could peep in on my most personal moments.

He would tear down the world if someone had done that to him.

Tear it to the ground.

My heart ached with the betrayal. My eyes stung with unshed tears. I'd always thought Austin and I were a team, the two normal ones in a maelstrom of weird. I'd missed hanging out with him something awful these last weeks. I'd longed for him to randomly call me, like he had at the beginning. Except it hadn't been random at all. He knew when I was okay. He even knew when I was lonely or sad.

Let's have some space, Jess, I imagined him saying. *Let's take a step back and clear our heads. But only you will feel lonely. I'll be good because I'll have the reassur-*

ance of your presence with me all the time.

This wasn't how friends treated each other.

I blinked away the tears and slowly blew out a breath. I hated that they could all feel my heartache and the cracks forming in a trust I'd once valued so highly.

Anger was less embarrassing than mopey sorrow.

"What a dick," I said to no one.

"Uh-oh. Looks like some fireworks are coming our way," Niamh murmured.

Yeah, it did. I wanted an explanation. I wanted a confrontation. I wanted him to make it better.

Before I could about-face and head straight to the bar, a knock sounded at the door.

I froze. Mr. Tom and Niamh looked between each other and me.

No strange presence stood on Ivy House soil.

A mage strong in magic had been able to fool Ivy House. My summons had been answered.

CHAPTER 4

"WE SHOULD…" I rolled my shoulders, pushing away my anger so I could focus.

"Let me." Mr. Tom moved to step in front of me, but I put out my hand.

"I will." I pulled open the door slowly, my face surely matching my mood—grim.

A guy of about thirty stood just off the front stoop, his light brown hair disheveled and sticking up at various spots, stubble adorning his sharp chin, and thin eyebrows sloping over light gray eyes. He had his hands in the pockets of his loose jeans.

He looked me over, his expression flat. Finally, he pulled his right hand free and dragged a blue note card from his back pocket. "You wanted me to make this potion?"

I frowned at him. "You're not glowing."

He glanced down at himself. "I altered the potion a little. Hope you don't mind. If you glow, you give yourself away as magical. People will know you're using a spell. This way, no one will know." He turned back and pointed at the ejection panel. "Otherwise the potion's kind of like that spell. Anyone who knows what to watch out for would avoid that."

"I know. That was on purpose."

He nodded, turning back. "I wanted to step on it, just to see what it did."

"It wouldn't have done anything. Ivy House can't sense your presence, so she wouldn't have known to trigger it. Otherwise, though, you'd fly like a bird and land on your butt."

He could give Austin a run for his money on expressionlessness.

"Funny," he said. "I would like to see that."

"Hang around for long enough, and you probably will. Do you know why you're here?"

He slipped the note card back into his pocket.

"Wait, I'll take that." I put out my hand.

He shrugged and handed it over. "I got a magical...summons, it felt like. It was like a tug, directing me here. I resisted for a while—my employer doesn't like to share highly paid employees—but..." His smile was crooked, as though someone else were pulling at his lips. "It got the better of me, didn't it? Here I am. You need some training or something, right?"

"Your employer..." I paused for a moment. "And

who is that?"

He opened his mouth, as though to answer, and then drew in a breath. He shook his head. "Can't tell, I'm afraid. Physically, I mean. It's a gag spell put on us when we sign up. He's more powerful than me or I'd find a way around it." He shrugged. "It's pretty standard practice for the higher-level employees."

"Probably should've expected that," Niamh murmured.

"Do you know the story about this house and who I am?" I asked.

He looked upward, leaning back to do so. "Creepy old house. It's cool. But no, I don't know more than that. This town is out of the way. Seems pretty small. Is it magical? I haven't heard of it."

"Not really. I mean, it's becoming magical."

I chewed my lip, feeling a strange sort of hesitation. Usually when someone answered my summons, I invited them in. Some of them got to live here until they were fired or accepted. But for the first time, I didn't want to push the door wide and usher this guy through. Maybe it was all the failed mages before him. Maybe I'd learned not to be so welcoming to strangers. Whatever it was, I didn't step back and play the nice host.

"You know what?" I said. "Why don't I have one of my team get you checked in to the hotel in town." I glanced back at Mr. Tom—a silent request for him to get Ulric or Jasper. "We can meet up at the bar in a few hours and chat. In the meantime, my person can fill you in on some of the particulars about this place."

He dug his hand back in his pocket to match the other before stepping back. "I already got a room there. I wanted to put my stuff down and check out the town before I showed up." He paused for a moment. "Precaution."

"Right, so"—Niamh stepped forward, past me— "let's go grab a pint then. C'mon, I'll tell ye all about this miserable place and the whack jobs running it."

A car rolled down the street slowly, a newer Ford in midnight blue, the figure inside scouting the houses he or she passed. When the car neared us, though, I nearly lost my stomach.

"It's Jimmy! He's here early!" Joy bubbled up through me, and I was shoving Niamh and the new guy down the walkway before I realized my rudeness. "Sorry, hey, what's your name?"

"Sebastian," the new guy said.

"Hi, I'm Jessie—"

"But you will call her 'miss,'" Mr. Tom cut in.

I didn't have time to get annoyed as Jimmy stopped in the street, looking through the windshield of his rental car before glancing down at the screen of his phone, trying to find the right house, not noticing me standing out front.

"Niamh, head to the bar with Sebastian and fill him in. I'll…" I grimaced. This was the first mage that had made it to the door, and he might be the last. He could help me, but if left solely to Niamh's devices, he might not stick around long enough to hear an offer. I had to meet them tonight to make sure he'd stick around.

Hopefully Jimmy would be tired from his journey. He'd come all the way from New York, a trip that would've taken a couple planes and a layover. He'd probably want to head to bed early. I could make the meeting work.

"Fill Sebastian in," I started again as Jimmy recognized my car in the driveway and then noticed us all standing near the front door. He frowned. I'd told him about the house—I'd even sent him a picture—but only an in-person tour could do this place justice. Jimmy was seeing why, from the magical shadow that unnaturally shaded the place, to the glowing attic light (which was rarely on), to the sheer size as it sprawled across the carefully tended grounds. "Get some food, maybe. I'll meet you all as soon as I can, okay? I just have to get my…visitor settled in."

No point in letting a stranger know how precious my visitor was. I wasn't important enough for someone to hunt Jimmy down all the way in New York, where he went to school, but if my son was on hand, and things went pear-shaped with this powerful visitor…

"He's a day early," Mr. Tom said, stepping farther out to see the car as it pulled into the drive. "Hopefully he didn't bring a cooler full of food and cheap beer like your parents did."

"Okay, see ye in a while." Niamh motioned Sebastian ahead of her.

"Are we allowed to come out now?" Ulric called from inside the house. "Also, are we in trouble? I promise I wasn't spying on you, Jess—miss. I did like feeling the spice, but I didn't want to feel your wrath, so figured I'd better close it down."

"*Shh!*" I batted at the air even though he couldn't see me. "Mr. Tom, tell him and Jasper to head into town to watch Sebastian. Tell Austin about him, too. He'll want to keep an eye on things. *Don't* tell Austin I'm going to ring his bell the next time I see him. I don't want to ruin the surprise. Hey, bud!"

I practically ran around the car to grab hold of Jimmy as he climbed out.

"Hi, Mom." He groaned within my squeeze. "This house is huge! Is it really yours?"

I reached up to put my palms on both of my son's cheeks, his scruff almost a messy beard, completely unkempt, and his sandy-brown hair falling past his eyes and over his ears. His hazel eyes matched mine, as did his thin nose, but he had his father's wide smile and height, over six feet tall.

I frowned at the hoodie draped across his bony shoulders and the jeans sagging around his hips. "Did you stop eating? What happened to you?"

"It's fine." He twisted out of my grip. "Cooking sucks. But seriously, is this really your new house? I got the pictures, but…"

"Yeah, this is it. Come on." I led him toward the front door as Sebastian and Niamh reached her house. She ran in to get something, and he turned to look at us, his gaze tracking me and Jimmy. I waved my hand, throwing up a magical one-way mirror, making it so nothing impeded my view of Sebastian, but he saw his own reflection instead of us.

"Well, hello, Master Evans." Mr. Tom bowed, his wings fluttering.

Magic sparkled along my spell, and it took me a moment to realize Sebastian's fingers had lifted from his sides, his spell work hardly noticeable. His magic and power filled in little spots and crevices in my spell that I hadn't even realized were there, strengthening it but also changing it. Enhancing it.

I paused as Jimmy reached out to fist-bump Mr.

Tom, turning back to see Sebastian's handiwork.

The image of Sebastian crystalized, like I was looking at a computer screen, the shadows of early evening now tinged lime green. He'd added a nighttime effect in addition to cleaning up the haze from my spell.

"Just a sec," I murmured, jogging out to the street. I couldn't pass up the chance to look at it from the other side.

I punched a hole through the spell so I could cross the threshold, the world snapping back to its normal appearance. Once I crossed through, the hole winked out, the spell weaving itself back together.

"Wow." Sebastian narrowed his eyes at the spot I'd jogged through. "That's incredibly advanced, being able to walk through a spell like this without tearing it down. Not many in the world would be able to do it. I didn't expect it with the rudimentary spell you'd erected."

"Let's just quiet things down." I made a sign like pushing down the air. "Not everyone knows I'm magical around here."

He frowned. "That's your son, though, right? He looks like you."

I didn't comment.

Apparently I didn't need to.

"How can you have this much magic without him knowing about it? Without him having some too?" he asked.

"Niamh will explain my situation. Keep your voice down, if you would." I marveled at the way he'd changed the spell. His side was no longer a mirror: I could see Ivy House, only Jimmy's car wasn't parked in the driveway and there was no sign of anyone in the doorway of the house. It looked as though Jimmy hadn't come at all and we'd all gone inside. "The work you did on that spell is amazing. How can you fix someone else's spell?"

He scratched his head, making another patch of hair stand on end. "I have a lot of power, and figuring out spells and duplicating them is kind of a hobby of mine. Patching up or fixing spells that have already been realized is in my wheelhouse."

"Can a lot of mages do that?"

"No. That's why I get paid so well. And why...whatever this is probably won't work out. I mean, from the summons I got the sense I'm supposed to train you or something, but..." He shrugged. "Like I said, I have a job."

"If it is just the money you're worried about, that's no problem." I blew out a breath, really wishing I could have him walk me through how he'd fixed my spell. Jimmy was waiting, though. "Listen, will you just hang around this evening long enough for me to meet up with you? After I get my houseguest settled, I'll head around to the bar. Please?"

Niamh stepped out of her house as the man's gaze rooted to mine, reading me. Or maybe reading the situation.

"Okay." He shrugged, still seeming so uninterested. Aloof. "I took a week off anyway, so I don't have to hurry back."

I had a week to determine if I could trust him, a week to win him to my side. The fact that he'd created a potion that hid him from Ivy House without making him glow like he was radioactive was eyebrow-raising, because even Elliot Graves, one of the most powerful mages in the world, hadn't pulled that off. But transforming my spell into something infinitely better? This guy could be my salvation. Austin could drag out my magic, Edgar could point me in the right direction, and this guy could help me hone my craft.

I couldn't help smiling at the thought. "I'll connect with you later. Get some food or whatever you want. I'll see you."

As Niamh stepped down to him, I waved and jogged back to the house. I punched a hole in the spell and saw everyone still on the porch, Jasper and Ulric included. Edgar had joined them.

I really hoped it worked out with Sebastian. He'd

give me the edge I needed to survive this crazy magical world. An edge I'd likely need once his obviously rich and probably high-powered boss found out I'd stolen his star employee.

CHAPTER 5

"THE CAPE IS dope, bro." Jimmy was sitting at the kitchen island, eating an apple while Mr. Tom made him sandwiches. He'd gravitated straight toward the kitchen. "Sometimes you just gotta let your freak flag fly. At your age, you've earned it."

"Yes, fantastic. Thank you for the vote of confidence," Mr. Tom said dryly.

"It isn't a cape," I said. My stomach twisted as I stood at the corner of the island.

I'd decided before Jimmy had gotten here that I'd immediately tell him about the magic. There was no point in the house playing mind games with him like it had with my parents, or with me trying to hide the nature of the mage that had just shown up at the door. I'd have to tell Jimmy about the magic eventually—my parents had proven that—so I might as well do it while he was tired from his already long day. He'd be less inclined to want to leave.

I hoped he didn't assume I'd gone crazy and immediately run for the door…

"They are wings," I said. "In his other form, they are wings, and when he's in this form—his human form—they look like that. Like a cape."

There were probably better ways to break it to him, though.

Jimmy snorted. "Like a gargoyle?"

Mr. Tom twisted to look back at him. He didn't say a word as he returned his focus to the sandwiches, leaving this to me.

"What do you know about gargoyles?" I leaned over the island.

"Remember that old cartoon? And come on…" He rolled his eyes. "How many movies have gargoyles with a cape that's supposed to be their wings? I've seen it in anime, too. You'd think someone would have an original thought. I mean, no offense, bro. If you're going to do cosplay, you kinda gotta go with what's established, right?"

"Only in the realm of make-believe does one require original thoughts." Mr. Tom set a plate down on the island, the porcelain clinking. "Would you like some chips? Tea?"

"Do you have Coke?" Jimmy asked.

"Yes, sadly. It will rot your teeth, but I did pick some up." Mr. Tom turned toward the fridge.

I clasped my hands as Jimmy took a much-too-large bite of the sandwich, filling his cheeks to the extent that he could barely close his mouth. He'd relaxed a few of his manners at college, that was clear.

"So...there've been some changes with me," I started. "It all started with this house..."

"I know." He struggled to swallow before taking a sip of the freshly opened can of Coke to wash it down. "You look really good, Mom. You finally had time to exercise and stuff, huh? You always wanted to get in shape."

"I wanted to be in shape, not get in shape, but...no. This house—"

"This house is rad. It's creepy as hell." He bobbed his head as he looked around. "It's huge."

"I'll leave you to it." Mr. Tom finished washing up. "I assume I will stay behind to watch the young master when you visit the bar?"

Jimmy's eyes rounded, but he didn't comment. There was no telling what, precisely, he was reacting to.

"Yes, if you don't mind. The others are already there, not to mention Austin." Anger flash-boiled my blood. I pushed it aside. "I'll have plenty of cover."

"Of course." Mr. Tom walked from the room with a straight back, raised nose, and grossly overdone stuffy English butler vibe. He did like to put on a show.

"You have your own butler?" Jimmy asked with a grin, his right cheek puffed out with food. "That is so fucking awesome."

I frowned at him. "When you are in this house, you will not curse. Have respect for me and your surroundings."

"Sorry," he mumbled, and finished off the first sandwich.

"I do have a butler of sorts, yes. He kinda...came with the house. He was employed here when I came. So was the gardener."

"Yeah, you have a huge yard." He shook his head. "Dad's house is big, but it doesn't even compare to this one. He lives in a ritzy spot, but he certainly doesn't have the money for a butler!"

"You went to his house first?" I tried not to let the disappointment show on my face. It was petty, but some things couldn't be helped.

"Yeah. I thought you knew? He kept pushing and pushing, and all the guilt trips..." He sighed, picking up the second sandwich. "Same ol' Dad. He hasn't relaxed with the new setup."

"So then...why are you early? I wasn't expecting you for another day."

"I could not handle Camila for one more second. She's too...*nice*! She was always around, smiling and chatting and wanting to get to know me." He shivered. "Dad was working like he always does, so it was mostly just me and her. I mean, she's great, don't get me wrong, but…" He shook his head and then took a bite.

"So…how long are you here? I'd thought you were going to leave from here to go there."

"The week, if that's okay? I fly out on Monday. After Easter."

I smiled and quickly walked around to wrap my arms around his shoulders and squeeze him. "Of course! We have plenty of room. But…" I sat at a stool next to him. "Like I was saying, there have been some changes."

"You found someone new?"

"What? No, not that. You see, I didn't actually pay for this house. It kind of…chose me."

His eyes narrowed, not out of suspicion, but like he was trying really hard to get my words to make more sense.

"Gargoyles are actually real," I said. "Magic is real. I didn't believe it at first, but… Well."

"Are you on meds? Is it for the depression? Dad said you were depressed."

My eyebrows crawled up my forehead, and a new flash of anger blistered through me. "Your father never bothered…" I pushed away the desire to talk smack, taking a deep breath. "I'm not depressed, no. I'm actually happier now than I've ever been. But the world as you know it isn't actually the whole story." I twisted my lips to the side, thinking. "Right, okay. Finish up. I'll show you. I didn't actually believe any of it until I saw proof."

"What kind of proof?"

"You'll see."

✦　✦　✦

"Miss, are you sure this is the best idea?" Mr. Tom stood in the large entryway, awaiting further instruction. "The game box is all cued up with his favorite game. Wouldn't he rather do that? Remember how your parents reacted?"

Edgar stood beside Mr. Tom with a supportive smile. He had no problem showing his supernatural abilities to a non-magical person.

"This is the only way, Mr. Tom, or Ivy House will just rattle him. You know she will." I pointed up at the panel arching above the entryway, bridging the gap between large, curving staircases. A lovely tableau of a meadow was etched into the wood, spring flowers covering the rolling hillside.

"Mom, you're starting to make me nervous," Jimmy said softly, and my heart squished because it was clear he was worried about me. He cared.

"*You're stealing all of my fun,*" Ivy House said to me in our magical way of speaking. "*I wanted to see if I could make him wonder if he was going crazy, like your father.*"

"*Which is exactly why I am telling him now,*" I replied. "*I want him to be happy here. To be comfortable. I want him to come back.*"

The house was quiet for a beat. "*Ten-four.*" An affirmative.

The flowers engraved on the panel swayed as if caught in a gust of wind, the carvings so lifelike that I could almost smell the floral aroma. I found myself assigning colors to them: buttery yellow speckled with loud fuchsia. Violet dotting the way.

A memory stirred, of sitting on a rock shelf above such a meadow, a similar array of flowers stretching away into the soft afternoon sun. Austin had sat beside me, easy and comfortable, a feast of meats and fruits and cheeses displayed in front of us, a crate of wine to one side. He'd given me the perfect date, as he'd set out to do.

"*You're choosing his side,*" I said to Ivy House. Usually her wooden carvings were of battle and death and heads on spikes or, if she was feeling less vicious, magical creatures in fantastical situations. She'd never displayed such a pretty, mundane scene. She always, however, liked to poke the bear and create images that would mess with me in some way.

"*Yes.*"

Understanding dawned. "*You knew this was going on, and you didn't mention it…*"

"*Obviously. I've been dormant for much too long. All of the guardians have. I need you alive, and the magical link gives them the ability to keep you safe. This was always in your best interest. Any magical person would've known that.*"

"*Which I've acknowledged. My arrangement with Austin was a bit different, though. I trusted him to be honest, and he purposely deceived me. I have every right to be pissed.*"

"*By all means. Kick his head in. Just don't kill him. I need him. He's the best chance you have at long-term survival. Above all others, above the mage that came earlier today, Austin is the man that I need the most. That you need. So give him hell, but let him explain. Unless his explanation is bad. Then let him use his mouth in other ways that will be much more enjoyable than talking.*"

I frowned at her. She was entirely too focused on getting me laid.

"*I will get to the root of that link so I control it from my end.*"

"*I don't doubt you. Ultimately, that power is yours above mine. Above theirs. If you'd just put your big-girl pants on and do the blood oath, you'd realize that the links you share are as much for them as they are for you. If they are ever in trouble, you will need those links to find them. To save them. You are a team, and you are stronger together.*"

"*I don't need to give blood to want to save my crew if they are in trouble. That's a given.*"

"*Then why are you so hesitant to take the oath?*"

A wave of unease washed through me, the price tag of *forever* weighing on me heavily. When Ivy House started making chicken sounds—"*bawk, bawk, bawwwwwk*"—I cut off the communication. She could be insufferable.

Reemerging into reality, I realized Edgar was talking, and likely had been the whole time I was communicating with the house.

"Yes, a *real* vampire. I'm one of the oldest alive." He smiled, his canines long and gruesome. "Usually when a vampire is turned out of their clan for being too old, they are hunted for sport and killed for fun. I found Ivy House, though. They don't think I'm great sport for some reason."

"Probably because you keep asking to be retired," Mr. Tom said. "It's no fun when the prey asks for it."

Retired meant killed permanently. Every time Edgar made a mistake, which was pretty often, he insisted that I kill him. It would've been a running joke if he didn't actually mean it.

"What was in that soda?" Jimmy asked softly. "I feel like I'm on acid or something." He rubbed his eyes, watching the wooden tableau move and shift, less like wooden carvings and more like a TV screen.

"Shall we?" Mr. Tom put his fingers on the buttons of his jacket, awaiting my directions. "I want to bring in Master Jimmy's things and get his room set up."

"Just call him Jimmy, Mr. Tom. And yes, that's fine. Edgar…" I motioned for him.

Edgar puffed into a swarm of insects.

"Holy—" Jimmy staggered backward. "What just happened? Seriously, was there something in that soda? Did I take an edible and not know it?"

So my son had tried edibles and hallucinogens— that was something I could've gone my whole life happily not knowing.

After a deep breath, I motioned for Mr. Tom to hurry up.

A hidden door popped open down the way, Ivy House wanting to show off her stuff as well.

"No, no. Why is he dropping trou?" Jimmy asked, backed against the door.

"*Hold off,*" I told Ivy House. "*Let's give him a second to adjust. Show him the hidden tunnels and whatever else after he's gotten used to the idea. He'll like it better by then.*"

The hidden door down the way clicked shut again. For once, she agreed with me.

The sound of boulders moving and scraping against each other filled the space. Mr. Tom, in his birthday suit, bent slowly, his skin mottling from pasty white to a deep coal as it hardened into a tough hide. His wings rose behind his back, taking shape and stretching out before he pulled them back in, something he could do even while changing forms. Large teeth protruded from his pronounced jaw, and his ears rose to points within his growing black hair.

"What in the..." Jimmy's breath went out of him. His mouth hung open and his wide eyes took in the slow transformation from man to gargoyle.

For a moment, Mr. Tom crouched on the floor, utterly still, hard stone. Then he straightened to his full height of nearly eight feet, propelled into action by my need for him to show his gargoyle form. Otherwise, if I didn't have the need, he would stay stone until naturally emerging, the time that took dependent on his age.

Given Mr. Tom's age, that would take a *very* long time.

"He looks like the gargoyles from the cartoon," Jimmy whispered. "Am I really seeing this? Am I tripping?"

"It's magic." I held out my hand, palm up. A foot from my skin, a collection of sparks popped and fizzed. "Edgar, change back."

The swarm of insects changed back into the stooped vampire with long fingers and nails and pronounced canines.

"My magic came from the house, but magic exists all through the world—they are proof." I magically extinguished the sparks and lowered my hand. "I didn't believe all this either, at first. Someone I know turned into a large rat in front of me."

"A shapeshifter," Jimmy murmured.

"That's right."

"They usually turn into predators," he said through a slack jaw. "I've never heard of a rat shifter."

"Who wants to write a story about a shape-shifting rat, you know?" Edgar chuckled. "But vampires *do* drink blood, so you had that right. See? You were already looking for magic in your reading. Now you've found it."

Jimmy looked at me with dazed eyes, completely gobsmacked, his mind in overdrive and ready to shut down.

The scene of a winery tasting room appeared in the wood on the archway, and I narrowed my eyes at it. Austin had told me about magic at a wine tasting. My mind had been in overdrive too. It had tried to shut down. Austin had been there to help me through it. He'd essentially held my hand, kept me level. He'd guarded my back while I learned about a whole new world.

When Ivy House picked sides, she really rubbed it in.

CHAPTER 6

MAGICAL PEOPLE CROWDED in the bar, unusually packed for a Sunday night. Austin pulled out two beers and flipped the caps off before setting them down in front of two women in their mid-twenties with roaming eyes and simpering smiles.

"Ten bucks." He knocked on the bar and moved on, knowing Paul or Donna would follow along behind him and grab the payment. Austin wasn't so much a bartender as the owner and peacekeeper. Tending bar helped him keep an eye on things without having to mingle within the crowd.

"Austin Steele." Down the bar, Niamh raised her empty glass, seated between one of the support beams and a guy in his early thirties with pale eyes.

Niamh still refused to call Austin alpha. If it had been anyone else, he might've pushed the issue and asked for the respect he was due, but he knew it was her way of honoring Jess. Of showing her pride in the Ivy House mistress, and maybe making a subtle statement that she thought Jess was the mightier of the two.

The sentiment probably should've enraged him, but it warmed him instead.

Austin refilled the ice in Niamh's cup, placed a bottle of cider in front of her, and then braced his hands against the edge of the bar in front of the mage, meeting that flat, watchful stare.

"If you're going to park here, you have to buy a drink," he said, which wasn't even remotely true. This mage was here on business, waiting for Jess. He could sit at the bar all night if he wanted to. Normally Austin would make sure he wasn't disturbed while he did it.

But something about the mage's cool demeanor set him on edge. Austin was typically an excellent judge of character, but he couldn't get an accurate read on this guy. He was dangerous, that was clear. The tang of his power, recently used, tweaked Austin's nose. He didn't show the usual swagger or overblown ego of high-powered mages—of high-powered *anyone*—but he had the power to back it up.

What really set Austin on edge, though, was the way the mage had been watching his every move, every interaction. He didn't glance away when Austin caught him, or lower his gaze in response to *the look*. There was no hostility, but there was also no fear.

This guy either had incredible confidence, or he

hadn't ever dealt with an alpha shifter.

Austin certainly hadn't dealt with a magical person like this mage. Then again, he wasn't exactly worldly when it came to powerful mages. Shifters and mages didn't usually mix.

"Scotch. On the rocks," the man said.

"That's on Ivy House." Niamh poured her cider over the ice cubes.

"Any particular brand?" Austin asked as Donna bustled by behind him.

"Glenfiddich. Please."

Austin held the man's stare for a beat, but he didn't sense a challenge. He wondered if the mage was simply inquisitive, like a child examining a colorful bug that he didn't realize was poisonous.

Whatever his purpose, the mage was treading a fine line. The staring had a time limit, and it was fast approaching.

Austin felt Jess winding her way closer to the bar. She'd started the trip by herself, but Jasper, who'd been outside the bar, blending in to the stone façade, had peeled away in his gargoyle form and flown to meet her.

In the beginning, Austin had only really felt a magical connection with Jess, but he could now keep tabs on the whole crew, something that helped him gauge Jess's level of safety. Her anger earlier in the day, for example, had been met with Jasper's confusion and wariness instead of alarm. Whatever she had reacted to, it wasn't a potential threat.

Austin set the glass down in front of the mage, meeting his gaze again. Increasing the weight of his stare, pouring power into it, Austin tried to force a reaction.

"Thank you," the mage said, but didn't reach for the glass. He didn't look away.

No spike of adrenaline came, no hint of challenge. No fear. No expression at all. Nothing!

This mage was an enigma, and in Austin's experience, enigmas were dangerous.

✧ ✧ ✧

NIAMH WATCHED AUSTIN Steele as he walked away to help someone else, his eyes lingering on the stranger as he moved away. That was odd. It seemed like the alpha couldn't figure out what to make of their new friend, and neither could she, truth be told. She'd yet to meet anyone else who could hold eye contact with Austin Steele like that. Besides Jessie.

She grunted and took a sip of her cider.

"What do ye think of the town?" she asked.

"It's…" The mage took a sip of his drink, watching Austin Steele go about his business. "This territory should be in its infancy, right? Isn't he a new alpha?"

"Yeah. What of it?"

He shook his head. "Looks like he's been running this town all his life."

"He's basically been running it since he got here, just without the title." She felt Jessie winding closer and wrestled a delighted smile off her lips. Niamh hadn't told Austin Steele why Jessie was so pissed off earlier. It would be a wonderful and probably extremely violent surprise.

"I don't know anything about shifter territories other than what I've read, but this place seems like a well-run magical town."

"Well-run? Do ye *hear* him?" she exclaimed.

"Who?"

He clearly wasn't familiar with that turn of phrase.

"The new people have made a right bags of this town—"

"A right what?"

"It's a fecking shitshow, so it is. Pure chaos. There are lads running all over the place with their willies in their hands, lookin' to fight. It's madness. Well…" She took a sip of her drink. "It's fun, don't get me wrong. It's like a game of Whac-A-Mole, but you have'ta play behind Austin Steele's back or things get ugly. When I'm in a mood, I can always find someone to pound on.

It's great craic."

"He seems to back people down with just a look…"

"Yeah. Take the hint."

She was met with silence. Clearly this mage was way out of his league when it came to shifters. That would work out badly for him if he stayed in O'Briens.

"When he's staring atcha," she said, "he's promisin' to put ye in yer place if ye don't mind yer manners. He's being nice to ye right now because of Jessie. It's the only reason he's ever nice. Otherwise he's a fair but hard-hearted el' bastard, so he is. Good man but as dangerous as they come."

"So staring is considered a challenge?"

"Yer not going to last long in this place, boyo, unless ye cop on."

He stared at the side of her head. "I'll assume that is a yes. So if he takes it as a challenge, what happens next?"

"Jaysus, Mary, and Joseph. Ye get a clatter, that's what happens. Ye try to see out yer ear after he thumps ye. Look." She turned a little so she could better see him. "Here's a word of advice. If ye want to try yer hand against a shifter, and I don't blame ya if ye do, pick someone else. *Any*one else. Don't start with him. Don't even *end* with him. He was born an alpha, and now he's actually trying a little. It won't be long before he tries a lot and claims the reputation he deserves. For Jessie's sake, stay away from him. She needs help, and ye can't do that if Austin Steele rips ye in half."

"All due respect, you aren't born an alpha any more than you're born a mage. You are merely born with talent. It's up to the individual to hone and shape that talent into a skill set."

"What are ye, a philosopher?"

"When I have nothing better to do...yes, I suppose so."

She grunted again. So much for idle chitchat.

"What made him...try a little, if I might inquire?" the mage asked.

She took a sip, debating how much information to share about the area and the people running it. Austin Steele might not know what to make of the mage, but he didn't seem to consider him a threat. Niamh never really tried to assess anyone, assuming everyone was an arsehole, but she had to admit that the mage didn't annoy her. He wasn't pushy, he wasn't too chatty, he drank when pushed—and a drink to be proud of, at that—and he just minded his own business when no one engaged him.

He did have a staring problem, though. He was as bad as the horny girls that filled this place, watching Austin Steele's every move, hoping to go home with him. Only this guy wasn't looking at Austin Steele's arms, back, or butt. He was paying attention to the way he handled people, taking in what the alpha noticed and reacted to.

That should've probably set off warning bells. It didn't.

"Are you using magic to alter the moods of the people around you?" she asked.

It was her turn to get analyzed. "You don't seem overly put out about the possibility."

She shrugged. "Ye're not annoyin' me. If it takes magic to make that a reality, then I'm not beat up about it."

A crooked grin worked at his lips, as though a novice puppet master were maneuvering his mouth. "What a strange place this town is. You aren't afraid of magic controlling you." It wasn't a question.

"Not afraid, no. Though that kind of thing can make a body irrational."

"Meaning?"

"If you were, and I'd had enough, I'd kill you."

"I would expect no less. In answer to your question, no, I'm not using magic to control you. I'm using it to eavesdrop around the room, but since I can hear you just fine, the spell isn't near you."

"Oh yeah?" She glanced at those flat gray eyes, his

face utterly expressionless except for that strange smile. "Hear anything good?"

"A great many ladies would like to bed the alpha."

"You don't need magic to know that."

"Well...*I* do. I'm not very good at reading social cues or understanding human behavior. I'm slightly...socially awkward, we'll say. Socially deficient, maybe."

"Jessie will be glad to hear it. What else?"

"A group in the back doesn't like the way the alpha is scheduling supervised fights to handle pack placement. Nor do they like the way he throws his weight around."

Niamh sniffed. "They don't like their own inferiority."

"Sounds like one of them's an alpha from another pack? I can't be sure, but..."

"Ah." She nodded. "A mediocre alpha and his best and brightest. They're more interested in fighting for dominance than in joining the pack, the maggots. Some alphas cannot stand the idea of someone being tougher or more powerful than they are. They likely take Austin Steele's newness to the post as a sign of weakness." She grinned. "That'll be some show. I hope they challenge him tonight."

"You want them to do it?"

"Oh yeah. When Austin Steele gets going, it really gets the blood pumping. I like watching—when it's got nothing to do with me, o'course."

"I see."

"Nah, ye don't. Shifters are a different breed. Though all creatures have their issues. Gargoyles are some lot, I'll tell ye. Only thing good about them is they are mostly quiet. Except for the thorn in me arse, *Mr. Tom.*"

"I've tried to read up on them—shifters, I mean. I've always been fascinated by the rift between mages and shifters, you see. And I think… I mean, I don't know… But after seeing some of the shifters in here, I think mages must be scared of shifters. I'm scared, at least. That must be the root of the prejudice. Magic like mine does not require strength. Magic does not require courage. We are cowards, most of us. Take away our magic, and you take away our…purpose. Our…"

"Bollocks?"

He huffed out a laugh. "Yes, I suppose. I am physically weak. I am emotionally stunted."

"Christ almighty, we don't need to get too personal—"

"I am socially inept. All I have is my magic. If that magic fails, a shifter, even one in human form, could rip me in half."

"Some of them would rip you in half even with yer magic. They might be half-dead before they finish the job, but by God, they would finish it."

"Yes. That's what I'm gathering. Mages have reason to be scared. A well-functioning pack led by a competent alpha would be a serious threat to my kind. They stand together, whereas mages stay solo. Even the Mages' Guild, which is supposed to be an association of our peers—" He huffed and shook his head. "Each one of them are in it for themselves. They aren't working as a unit; they are strategizing against each other, supporting each other only when it is clear they'll get something out of it. They make deals that will help themselves under the guise of helping mages everywhere. The rest of us might work with other mages on things, but it's out of necessity, and the sum total is equal to its parts. With shifters, the sum total of a pack is greater than its parts. Do you see what I mean?"

"And here I thought you weren't chatty."

He wiggled in his chair a little, the only time he'd really moved since sitting down, other than bending forward and looking aloof. "You say this town is in chaos. This is a normal magical town to me. The strong prey on the weak. The weak get out of the way. Law and order is present to some degree, but only when the powers that be feel like keeping the peace."

"Well. If ye hang around, you'll see what a well-functioning town looks like. Austin Steele will sort it all out."

He was quiet for a moment. "You've heard of Momar?"

She squinted, trying to place that name. "A powerful mage, yeah? Last I heard, he was organizing his forces to take over the crime world from Elliot Graves."

"Your information is outdated. He *has* mostly taken over the crime world. Elliot Graves has slunk into the shadows. I heard he's doing just enough to get by. His defenses are up, so no one can get to him, but he hasn't been pulling jobs or leading teams. He's a has-been."

Niamh couldn't help but give him a funny look. That account didn't match with what Ivy House had seen. Was someone throwing Elliot Graves's name around to push them off the true scent of whoever had been behind the attacks?

"No, *Momar* is mostly in power now," the mage said. "He is considered the most powerful mage in the world, not because of his magic—that title still belongs to Elliot Graves, no matter how hollow it is—but because of his holdings, his money, and his magical influence."

"What's yer point?"

"He is so powerful that he should fear very little, but

he hates shifters. *Hates* them. When he can, he destroys entire packs."

Niamh frowned. She'd been hibernating in this small town for far too long. She hadn't heard any of that. Knowledge of the magical world had gotten away from her, probably because she'd been contemplating retirement before Jessie had shown up. If she stuck her head out of this little divot in the ground, she wouldn't recognize the politics of today. That could be a dangerous situation for Jessie. With as much power as she'd inherited, she was part of the magical world, like it or not.

Niamh needed to amend this gaping hole in her knowledge. Become the expert she used to be.

"Why is that, then?" she asked.

"I've always wondered that very thing. What if it's all rooted in fear? Fear of their strength, of their courage and loyalty to each other. It doesn't hurt that Momar's father was killed by one. From what I've read, it sounded like Pappy Dearest got what he deserved—he'd been bleeding the town dry in taxes, forcing the hungry and desperate to rise up against his tyranny. Regardless, Momar would like to rid the world of shifters, but if he kills too many too fast, they will band together. I am starting to understand just how dangerous that would be for him." The mage went on watching Austin Steele.

"So instead, he's been drumming up reasons to attack smaller packs. Still, it's only a matter of time before he develops the resources to go after the larger ones."

"And ye think this guy will see Austin Steele as a small pack to go after?"

"I don't know. If the alpha is as good as you say, now would be the time to act, before he gets his feet under him. But who knows of this town? No one. I'd always thought it belonged strictly to Dicks and Janes. I was utterly confused by the summons."

"It mostly used to. Things are changing quickly now, though."

"Yes. One hopes, then, that it becomes powerful before Momar realizes the threat."

Niamh looked at her glass without comment. This new crime boss wouldn't just be interested in Austin Steele—Jessie would add to the flavor. Clearly they needed to keep this area as low profile as possible for as long as possible. Keep their heads down and plod along, building strength quietly.

She needed to mention all this to Austin Steele, and also tell him to keep an eye on this new mage. He seemed okay, but he could be influencing them with magic. Until Jessie was up to speed, there was no way to tell. If he was gathering information for someone, they could be in a world of hurt.

Especially if his boss was Momar.

"I am almost tickled to see how it all turns out," the mage mumbled, as though to himself, ever mindful of Austin Steele. "If I live that long, obviously."

"Why wouldn't ye?"

"You've already mentioned killing me. It sounds like I don't have great odds of leaving this town alive."

Niamh looked over his plain face, the button nose the only cute thing about him. His messy hair, sticking up every which way. His expressionless eyes, not the dimmest twinkle within them. "I can't tell if yer jokin'."

"Neither can I. Sometimes it creates problems."

She lifted her eyebrows and turned back to her cider.

"You don't have to worry about me," he said, as though picking up on her uncertainty about him.

"Is that right?"

"My life will be forfeit should my employer find out I'm here. He will assume I'm sharing information. I shouldn't have come."

"Then why did you?"

He shook his head, small movements, his eyes rooted to Austin Steele. "Pandora wasn't the only one with curiosity. Now I'm worried I'm hooked. So whatever goes on here is safe with me."

"We'll see."

"Fair enough."

Jessie slowed as she neared the bar, Jasper peeling off to blend in with the side of the building and Ulric already stationed at the other end. Niamh could feel Jessie's anger—a coil ready to spring. Austin Steele stopped helping people and stepped back, his gaze on the door.

Right now, Jessie's anger was on a tight leash. But one wrong word from Austin Steele—*one* wrong word—and that leash would snap and the fireworks would ignite.

Niamh couldn't wait for the show.

CHAPTER 7

JASPER BLENDED INTO the building as I approached, and I caught sight of Ulric at the other end, his blue and pink hair subdued in the shadows. Mr. Tom had stayed home with Jimmy, who had decided to play video games and escape into a reality he understood. He'd done a lot of far-off staring, paired with some adamant head shaking, but I firmly believed he'd come around. I had to.

Sasquatch stood outside of the door, his hand at his side and a cigarette trailing smoke between his fingers. He looked up as I approached, and his features pinched into a mask of distaste.

"That was my favorite knife," he said.

"Then you shouldn't have stuck it in me and stepped away, huh?"

"I would've taken it back if you hadn't used your magic."

"God you're dumb." I shook my head, anger pulsing within me. "Austin has your knife. Ask him for it.

Though how a rusty knife could be your favorite, I do not know."

"It wasn't that rusty."

I pushed past him and then stopped, sticking out a finger. His flinch buoyed my mood a little.

"You know what? I want you to keep playing that game with me. I'll make sure you get your knife back. If you catch me, fine. Stab me. But if you can't, and I catch you instead, I'll be the one stabbing *you*."

His eyebrows lowered. "You're going to be in a world of hurt. You're terrible at your magic."

"I'm terrible at my magic? What, did you throw yourself at the wall earlier? Is that why you whined to Austin about me?"

His eyes narrowed. I stared him down, waiting for a rebuttal, but he just turned away, pulling a long drag off his cigarette as he left.

Ha! Point to me.

Sucking in a deep breath, I entered the crowded bar, standing room only. I recognized a few faces, but no one nodded to me as I passed. They seemed almost…nervous. Schooling my expression, trying to wipe off any residual anger or frustration, I threaded my way through the crowd. Despite the vibes I was apparently giving out, I wasn't here to talk smack to Austin, and I definitely didn't intend to yell at him in front of all of his customers. I would do that in the privacy of Ivy House property, thank you very much.

I was here to see about a mage.

The crowd parted as I walked through. Puzzled strangers or wary regulars shifted out of my way, giving me a view of the bar. Austin stood behind it with a wide stance, popping muscles. His hard expression indicated he was preparing for battle.

I glanced around, getting the sense that my bad mood wasn't the only trouble brewing. A quick blast of magic helped me find the source: a table at the far back corner of the main room, against the wall that led to the pool room and bathrooms. I couldn't see any faces through the crowd, only a glimpse of a red cotton-clad elbow, but I felt dark energy radiating from the people sitting there, like oil slicking across water.

Niamh sat in her usual spot, the support beam at her left and a little removed, preventing anyone from sitting too closely on that side. Her fingers curled around her glass, the ice cubes jockeying for position within the fizzy amber liquid.

Sebastian twisted in his seat beside her. I thought he'd look at me, but instead his eyes did loop-de-loops, tracing something through the air. His fingers wiggled in a way that suggested he was doing magic, but I couldn't see or feel it. He was way more experienced than me. More powerful, too.

"Hey," I said softly, stopping behind them, my hand coming to rest on the back of Niamh's chair. The bar chatter, which had quieted down when I first walked in, now cut off entirely, as though the room was holding its collective breath. "Did I get here at a bad time—"

"Jess." Austin stopped in front of me, his stare beating into me like a palpable pressure. His power pulsed and slammed into me, turning my blood to gravy. His commanding presence, his air of dominance, pressed down on my chest. On my shoulders. It seemed to say, *Submit, or I will make you submit.*

Like a spark igniting deep within me, anger flowered up and blossomed out, covering me in shivers, shrugging off his imposing power.

"You good?" His words were clipped, tone rough.

My fingers tightened on Niamh's chair. "Is that how you greet a friend?"

His jaw clenched. He didn't move. He just stared me down like I was a stranger causing a ruckus.

His silence punched straight through my middle.

Anger rushed in to drown out the hurt. Red tinged my vision.

"Bros before hoes, is that it?" I asked, my anger blazing brighter and hotter, my pain lodged firmly in my throat. "Don't you know how I'm doing? My block has nothing to do with your side of the link, so aren't you well aware of what I'm feeling?"

His flinch was so slight that I almost thought I'd imagined it. But I ripped away the block on the link, and guilt gushed through it.

Unlike Mr. Tom and Niamh, Austin felt bad for what he'd been doing. He'd known it was wrong. He'd known he was violating my trust.

My eyes stung and my magic ballooned around me, my control wobbling—my heart aching and my rage compensating.

"Why did you never tell me?" I asked the dead-silent room. I wrapped a bubble of silence around us, letting the walls shimmer so he knew what it was. "How could you let me continue believing I was giving us both privacy when you knew it was completely one-sided? The new guys listened in to my...*private* time, Austin," I said with a tightening throat, the embarrassment almost choking me. I'd tried to push that aside earlier, but the thought was mortifying. How often, how long... "Can you even fathom how embarrassing that is?"

White-hot rage sparked in his eyes.

"Oh no." I held up a finger, power pumping out of me in heady waves, more now than I'd ever felt. "No way. You get to apologize, you get to make it up to me, but you do *not* get to be angry. Do you understand me,

Austin Steele? If you don't listen, I will give you the beating of your life. I'll be the fire that melts your steel into a puddle. Try me and see if I'm lying."

"I overheard Mr. Tom, Niamh, and Edgar discussing the way they control their link to you," he said, his voice so rough it sounded like a growl. "I assumed they'd passed that on to Jasper and Ulric. Those guys should not have access to…" His hands fisted and the weight of his power threatened to push me to the floor. My limbs started to quiver, my reaction to him entirely primal. "I will ensure that ends immediately."

"None of you should have access to that time, least of all you, considering how desperate you've been for distance from me. But *you* won't do a damn thing. You don't rule me, Austin Steele. You don't control my life. *I* will ensure that ends immediately. In the meantime…"

I stared at him, grappling for a threat of some kind. I'd overshot my tirade and left myself dangling.

"Go to hell," I finished lamely.

And then kept standing there, because I had business in the bar. This had to be one of the world's worst standoffs. No wonder my ex had always won our arguments. I was just plain bad at them.

"Can I speak to you outside, please?" Austin said, his voice softer, more subdued. "We're making everyone incredibly uncomfortable." Guilt still pumped through the link. Guilt, discomfort, anger, and regret.

"You don't really want to start a fight with me right now," I warned him.

"I don't ever want to start a fight with you, Jacinta. I'd never lift a finger to you outside of training, you know that. You'd pummel me."

"Don't be cute." I tore down my privacy spell—the irony was not lost on me—and nearly staggered into Sebastian, knocked forward by the menace pulsing from the corner of the room.

"That's a neat spell you devised," Sebastian said. "I made it better. Maybe I shouldn't have. It's a little too strong right now."

The spell I'd used to lock Austin and me in a soundproof bubble had also blocked my awareness of the other spell, the one I'd sent to suss out trouble.

"You just made Austin Steele look incredibly weak to those who don't know him," Niamh said with a little smile. "Or you."

I'd seen that smile before, usually before Edgar got the brunt of one of her violent practical jokes.

Austin's gaze snapped to the corner. He didn't need a spell to feel the danger.

"Oh wow, interesting," Sebastian said, watching Austin with thinly veiled fascination. He'd realized the same thing.

"Get out of the bar, Jess," Austin growled, putting out his hand to nudge Paul to the side. Donna, the cute twenty-something bartender who'd turned into a rat to induct me into the magical world, had already scattered, leaving Austin alone behind the bar.

"Ye'll want to clear away now, lad." Niamh nudged Sebastian before standing, her full glass clutched in her hand. She didn't leave drinks behind. "They're about to make bags of the bar."

Sebastian rose, his movements surprisingly unhurried, and followed Niamh to the side as the menace from the back worked its way forward, one guy at the front, two flanking him, and three more at their backs. People had stepped aside for me earlier, sensing my mood and knowing my power, but now they were tripping over each other in their haste to clear the way for this crew. They poured into the pool room or out of the front door.

"Jess, get out of here," Austin said, and I felt the command down to my toes.

It took everything I had to stay put.

"No."

I stood tall, back to the bar, watching the tide of muscle coming toward us. Those in the back of the group topped Austin's six-foot-two frame by a few inches, but their thick bodies were layered over with fat.

The man in front was made of iron. Pecs popped under his tight black shirt and robust thighs strained his snug trousers. Those to his sides were shorter and stockier, blocks of muscle with smooth grace. They'd be trouble in a fight.

Adrenaline coursed through me, followed by fear. The fear of the woman I'd been rather than the woman I'd become. This was always the way before action. I'd snap out of it. Usually I had Ivy House at my back, but Austin would do just fine in a tight squeeze. If worse came to worst, I knew Niamh could change into her second puca form, the horrible little goblin with razor-sharp teeth. That thing loved tight spaces.

"You have a pretty little territory here, *Austin*." His use of Austin's name rather than his title was an insult. A challenge. "Thanks for setting it up for me."

"Bit early to move in." Austin put a hand onto the bar and launched himself over it, sticking the landing right next to me. He took a step forward before reaching back, his hand connecting with my hip and then tucking me in behind him.

I wrapped my hand around his arm and pushed, but it didn't budge. Luckily, I didn't need to be face to face with these guys to work my magic.

"I've barely mapped everything out," Austin said.

The guy to the leader's right, a guy whose buzzcut

drew attention to his pinhead, smirked at me as I peered out from behind Austin's broad back.

"Looks like he's got a mate all picked out for you, too, alpha," Pinhead said. "Pretty, but you'd better bed her quick if you want heirs—"

Austin moved so fast that I jumped. With a vicious growl, he grabbed Pinhead by the shirt, and in a show of savage aggression that had the guys in the back widening their eyes, he slammed his fist into Pinhead's face three times in quick succession before lifting him and throwing him into the wide-eyed guys.

The leader barely had time to flinch before Austin was on him, one hand at his throat, the other at his nuts. He squeezed, and a strangled, high-pitched shriek barely made it past the guy's lips. Austin used him as a club, swinging and hitting the last man standing, knocking him toward the bar. Another step forward, and Austin threw the leader against the wall so hard that the entire building shook. He was on him again a moment later, pummeling him with a fist before lifting him, swinging him, and throwing him out through the door.

The three guys pushed Pinhead off and struggled to their feet.

Too late.

Austin was like a tornado of rage and power and

destruction, touching down on them before hurling them out through the door, one after the other. The guy that had staggered into the bar tried to crawl out, desperate to get away, but Austin delivered a few more strikes before evacuating him.

Pinhead was left cowering on the ground, a dark stain down the insides of his pants.

"Please, alpha." He lifted his hands over his head. "Please, alpha."

Austin stalked toward him like a wild thing, savage and untamed. Blistering rage burned in his eyes, and a killer's grace sang in every movement. The predator had sighted his prey.

"You dare disrespect her?" His voice was not his own, fueled by the darkness within him.

Austin grabbed Pinhead by the throat and held him above the ground, his feet dangling.

I felt my eyes widen and my heart pound. I'd seen Austin on the warpath, but never like this. Not in human form, anyway.

"You dare come into my territory, my bar, and disrespect someone as pure and good as Jacinta." He squeezed.

The man kicked, his face turning red. He grabbed at Austin's hand, his wrist, and tried to push at his face. His strength was draining.

"Say you're sorry," Austin seethed.

Pinhead's mouth worked, but no sound came forth.

Austin shook him as if he were a mouse, not a shifter made of solid muscle.

The shifter's slight to me had been enough to completely derail Austin's control. What Pinhead had said had pushed Austin into his dark place, creating an opening for the beast to emerge.

Austin had allowed himself to get too close to me, and hearing someone belittle me had sent him into a tailspin. It had brought one of his greatest fears roaring to life. He had lost himself.

I had to set him to rights. If I didn't, he might never forgive himself for the loss of control. He'd think all of his years of penance had been for nothing.

I shoved a few spectators out of the way and slammed the door shut, locking it. Like a shepherd, I herded everyone who remained inside, Niamh and Sebastian included, into the pool room. Once they were safely tucked away, I sectioned them off with the spell Sebastian had devised earlier that day. They would not see or hear us. I worked quickly, knowing Pinhead's time was running out.

"Enough, Austin," I said softly, walking closer with slow, even steps. I didn't want to startle him. "You've made your point." I dropped my hand to his shoulder, my breath hitching when Austin shook the man again. "It's time to stop this now. Let it go."

Radiating calming emotions through our magical link, I rubbed up the center of his back and then reached around and put my other palm over his chest, the beat of his heart filtering through me until it almost beat in time with mine. Until I felt our connection in my center.

"That's enough, Austin, please." I slid my palm up his chest and cupped his chin, ever so gently pulling his face toward mine. I threaded a little command into my tone, just enough to get through to him. "Look at me, Austin."

His arm dropped a little. His fingers relaxed, but not enough. Pinhead slowly stilled, just about out of air, his legs barely kicking now.

"Look at me," I whispered, applying a little more pressure to Austin's chin, turning his head. His eyes, dazed with violence, lost to his primal side, weren't focusing. "Come back to me. Remember the meadow with all the flowers? Remember that perfect day, with the sun and the wine? Remember how sublime it was, how peaceful? I need you to return to that headspace. Come back to me, Austin."

His eyebrows dipped, and I took my hand from his chin and ran it down his outstretched arm, the one that was choking Pinhead.

"You've made your point. You're worrying me. Let's let him go." By the time my hand reached his, his arm relaxed, dropping, letting go.

The man fell away, a puddle of flesh and bone, gasping through a tight, bruised throat. But he was alive. He'd heal, he'd live, and, if he were smart, he'd never show his face in these parts again.

As Austin's eyes cleared, blinking down at me, I acted quickly—using my magic to rip open the door, fling Pinhead out, and slam it shut again.

Putting my hand back on Austin's chin, I ran the other over his shoulders and down to the base of his neck. His arms came around me then, pulling me to him. He dipped his head and his lips claimed mine, possessive, insistent. His tongue ran along my bottom lip, demanding admission.

Surprised, I opened to him, feeling his tongue plunge in before sweeping through, striking up a deep rhythm that stole my breath and made my heart thunder in my chest. I tightened my arms around his neck, rewarded with a deep, masculine growl, his kiss deepening, his hands splaying across my back. The world turned sideways, and all other thoughts fled as I fell into the feel of him, hard against my body. His taste overwhelmed me, spicy yet sweet, and I melted against him, utterly lost.

I'd forgotten how good this felt. How unbelievably he kissed, claiming all of my focus and stealing my breath.

Too soon he pulled back, gently biting my bottom lip, hot and passionate one moment, sultry and sanguine the next. I ached to find out if he was as good within the sheets as he was with his lips.

"Sorry," he murmured. "For all of that. For this, for everything. I didn't know how to tell you about the link. At first I didn't intend to use it. But you'd been kidnapped under my watch, and I was terrified of it happening again. I'm trying to give you as much privacy as I can. I don't know how to muffle it automatically, so whenever it feels like you need your space, I push the link away. I ignore it. Please believe that. This isn't about me spying on you."

"But why didn't you mention it? I would've understood."

He shook his head. "Embarrassment, at first. I'd made such a big deal about Ivy House, and here I was, sticking my hand in the cookie jar. But after that…" He took a deep breath. "Someone suggested to me that it would be dangerous for you to know. That you might figure out a way to cut yourself off from us if you found yourself in a sticky situation. Which…you would. We both know it. You'd worry more about us than whatever was happening to you."

I grimaced. That "someone" was likely Niamh, given she'd said the same thing. They weren't totally wrong, although I'd evolved in my thinking.

He traced his thumb along my bottom lip. "I will accept your wrath. I deserve it." He kissed me again, so incredibly open in his physical intimacy at the moment, which he would have usually shut down by now.

"What should I expect from what just happened?" I pulled my hands down his chest, realizing I didn't want to pull back. I didn't want to step away. Keeping my distance from him for the last month and a half had been excruciating. Just work and no play made this former Jane a very dull girl. I was going crazy with only the Ivy House staff to hang out with. That way lay insanity. I'd end up asking to be retired like Edgar always did.

Shadows passed over Austin's eyes, but before he could answer, I said, "I want you back. I want our friendship back. I've missed you. I want you hanging around again. And I want to help you with your territory…if you'll let me."

His gaze was deep. "What can you expect from what just happened? Nothing. Once they challenged me, their lives were in my hands. Every last one of them. I could've killed them without remorse."

I frowned at him. "No, I meant, will you freak out that you got lost to your dark side?"

The shadows returned again, and he looked at me for a long moment, as if debating. "Yep," he finally said. "And you are the only soul who will hear that truth. I trust you won't pass it on."

"Okay, well...how do I help with that?"

His smile was soft. "You already did. You pulled me out of it. I can't remember a single person, besides my little niece, who has ever been able to do that. You are a remarkable woman. But I'll need to think on what happened and why. I have to make sure it doesn't happen again, or I'll need to step down as alpha. These people deserve more than someone who loses control."

I nodded slowly, basking in his heat, seeing the cool logic return to his eyes. He took a step back.

"As for our friendship... I've missed you too." He shrugged, a smile flitting across his lips. "Maybe we're just friends who kiss from time to time. It happens."

I released a breath I hadn't known I was holding. "Yeah. It's worked for us so far."

"Thank you, for pulling me back," he said seriously. "For knowing when...and how."

"You've had my back enough; the least I could do was return the favor." I turned and headed to the bar. I needed a drink after all of that. "Ivy House took your side, by the way. When I was mad."

"Oh yeah?" He pulled out the seat Sebastian had been using so I could sit down. It was my regular seat. Sebastian would have to understand. Surprisingly, Austin took the one next to it.

"Yeah. She says she really needs you, which apparently means you can get away with almost anything. I mean...she said I should beat the crap out of you, but that I need to forgive you in the end."

"That's a comfort. Do you want to let everyone back in?"

"Oh yeah, sorry. Are you...?" I nodded at the chair.

"Taking the rest of the night off. I need to catch up with an old friend. I might even get to slip in a smile or two. After what I did to that guy with the terrible haircut and all his friends, I'll get a few days' leeway before someone else acts the fool."

It was clear he hadn't processed everything. He was trying not to think about what had happened, but I knew he'd turn a corner at some point and find himself in that dark place. The best thing I could do for him now was stay by his side and help make that transition as easy as possible. Because, honestly, that had been *crazy*. I'd never seen Austin react like that, like some kind of movie villain. And yet...I hadn't been afraid for one moment, not for myself and not for the people tucked into the other room. I'd only worried about the man hanging from his vise grip.

No, that wasn't quite true. I'd mostly been worried about Austin, and how far into the shadows he'd charged.

I had caused him to do that. I had to own that. He'd only lost control when the conversation had turned to me. I'd caused it, and I would help fix it.

Niamh was the first to stomp back into the room, her glass empty and her expression closed down in irritation. "What took yis? Stop playing with your food, Austin Steele, or do it somewhere else. I'm *choking* with thirst!"

Sebastian drifted in slowly with his hands in his pockets, slightly bowed, his hair still sticking up all over, and his gaze rooted to Austin.

"I want to thank you," he said when he got within range. "I haven't felt proper fear in a very long time. I was a little afraid when I saw all the fierce muscle in the bar, just knowing what could happen, but *seeing* it..." He shook his head, then shivered. "Thank you for reminding me what it's like."

"He'll fit in with Ivy House at least," Austin murmured, turning away as Donna bustled in behind the bar.

"What can I get ya, alpha?" she chirped, as though nothing had happened.

Everyone else filed in from outside, and I was surprised when there was even less room in the bar than before. I'd expected people to go home in fear or boredom. From the looks of it, they'd called their friends.

After Austin ordered a round for everyone on the house, I reached in my back pocket and pulled out a bent invitation Mr. Tom had given me a couple of hours before. It had come by courier, apparently, something I'd totally missed in the midst of my twelfth attempt to explain my newfound magic to Jimmy.

"Okay, let's get down to business. Two things..." I pointed at Sebastian. "Are you up to speed regarding Ivy House and my role there?"

"Not your role, but Niamh did tell me about your introduction to magic," he answered.

"Yeah, I don't even really know much about my role. I've been avoiding it. Good call. Okay, so I'd like to beg your help in training, because I need to get ready for this." I straightened the thick, smoky-colored card stock. "For the first time, an interested party isn't planning on attacking. They are, instead, formally inviting me and my people to a weekend at their estate. Apparently he wants to...get to know me."

"Form an alliance, maybe?" Niamh asked, peering over. "Did he say how he heard of ye?"

"No, no information. Just a meet-and-greet situation." I shrugged. "To get to know me," I repeated. "It's a chance at a friendship, maybe. Or at least make a connection. Maybe I can get my foot in the door with mages."

Sebastian leaned forward, peering over my shoulder at the swirling font. "Domino Kinsella would stab his granny in the back if she had something he wanted."

CHAPTER 8

"I F SOMETHING GOES wrong, or his intentions aren't pure, we don't have the numbers or the setup to make that visit." Austin took his drink off the bar, swirling the dark brown liquid. The people trying to get to the bar for their free drink gave our group a wide berth, but several of them shot furtive glances at Austin and me. "I have a few guys who can operate well in small spaces, but they won't show well in an affair like that. They have more raw talent than honed skill. Do we know anything about this guy's magic or power level?"

"Mid-level mage, I think." Sebastian put his hand up and teeter-tottered it back and forth. "I know him only by reputation. He's made it farther than a man of his stature normally would, and it's because of pure viciousness."

"I really need to stick me head out of me arse and get better acquainted with the magical world again," Niamh murmured.

"I was just thinking the same thing," Austin said, his

expression troubled. He glanced to the side as someone slowly shuffled by, watching Austin with tightly pressed lips. His expression smoothed over into the hard mask.

"My side of the link is going to stay open now, I hope you know." I reached for my bottle of beer, the dark brown glass sweating. I felt like something a little lighter than my normal glass of wine. "It's only fair."

"Oh, ye worked that out, did ye?" Niamh twisted her mouth to the side in distaste. "I wanted to see that go down."

"What would be the downside of putting off the visit?" I asked. "Would he lose interest, do you think?"

"Are ye *jokin'*?" Niamh tsked. "He'll surmise ye don't have the forces to keep yerself safe. I may not know much about the current players in the magical world, but I doubt the game itself has changed. Ye are new and untested, mostly. So far as he has heard, anyway. He wants to get a gawk. He wants to size you up. If ye snub him, fine, but ye better have the power to swat him away if he takes offense and paints a target on yer back.

"Now, maybe he doesn't know if he wants anything a'tal. Maybe he's just sizing up the new kid. A few vicious shifters led by Austin Steele will make a statement. Then there is the house staff. We have a lot of experience. We might be able to make it seem like we are—Well, no." She batted her hand through the air. "I'm full of shite. Earl has lost his marbles, I'm out of the loop, and Edgar will just make them feel sorry for us. We're not enough. We need a few more powerful fliers, another mage or two who's not so wet behind the ears, and some stronger units on the ground for Austin Steele. We go like this, and we'll look like a rinky-dinky, two-bit circus they can hang upside down by the ankles and shake all the money from our pockets."

The digits from the ledger rolled through my mind. A cold sweat broke over me. "Would they actually try to steal Ivy House's money?"

"If there was enough of it, yes," Niamh said. "Or...they would've back in the day. Not sure now. Maybe there's a different commodity the magical world is into."

"Money and power will never go out of style," Sebastian said, looking at his feet. "I didn't realize at first how much power you had, Miss Jessie."

"You can just call me Jessie."

"You do a good job of masking it. When you opened up and let it roll out earlier with the alpha, it blew my hair back. Figuratively speaking. You'd want to be careful showing off that much power without the knowledge of how to properly use it. Your power is worth more than Ivy House's money."

"Speaking of…" I traced my finger down the side of my bottle. "I could really use help with that. You said you'd give me the week, right? What if we treat it as a trial run? We train with magic once a day for two to three hours—whatever we can handle—and the rest of the time is yours to do with as you please. We can have a chat at the end of the week, see where we are and what you're thinking."

He shrugged, watching the people in the bar. "The week, sure. I've never been given an apprentice. I've always wondered about the apprentice/master bond." Austin stiffened before leaning an elbow on the bar, looking away. Sebastian noticed it. "I came here, to this tiny town in the middle of nowhere, to satisfy my curiosity. I fully intended to leave at the end of the week." His eyes were still on Austin. "But that display earlier… I've never seen a shifter at work. I am…*fascinated*. Their magic is built in. They don't need spells and incantations, potions and magic-built eyes in the back of their heads. Their primal senses fill that gap. Their strength and speed—if I had been that man with the odd haircut, my neck would've snapped before I even realized I was in trouble. I am not that fast on my best day. My very best day. Even standing here, now, I am holding on to courage with two fists. I am worried about his temper breaking and killing me before I can even think of a magical deterrent." He shivered. "I rather like the feeling. I feel…alive. Reinvigorated."

Austin had turned slowly to look at Sebastian, his face unreadable but his emotions akin to what he felt when listening to Edgar talk about his flowers.

Niamh mumbled, "He's as mad as a hatter."

"I find it," Sebastian said, dropping his gaze to his shoes, "very surprising, all of this. But I have a very cushy job, separated from the more unpleasant parts of the magical world. It would be quite a change to come here. However, I will not close my mind to the possibility. I agree to the trial period, and I'll decide what to do at the end of it."

"Maybe you'll find the small-town life suits you," I said. "I have, for what it's worth."

Sebastian looked around again. "Do you even have delivery?"

"Ah, sure, just stop by Ivy House and have that eejit *Mr. Tom* make something for ye." It was probably the first time I'd heard Niamh use his made-up name. She was making fun of the idea, yes, but she'd still used it. Baby steps. "That's his only real use these days, anyway."

Austin pushed his glass to the top of the bar and connected eyes with Paul, silently asking for another, before resting his elbow on the edge again. "You do need better fliers, Jess. Jasper and Ulric have their uses, as do Mr. Tom and Niamh, but they won't be enough to protect you when you are forced into aerial combat. That is where you're weakest."

I sighed, finishing off my beer. I pushed the bottle away.

"Here, Donna, swap this out." Niamh pointed at the bottle. "Thanks so much."

"No, no," I said. "I'm done. I need to head—"

"You might as well, like." She motioned for Donna to step to it. "That lad of yours will be fine on his own. He's got enough to be gettin' on with, seeing as Earl bought out that store for video games. Besides, he's probably sleeping. You're grand. Two won't hurt ye."

"No, honestly, I need to be…" Donna deposited another bottle in front of me. I wouldn't be going anywhere. That was always the hazard of drinking with Niamh.

"Okay, then, what sort of fliers do I need?" I asked.

"Masters of the sky," Austin said.

"Formidable," Niamh added. "Ruthless in battle."

"Even better if they can also fight on the ground in human form," Austin said.

"What we need is pure power." Niamh wiggled her drink, the ice tinkling against the glass. "We have Ulric for maneuverability, we have Jasper for coasting, but we need someone explosive. Thunderous in power."

"How about someone who seems like they're beneath notice but transitions into a form that wreaks vast damage?" Sebastian asked.

"All good ideas." I chewed on my lip. "And I need another gargoyle. Ivy House said so when Ulric and Jasper were given their place."

"You can speak to the house?" Sebastian asked. His slate-gray eyes showed no surprise or disbelief, but his tone was one of delight. He really could take crazy in stride. That could only help him with my crew.

"It's not a normal house." I thought about everything that had been said, then went over what I knew of gargoyles. "How many big personalities can I handle, do you think? People who might keep trying to push for the alpha role?"

"You?" Niamh shook her head. "None. Ye don't understand the subtleties of the magical world or those who are ruled by, or rule as, alphas. Dalmatian or whatever his name was proved that. He was trying to subtly manipulate ye the whole time. Good thing he was piss-poor at romance and not so bright."

A black cloud of rage rolled through Austin, though his appearance gave no sign of it. He hadn't been a fan of Damarion—both were natural alphas, and neither had wanted the other in his space. It was still a sore subject, even more so now that Austin had stepped up to take the title.

"He always did what I said, even when he didn't want to," I replied.

"See?" Niamh tucked in her lips and lifted her eyebrows, as though I'd made her point for her.

"If he was trying to manipulate me, where were you? You never said a word."

"I agreed with Austin Steele about the way the eejit was training you, and I said so. I didn't bother me arse about the subtle manipulation. He was romancin' ye to win ye over. Ye weren't havin' it, not that I blame ya. That lad didn't have a clue. Not one clue, boy. Would've been nice if ye'd relieved a little stress, though, if ye know what I mean…"

Another blast of rage rolled through the link.

"Great, super. Thanks again for all the help." I smoothed my hair back in annoyance.

"How many could Austin Steele handle, though?" Niamh knocked on the bar. "Well, now we've got a real question, haven't we?"

"As many as you need." He rested his hand on his thigh, looking at me. "I can handle whoever and whatever you call in."

"Is it confidence…or ego?" Sebastian mused aloud. Austin swung his gaze Sebastian's way. The mage flinched, and then the crooked grin worked at his lips. "I spent some time as an adrenaline junkie in the past—"

"Oh no, he's on about his past again," Niamh drawled, and then chugged her cider.

"After a while, you can't find anything to get the blood pumping again." Sebastian's eyes flashed, the color almost morphing into blue for a split second. "I wonder when this will wear off."

"It won't." Niamh tinkled the ice in her empty glass. Paul hurried over. "Trust me on that. It's annoying as all hell."

I lightly touched Austin's knee to bring his attention back to me. He flinched, and wariness roiled through the link.

"Are you always this jumpy after a challenge?" I asked, trying to make light of it.

He didn't respond.

"Are challenges typically six-to-one odds or similar?" Sebastian asked. "I thought I'd read somewhere that two alphas fought for territory…"

"It's supposed to be one on one," Niamh said. "That's the only way it truly counts. They must've known they couldn't handle Austin Steele that way."

"What happens if a challenger wins by cheating?" Sebastian asked.

"If it's not an honest win, the people don't have to

recognize the winner as their new alpha. Of course, it doesn't always work that way in practice. A cheating alpha doesn't just go straight once he or she gets ahead. They usually get the territory, and it almost always fails."

"*Fasci*nating," Sebastian said. He started to ask another question, but I tuned him out. While this was all probably good to know, I had other things to settle before I snuck out.

I lowered my voice for only Austin, shrouding us in a protective magical bubble. "Are you sure about the level of power I might call in? You have your territory to set up. I don't want to be taking your bandwidth."

"Jess, you've inspired me to challenge myself, to rise to my potential. It would be easy to run a small territory like this one, with a few towns and only a few idiots challenging every once in a while. My role is more complicated because my pack needs to be strong enough to defend Ivy House, but that's still well within my abilities. To do all that and also manage the powerful creatures you need for your council? That will certainly be a challenge. Given that a challenge is what I set out for, I hope you call in the biggest and baddest you can find. You charmed a basajaun, of all things. What other surly creatures can you collect?"

"I don't think you want to ask that question."

He winked. "I'll handle whatever comes, Jess. That's a promise. Call in whatever you need. Call in the best."

It wasn't Austin's ego speaking. He'd earned his confidence. It was built on a foundation of years of experience and trials, and there was no question he also had a firm grip on his weaknesses, most of which stemmed from his past. He was not a man to falsely dress up his nature. He was quicker, in fact, to tear himself down.

The summons exploded from me without warning, Austin's green light allowing my magic the freedom to search. Those who fit the requirements we'd discussed would be called. The gargoyle would likely come immediately, Ivy House and its mistress figured largely into their lore, but the others... Well, I hoped they were just as curious as Sebastian.

I sucked in a breath and let it out slowly, dissolving the spell bubble around us. "Now we wait. Again. I hate this part."

"That's how you called me?" Sebastian asked.

"Yes. You and everyone else."

"So what are we going to do about that invitation?" Niamh asked, eyeing my beer. She clearly knew I was planning my escape.

"I can put him off." I touched the edge of the invitation. "I can say that Austin is forming his pack and it's not a good time to visit."

"In other words, we are vulnerable," Niamh said.

"So maybe he'll attack Ivy House. It won't be any different than the other times we've defended her. Probably easier, since we've had more experience fighting as a team."

"Why not just bring him to town?" Sebastian asked. "They wouldn't be able to bring too many people because of the town's size and lack of accommodations. You can even control how many rooms are available."

"All of the Airbnbs are full," Austin said. "House inventory is very low with everyone moving into town. He could put people in the other towns, effectively spreading them out. We'd let him, saying the size of his team is only an issue because of available space, not because we aren't set up to defend against it. The problem would be when we all meet up. And if his people wandered the streets, intending to cause trouble..." He tightened his lips and minutely shook his head. "Let me think on this. But it's a good idea. Bringing them here is probably the safest bet."

"This place is like the Wild West right now," Niamh said. "Ye can't have a well-established magical muckety-muck coming through here. He'll think we're easy for the taking."

"He's a mage," Sebastian said. "I don't know about

his setup, but mages don't typically have shifters on their teams, as I said to…the Irish lady—"

"After all we've been through, you don't remember me name?" she cut in, and I could tell she was delighted for reasons unknown.

"He'll probably buy this as a normal shifter setup," Sebastian continued, ignoring her. "I thought it was. It wouldn't even matter if it were less…respectable. You turn into animals—why not live like animals?"

"Animals are typically much more organized than people," Austin said, almost a growl.

"Someone give me a heads-up when I say the wrong thing," Sebastian whispered, "so I can get ready to run or put up a spell or something."

I spat out a laugh, not expecting that little bit of humor, made funnier because he was dead serious.

"Ye still need a good team in place, Austin, and ye don't have it," Niamh said.

Austin nodded and took a slow sip of his drink.

I wondered if that was his way of saying, *Hold my beer.*

✧　✧　✧

LATER THAT NIGHT I tucked myself into bed, my brain a little fuzzy from alcohol and my son thankfully asleep in his room. Niamh had strong-armed me into another couple of beers, Sebastian hadn't escaped without another scotch being forced on him, and Austin had eventually walked me home, Ulric and Jasper flying high overhead. We'd all separated with the question remaining—how could we possibly play host to an established mage and not look like a Podunk outfit? Niamh didn't think there was a way—she thought we should come up with a good reason to keep him waiting.

The question was, what would happen when he got tired of waiting?

I pulled the covers up to my chin, my eyes on the soft moonlight shining in the many windows of the largest room I'd ever called my own. I nestled into the soft bedclothes and fluffy pillow, thinking about the events of the night. As sleep dragged at me, warmth sparked down low and curled up through my middle. It spread, saturating my body, a deep ache tightening my core.

Pleasure came next, forcing out a gasp, localized between my thighs. I pushed my legs together, twisting as though I could move away. A sudden urge for fast, hard contact bled through my thoughts.

I gripped the sheets, trying not to give in to the sensations, which had come out of nowhere. At this point, everyone knew not to spy on me during certain times, but until they learned how to magically control the link to automatically shut down in private moments, Jasper and Ulric would know what I was up to before they could sign off.

Realization dawned.

I checked the links, the pleasure pumping higher now, consuming me. It was pounding between my thighs, massaging the bundle of nerves at my apex. I stifled a moan as I blocked my magical connections to Jasper and then Ulric. These feelings weren't from them.

Half grossed out, I blocked the rest, the pleasure cutting out immediately, leaving an absence in its wake.

Panting, now off-kilter, I felt Mr. Tom downstairs, tidying up the kitchen after making me a late-night snack. Wasn't him, thank God, something I was happy to ascertain through his position in the house and not through the link. Edgar was out in the wood, doing God knew what, but he was walking around. Couldn't be him.

"Please don't be Niamh. Please…" My stomach twisted in distaste.

I couldn't not know. I couldn't have that hanging over my head as a maybe.

I unblocked the link and blocked it back up super quick, the briefest of feelings. Nothing. She was probably asleep.

"Thank all that is holy," I said, heaving out a sigh. I wasn't sure I would've ever recovered from…

My phone vibrated on the nightstand. Frowning, I pushed up to an elbow to peer at the screen.

Text from Austin: *You okay?*

I frowned harder. When I unblocked the link between us, the pleasure didn't resume. He must've felt my distaste.

Phone in hand, I was about to text him a quick answer and let him get back to things, but…

A spike of unease pierced my middle. What if he was with someone?

It felt like acid dripped down through me.

I wasn't, by nature, a jealous person. Never had been. Boyfriends had flirted with other women at parties and my ex-husband had been known for his "charm." I'd never worried about it.

I didn't have any right to Austin, but I hated the thought of someone else sliding against his amazing body, or delighting in his expert, passionate kisses.

My stomach turned at the thought of him taking someone else on the perfect date, or directing her with a gentle but firm hand on the small of her back.

The phone rang this time, vibrating in my fingers. Austin's name was on the screen.

I slid my finger across it, answering the call.

"Hey," I said, uncomfortable, hating that I felt this way.

"Hey." His voice was thick, rough. His breathing came faster than normal, like he'd been working out. "You okay?"

"Yeah. Sorry."

"For what?"

"I… Uhm." I swallowed. Now that I was in this position, I suddenly understood why he'd been hesitant to tell me about listening in through the link. "I accidentally forgot to close down everyone's links, so…"

A rush of heat flooded my body from Austin. He'd liked hearing that.

His voice lowered, his tone softer now. "Is that why you felt so disgusted?" I could hear the teasing.

"I didn't know who was…" Another rush of heat. I barely stifled a gasp. "I usually only have one or two of them open at a time, so I haven't practiced deciphering who is who when they're all open. I closed them all—"

"How'd you know it was me?"

Another sheen of sweat broke out on my forehead. An insane part of me wanted to dip my hand south, like we were in college in different dorms, unable to stand the distance separating us and desperate for the time when we could feel the rush of each other's bodies again.

"I had to check each person. It came down to you and Niamh, and I couldn't live with the not knowing... I had to know if I'd ever be able to look her in the eyes again." I laughed nervously. "But anyway..." I licked my lips, needing to know. Not able to help it. "I should let you get back to your date."

"I haven't had a date since the one with you."

"You know what I mean."

"Yes, I do. I haven't had a date since the one with you. There's no one here, Jess."

Heat coursed through me, my own this time. His groan was soft, and suddenly I didn't know what we were doing. I didn't know if I was about to make a big mistake.

I was certain I didn't care.

"Have you ever listened in on me?" I asked, my voice belonging to another woman, thick and sultry and wanton. "Through the link, I mean. When I've..."

"Yes." His voice dripped with arousal. My nipples tightened and I rubbed my thighs together, unable to stand the pounding heat.

"I should be mad at that," I whispered.

"Probably," he replied, and pleasure once again swirled between my thighs. I moaned, the feeling threatening to sweep me away. "It happened by accident at first. I was reading and the pleasure caught me off guard. Most of the time I block the link, but sometimes…"

I sighed at the pounding deep inside of me, my knees parting, my hand slipping down my stomach and between my legs.

He growled into the phone.

"Does it feel like someone is touching you?" I asked, arching.

"It feels like *you* are touching me. Sometimes it feels like you are sliding onto me. I assume that's when you use…help…"

I should've been embarrassed, definitely. But I groaned into the phone.

"During these times, the feelings from the link are heightened. Incredibly heightened. It feels like you're lying beside me. Or straddling me. The feeling of you when you aren't here is better than I can remember anyone else feeling in the flesh. More consuming."

I squeezed my eyes shut, my hips jerking against the mattress. "I don't think it's like this for everyone. From what Jasper said—"

A spark of rage blistered through the link, and strangely, any embarrassment that lingered from the conversation with Jasper eased, almost like Austin was squashing it dead.

"Thinking someone was there with you… I didn't like it," I admitted. "I'm not usually jealous, but…"

"Thinking of anyone with you…"

Another wave of rage pushed through me, sparking my adrenaline and heightening my pleasure. I didn't understand why. I should be worried or afraid, ready to step in and calm him down. Instead, I could barely focus as I imagined his hands on me, his body filling mine.

"It's your primal response to my primal reaction," he said, clearly having deciphered my feelings. "My unconscious rage stems from wanting to crush any competition that seeks your hand. To claim you as mine. Your reaction to that mimics your desire for it to happen. If you were angry or scared, it would mean you didn't like the match. It would mean you were worried about being taken by an alpha by force. Your pleasure means you'd welcome it."

His rough tone caressed me, and while I was pretty sure I needed to be a shifter to feel and really understand all he'd said, there was no denying the aching rapture of his reaction.

"Friends that kiss and sometimes have late-night phone conversations," I choked out, the feelings consuming, my thoughts frazzling.

"There's no point in pretending anymore, Jacinta. Not after what happened at the bar."

I meant to ask for clarification.

I ended up begging for more.

CHAPTER 9

"HEY, MOM." JIMMY trudged into the kitchen, a cup of steaming coffee in his hand. Mr. Tom's notable absence meant he was probably already ransacking Jimmy's room for dirty clothes and dishes and whatever else he could clean. He probably worried Jimmy would be like my parents and try to clean up after himself. Or worse, clean up after Mr. Tom.

"Hey, bud. You hungry? Mr. Tom made some eggs and toast."

He squinted at the digital clock on the oven. "You're not pissed I'm up so late?"

"Ten thirty is about normal for me these days. We all keep late hours."

"Sweet." He opened the microwave. "Where?"

"Oven—"

"I'll do that for you, don't you worry." Mr. Tom bustled past the kitchen in the hallway, heading for the laundry room with a hamper. "Just have a seat and I'll be right there."

Jimmy stared after him, his hair standing up in all directions, much like Sebastian's last night.

Last night.

A wave of emotion rolled over me, both from my tandem release with Austin over the phone and also what he'd said. He'd promised he would see me today, and his voice had been rough and raw when he spoke about my reactions to him.

Something had shifted between us last night, and I wasn't sure exactly what. We'd certainly muddied things with that phone call, but the physical stuff hadn't been the deciding factor for him. He thought we'd turned a corner for other reasons, and I wasn't sure what those were. I was nervous to find out what. Just as nervous as I was to climb the stairs and go into the office, to take the blood oath and accept my permanent place at Ivy House.

"Mom?"

"What's up?" I straightened up from where I'd been slouching and lifted my eyebrows.

"I asked what the deal is with that butler." Jimmy sat down beside me, content to have patience when there was the prospect of being waited on, just like his mother.

"He's as weird as they come, bud. No other explanation for it."

"But you pay him?"

"Kinda. The house funds pay him. He kinda…came with the house, like I said yesterday. Because of the…"

"Magic, yeah. I'm still trippin', trying to piece reality back together. Like…Xbox doesn't seem as interesting when you've seen a gargoyle, you know? *I've seen a gargoyle!*" He bent over the island. "I have seen…a *gargoyle.*" He swore, and I let him have that one.

"Now." Mr. Tom reentered the kitchen, as pleased as I'd ever seen him. "What are we thinking, Master Jimmy? The works? You ate enough to feed an army last night; I can only assume you'll eat all I've prepared for you today."

"Yes, please."

"There." Mr. Tom nodded. "Manners. That is much better than the foul mouth I heard a moment ago."

"What did you want to do today?" I asked as Mr. Tom compiled enough food for two. I knew none of it was for me. Apparently he wanted to test Jimmy's stomach. "Do you want to check out the town, or—"

I felt Austin's feet touch down on the walkway leading to the house and butterflies swarmed my stomach, quickly turning ravenous and beginning to eat through my stomach lining. My links were all closed down out of habit. I hadn't expected him.

"Or a hike, maybe?" Jimmy said. "Mom?"

"Yes. Sorry. Yes, a hike would be great. Want to meet a Bigfoot?"

Jimmy just gaped at me.

"He is a basajaun," Mr. Tom said with a sniff. "You'll slip one day and call him Bigfoot to his face, miss, and then he won't want to help you anymore. You'd better be careful."

"He doesn't know what a basajaun is—"

"I know what that is," Jimmy cut in. "I can't remember where it's from."

"Basque mythology portrays them quite well," Mr. Tom said.

"Right, right." Jimmy nodded as Mr. Tom delivered a heaping plate. "Mythology class, that's right. Or maybe it was a dude in D&D who mentioned them. It's bigger than a Bigfoot, right? Meaner?"

"He is very mean, yes. When you aren't on his good side, at least." I magically opened the front door as Austin reached it. "He loves magical flowers."

"This is a trip. You are living the absolute best life."

I glowed from within, trying not to preen at being the cooler parent for the first time ever. "It's a crazy life, and it has some serious dangers." Austin walked down the hall toward us. "It's not all fun and games."

"Well, I mean..." Jimmy pushed food into his cheek. "It is for me, right? Because I'm just visiting."

"Smart boy." Mr. Tom snapped up straight and turned toward the door as Austin entered. "Hello, Austin Steele, can I get you something to eat?"

Austin's cobalt eyes burned as they beheld me, tracking me like prey, and I didn't dare peek at the link.

"Hi," I said, suddenly unsure where to put my hands. He'd always been the one uncomfortable with our closeness. I'd been the blasé one. The sudden shift wigged me out. Made me feel like a high schooler with a crush.

Jimmy's fork slowed on the way up to his mouth, his eyes widening and the rest of him freezing.

"Hi. I'm Austin." He put out his hand for Jimmy.

"They prefer fist bumps these days," Mr. Tom said as though he were the leading expert on college-aged kids. "Or high fives."

My son shook himself, lowering his fork. "Oh." He pushed to standing, his face suddenly flushed. "Hi. Hello, sir." He grabbed Austin's hand, offering a hearty shake.

"It's good to finally meet you. I've heard a lot about you." Austin let go of Jimmy's hand and stepped back, giving him space.

"Oh, yeah. That's my mom." Jimmy absently gestured at me, bending like a gawky teen. "You don't... Ahhhmm." He pointed at Austin's chest. "I don't see a cape—er, wings. Or…a cape?"

I frowned at him. When had he inherited my social awkwardness? He usually charmed the room like his father.

Austin rested a hand against the island. "I hear you got the lowdown on the hidden world within the world. I'm what's called a shifter. I—"

"A shapeshifter, yeah." Jimmy grinned. And then his lips went slack. "Sorry, sir. I didn't mean to interrupt."

Still frowning, I reached out to touch Jimmy's arm. "Austin is a good friend of mine. You don't have to be so formal."

"Oh right. Yeah." Jimmy slowly slid onto his stool, anything but comfortable. He was clearly reacting to Austin's raw power, the lethal confidence he didn't try to hide. "Sorry. Um, what do you turn into? If you don't mind me asking."

"A polar bear."

"Oh…" Jimmy's brow furrowed. "Aren't you always hot?"

Austin spread his hands. "I'm magical. I can control that stuff."

"Right, yeah." A nervous laugh rode Jimmy's exhale.

Austin's attention shifted to me. Butterflies flitted against my ribs.

"I wanted to let you know that I'm bringing the shifters to train in the woods today. I'll take them through the front yard so that there is plenty of warning. Just in case Ivy House is temperamental."

"*I'm feeling just fine,*" she murmured.

"You're good," I told him.

"Also…" His eyes flicked to Jimmy and back. "I wondered if I might have a word with you?"

Nervousness filled me and I gulped.

"It's not all that bad," he teased, his eyes crinkling.

It felt like I couldn't breathe. Like the world was imploding, and Austin was the only thing left to grab on to.

"Yeah, sure. I'll be out in a sec," I managed, trying to get a grip. Trying to figure out what was going on with me. This wasn't a normal crush. This was… Magic had to be involved in some way. Or maybe I had a late-onset behavior disorder. Who could blame me with all that had happened in such a short time?

He nodded, said goodbye to Jimmy, and stalked out of the kitchen, a busy man with places to be and heads to bust.

A gush of breath exited Jimmy. "Wow," he said. His eyes rounded as he picked up his fork. "That guy is intense. In-*tense*! Is that your boyfriend?"

"No, no, he's just a friend. One of the first friends I

made after moving here."

Jimmy rolled his shoulders. "He's big. Fit. He's your age, though, huh? He looks your age, but *wow*. He's keeping it together. I hope I look that good when I'm forty. Or is that just what shifters look like?"

"Not all of them, trust me. They can get out of shape just like the next guy."

"When that guy looks at you, your bowels get a little soggy, am I right?" A smile worked at his lips. "He's the type of guy you want on your side. Is he single?"

"Why, do you want a date?" I laughed, standing.

"If he's single, you should go after him. I'm confident enough in my masculinity to say that he's a good-looking dude. You could do far worse."

"I thought sons were supposed to be protective of their moms? You want me to just jump back on the wagon?"

"If it means you're happy...yeah."

I blinked at him for a moment, surprised to hear that. "You're not pissed at your father and me for splitting up? I know you said that, but..."

He shrugged. "You spent half the time fighting, and the other half ignoring each other. He was never home. He's *still* never home. You deserve to find someone who devotes time to you and makes you happy. You seem really..." He flared his arms while wiggling his shoulders. I shook my head, no clue what that meant. "Like…light and easy. You seem more chill. I can tell you're happier." He shrugged again. "It's probably for the best, you know? So if you *are* going to climb back on the…wagon, if you want to use that ancient metaphor, he's probably a good guy to do it with."

I mussed his hair, which I knew he hated. "You barely met him. How would you know?"

"I don't know. You meet that guy, and you expect to be told what to do, and you just know you're going to do it. I wouldn't even be pissed to do it—I'd just get it done and get out of his way, know what I mean?"

"She doesn't, young master. She has no clue what you mean," Mr. Tom said solemnly. "She barely knows how to get out of her own way."

I rolled my eyes, making my way out of the kitchen and into the front yard. Two dozen men and women waited on the street, dressed in sweats and loose shirts, standing in clusters and murmuring softly, clearly waiting. Austin turned to me when I stepped outside, his gaze sweeping my body before burning into my eyes.

I braced myself, not sure what he was going to say, how I'd react to whatever it was.

"Listen, I've been thinking. I might have an…unorthodox solution to our problem." He turned his back on his waiting people, facing me.

I wasn't sure which problem he was talking about. "Oh?"

He shook his head a little, flexed, and gritted his teeth.

Despite myself, a smile crept onto my face.

"Run your fingers through your hair?" I guessed. "Was that what you stopped yourself from doing?"

He looked down at me, mirth sparkling in those beautiful eyes. A ghost of a smile crossed his lips. "I was going to brace my hands on my hips. This is a bit…" He shook his head, the humor fleeting. "The mage who sent that invitation might not be significant, but I think we ought to host him sooner rather than later. If we can grab him as an ally, great. If not, we need to make a statement, to rattle him to the point that his allies and competitors don't want to mess with us. We have to be prepared in case of the latter."

I let out a shaky breath. He didn't plan to bring up last night. At least not right now.

Why was I so relieved about that? Why was I so nervous?

"That all sounds great, but don't we lack the power to make a statement?" I asked.

"That's what I wanted to talk to you about. I wondered… What would you say to pushing that meeting out a month so I can bring in some temporary help to fill my ranks? I'll have the people on the ground even if you don't have everyone you need in the air yet. When we've made our point, we can disband them."

"Do they have that? Shifter temps?"

He swallowed, his eyes creasing at the corners. I finally opened the link, feeling the discomfort pouring from him. "I was thinking about calling in a favor to my brother."

CHAPTER 10

THE WORDS TASTED sour on Austin's tongue, but he couldn't see any other way to make this work. Even to get this mage as an ally, they'd need a show of power. They'd need to show they were someone worth knowing.

But if things went wrong and Austin didn't squish that threat immediately, it would be open season. Shifters from all over would think him weak, coming to test him, to invade his territory—more so than the normal startup growing pains. Much more so.

That wasn't the biggest concern, though. If Jess showed off her power—and she would as soon as she did a spell—that mage would know what a powerhouse she was. He'd soon also realize how inexperienced she was. How magically naïve. How great she'd be to train up and force into a position on his staff.

It ultimately didn't matter which way the meeting went. Austin needed experience and power on his side. He needed a steady, reliable, strong defense. He needed to guard Jess in case the worst happened, and with mages, there was usually a high probability of that.

"Would he be okay letting you pull rank?" Jess asked, her deep hazel eyes full of concern.

He wanted to run his thumb across her chin, then her lips. Given she wasn't his mate, and his pack was standing behind him, he did neither.

"I can't say for sure, but I'd bet a million dollars that he would. He isn't like me. He doesn't push for dominance without meaning to. He's logical and balanced. And helpful. He never turns his back on someone in need."

"Then yes, if you think it'll work."

He very nearly reached forward to grab her hand.

"Fingers through your hair?" she asked with a devilish grin.

He barely stopped himself from smiling. "You're not great at guessing my reactions. What's the schedule for your training? With the weird mage?"

"Oh." The word rode a release of breath. "I want to spend some time with my shell-shocked son, who met you for only a couple minutes and thinks the sun shines out of your butt. I hoped to show him the town, or maybe take him to see the basajaun."

A shock of fear coursed through him. He played it cool, though he couldn't hide the growl. "Why don't you wait until I can go with you for the basajaun? The basajaun can be unpredictable with strangers, and you don't know enough magic to both combat him and protect your son at the same time. Just in case, I'd like to be there."

She shrugged with one shoulder. "It's pretty far anyway, not to mention we'd have to fly, and I'm not so sure he's ready to be carried by a gargoyle yet. He is quickly coming around to magic, but that might be pushing it. So maybe we'll do the town today and hit that tomorrow or the next day?"

He fell into that open gaze. She was so easy to work with. She wasn't stubborn when someone suggested a change in plan, but would push for all she was worth if she knew her plan was better. He respected that. He respected her.

Which was why he'd unwittingly grown close to her over the past half-year. She'd slipped under his defenses and wound herself through his very person, touching heart and soul. He'd tried to put distance between them to cool things off, but the damage had been done, something that had become incredibly apparent last night when he'd lost himself to blind rage. Hearing that clown speak about her like that...

Rage kindled down deep, barely controlled, threatening to rise.

Mine.

"You okay?" she asked.

She'd pulled him out of it last night. She hadn't goaded him on like his ex, Destiny, would've done. She hadn't watched it happen in horror, either, too scared to intervene. She hadn't even forced his hand, which she could've. She'd kept her composure, cleared the room, and brought him out of the darkness. She'd known exactly how to handle it, and she'd even helped him deal with the fallout.

The situation last night had left little doubt of what he had to do next. But he didn't trust himself. Not when he'd made such poor decisions in the past. He needed a second opinion. He needed to know if it was safe to continue down this road, or if he was putting Jess and everyone in this territory at risk.

There were few things in the world he dreaded more than asking his brother to help him with that. But Kingsley was the person best poised to help.

"I'm good," Austin said. "Let me know what time you want to train with the mage. I'm curious to see what he can do."

"I'll text you."

"And I'll let you know about my brother. Depending on his answer and his schedule, you'll have a better idea for that RSVP."

She bobbed her head, her eyes tightening again. Nervousness flared through the link. She was probably wondering if he'd mention last night.

His answering hunger made her gasp.

He about-faced and walked away. Safer to keep those things at a distance until Kingsley arrived. He had always been the logical one, preferring to think things through rather than rushing in headfirst.

Of course, it remained to be seen whether he would come at all, given the way Austin had left.

CHAPTER 11

"OKAY, READY?" I asked Austin, who stood across the clearing in the woods behind Ivy House with a knife in hand.

My son, tired from touring the town and surrounding nature on foot, had been content to play his video games for a while, so I'd snuck away to train. I wasn't ready for him to see me bumbling around with magic. It would strip my new "rad mom" tag right off.

"Go for it." Austin flared his arms from his sides a little, ready for my pounding.

"Now, Jessie, remember what the book said." Edgar hunched over the large volume of the second training book, tracing the lines he'd recently translated. The spells in this book were much easier for him to read than the ones in the first volume. "It's a spell meant to disarm. Too much power and you'll literally rip an arm off. We're starting to get into the big leagues now."

"She'll have this one just fine," Niamh said, standing to the side with Jasper and Ulric. Mr. Tom stood behind

Edgar, peering over his shoulder. "She has no problem following directions. It's when she tries to change the spells that everything goes tits up."

"Yes, thank you for that lesson on what we already know," Mr. Tom said.

"If he knew it, why'd he say that?" she snapped.

I flexed my fingers, chancing a glance at Sebastian, who sat to my left on a log, placidly watching us. He'd suggested that I train as usual—he wanted to gauge where I was, magically speaking, before he gave any suggestions.

"You sure you're ready?" I asked Austin, licking my lips. I hated this part. He was my human guinea pig, and most of the spells I tried out caused him pain or discomfort.

He nodded, and nothing but expectation and support swirled through the link.

Why did the connection feel so completely different now than it had last night? It had almost felt like his actual hands were cupping my breasts, and his slow thrusting—

"Where did yer mind go?" Niamh shouted, bracing her hands on her hips. "This isn't the time to think dirty thoughts, girl. Keep yer head in the game!"

My face flared with heat and lust blasted through the connection from Austin.

"*I made it different. I know how to control the link, and you don't,*" Ivy House said. I'd apparently broadcast my internal debate to her. I occasionally did that without realizing it. It was like talking to myself, but with an audience. "*You've been a prude for far too long.*"

I formed the spell without thought. Niamh was right—I could always perfectly execute the spells in the book. The act of Edgar reading them planted them in my brain as if they'd always been there, waiting to be released.

"*You know how to alter the link?*" I asked as I released the spell.

"*You don't?*"

I frowned at her as the spell reached Austin. It swirled around his body. The knife fell out of a suddenly limp hand. His expression didn't change, but pain bled through the link. He sank to his knees, his muscles popping, straining his tight white T-shirt and pushing at his sweats. Trembling, he struggled to stand.

"What's happening?" I asked, my focus narrowing in on him as I jogged over. "What's it doing? I thought it was supposed to just disarm him."

"He's a shifter," Sebastian said. "His animal is a weapon."

"But…" I looked at Edgar. "What's it doing to him?" I shouted.

"Let me just…" Edgar's finger moved faster over the book.

"I'm…good…" Austin wheezed, on his hands and knees, head bowed. Pain drowned me through the connection.

I could fix his pain. I could numb him. But I worried that if I did, he'd stop fighting against whatever the spell was doing. If I numbed the sensations, I worried the spell might kill him.

Fear ate at me as Edgar said, "Here's the counter-spell."

"No—"

A flash of blistering heat and a blinding light cut off Austin's voice. Fur erupted from him as his body shot up and out, his animal form taking over. Suddenly, a massive polar bear stood in the clearing, much bigger than its counterparts in the natural world. His shoulder was at about the level of my head.

His roar thundered through the woods. The pain fizzled before dying, shed from him like a snake shed its skin. He shook himself before standing on his hind legs, a second roar shaking my bones and jittering my nerves.

Yesterday, I'd thought I could tango with this massive beast. Clearly it had been too long since I'd seen him in his animal form. Raw power pulsed into the clearing, squeezing something inside me left over from my ancestors. The fight-or-flight response to danger in the wild. Right now, it was screaming at me to run.

He lowered back down to all fours before huffing, the clearing dead quiet. A moment later, the heat and light made me flinch, and there was Austin again, his ripped and ruined clothes at his feet, his robust, muscular body on full display.

I was too frazzled to take notice.

"Wow." Sebastian ran his fingers through his messy hair. "That was..." A cockeyed grin spread across his face. "Very cool. I am literally shaking right now." He held up this hand. "I am so scared that I am literally shaking. I honestly do not know if I could magically fight that monster." He paused for a beat. "No offense intended, sir. Just... *Wow*."

"Take a number." I blew out a breath. "Someone run and get him some new sweats. Try to find something other than purple, if you can. He hates the purple ones."

"I have gray for him, in the laundry room with the others," Mr. Tom said as Ulric straightened out of a crouch and took off jogging. "Mind the size. I ordered the wrong size the first time around. Get the larger ones. He's bigger than you—"

"He's already gone; he can't hear ye anymore,"

Niamh said, waving her hand to quiet Mr. Tom. "Austin, what happened there, then?"

"The spell was trying to cut out my ability to shift," Austin replied. "Fighting it…hurt."

"Saying it hurt is a severe understatement," I said, bracing my hands on my hips. "I didn't want to numb you and possibly cut out your resistance. Was that a good idea or bad idea?"

"Numbing the pain would've made me submit to the spell. It was working through my limbs to my middle. If I hadn't been able to feel it, I wouldn't have known how to fight it."

"Why fight it at all?" Sebastian asked. "It would have kept you from shifting, sure, but the effects would have been nullified by the counter-spell."

Austin studied him for a moment. "I don't like being controlled. I would succumb if Jess explicitly asked me to, but she is the only person in the world I would allow to have that much control over me."

"So if I tried that spell on you?"

"I would not stand still to fight it like I just did. I would fight it as I ripped your throat out."

Sebastian shivered. "Jesus, you're intense." He draped his arms across his thighs. "She said you were in incredible pain. I couldn't tell."

"Thanks for the update." Austin looked back at me.

"What's next?"

"Are all shifters this selfless?" Sebastian asked. "Allowing someone to magically experiment on them even though it causes them great pain? I assume this isn't the first time you've done this."

"To be an alpha is to sacrifice," Austin replied. "If I can help Jess by undergoing something so trivial as pain, then it's an easy decision."

"Many shifters will tolerate a great deal to help their packs," Niamh said. "Most successful alphas will sacrifice a great deal more, like he said. But only one in a million could endure the sort of magical treatment Jessie throws at this great lummox, and still he comes back for more. Some of the spells are brutal. Sometimes I wonder if he's touched in the head."

"That started out so promising," Mr. Tom mused. "But I see you quickly slid back into your trough of bad manners and name-calling."

"Ye are much too sensitive, ye donkey," she replied.

"Yes, that's the ticket, double down on the bad behavior. Fantastic. I do so enjoy your company."

"Yer about'ta enjoy my foot up your hole in a minute."

That crooked grin worked at Sebastian's lips as he watched them argue.

"Right." I took a deep breath and shook out my fingers. Now for the hard part. "While Edgar translates the next spell, I should probably work on tweaking this spell so I can use it for smaller stuff. Like knocking away your knife without taking away your ability to change. Or"— I snapped—"I know. It would be really good to quickly know what sort of dangers a person is hiding. This spell, if tweaked just a little, should be able to tell me that."

Austin nodded and looked down at the knife. "I don't have anywhere to put this at the moment. Maybe we should wait until Ulric is back with the sweats so I can hide it on my person?"

"Well...ye *do* have somewhere to put it. It just won't be entirely comfortable." Niamh's eyes flicked down and then back up.

"I'm not going to make him put a knife up his keister, Niamh." I rolled my eyes. "Okay. Sebastian, this would be a great time for you to instruct me so Austin doesn't get hit with something ugly."

"I want to see how you problem-solve. I don't want to teach you spells; I want to teach you how to *create* spells. How to figure them out. You'll be able to make your own, improve others', and tear them down."

"Give a man a trout, fill his belly for a night," Edgar muttered, still looking at the book. "Teach a man about trout, fill him for a lifetime."

"Something like that, sure." Sebastian chuckled.

I dragged my teeth across my lip as I faced Austin again, his emotions expectant and patient, with a trickle of leftover heat worming through. The goal was not to hurt him, obviously. Instead of knocking away his weapons, I just wanted to see which ones he had. This was informational, that was all. And sure, I hadn't waited for the sweats, and I could literally see what he was packing—all of it—but that shouldn't matter.

"Here we go," I said, breaking out in a sweat, reminding myself of the trickle of power I needed. That was it, just a trickle. Anything more would turn the spell into something dangerous.

Spell ready, I reduced the power a little more, just in case, and let fly.

The spell hit a magical wall three feet from Austin. Sparks fizzed and sputtered. Fire flared before purple smoke curled into the air.

"You were really going to let her hit you with that?" Sebastian said to Austin, awestruck. "She cannot control her power, she just made up an intricate spell, willy-nilly, and you were going to let her fry off patches of your skin?"

"Is that what it would've done?" I asked, aghast.

"He's had worse," Niamh murmured as Ulric jogged back toward us, sweats in hand.

"I thought you all were showboating. I didn't think

she'd actually do it. But clearly this is how she's been training, huh?" Sebastian shook his head, looking down at his feet. "This would *never* happen in my world. Mages and shifters working side by side. The intricacy of spells and potions mixed with brute strength and iron-clad courage. What an army that would be."

"That's not true, about shifters and mages never working together," I mumbled, half my brain still thinking about where that spell might've gone wrong. "This house was attacked by a mage and some shifters."

"Those shifters were brought to die," Ulric said. "They weren't working together. That mage was offering them for slaughter."

"Yes, that sounds more likely," Sebastian said, still studying his shoes. "That spell had the right qualities, but you used way, *way* too much power." He put his head in his hands. "You have a deep well of power within you—very, very deep—but it's mostly below the surface, like an iceberg. It wasn't until you opened up with spell work that I glimpsed your raw strength. You aren't using all of it yet, but I know you will be more powerful than me when you eventually do. I could feel the currents of it when it hit my spell."

"Can you still teach me what you know?" I asked softly.

"Yes." He scrubbed at his hair and sat up, looking

away, his eyes distant. "Why hide your magical ability? A mage's power level scares off potential attackers half the time. Only the worthy need apply."

"For now, her biggest strength is in being undervalued," Edgar said, sitting back on his haunches. "It's best if people think she isn't anyone of consequence. But that aspect of her magic is at her discretion. When she's ready to show what she's made of, she can."

"How come you never told me that?" I asked.

Edgar shrugged. "It never came up."

"That makes sense." Sebastian's eyes rested on me, and for the first time I could remember, they weren't flat and affectless. They looked almost blue in the slice of sun that cut down his face, and they shone with intelligence and cunning. "You can release the alpha. You can release everyone but the vampire and his book, actually. I won't need their help."

I offered him a relieved smile, thankful he was sticking around. "Austin draws out my magic, so he has to stay." I glanced at Ulric and Jasper. "I'll call you when it's time to fly."

Before I could turn to Niamh, she said, "Nah. Don't bother. I'm not going anywhere. I want to see how ye get on. Besides, if that mage turns into a nutter and tries to bring you down, I want to be on hand to watch Ivy House deal with him."

"There is no way I am stepping out of line with the alpha on hand, I assure you," Sebastian said, flicking a glance Austin's way. "Seeing his polar bear form rattled me, and I don't mind admitting it." Sebastian rose, slouching as he walked toward me. "He doesn't need to stand there. You shouldn't practice on him anymore. He distracts you, and the worry of hurting him makes you hold back. I could see it in your body motions and positioning. Believe it or not, the positioning of your body matters when making a spell."

Austin nodded and moved toward Ulric, putting out his hand for the sweats.

"You will cast toward my magical backdrop." Sebastian stopped beside me. "First you'll do a spell from the book that you know and have no trouble with—I certainly wish I'd had a book like that—and then you'll create something similar from scratch. See how you measure up."

"Measure up…meaning what?" Mr. Tom asked. "To what?"

"Training by committee. Interesting approach." If Sebastian was put out, he didn't show it. "You saw what happened when a spell with too much power hit my wall. Fire. The color of the smoke informed us of the nature of the spell—violence lives in purples and blues. More benign spells come in yellows and oranges, and so on. But talking only achieves so much in the realm of spell-making. It'll be easier for me to teach you if I see you cast." He put his hands behind his back and clasped his fingers. "So let's see what we've got, okay?"

We had a lot of violence, that was what we had. I'd learned attack spells through the book and on the go. I also knew a lot of defensive spells, which were apparently in the red family. I didn't have a lot of knowledge to go with either variety. Most of the things I tried I got wrong, but occasionally I got something right.

I was panting and sweaty toward the end, something that had never happened to me before while practicing magic.

When Sebastian finally declared we were finished for the day, he was fresh-faced and with sparkling eyes. He wasn't tired in the least, but he'd clearly had a good time. That was a relief.

"Now you fly?" he asked, reseating himself on the log.

"Yes. I have to learn better aerial maneuvering." I hesitated in shedding my clothes. It was hard enough to disrobe around shifters, who were used to seeing others naked, but Sebastian's fixation on his shoes earlier had shown how uncomfortable he was with Austin hanging around naked. I wasn't in the mood for a peep show.

As if realizing it, Sebastian rose, stepped over the

log, and sat with his back to me. "That has to be so weird, going from not even knowing magic exists to all of this."

"Very weird, yes." I hesitated for a moment, just to make sure he didn't turn around.

Austin repositioned himself between us, cutting off Sebastian's sight even if he did peek.

"I don't much like an alpha at my back," Sebastian murmured. "I can feel him there somewhere. The small hairs on my neck are standing up like I'm about to get attacked."

"If you plan on staying peaceful, it's not me you need to worry about. You'd do best to keep an eye on Niamh," Austin said. He'd pulled on the sweatpants but hadn't bothered with the shirt, his big, broad back corded with muscle.

"Don't ruin the surprise," Niamh said, removing her clothes.

Clothes off, I shifted to my gargoyle form. My face didn't protrude quite so much as the male gargoyles' did, my wings were smaller, and I put out a sort of swirling light show when I moved. Jasper and Ulric changed with me, the sound like boulders moving against hard-packed dirt.

"Can I turn back now?" Sebastian asked, and I took to the sky. When he saw me, I could just barely see his mouth go slack and his eyes widen. "That is every bit worth the price of admission," he said, and then I was up through the trees, out of hearing range, soaring with my kind, wind against my wings, savoring a sort of freedom I couldn't express in words.

If Austin called in his brother, my ground game would be covered, but I still needed more fliers. Up here, soaring through the air, I realized how important that was.

My blast of magic nearly knocked Jasper and Ulric from the sky.

Hurry up.

An answering blast nearly froze my blood. I was calling in the best, and they had answered. They were on their way.

I sure hoped Austin could handle them.

CHAPTER 12

M R. TOM LEANED over the young master, sleeping more soundly than Mr. Tom could recollect anyone sleeping, ever. If an attacker waltzed into this room, it would be open season. Luckily, Master Jimmy had the house and his mother to look after him. He'd be safe as long as those held up.

"Young master," Mr. Tom said softly, something that usually roused the miss when she didn't sense him lurking over her. Not so much as a twitch.

"Young master," he repeated, a little louder this time. At least this boy approved of being called the proper title. Much less fussy than his mother or grandparents. He could get used to the boy staying in the house. It made Mr. Tom feel all kinds of useful.

Except when he wouldn't wake up.

"Master Jimmy!" Mr. Tom kicked the bed.

"Hmm?" The young master slowly opened his eyes. "Hah!" He jutted out his hand in some sort of karate chop move he must've learned from his mother.

"We need to start training you in combat ASAP," Mr. Tom said with a sniff. "No one connected to this house should go around cartoon-style karate-chopping at people. It's embarrassing for all of us. Now." Mr. Tom straightened up as the young master rubbed his eyes. "There is coffee on the night table for you and breakfast waiting downstairs. Best get moving. You're off to see the basajaun today. Austin Steele will be going with you just in case the insufferable flea magnet decides it doesn't like strangers and attacks. You never really know with them. This particular one has been downright tame compared to some others I've heard about, but I would still refrain from turning your back on it."

The creature still hadn't, after all this time, so much as told them its name. It was very odd. Good to have on one's side, though.

"Ohhhh-kay."

Mr. Tom nodded, picked up the dirty clothes strewn around the floor, and headed downstairs. In the kitchen he found the miss, eyes puffy and head drooping, clearly tired from the night before. She'd gone to bed earlier than usual, but the automatic link dampener had stayed in place until very late. When she'd clicked back onto his radar, it had woken him up.

Her refusal to just use one of the gargoyles for sexual stress relief was such a mystery. Clearly she needed it, if she spent all that time at it alone. Janes were very odd about those things.

"Do you need another cup of coffee, miss?" he asked after seeing to the laundry.

"Yes, please."

The RSVP from the mage lay off to the side. He had accepted their offer to host him, rather than the other way around, and would be coming in a month. Plenty of time to get things ready, assuming that insufferable Paddy next door was researching the mage's character.

"I woke the young master. He'll be down shortly." He filled her mug. "You know, he is taking to this magical idea very quickly. One wonders if he might belong in the house permanently…"

She took a deep breath. "That would be nice, but he's in college. He needs to be out on his own. Maybe he'll come back for summer, though."

Misery lined her face. She only had a couple more days with her son, and the prospect of saying goodbye clearly caused her pain.

She needed a distraction.

"Here." Mr. Tom dropped the furniture catalog in front of her before taking two eggs out of the fridge. Some things could be cooked beforehand and kept warm, but eggs really needed to be fresh. He set them on the island and monitored Master Jimmy moving around his bedroom.

"What's this?"

"I was thinking. Of *course* you don't feel comfortable looking over the ledger in that office. The furniture in there is very old and out of date. In fact, most of the furniture in this house needs updating. Maybe if you freshened everything up—made it yours instead of just a magical house you moved into—it would make the desire to properly run it less tedious."

The corners of her mouth turned downward and her eyebrows pinched together. She pressed her palm against the shiny cover featuring a lovely bedroom setup before sliding it out of the way.

"Good thinking. As soon as Jimmy leaves, I'll..." She paused, her expression that of someone who'd eaten something unsavory. "I'll go through this and pick some things out."

"There are many stores to choose from. Just say the word and I'll sign up for catalogs for others."

"I can just use the computer," she said, looking down at her coffee.

"Also, it seems next week Austin Steele will need you to sign some paperwork regarding the winery."

Her cheeks colored, something that was happening a lot lately in discussions of or with the steadfast alpha. "Sounds good."

Mr. Tom studied her face while focusing on the link. Her emotions seemed muted, but he could plainly see something was bothering her.

He wondered if that awful woman next door had given the miss a hint on how to control the link. The miss ultimately had the power to do whatever she wanted—turn the "volume" down, mute it, block it entirely, or turn it up full blast until an errant thought about poking someone in the eye would translate into a jolt of pain. There would be no eye damage, of course, unlike with a real finger, but it would still smart.

Master Jimmy walked in a moment later, the shadows lingering on the miss's face scattering until pure joy took over. Mr. Tom's heart warmed to see it. A mother with her child was such a beautiful thing to witness.

"Here we go." He grabbed up the eggs. "How would we like our eggs cooked today, young master?"

✧   ✧   ✧

A COUPLE OF hours later, Austin Steele stalked onto the property, his movements purposeful and his steps eating the distance to the door. Mr. Tom couldn't see him physically, but he knew how the alpha walked into a scene.

"Master Jimmy, come out of there now," Mr. Tom called to the boy, who'd been wandering the secret hallways for over an hour now. Ivy House had opened the doors to him, and he'd charged in with the delight of a little boy. "It's time to go. *Finally.*"

Master Jimmy hurried out, a lopsided grin on his face. "That is wicked! This house is incredibly cool. How does it know where I am? It literally just led me to you with the lights."

"It's magical. Come now. Is that what you're going to wear?"

The boy looked down at his jeans and T-shirt. "Yes. Should I put something else on?"

Mr. Tom held out the boy's jacket. "You'll want this."

"It's a really nice day, though."

"On the ground, yes. Up in the air where you'll be, no. Come along." Mr. Tom led the boy out of his room and down the hall.

"What's with my mom and that alpha guy? She said they're just friends, but they definitely don't have a just-friends vibe."

"Austin Steele is a solitary sort of man. He might have feelings for her, but he will not allow himself to act on them. He is very hardhearted in that way. Trust me, he's been pursued by every woman in this town, young and old, resident and tourist. He very rarely goes on more than a couple of dates with any one person."

"Has he taken my mom on a date?"

"Not romantically, no. They have a strictly platonic friendship." Mr. Tom led the way down to the ground level as the front door swung open, not mentioning that the miss would need to play the field for a while. From what he'd always heard, female gargoyles typically treated men like hats for a long period of time. They picked them out, tried them on, put them back, changed them with outfits, borrowed them—what have you. Eventually she would find that perfect hat, and that was when the mating dance would begin.

Female gargoyles usually chose male gargoyles, from what Mr. Tom had understood. She chose the strongest alpha her kind could muster, someone to protect her better than she could protect herself, which was a tall order because of her power and magic. A shifter was just another hat, no matter how powerful Austin Steele was.

Then again, the Ivy House heirs in the past had chosen mages. Powerful mages who could certainly protect them, but who weren't trustworthy. Those mages had eventually led to the heir's demise, so clearly the heirs would've been better off sticking with their own species. The proof was in the pudding.

Austin Steele stood in his sweats, his power surging around him, raw and potent, filling up the front entryway and then some.

Usually he was better about keeping it contained,

but now it pressed on Mr. Tom, a dominating force. Something had gotten his dander up. Probably the challenge in town that had made him late.

The breath went out of Master Jimmy, and he slowed, his eyes wide as he beheld Austin Steele.

"Yes, okay, you've made your point," Mr. Tom said as the miss left her room upstairs. "You're not in your territory anymore, though, Mr. Steele. It is time to rein it in."

That ruthless blue gaze shocked into Mr. Tom, like a predator zeroing in on his pray. Mr. Tom's small hairs stood on end, and he had a sudden impulse to change shape and protect his territory. But the alpha's focus shifted upward to where the miss was just reaching the landing.

She stopped dead, her hand on the railing, her gaze rooted to Austin Steele's. The air heated up around them, catching Mr. Tom and Master Jimmy in the crossfire, magic swirling, pressure building. Within their gazes, within their connection, something urgent and needy pulsed and boiled. Her cheeks flamed. His body tensed. Arousal bled through the muted link.

Oh, good, maybe the miss would finally try on a hat and reduce some of that sexual tension while she looked for her mate. It would help her calm down a little, which would help everyone.

CHAPTER 13

I OPENED MY eyes to the familiar face of Mr. Tom, someone I didn't really feel like seeing at the moment. My heart hurt. Today was Sunday, the last day before Jimmy had to leave for who knew how long. At least we'd spent some really great quality time together, more so than any other time since he'd approached teen-hood. We'd taken hikes and hung out around the town; we'd had picnics and wandered through the woods. He was not only getting used to the idea of magic, it clearly made me more interesting to a nineteen-year-old boy. Win-win.

The only part of my plan that hadn't worked out was the trip to see the basajaun. It hadn't mattered much—rather than hitch a ride to the mountain with one of the gargoyles, Jimmy had ridden Niamh's nightmare alicorn like a pony. We'd wandered the mountain, touching trees and brushing leaves, hoping the basajaun would come out or that Austin might scent him. No such luck. At dusk we'd had no choice but to turn back. Jimmy and Niamh had apparently bonded, though, because that night he'd chosen to forgo video games in favor of sitting with her on her porch, throwing rocks at the mages who were flung away from Ivy House. (Yes, mages still trickled in, none of them with enough magic.)

"Not now, Mr. Tom," I said, rolling my head the other way, looking at the buttery sunshine layering the cream windowsill.

"Yes, miss. I brought you some coffee." He didn't turn away.

"'Not now' means I'd like a little alone time before I get up."

"Yes, miss. And why wouldn't you, with that mage always staring, or Austin Steele throwing his weight around, making everyone nervous."

"Sebastian is a godsend, and he only stares when he's trying to figure something out, like why I keep messing up spells so he can teach me to do it better. Which he does. Austin isn't making anyone nervous. He's the same guy he's always been. Just…hotter, somehow."

"He might not be making *you* nervous, but everyone else is on eggshells when he's around. He's gotten much more intense."

I shrugged. I hadn't noticed.

"I'll be down in a minute," I said.

"Yes, miss. Pastries are ready and waiting, and we'll have a nice brunch in an hour or so. Master Jimmy is up and at 'em, in the shower and getting ready for his egg hunt. I've taken the liberty of—"

"Egg hunt?" I rubbed my eyes to try to rid them of sleep. Normally, I'd sit up and reach for the coffee, but my stubbornness had kicked in. I wanted a moment to pity my situation before I put on a brave face, and I wanted to do it in silence.

"Yes, miss. It's Easter, remember? Egg hunts are a customary tradition for Dicks on Easter."

I stared at him for a beat, reading nothing in his placid expression.

"When did you dye Easter eggs?" I finally asked.

"Oh no, miss, don't be silly. I'm not in the habit of throwing away food, and there are only so many boiled eggs and egg salad sandwiches a person can eat. No, I used the plastic eggs and put money in them. Master Jimmy said that was his favorite type of Easter egg hunt growing up. I hid the golden egg very well, trust me. It'll take him all day. I haven't hidden the Easter basket. I don't quite understand why you'd hide one Easter item and not the other, but Dick and Jane customs can be head-scratchers. As for Easter brunch, I've had Edgar set up the garden tent on the lawn. As soon as we move out that way, I'll slip a mimosa into your hand, don't you worry. There is no reason to be sober for this year's Easter when you haven't been sober in years previous. Now, if you'll just rise and get ready, we can kick this day off to a smashing start."

My heart ached and my lower lip trembled. He'd said he had taken care of the Easter basket, which was the only tradition I'd kept up after Jimmy was grown, but he hadn't told me about everything else. I should've known Mr. Tom would find a way to make Jimmy's last day perfect.

"Okay." I pushed up to sitting and reached for the coffee. "Give me a moment."

"Of course, miss."

I showered and freshened up, pushing away the sadness of Jimmy leaving and trying to focus on being thankful he'd gotten to stay for so long.

In the kitchen, on the table by the window, waited a lovely wicker basket with a pink bunny propped up inside. Chanel sunglasses sat beside a royal-blue box of exotic truffles. A Louis Vuitton scarf took up the edge, with a black jewelry box resting on bright lime Easter basket filler.

"Mom!" Jimmy stood at the island, the contents of his basket spread across the surface, his hands out and fingers splayed. The same lime filler lay discarded on the island in tufts, his much larger wicker basket pushed aside and his stuffed bunny leaning on its side. "What did you do? You can't afford all this!"

Closed jewelry box in hand, I leaned around him to check out his wares. Beats earphones, an iPad, Prada sunglasses—

"Are you serious with this?" He shook a box at me, forcing me to lean back. His smile took up his whole face and his eyes gleamed, reminding me of the Christmas he got a Game Boy and about peed himself with excitement. "*Are you serious with this?*"

His hands kept moving, shaking the box, and I squinted to see the jiggling lettering.

"Virtual reality gaming!" he said, and widened his eyes. "*Virtual reality gaming.* My buddy wants one of these so bad. He was just telling me the other day how awesome it was. How'd you know?"

Mr. Tom pushed aside some of the basket filler so he could set down a silver tray filled with an assortment of pastries, breads, cheeses and jams. His expression was smug.

"Mr. Tom was probably listening at your door when you were talking," I said with a chuckle, the jewelry box groaning as I flipped the lid. A diamond tennis bracelet surrounded two diamond studs, glittering in the sunlight streaming in behind me. "Oh wow, Mr. Tom, these are beautiful."

"Yes, miss. I have excellent taste."

I gave him a flat look, but showed Jimmy.

"Oh crap, Mom. Did he buy all of this?" Jimmy touched each item in front of him before picking up the sunglasses. "Do I have to give it back?"

"The estate bought all of this," Mr. Tom said, "and as soon as your mother finally gets around to officially transferring it into her name, she can take credit. Until then, your thanks will have to wait in limbo, with her best of intentions."

The flat look continued.

"That is awesome." Jimmy put on the glasses. "I'm going to look so dope in these. They're designer! I've never had anything designer before. Girls love a guy who has a little bling."

"Well, if that's the case, then—"

"No, no, Mr. Tom." I held up my hand. "This is plenty. You'll have to wait until his birthday to continue spoiling him."

"She really can kill the mood, can't she, Master Jimmy?" Mr. Tom tightened his lips while grabbing a bottle of champagne. "When you two are through, you may head to the back garden and begin the egg hunt."

Jimmy laughed with maniacal delight, snapping a picture of the headset with his phone. "Max is not going to believe this. He's going to be so jealous."

"Share with him." I touched Jimmy on the shoulder. "It's okay to celebrate good fortune, but it is not okay to hold it over other people. You need to share."

"Yes, Mom," he replied dutifully, ever the sullen teenager when he wanted to be.

Mr. Tom hadn't been kidding. He slipped a mimosa into my hand the second we reached the lovely white tent arching over a rectangular table surrounded by foldout chairs. White netting draped to the sides, secured to the tent poles with large cream bows, leaving it all open. Jasper and Ulric, both dressed in white slacks and tweed jackets, outfits that had undoubtedly been picked out by Mr. Tom, milled around the grass in bare feet, sipping their own mimosas. I wondered if they'd gotten baskets. Given they were both from towns that were mostly magical, where people didn't seem to celebrate the same things, they probably thought this was yet another example of Dick and Jane oddity.

They were still looking, though. Our traditions might seem strange to them, but that didn't mean they weren't fun.

"Now, Master Jimmy." Mr. Tom stood next to the tent, straight as a board, his black tux swapped out for a cream one. "The eggs are hidden in this section here." He put his arms out to the sides. "Starting from the house and going to the edge of the wood, not beyond. I've hidden a hundred eggs, containing various denominations of—" He cleared his throat. "The *Easter Bunny* has hidden a hundred eggs, and he—it?—*told* me that the eggs contain various dominations of money and gems."

"Gems?" I asked, slipping out of my shoes as well. I hoped Niamh hadn't put nails in the grass again.

Mr. Tom half turned to me. "Do you not have gems in Easter eggs? They are worth money, so I assumed that counted? We have a ridiculous amount of them in the attic, too big or cumbersome to fit into proper jewelry. The heirs of the past accepted many gifts from hopeful suitors throughout the years, something you will likely miss out on, since you seem to be settling so early. A shame."

"Gems...like rubies and diamonds?" I clarified. I had no idea what he meant by the rest of it, and I didn't care to ask.

"And semi-precious stones as well. Is that not...how it's done?"

Jimmy's face had gone slack as he stared at Mr. Tom.

"Be careful when you open those eggs," I told Jimmy. "We'll swap out the gems for paper money. Mr. Tom is not really...in touch with real life."

"Well, whose fault is that?" Mr. Tom grumbled. "I'm not the one that's supposed to be making these monetary decisions. Honestly, miss, you can run into battle, but you can't take a blood oath? It's only a little blood. Hardly a slice of the finger. You invented a game so you could get stabbed—what's the big deal?"

"Go." I waved Jimmy away. "Go! Go find money. Mr. Tom certainly put way too much in the eggs."

"Did he say…" Jimmy shook his head and turned. That had done it. There was too much to unpack in what Mr. Tom had said, and Jimmy's brain had shut down. It happened about once a day.

"It's not the blood I'm worried about, Mr. Tom," I said through clenched teeth, then drained my mimosa. "It's the responsibility. I'm being asked to make a choice that will shape the rest of my life. I won't be able to get out of it until I *die*. I know I took the magic, but I guess…" I pushed my hair over my shoulder, turning so the cool breeze could stroke my face. "I guess I didn't realize the magnitude of it. I just need… I don't know, I need a little more time, I guess. It's thrown me for a loop."

"Well." Mr. Tom pulled the champagne bottle out of a silver ice bucket on the grass at the corner of the tent. "You can redo the house in your style of choice, and when you are ready, which will hopefully be soon, we can get everything squared away. A little permanence would do us all some good."

There was nothing little about this sort of permanence.

CHAPTER 14

AUSTIN CHECKED HIS watch as he climbed out of the Jeep, careful not to touch anything that might transfer dirt onto his crisp white pants or sky-blue polo shirt. He felt a little ridiculous in these preppy clothes, but Mr. Tom had assured him this was Dick and Jane Easter attire, similar to a garden party, and they'd all be celebrating in order to give Jimmy the best send-off they could.

Austin could use a little distraction today. His brother hadn't just accepted his invitation—he was already on his way, expected to arrive tomorrow. Austin got the feeling that Kingsley was curious to see what Austin had made of himself. Which made him more than a little anxious, given the state of his territory. Every dick-slinging hotshot across the world, it seemed like, women as well as men, wanted to pull off Austin's newly created mantle. Once subdued, they fell in line, but the constant challenges of lesser-powered shifters were starting to wear on him. It was tedious at best, and it sucked focus and time away from matters that desperately needed his attention, like organization and enterprise.

He caught sight of Niamh across the way, exiting her house in black pants and a black T-shirt, a small hat with a black veil pulled down in front of her face. She looked like she was headed to a funeral.

When she reached him, she said, "Well, what's the craic?"

"Not a thing. I see you dressed for the occasion."

"That bollocks is thick if he thinks I'll dress how he says."

"I did it for Jess and Jimmy. This is apparently what people wear at Easter parties."

"What is the deal with the Easter Bunny, do ye suppose?" She headed for the side gate leading to the backyard, where the house crew had fanned out.

"What do you mean?

"Well…it's a bunny that secretly lays eggs. Is it some sort of science experiment gone wrong, or have we gotten the laws of nature wrong, and the proof is in the mutant bunny?"

He laughed, the decorative gravel along the side of the house crunching under his feet.

"Jessie is goin'ta be a puddle of sad when the boy leaves." Niamh slowed as they reached the grass. "She almost seems…softer when he's around."

Jess stood in the center of the bright green grass, dressed in a cream summer dress flowing in the breeze, two little straps clinging to her shoulders and the bodice hugging her torso. Golden light glinted off her shoulder-length brown hair, and she had a hand perched over her eyes, shading her beautiful face from the sun. Her smile lit up the yard, outshining the bright pops of fragrant flowers hugging the grass.

"Her softness seems to make yer personality a wee bit harder, no?" Niamh said.

"I hadn't noticed her being softer, just happier. And no, it doesn't make my personality harder." He gritted his teeth, trying not to complain about his job. Then, because they were technically in Jess's territory and he wasn't the alpha here, he just admitted it: "Having to ask my brother for help with defense makes me want to scrap the whole alpha thing and go back to my old life, where I had very little responsibility."

"Ye were wasted in your old life. Look, it's a load of shite right now, with all these people creating hassle, but as soon as you get a few capable people in yer top tier, it'll take the load off. I think yer just about to turn the corner, so I do."

He really hoped she was right. Because he was about to face his successful, good-at-everything, stable older brother, and Austin didn't have much to show for himself. He wondered how long it would take before he got the disappointed look he remembered so vividly from his youth.

"Who died?" Mr. Tom asked Niamh as they neared the tent setup on the lawn, fluffy pastries and square-cut cheeses laid out on a tray. "Couldn't be your good mood. That has been dead since I've known you."

"Yer sense of humor died, actually," she replied. "May it rest in peace."

"Hey!" Jess turned, her eyes sparkling with merriment. Austin stared for a moment, unable to help himself, lost in that glittering smile. "I didn't know Mr. Tom invited you. I see you put on your garden attire."

"Hey, alpha." Ulric walked up with a fuchsia plastic egg in his hand, no shoes on his feet, and a sense of ease that Austin admired. "Good of you to join. We've just about found all of the eggs, but there might be one or two more if you want to help? At first we weren't allowed to help, but Mr. Tom got a little too creative when he was hiding them, so Jimmy had to call in aid."

"Yeah, sure." Austin shrugged, falling in beside Jess, his arm brushing against hers.

"Only you could make that outfit look good," she said softly as they strolled across the grass, eyes down but neither of them really looking.

"What do you like best? The nearly see-through pants?"

She laughed, hooking her arm through his, sending shivers racing across his skin. "I think the shirt that screams 'I'm a nice boy' really does it for you."

He let himself smile, something he could no longer do outside of this property. "I'm just hoping to throw people off the scent."

"Make them think you're nice and then offer them a beat-down?"

"Works every time."

They stopped at the flowers near the woods, and she leaned around to look at him. Their gazes locked for a moment, and his world spun.

"A deeper blue would really suit you," she said. He turned so they fully faced each other, their bodies close. "It would bring out your eyes."

Unable to help himself, he reached up and traced his thumb across her full bottom lip.

"When you became alpha, was it forever?" she asked, so softly that he had to strain to hear.

"Being an alpha is never forever. It is until someone tears you out of your position, sometimes taking your life to do so."

"So if you don't like being alpha, you could just step down?"

He trailed his fingertips along her jaw before skimming them down her throat, running the pads of his fingers over her jugular. A shifter would only allow someone they trusted implicitly to touch so vulnerable a place. She didn't know that, of course, but his body responded like she did know, hard in some places and languid in others, savoring the touch. The heat of her skin.

"No, it's not that simple. I couldn't just let someone else challenge me and take it, either. In becoming alpha, I've drawn people to the area, violent people, who need a strong hand to lead them. I've bought businesses and am helping others flourish. If I were to pull out, or allow someone unworthy to take my place, it would have negative effects on the community. It would hurt the territory and, most importantly, the people living here. I'm in it too far now to responsibly back away. Which is starting to chafe at present. No one told me the growing pains of starting a new territory would be so...arduous."

"Uh-oh, you're bringing out the thesaurus. You must be getting diplomatic on me."

"Can you guys stop gazing into each other's eyes and help me?" Jimmy threaded through the flowers at the edge of the wood. "This is way harder than when I was a kid."

"Oops, Master Timmy, no." Edgar jogged to the

edge of the grass.

"It's still Jimmy, bro," Jimmy said dryly, moving on. "Just like yesterday, and the day before. Do vampires have terrible memories?"

"It has nothing to do with the memory," Niamh said, hunting around the edge of the hedge labyrinth off to the right. "That one is just Froot Loops."

"I really don't think he'd hide anything in the flowers, Master Jimmy." Edgar leaned over the flurry of color, his flower design like a flower fairy had drunk too much, stumbled to the area, and thrown up all her seeds in one go.

"Ah-ha!" Jimmy reached down and plucked a pastel purple egg out of the flowers. "Got it."

Edgar's brow lowered. "I'll need to have a word with Mr. Tom about that next year. My flowers are not the correct place for fun and games. They are prizewinning flowers, and they should be treated as such." Still grumbling, he wandered away.

Jess gave Austin an apologetic smile and turned, back to scanning the ground.

"Are you having second thoughts about this place?" Austin asked quietly, keeping pace. He could smell Mr. Tom's scent, fresh in some places and stale in others, working around the garden in a set pattern. It wouldn't take long for him to find all the eggs, even if blindfolded.

"Just." She took a deep breath, stopping again and looking out at the woods.

It took him a moment to feel it, a creature crossing the threshold at a fast clip, headed straight for the house.

"He must've realized we were looking for him," she said.

"The basajaun." Warning shocked through him and he glanced around the large garden, noticing the positioning of everyone he would have to protect if things went wrong. The mage wasn't here, either not invited or not interested—he really only hung around when training—which was a pity. He was powerful and precise, his magic incredibly effective. He could've helped end any sort of altercation much more quickly. A prolonged battle might scare Jimmy for life. He may have enjoyed his introduction to the fun side of magic, but he wasn't ready for the horror show it could devolve into.

"It's good." Jess laid her palm on Austin's forearm. Electricity zipped through his body, tightening his gut. "Even if he turned violent, Ivy House would handle it. She'd love to, actually. She's much too violent, if you ask me."

"I wondered…" He barely felt the anxiety coiling

within him, wrapped up as he was in those shimmering hazel eyes. "If my brother doesn't use my invitation as his opportunity to beat me senseless for what I did to him when I left…" A crease formed between her brows, but she didn't say anything. "You need to meet him in a professional capacity, but I wondered if you would also have dinner with us. Just us. Family and…friends."

She blinked at him, as though realizing the importance of what he was asking.

"Of course," she said. "Should I bring clam dip? In a cooler?"

The laughter bubbled up unexpectedly. When Jess's mother had come to visit a couple of months ago, she'd brought her dip and eggs, repeatedly talking about belated Christmas.

His smile dripped away. "My family isn't like yours. I'm from a long line of alphas, and they—we—are trained young not to show too much emotion. We're not welcoming and warm, not with smiles and hugs, at any rate. My brother might seem a little…cold, but just know that it isn't personal."

"Cold? Well, where did you go wrong? You were smiling and giving muscle shows the first night I met you."

Austin should've known it then. He should've known what she'd become from that very first night.

She'd started seeping into the cracks in his defenses from the word go.

What the hell was he going to do if his brother thought he was too unstable around her and advised him to cut ties in order to keep her safe? His heart ached at the thought. He'd do it—for her, he'd do anything—but it would break the last shred of him that still hoped for a normal life.

"You okay?" she asked.

The basajaun drew closer. Having entered the property at a full-out run, he'd slowed to a crawl as he edged up to the tree line, closing in on Jimmy, who was bent over, hunting through the flowers. Austin turned in that direction, not far from the young man and easily able to rush in front of him if something were to happen.

"No, no," Jess whispered, laughter in her voice. She plucked at Austin's stupid shirt. "Wait."

"I really don't think—"

"It's fine. I have a protective wall up. I'd singe every hair on that basajaun's body. The smell would be terrible. But can't you see? He's doing his sneaky thing." Her grin was evil. "Can't you see him, slowly moving up through the trees?"

Austin could smell him, and he could feel him with Ivy House's magic, but he couldn't see anything but trees. No movement, no big, hairy body, nothing. He shook his head, continuing to look.

"Oh, right," she murmured. "With Sebastian's help, everything feels so second nature now. I just did that spell for finding dangerous things, and now I can see him, clear as day. Watch." She looped her arm around his again.

"Got another one." Jimmy straightened up and wiped his head. "This is tough. Good call on making them money eggs. Otherwise I don't know that I'd keep going."

"Why not?" Niamh called, near the house now. A sparkly pink egg caught the light from the grass a few feet away from her. She'd clearly thrown it after finding it, since Mr. Tom hadn't made any eggs that easy to find. "This is good craic. We should do this more often."

"If you followed Christianity, you'd go straight to hell," Mr. Tom said, readying another mimosa. Jess's was getting low.

"Shows what ye know, now doesn't it? Ye don't go to hell until ye die. I'd have a lovely, long life being perfectly wicked, and then I'd head down under and pull on the devil's whiskers."

"Down Under is Australia."

"Same difference. Hot as the bejesus."

"Look," Jess whispered. "The basajaun wiggled a

branch. Just one. Jimmy didn't even notice."

Jimmy sure didn't. If this were a dangerous situation, he wouldn't stand a chance.

"Are there more over here?" Jimmy called.

"Another branch," Jess said. "A bigger one."

"I heard it," Austin said. The branches were scratching each other, the leaves rattling.

"Just one more to find before you look for the golden egg, Master Jimmy," Mr. Tom called. "It's hidden over there somewhere. Or maybe a little closer to the woods."

Jimmy took a big step over a tightly packed bunch of flowers and then stopped abruptly, looking down between them. The basajaun pushed forward, put out his hands, opened his great mouth, showing his large teeth and longer canines, and softly growled.

Jimmy's head snapped up. His body tensed. The large wicker basket in his hand dropped and plastic eggs tumbled out.

"Mom!" Jimmy yelled, back-pedaling over the flowers, crushing them under his feet. "Help! Mom!"

"Oh no! My flowers!" Edgar darted from the hedge maze.

The basajaun straightened up, all nine feet of him, and roared, filling the space with his mighty frame before he bent forward. Jimmy, face white and eyes wide, raced for his mother and ducked behind her.

Niamh cackled from beside the house.

"Now, that's not funny," Mr. Tom called. "The poor master will have nightmares. I feel guilty for the part I played, however almost innocently."

The basajaun's roar turned into hearty chuckles. He shook with them, bending over his knees and shaking his head. "Did you see his face?" The basajaun's laughter increased in pitch. "*Did you see his face?*"

Jess turned to comfort her son as the basajaun finished laughing and straightened again, his gaze coming to rest on Austin, not Jess.

"Alpha. Per our agreement, I must tell you that a band of shifters was in the process of crossing my mountain when I returned from my family reunion in the Redwoods. They were headed in this direction, though they were not hurrying. The most powerful of them traveled at the front until they crossed my scent. He then altered their course and repositioned his people so that he was always closest to my scent. I watched from high in a sycamore tree. He respected my claim and removed his people from my territory in the fastest way possible. He does not owe me blood."

"What did he look like, the one in lead?" Austin asked.

"A great tiger, strong and fierce." The basajaun

scratched his chest. "This one would give me trouble. Not the sort of trouble you would give me, but nearly."

Adrenaline flooded Austin. He should have known his brother would show up a day early and sneak in through the back door. He'd want to test Austin's territory borders. He'd want to see what resistance stood in the way.

Austin had some good people already, but he'd expanded the size of the territory quickly, and they were stretched thin. If Kingsley hoped to be impressed, he'd be left wanting. Still, it was worth trying to rally the forces and present a good defense to outsiders. Austin would need to show Kingsley his best if he expected help.

Or maybe it would be better to display his weaknesses. To be humble.

"Help yourself to a few flowers," Jess said, Jimmy now back with Mr. Tom, staring for all he was worth. "It was a long journey."

"Oh. You are so kind." The basajaun offered her a toothy grin. "Very generous. A great hostess." The basajaun picked up some of the smashed flowers Jimmy had crushed in his haste to get away. "Since I was the reason behind this catastrophe…"

"Yes, fine, that'll work, I guess," Edgar said, wringing his hands as he watched.

"Jess." Austin squeezed her upper arm gently. "That'll be my brother. I have to go. I need to make sure everything is set up for him. I wanted to spend the day with you guys, but..."

"Of course you have to go," she said. "I doubt your brother is that far behind the basajaun. Do you need anything?"

"Rain check?"

She smiled, and her lashes fluttered, a pretty gesture that thawed something inside of him. "Easter only comes once a year, but...I'm sure there's some way you can make it up to me."

He ran his thumb across her skin before pulling his hand away. "In the coming days, depending on how it's going, I might need you to show off your power and your people and your house. I might need a spectacle."

"I say, if ye want to make an impression, don't invite us all," Niamh said. "Some of these clowns would only make yer brother pity yer new setup."

"Speak for yourself, old woman." Mr. Tom sniffed. "*Most* of us are housebroken."

"Says the eejit who names his weapons." Niamh shook her head and went back to looking for eggs. "Ye didn't even think up good names, either. Who names a bludgeon Ron, fer feck's sake?"

"People have spirit animals, and weapons have spirit people. How is that so hard to grasp? I simply evoked their human likenesses."

"Ye and the vampire. Ye've both lost yer marbles. This house has gotten to yis. Why do ye think I never moved in? I know why."

"You throw rocks at tourists. You don't know why."

Austin pulled himself away from the fight. When they got going, it was hard to drown them out.

He squeezed Jess's arm again. "We're in the same boat. We just have to do what we can with what we have."

She laughed, but nervousness bled through the link. It felt muted, which meant she'd learned to turn it down. That was probably good. Hopefully it didn't extend through bedtime…

"Good luck," she said as he turned.

He stopped in front of Jimmy, the kid now in rapture, staring at the basajaun like, well, like someone who'd just found out Bigfoot was real. His gaze slowly shifted to Austin.

"Enjoy the rest of your day. The golden egg is at the center of the labyrinth, or near enough—"

"Austin Steele, that is cheating," Mr. Tom chastised.

"Maybe have the basajaun go with you to find it," Austin continued. "He can nearly see over the hedge. I will be here tomorrow for a proper send-off."

"Okay." Jimmy leaned forward and lowered his voice. "Just so you know, my mom's dream has always been to find a man that cooks her dinner. She likes romance, too, like roses and candlelight and stuff. I mean, all girls do, right? But I've always heard her say that she loves the idea of a man in the kitchen." His face colored. "I don't know, she's just always wanted someone to cook for her, I guess, and she never got it with my dad. My dad always said it wasn't his job. I don't think she liked that much. But, you know..." He shrugged. "If you wanted an *in* with her..."

"Well." Mr. Tom puffed up. "It's good to know I'm appreciated."

"No." Jimmy placidly pointed at Mr. Tom. "I mean, you are, but I meant—"

"I know what you meant." Austin winked at the kid. "I'll take care of it."

Jimmy smiled, and it was the look of a boy who thought something good was going to happen to the most important person in his life.

Austin hoped he could make good on his promise.

CHAPTER 15

I T WAS THE day after Jimmy left, and I'd decided I wasn't going to mope around the house anymore, teary-eyed from the image of his car pulling away. It was time for action.

I would head into town and challenge Sasquatch, owning my gargoyle mantle and blending invisibly into the buildings. I'd lie in wait for Sasquatch to sneak by, and when he was nearly past, I'd stab him right in the back. It was the sneaky, underhanded sort of thing that my mood dictated right now. Stabbing him from the front might scare him a little more, but I felt like pulling a *Psycho* from behind.

I patted Cheryl, nestled in the back pocket of my jeans, the spring-loaded pocketknife with a razor-sharp edge. She'd cause a problem if anyone would.

After that, it would be off to the bar for a hundred and two libations, followed by an alcohol-induced coma. Drown the pain. Hopefully, my plan would bolster me enough that I could meet Austin's brother tomorrow. I'd play ambassador to Ivy House, then we could sit down and talk about the mage's visit. We'd need to set up dinners and…

I didn't even know what. Clearly I'd need a lesson on what to expect from a formal meetup.

But all that could wait until tomorrow. We had a month to plan. One day of furlough wouldn't hurt.

"It's going to work this time." I made a fist as I headed out the door, Ulric and Mr. Tom in tow. Jasper was already downtown, having organized the "game" with Sasquatch. "I'm going to become the stone."

"You don't actually become stone, miss," Mr. Tom said.

"Yes, Mr. Tom, I know that. It was just a figure of speech."

Sebastian met me on the porch, and I had a surge of hopefulness. His week had officially ended yesterday. Did this mean he would stay?

"What happened to your hedge maze?" he asked as he kept pace, having decided to tag along even though it wasn't a traditional training session. "I ducked back there to give Edgar a new growing serum and saw him fretting over a huge hole in the side."

"The basajaun did that," I said. "Mr. Tom hid the golden egg—which was a solid gold egg, by the way."

"How was I supposed to know the situation didn't

call for an actual *golden* egg?" Mr. Tom said, outraged. "You told me about your traditions, but you left out vital information."

"You should've seen the look on Jimmy's face," Ulric said, laughing. "At first he was incredibly confused, then he thought it was fake gold. It wasn't until he found out it was real that the facial gymnastics started. I think he was afraid to hold it."

"Of course he was afraid to hold it!" I said. Niamh wasn't on her porch. It was only midafternoon, but maybe she'd already headed to the bar. Jimmy's departure had affected everyone. They'd liked having a younger person in the house to fawn over, like a bunch of grandparents. "He's never seen that much gold in his life, not to mention the amount of money it represented. We were comfortable, the ex and I, but we were not rich by any means. Jimmy hasn't ever seen the kind of money this place has just loitering around the attic."

"If you would just finish the transition and officially transfer the—"

I held up my hand. "Not now, Mr. Tom. I don't want to hear about that today." If Austin and his brother had set up more robust defenses already, nothing had notably changed along my street. The houses ended and gave way to woods on both sides, sunlight fighting through the dense canopy, struggling to the ground. "Sebastian, to answer your question, the basajaun made that hole. He went into the maze with Jimmy to help find the egg. Once inside, though, they couldn't find their way back out. Before Edgar could go in and retrieve them, the basajaun roared like he was being attacked, picked Jimmy up, and burst his way through the sides until he was out. Once there, he cleared a large patch of flowers and then drank all the champagne. Apparently he didn't like being trapped in the maze."

Sebastian threaded his hands into his pockets. "A basajaun, huh? I'd like to meet one of them someday. I've heard they are fearsome."

"Yes. And incredibly violent when they get their dander up." I peered through the trunks and leaves as we walked. "I need to put a spell around the woods at the end of the street to warn me of approaching danger. But hikers and animals and all sorts of people wander around this area before setting foot on Ivy House property. How do I pinpoint what's actually danger-ous?"

"Remember that spell you learned for sussing out weapons and dangerous things?" Sebastian asked lightly, looking the other way, as though envisioning the possibilities.

"Yes."

"And a tripwire. I'm sure you know how to do a tripwire?"

"Yes."

"So…" Sebastian looked straight ahead again.

"So I tie those two spells together and *voila*." I shook my head, annoyed at myself. I should've been able to deduce that.

"I have a couple of spells that might work better, though," he said as we reached the end of the street and turned toward downtown. "They are advanced, but with practice, you should be able to get them. Then we need to get into elixirs and potions. Believe it or not, potions are much harder than spells. They are an art form. If you get good at potions, the world is your oyster. You can make a living wherever you go. A good living, too. You won't have a care in the world. Well…" He shrugged his left shoulder. "Except for being killed by a rival organization trying to cripple the organization you're working for."

"That's a thing?" I asked.

"Of course that's a thing. To have power in the magical world is to accept danger. The people who want it will kill to get it, and the people who have it will kill to keep it. Everyone else is in the crosshairs. But if you are a master at spells and potions, you can protect yourself. Master both, and you are someone to be reckoned with."

"Are you someone to be reckoned with?"

"Yes. When I want to be. Which isn't often. It's tedious. I much prefer working in my lab with my head down, creating new spells and potions."

I bit my lip. It really did sound like he planned to stay.

I took a chance. "You'll need a lab, then. And a paycheck." I ran my fingers through my hair as we neared the downtown area. "I'm sorry, I've been distracted with my visitor. I lost track of time."

"So far you've paid me in other ways. We'll figure it out. But yes, a lab would be nice."

I almost asked what other ways he was referring to, and if that meant he was for sure staying, but I wasn't in a great frame of mind right now. So instead I just nodded and let silence settle over the group. I'd add a serious sit-down with Sebastian to the growing list of things I needed to accomplish tomorrow.

A few streets over from the main drag, a hard-faced shifter I didn't recognize walked down the sidewalk toward us. Tall and broad, he had a gently lined face that showed his years, mid-forties, and eyes the color of onyx. He glided like the lethal killer he likely was, his gaze passing through our crew quickly but efficiently, showing experience. Shoulders back and limbs loose, his confidence was no small thing.

I gulped. This had to be one of the shifters Austin's brother had brought in. He wasn't here to cause trouble or challenge for a place in the pack. He was here to keep order and establish a presence. Given the sudden coiling of my body—half of me wanting to laugh manically and then sprint away, and the other half wanting to laugh manically, brandish Cheryl, and sprint toward him—he was damned good at his job.

"Time check," I said, the shifter's eyes coming to rest on me. I made myself keep walking, swinging my lead feet, tamping down that maniacal laughter. My small hairs stood on end, as though a battle drew near.

"You have five minutes, miss," Mr. Tom said. "You might as well start now. That horrible little man is probably already in place. He has been a cheat for as long as I've known him."

I expected the shifter to continue walking down the center of the sidewalk, a bit of posturing that would force us to either step aside or fight. I expected to play chicken with his barrel chest and thick, muscular body, using magic to ensure he lost. I would not be pushed around in my town. Not by someone I knew, and especially not by an outsider. I knew enough about the magical world to know you couldn't always be polite, and you shouldn't always take the higher ground.

Sometimes you had to fight for your place.

Surprisingly, though, he slowed and stepped to the side, taking the curb so we didn't have to move.

"Ma'am," he said, nodding.

"Good day, sir," I replied, then couldn't help making a face like I'd just sucked on a lemon. "*Good day, sir?*" I muttered after we'd passed and were beyond his hearing. Hopefully. You never knew with shifters. "I held his gaze, won my place, and my celebratory salutation was *good day, sir?* What am I, Charles Dickens?"

"Technically, that is a who," Ulric said. "That must be one of the new guys. He was the right amount of intense for the town at present."

"I thought you did very well," Mr. Tom said, and although he was behind me and thus out of sight, I knew his chin was raised in snobby disdain. "You showed the shifter that the mistress of Ivy House does not cower within a dominating stare."

"Sure, but now he's probably wondering why I didn't stop and extend a lacy, gloved hand so he could kiss it before I walked on with my parasol," I muttered. "I told Austin I'd show off my power and my people. Hard to look awesome when I say things like that."

"People are wary of the unpredictable," Sebastian said, hands still in his pockets, turning to look behind us. "You're good. Keep being weird."

"You say that as though you think she has a choice in the matter," Mr. Tom said, and I got the feeling he was trying to help in some way.

"Okay everyone, disperse." I waved them away, pushing back against the wall.

An older man and woman walked along the sidewalk on the other side of the street. They glanced over, and I gave a little wave before pulling my power around me and sinking into the elements. They waved back, and if I'd just rendered myself invisible, they would've given a sign.

"Dang it."

I watched Mr. Tom don a bowler hat and a pair of thick-rimmed glasses before wrapping a yellow and maroon striped scarf around his neck. He rolled up the sleeves a little on his tux jacket and then hoisted one of the pant legs to his shin. That done, he drifted back to the wall.

"Become the stone." Mr. Tom's voice was soft and hollow, as though lending credence to his efforts. "Soak into your surroundings. Wrap the magic around you like a cloak."

"Huh," Sebastian said as Mr. Tom disappeared. I could still see him, of course, with my magic, but when they were in this element, there was a sheen to their appearance. It helped me identify when they were hiding and not. "That's pretty slick. I can't make him out at all."

"But you can make me out?" I asked as Ulric crossed the street and then blended in on the opposite side.

I felt Jasper on the main drag, probably halfway between Sasquatch and me. He always made my opponents start at the other end of the downtown area so I had a chance to figure things out. Hadn't happened yet, but today was the day!

"Yes. Why does Mr. Tom put on all that garb?"

"I have no idea."

"And why did he roll up his coat sleeves and one pant leg?"

"Look, when it comes to Mr. Tom, or Edgar, or Niamh, you really just need to roll with it. They don't make any sense at the best of times."

Sebastian's crooked smile was back. "You might have the most eccentric organization of them all."

"That's a very nice way to put it. Okay, you gotta scram. I can't have you hanging around, chatting to me. You'll get me caught."

Sebastian took a step away, but he paused and pulled a small vial from his back pocket. "I don't have magic to blend into stone, but when you get good at potions, you can use magic to make you disappear. I won't get you caught. Give me a sec."

He pulled out the cork stopper, tilted the vial up, and dribbled the contents into his mouth before he swished twice, sucked air in through his lips, and then swallowed it down, all without letting any liquid dribble from his lips.

He saw me watching. "Sometimes it's not just the potion, it's how you take it. Aerating that one right before swallowing keeps it working for twice as long. Don't tell anyone, but I found out accidentally. It's a secret."

His body shimmered and then the image of his face went hazy. A moment later, his physical being bled away, out of sight. He'd become invisible through other means.

"Does that mask your scent, too?" I asked, remembering when spells like that had been used against me.

"Scent, yes," came his disembodied voice. "Not sound, though. For some reason, I can't get this potion to cut out sound."

"Maybe you don't have enough power?"

"I can do a soundproof potion, and the two can be taken together, but the soundproof potion doesn't respond to aeration, and, strangely, stops the other from responding as well. I have no idea why. It makes no sense. So when I use the soundproof potion, the invisible potion doesn't last as long. I don't figure I need it here, though, so it doesn't matter. I'll be quiet."

I shook out my hands, noting Mr. Tom had drifted down the way a little, giving me space.

"Here."

The bit of sidewalk where Sebastian had stood looked completely empty. "What?"

The sound of glass met concrete. A shoe sole scuffed against the path, and a little vial appeared at my feet.

"So you can see me, and also get used to needing a defense against invisibility potions. They are heavily used within the magical world." His foot slid further away, giving me space. "You have to be careful with this potion—the one I took. It isn't just your body that disappears. It's almost like a cloud extends around you. Not far around you, but you will make things within the cloud disappear. A cunning eye will spot that, and an experienced magical worker will look for it. That vial at your feet holds a counter-spell to the potion I took. If I drank it, it would nullify the effects of the spell I have consumed. If *you* take it, it will allow you to see through the effects of the potion I'm using. There are a few varieties of invisibility potions, and the counter-spell will reveal them all in different ways. That's a secret, too. Most counter-spells are just that—counter-spells—

but I added a twist to this one. It's more helpful that way. Plus it tastes better."

"You guys must all want to sneak into each other's labs and steal each other's stuff, huh?" I picked up the vial and pulled out the cork.

"In most cases, yes. Which is why our labs are so well warded. Break-ins usually only happen to newer mages, and they don't have much to offer. Anyway, don't let me keep you. I didn't intend a lesson on invisibility potions, I just figured…since the case presented itself…"

"I hope this isn't poison." I upended the vial. The taste of black licorice exploded in my mouth, and I forced myself to choke it down. My face screwed up and I shook my head. "If that tastes better, I don't want to know what it tasted like before."

"Don't like black licorice? Huh." He took the empty vial from my hand, his fingers brushing against mine. I flinched as half my hand disappeared. "Also, no, it is not poison. I don't want to even contemplate what it would be like for that alpha to come after me. I will never hurt you, as long as I live. I swear that, both because I have decided to take you as my student, and also because I'm terrified of what that alpha would do to me. The more I learn, the more I realize how even-tempered he is around you. I do not want to make him angry."

"No, probably not. He gets crazy." The street shimmered a little before settling back to normal. The shape of Sebastian manifested near my elbow. A little hazy, orangy and sparkly, but there. "Cool."

I gave a thumbs-up and tried once more to blend into the stone, remembering what Mr. Tom had said. Feeling the stone. Turning into the stone.

Shivers coated my body. Was it finally working? Either way, I needed to get closer to the main drag.

I crossed the street at a jog, then flattened against the wall of an old house turned orthodontist's office. Shivers still danced across my skin. I chanced a glance at Sebastian, standing about ten feet away, looking right at me.

"Dang it. You can see me?"

"Is it cheating if I tell you?"

I narrowed my eyes at him.

He looked away. "That's a yes, then, it is cheating. Your expressions come in handy."

"Dang it," I said again, aiming for the alleyway down the way. Ulric drifted back, scanning the street, on bodyguard detail. Mr. Tom slunk across the street after us, following at a distance.

"Oh, I see," Sebastian said, at my back. "He is disguising himself for when he can't blend into buildings.

Though…who is he trying to look like? And the rolled-up sleeves and pant leg still make absolutely no sense."

"Can't people still hear you?" I asked.

"Sorry," he whispered. "Though I'm still unclear on what we're doing. Other than failing to blend into the stone."

"Just *shh*." I moved slowly, digging down deep inside of me, bypassing the sorceress magic to access the gargoyle part of me. The part with the wings, tough skin, and ability to fly. I called it up, glowing with the feeling. The desire to change form and take to the skies overcame me. To rise above the buildings and hunt…

That was probably a good sign.

"Can you see me?" I whispered.

"*Shh*," Sebastian replied.

I rolled my eyes, halfway down the alley now, focusing on the street. Someone passed by, straight and tall, muscular. Definitely not Sasquatch.

Farther along, I caught sight of the vacant wine-tasting room. The empty barrels had all been cleared away, the area swept. Once I signed the paperwork, I'd own half of a winery. Austin and I would need to settle on a winemaker, update the tasting room, and get the word out. It would be a lot of work.

Why didn't that scare me as much as officially transferring Ivy House into my name?

Because you could sell the winery, but Ivy House comes with a blood oath and a contract term of "forever unless killed."

"Oops. Where did your mind go?" Sebastian whispered. "You'd nearly done it. You'd blended in for the most part. If I hadn't been watching, I probably wouldn't have noticed you."

"Sorry," I said, pushing the thought of my duty away. But it refused to release its grip. The time had come for me to become the leader my people needed, the leader they deserved. I had to do what Austin had done and claim my position fully, balls to the wall. Only it was easier said than done.

I reached the edge of the alley, fighting to keep my focus, and losing.

Jasper waited just down the way, Mr. Tom was behind, and Ulric was…in the air?

I looked back, catching a glimpse of him just as he jumped from one rooftop to the next, his wings snapping out so he could soar the last few feet before his feet touched down. He held his clothes in his hand, and the second he landed, he disappeared into the wall next to him, his bright pink form blending in effortlessly.

Why hadn't he just followed behind Mr. Tom?

I turned back to the street, my gargoyle magic pulsing, as if I'd unburied it earlier and made it easier to access. Actually, it felt like when I was in the middle of changing, the power surging.

Ready to grab it up and drape it over me like a cloak, hoping for more than just *nearly* working this time, I froze.

Sasquatch stood right in front of me, an evil smile curling his lips. Triumph lit his eyes.

"Dang it!" I yelled.

CHAPTER 16

"MISSUS HIGH AND mighty can't use the magic she was given," Sasquatch said, his mustache moving as he spoke, the motion wiggling a clump of food stuck on the end.

"You couldn't be grosser if you tried." I spread out my arms. "Go ahead."

"Let's hear it."

I lifted my eyebrows, my mood blackening, which was saying something, because it was already in the dumps. "Hear what?"

"That I won."

"You get to stab me. Isn't that proof that you won, you dangling dingleberry?" I spread my arms wider, aggressive now. "You won. So go ahead, claim your victory."

His smile widened. "Get back into the alleyway more. The alpha said we can't do this where people can see." He pulled a pocketknife from his back pocket, a different one than before, and extracted the blade before motioning me on. "I'll follow."

"If you stab me in the back, so help me God, I will tear it out and fill you full of holes. I am not in the mood."

"I can stab you wherever I want. That's the deal."

"I didn't make that deal."

"Your man did. Quit stalling."

I huffed, the sound turning into almost a growl before I trudged to the back steps of the vacant tasting room and faced him again, out of patience. Sebastian, his interest clearly piqued, stopped a couple of feet away, still undetected by Sasquatch.

"There." I spread my arms once again. "Go for it. Also, your knife is stupid. Have a little pride in your weaponry."

His bushy eyebrows dipped and his gaze slipped down to the plain brown handle peeking through his chubby fingers, the dull blade about five inches long. If it had a name, it would be Pat. And if I started naming all my weapons like Mr. Tom did, I didn't know what I would do with myself.

He braced, and I readied for the flash of pain. For the terror of a knife speeding toward my flesh.

But the only movement I saw came from the corner of my eye. A massive shape rushed in, too fast for my reflexes, and I jumped in surprise as a large hand shot out and gripped my nemesis's front. A powerful body followed, brushing past me, and Sasquatch was ripped away from me and slammed into the fence to our side.

Sebastian dove to the ground, magic curling around him, whatever spell he'd tried to fire off floating away in a cloud of smoke. His eyes were wide, and for a moment his face seemed to wobble, as though it weren't attached, his skin still sparkling tangerine. My potion was clearly running dry.

The shifter from earlier, his dark eyes flaring with violence, had Sasquatch pinned.

Sasquatch stood frozen, arms at his sides, as though he didn't trust himself to even take a breath. His knife stayed clenched in his fist, although it was obvious he didn't intend to use it in self-defense. His eyes were so big that they looked like they'd pop out.

"That kind of behavior no longer exists in this town." The shifter's voice was a low growl that fluttered my stomach, dangerous and dark, capable of incredible violence.

Unlocking my limbs and forcing myself into action, I stepped closer and lightly put a hand on his arm. "It's—"

He didn't flinch, but the air of his static aggression changed, now encompassing me. He turned his head slowly, his warning very clear. He punctuated the message by dropping his gaze to my hand.

"Whoops. Not a touchy-feely kinda guy, huh?" I pulled my hand back.

Still holding Sasquatch, who looked stiff as a board, the shifter beat that aggressive stare into me, silently commanding me to back down.

"Right, yeah, I read you loud and clear," I said, "but here's the thing: this kind of behavior has never really existed in this town, except for this particular training exercise. Austin knows about it. He's asked that we carry out the punishment portion out of sight, so that's why we're here."

His stony expression didn't change. His hand didn't give Sasquatch any slack.

"He won the game"—I pointed at Sasquatch—"and now he gets to stab me. Those are the rules."

"You have a mage in the area." It sounded like each word was dragged over gravel, something that should have been unpleasant but wasn't.

"Yes. He's crouching on the ground just…" I moved to point, but Sebastian waved his hands at me in alarm, shaking his head. "Well, I'm sure you smell him. Oh, wait, you can't smell him."

"I heard him. I know where he is."

"How do you know it's a mage?"

"Invisible and clumsy, and I felt the brief sting of

useless magic."

I frowned at him. "The sting of magic? What's that like?"

"Gargoyles, too."

"Yes." I pointed. "There's one right on the roof, looking down at you."

The shifter didn't so much as flinch. If he wanted to look up, there was absolutely no sign.

"And another at my back," he said. "That's a very dangerous place to be."

"Oh no, I assure you, I mean no harm." Mr. Tom's magic wavered and then slipped away as he moved toward me. "I am merely standing by in case the miss needs something."

The shifter's eyes flicked over, and he did a double take. He'd only meant to sneak a glance, I knew, but Mr. Tom's get-up created something of a disconnect between the brain and the eyes. The shifter craned his neck for a better look.

"That's Mr. Tom, my butler," I said, knowing that wouldn't really ease the blow.

"What kind of dog and pony show is this?" the shifter ground out.

"It's…" I grimaced. "There really aren't words. Listen, thanks for trying to help, but I'm magical. I'll heal the stab wound right up. No biggie."

The shifter leaned back, releasing Sasquatch, who still didn't move. The stranger's dark eyes held mine before roaming over my face. I felt Jasper move into the alleyway. The shifter made no sign that he knew, though I suspected he did.

"What sort of game ends with a beautiful woman getting stabbed?" he asked.

Heat bled into my face. "I call it a game, but it's actually training. It's like hide 'n' seek. If I can't properly hide, I get stabbed by the worst human being this town has to offer. If I do, I'll get to stab him, something I dream about."

"He can smell you. How could you possibly hide?" A crease formed between his brows. "What are you? I haven't smelled magic like yours."

"She is—"

"A nutcase," I said, cutting Mr. Tom off. If this guy didn't know who—and what—I was, there was a reason. Austin wanted to keep it a secret. "Listen, if you don't mind, I'd like to get this game over with so I can meet my friends at the bar. We're out of the public eye, as Austin requested, so we should be good."

The shifter studied me for a long moment.

"Shall I walk five paces, turn, and blaze you with my peashooter, mister?" I asked, once again ruining my hard stare with my big mouth.

He held out his hand to Sasquatch. Without needing to be told, Sasquatch filled it with the knife.

"All due respect," the shifter said, "I wasn't told about this activity. I'll need to clear it with the alpha. I would recommend, however, that you find a different way to practice. Being stabbed is probably more detrimental to your training than it is helpful."

"Maybe, but I will stab him one day, without Austin having to raise a fuss, and it will be glorious."

"Austin…" The shifter was staring at me with renewed focus. His expression was locked down tight, and I didn't have a link with which to read him. "Does the alpha know you use his name so frivolously?"

"If he didn't, would you tell?"

"Yes."

"No one likes a tattletale." I took a step back. "Thanks again. For trying to help, I mean. You couldn't have known this idiot had the green light to stab a bitch."

"How did you know to intervene?" Sebastian asked, then sucked down the liquid from another vial.

"Reveal your—" The shifter cut off as Sebastian slowly hazed into focus, standing now. He tucked the empty vial into his back pocket.

The shifter didn't speak for a moment, scrutinizing Sebastian. Which was understandable. He didn't telegraph his emotions much more than shifters did, and his crooked smile didn't reveal the fear I knew he was feeling.

Finally, he said, "It's my job to know." He nodded at me. "We'll have to have that duel at high noon some other day, when I've had a chance to bring my pistol." He mimed tipping a two-gallon hat. "Ma'am."

He left the alleyway and turned right down the street. I watched him go, taking in the sleek grace of his movements.

"He's good at his job," I said.

"He literally came out of nowhere." Sebastian ran his fingers through his hair. "He could've killed me if he'd tried."

"You weren't expecting him," I said, taking Cheryl out of my pocket. I held it out for Sasquatch. "Here, do it with my knife."

"A-are you k-kidding?" Sasquatch stuttered.

"Oh. He lives," Mr. Tom said.

"He said no." Sasquatch wiped his hand down his sweaty face. "You don't defy the order of the pack."

"Or what?" I asked.

"Or you get punished, obviously."

"Yeah, but...that's just, like, the law, right? You shouldn't do it, yes. Fine. But if you don't get caught, who's the wiser? In two seconds, there will be no proof.

I'll hold up my shirt so I don't get blood on it. Besides, they can't tell me who can and cannot stab me."

"No way." Sasquatch shook his head and hurried away. "I'm not playing anymore!" he hollered over his shoulder as he left the alleyway.

"Great. Just great." I closed up Cheryl and jammed her into my pocket. "That shifter just screwed up my plans to stab Sasquatch. That's such crap." I stormed out of the alleyway, and everyone except for Ulric followed me. He was hunched on the roof, changing back to human.

Somehow he was still the first person to try to talk sense into me.

"No offense, miss, but it makes sense," Ulric said, catching up. He pulled his shirt over his head, having already put on his pants. "If the new people catch wind that this sort of violence is tolerated, things could get hairy really quickly."

"I don't care about that. I had a training system in place, and these new people are just going to march in and tear it down?"

"I agree." Mr. Tom nodded. "This is no time for sense and logic."

I sighed. "I'm going to go find Niamh at the bar. I've about had it with today."

"I don't know why you'd want to take a bad mood

into her company," Mr. Tom said. "She'll just drag it down until you say uncle."

"Where do you want me?" Jasper asked.

"I mean…" I threw up my hands, feeling annoyed, hungry, and just all-around unsettled. Clearly I wasn't done moping. "I should be plenty safe in the bar with all the shifters hanging around. Unless Austin's brother is setting him up, but if that's the case, we're all screwed."

"Maybe we'll hang out at the bar, Jasper, huh?" Ulric said. "Sebastian can come. Mr. Tom, maybe you should head to Ivy House in case more mages show up or someone responds to the last summons. Or, hell, someone could come to attack. You really just never know with that house."

It was an obvious excuse to get rid of Mr. Tom, but he was happy enough to accept it. He clearly didn't want to have his own mood dragged down. "Yes, that sounds fine," he said, peeling away.

"I'm still the alpha," I said, only because it felt like I probably should. I certainly didn't feel like much of an alpha. A high-powered shifter had crashed my pity party, and I'd had no idea how to react to him. No wonder Austin had offered to handle any big personalities that showed up in answer to my summons.

I'd have to get better at reading people. That thought in mind, I ran through everything that had happened with the new shifter.

"That's why he called me beautiful," I muttered. "I wasn't backing down from his stare, so he tried to disarm me another way."

"He wasn't trying to disarm you," Ulric said, "or manipulate you—he was giving you a very obvious hint that he was into you when all his other much-too-subtle hints didn't land."

"What subtle hints?" I glanced back at him.

"Exactly," he replied, smiling delightedly.

"But he was trying to dominate me, right?" I asked, hitting the edge of the street and turning left toward Austin's bar. I felt him on the move, but I couldn't tell whether he was coming back to town or headed somewhere else entirely.

"Yes," Jasper said.

"Have you learned nothing, Jacinta?" Ulric asked. His joyful mood was starting to annoy me, something I knew better than to admit, because it would just tickle him. "Packs have a hierarchy. Tiers. Levels. Gargoyles do too, but not to the same extent. Every time a shifter meets someone magical, you can bet they're going to size them up. Test them. The new shifters the alpha brought in have a lot more experience, and they're used to dealing in a lot more power. They're reading that in you. I doubt they are allowed to actually challenge you—no way would the alpha allow that—but they'll keep testing you. It's their way. It's ingrained. If it weren't for the setup, testing would likely evolve to challenging."

"What about me?" Sebastian asked.

"I'm sure you've guessed that shifters don't like mages any more than mages like them. But the alpha has allowed you on his turf. The smart ones will just sneer at you or ignore you completely. The idiots will wait until no one is around to tattle and try to kill you. The good news is that only the weaker shifters will come after you, the ones who don't have great standing in the pack. They're the sort that'll pick on anything they don't like or understand."

"How do you know all this?" I asked Ulric.

"I'm someone a shifter might want to pick on. The second I got here, I started learning all I could."

"The shifters you mentioned...the bullies..." Sebastian paused, and I slowed down, nearly to the bar and sensing he wouldn't want to advertise what he was saying. "Would they be missed?"

Ulric chuckled. "The ones I've come across haven't been..."

I widened my eyes. "When was this? Why didn't you tell me?"

"They picked a fight with the wrong guy. I handled the situation. What's there to tell?"

Jasper snorted, nodding.

"You too?" I asked him.

He shrugged. "They weren't a problem."

"Well, clearly I don't even know what's going on under my nose." I started walking again. "I'd be a terrible alpha of a shifter pack."

"In fairness," Ulric said, "the alpha didn't know about it either. Maybe he's guessed why a few people didn't show up for duty, but…"

A woman walked down the sidewalk on the other side of the road and pinned us with a stare that seemed to say, *I see you, and if you step out of line, I'll be on you like white on rice.*

I glared back and thought about snapping a tiny spell at her to dislodge those peepers.

"That's going to get old," I murmured.

We slowed near the bar door, Ulric and Jasper stepping to the side, not planning to go in.

"This won't go on forever. Once you're established as"—Ulric's voice hitched and he scratched his head, watching the shifter across the street—"whatever status you end up claiming, then it won't be so dramatic. They'll check the status quo, but they won't police you like that very attractive, clearly very confident lady is doing. Dibs."

"Damn," Jasper said softly. "I had my eye on her."

"I don't mind sharing if you don't find anyone else."

"Wow. And that's my cue to go inside." I turned and strode forward, only to walk into a wall of man.

CHAPTER 17

"E XCUSE ME," I murmured, putting my head down and scooting to the side, my default for when I've smashed into someone and want the brief awkwardness to quickly pass so I can continue on my way. No need for forced conversation or over-the-top apologies—better to just be embarrassed and then move on with life.

Only, the wall of muscle didn't move. Nor did the people behind me edge forward. They didn't even shift their weight in impatience, instead pushing back and giving us room. They clearly didn't think I was going anywhere.

I gave a cursory glance up, the guy's wide chest and broad shoulders taking up a good portion of the doorway. I wouldn't be squeaking by him, and given that he was just standing there, silently expecting something to happen, he clearly didn't intend on brushing past me.

He looked down at me, his piercing blue eyes and

stony expression pegging him as one of Austin's brother's people, and his air of patient importance and raw intensity marked him as someone powerful who thought the sun shone out of his ass.

Or maybe that was just my bad mood and fraying temper.

"Apologies, my lord. Please, let me humbly stoop out of your way." I took a step back, using my magic to shove the people who'd lined up behind me, Sebastian included (I'd have to apologize later). I bowed with a flourish and swept my hand out, indicating he should walk on.

"You are?" the man asked.

"Late for tea." I straightened, about at the end of my tolerance, and met his stare with one of my own.

"We don't allow mage magic in this bar."

"I'll use my mage magic to throw you out of that bar if you push me. Otherwise, please move aside. I'm a regular."

Dead silence rang in my ears, hinting at the very bad decisions I was currently making, but I didn't care. I could just hear Niamh hassling Paul about getting her another drink, and I wanted to sit among familiar company and complain a little.

"I will let you in, but know that the alpha is on his way. He might not be as forgiving as I am."

"Awesome. Fantastic. Can't wait."

He continued to stand there.

I let my eyebrows climb. "Are you waiting for a red carpet, or did someone flip your switch and you don't know how to get started again?"

"That mouth will get you in trouble one day," he growled.

"Let's hope so. I haven't been in a fight for a while. I might forget how."

He backed up, one precise step at a time, his body moving in perfect harmony, his age, early fifties, only showing in the lines on his face and the graying at the temples of his otherwise sandy-blond air. Next to no fat padded his body, and age didn't seem to have touched his powerful physique. He'd be a handful in a fight. Cheryl would be outmatched by sheer brawn.

He turned sideways and gestured me into the bar.

"Please."

I narrowed my eyes at him. It sounded more like a command than polite manners or a gesture of goodwill.

I returned the favor, only my tone suggested where he could shove his command. "*Thanks.*"

People glanced up as I came through, although, thankfully, most of them were people I knew.

As I approached Niamh, I kept an eye on the mountain by the door. He'd taken up a position against the wall, hands clasped in front of him, eyes firmly on me. Sir Stares-a-Lot would be watching me all night now, or until Austin got here and hopefully shooed him away.

"Well, Jessie." Niamh pointed her thumb at me before turning to the short-haired thirty-something woman on the stool next to her. "Here, you, move down, would ya? I've got a friend coming through."

The woman was also clearly imported, with the same staring problem.

"If ye are looking for sign language with all that gawking, I'm sorry to disappoint," Niamh said, sounding just as surly as I felt. "All I know how to say with my fingers is *feck off.*"

"Faith," the man by the door said, not a bark of command or even very stern, just the name, delivered with a crack of power.

Her lips tightened, holding something back, but she pushed herself up using nothing but her heavily muscled arms, and, still just using her arms, "walked" herself to the open seat next to it and slowly lowered back down.

"If yer trying to look intimidating, you've gone and missed the mark, love," Niamh said, reaching for her drink. "It's foolish ye've managed."

"Keep it up, old woman," the woman said, so low I barely heard. "I won't be on a leash forever."

"What are ye going to do, do bar handstands and hope I die of fear?" Niamh shook her head.

"Going great here, then, hmm?" I slid into the seat. "Thanks," I told the woman.

Her lip pulled up at the corner, like she was snarling.

"Don't even bother, Jessie. She's been at me all afternoon." Niamh waved it away. "She's trying to push my buttons, hoping I'll start a fight. What a load of hassle that would be."

"Miss Jessie!" Donna smiled at me. "Haven't seen you in a while. What can I getcha?"

"Umm…beer, I think. Something strong."

She nodded and moved away.

"Uh-oh, beer, eh? Not wine?" Niamh glanced over. "You're going to be here for a while?"

"Yes, but not so long that I can't get home."

"Ah, sure, Austin Steele will make sure you get home."

"Call him alpha," Faith grumbled.

"He's not my alpha, and you're not in his pack," Niamh replied. "But helluva try, girl. Helluva try. Drink up. Maybe you'll be pleasanter when yer drunk."

"All these new people do is stare," I murmured to Niamh. "It's really annoying."

"Aye, it is. They aren't allowed to make challenges,

so they glare down powerful people and hope for the best."

"And when nothing happens?"

"Well, Faith there just keeps at it, and it seems the bollocks behind ye isn't giving up, so I'd say we're in it for the long haul. Just ignore them. It's more fun when they grind their teeth in frustration."

"I won't always be on a lea—"

"Yeah, yeah, I heard ye the first time. Janey Mack, she's something." Niamh rattled the ice around in her glass. "Paul, if you please. A whiskey, too. I need a little help drowning out my new dear friend."

"Fancy meeting you here."

I recognized that voice, like a growl, but not angry. Not unpleasant.

Turning, I scowled at my "rescuer." "You scared off my nemesis," I said. "Now how am I going to find a way to stab him without getting in trouble? He tattles."

"May I sit with you?" He stood straight and tall, as though at attention, waiting patiently for the verdict. His face was a closed book, no hint of the easiness I'd heard in his tone.

"Sure, why not, invite all yer friends," Niamh said dryly.

He ignored her, continuing to wait for my response.

"Yeah, sure, if you want," I said.

He nodded, grabbed a chair from down the way, and placed it behind us, forming a triangle. I scooted out and turned my chair a little out of politeness. Niamh didn't move.

"I came to ask the alpha about your game," the man said, and then stuck out his hand. "I'm Kace."

I shook it. "Jacinta. Jessie to those in the know."

"Miss Jessie, eventually, when that God-awful butler makes his rounds," Niamh muttered.

"That's Niamh." I hooked a thumb at her, belatedly realizing Sebastian hadn't come in with us. For a guy who didn't usually feel fear, he'd sure gotten a wake-up call on this trip.

"Sebastian is going to train me," I told Niamh while he was on my mind.

"Oh yeah? That's good news, now. As odd as they come, make no mistake, but he does know his stuff."

"Sebastian, is that the mage?" Kace asked, interested rather than aggressive, his mannerisms subdued, not at all like he'd been with Sasquatch pushed against the fence.

"It is, yeah," I answered. "He hasn't been here long. Where's Sasquatch, Niamh?"

She huffed out a laugh. "He came in here shaking like a leaf, so he did. Pure terrified of something. He took one look at my new friend Faith there, sitting next to me, turned around, and walked out. If Faith weren't the worst thing to happen to sunny days, I'd be relieved for the peace and quiet."

"Just wait until my—" Faith started.

"Yeah, yeah, yer leash. Jaysus, do ye not get out much or what?"

"Kace did that." I thanked Donna for the drink and then pointed at Kace. I didn't really want to play conversation host to a stranger today, but he'd been trying to help, and the least I could do was be polite. If I'd actually been in trouble, he would've been a welcome sight. "Whatever he wants."

"No." Niamh put out her hand. "She doesn't know shifter rules. She is offering because of Jane manners."

"What's the matter?" I asked, pausing with my beer raised, ready to pour it into the glass Donna had provided.

"Let me get the round," Kace said.

"No." Niamh shook her outstretched hand. "No. She stays on my tab, and that is that. She will neither buy nor accept drinks from nice-looking gentlemen who gave Sasquatch a good clatter across the head."

"I didn't—"

I waved Kace away. "Let her dream."

He shrugged at Donna. "I'll have a beer. Bud." Kace nodded to Donna.

"What's the deal with buying drinks for a shifter?" I asked.

"We—"

"No!" Niamh half turned so she could glare at Kace. "Fer feck's sake, lad. Do ye have no sense? Leave her be. Mind yer business."

"Today is getting on my last nerve," I said.

I finished pouring my beer into the glass and took a large gulp as Niamh said, "I am right there with ye."

Too bad she was part of the problem.

✧ ✧ ✧

A COUPLE OF hours passed, and the drinks were still flowing. Kace turned out to be pleasant company, but I was tired and still heart-sore, and I honestly didn't want to have to try so hard. Being polite wasn't normally a lesson in patience, but Kace had caught me on a bad day, and Niamh definitely wasn't helping.

Thankfully, Austin was finally getting close. He'd answer Kace's question, and then Kace would be on his way.

Except I knew that wasn't quite true. Kace was trying to get to know me, and since he hadn't come right out and said he was interested, I couldn't think of a polite way to tell him that I wasn't.

"I'm going to head to the bathroom," I said, and slid

off my stool, squeezing between his left leg and the back of Niamh's chair.

Kace twisted his knees to the side and lightly touched the top of my hips to help guide me through.

"I'm good, thanks," I murmured dismissively, stepping away from his touch.

I might not be great at subtlety, but I did know when someone's interest was piqued. His touch, more intimate than helpful, confirmed what I'd already suspected. Crap. I wasn't in the mood to gently rebuff someone. He might react badly, and then I'd feel threatened, and then magic would start flying around, and suddenly it would be a whole thing. What a mess.

Still mulling over how to get out of this situation—I had to do something, because I didn't want to lead him on—I used the restroom and made my way back, feeling Austin nearby. His progress had stalled, though, indicating he was probably talking to someone outside.

Sir Stares-a-Lot still stood by the door, and I found myself veering that way. His presence actively squashed mirth, and his watchfulness had been overwhelmingly applied to me for the last couple of hours. I didn't know why he was so bothered by me—I was clearly not a shifter. I should've escaped his notice altogether, unless he was that worried about naïve mages without much magical experience. Regardless, full of liquid courage and a black mood, I decided it was time to put this to bed.

"Hey," I said, stopping beside him, leaning against the wall.

He didn't respond.

"Why do you keep looking at me instead of spreading your attention around the bar?" I asked.

"I am learning this territory and the people in it." He angled his body, his presence overbearing and his height topping mine by about half a foot. Although not as tall as Austin, he was just as broad and muscular. I felt his focus beating down on me, his dominance almost a palpable thing.

I just was not in the mood to pay attention.

"Rather than stare at me all creepy-like, why don't you just ask questions?"

He was silent for a beat.

"What are you?" he finally asked.

"Amazing." I spread my arms. "Also a female gargoyle."

His face might've been painted on for all the emotion he showed. "I haven't heard of a living female gargoyle."

"It's a new situation."

For the first time, I saw a flicker of something on his face. Doubt and maybe annoyance. I narrowed my eyes, now watching for all I was worth.

"I am staring, ma'am," he said, his voice rough, "because I monitor dangerous things. Within this bar, you are the most dangerous thing. You are wild and unpredictable, mouthy without worrying about the consequences, and too confident for your own good. I can't sense much power in you. You'll be killed if you keep this up."

"I'm the most dangerous thing in the bar, but you're worried I'll be killed?"

"You are the most dangerous thing because you'll incite violence. You'll say the wrong thing and set someone off. If not for my control of the situation, you would've created a problem already. Tensions are high in this territory. There is a lot of power, strength, and aggression with a lack of proper higher structure to keep it contained."

I lifted my eyebrows, thinking about defending myself. About telling him that he had it wrong, and even if he didn't, I'd be just fine to defend myself, thank you very much. I'd lasted this long—I could keep going a while longer. But Austin was approaching the door now, and I figured he could weigh in.

I gave Sir Stares-a-Lot a thumbs-up and stepped away, looking out the door. Austin approached with a short, bull-faced woman who was nodding at whatever he was telling her. His bearing was stiff, and I saw the fatigue lining his eyes. Stress. He was under pressure.

Kicking myself for not having noticed that before, I pulled the mute off his link and trickled healing magic into him, taking the edge off. Soon he'd be right as rain, still stressed but less tired.

His gaze snapped up, pleasure and gratitude filling the link. He nodded, the gesture barely perceptible.

I gave him a little smile and couldn't help a stupid wave. He had plenty to do, though, and I didn't need to bother him with my stuff. I ignored Sir Stares-a-Lot and made my way back to my seat, having to squeeze in again, this time pushing more toward Niamh's chair so I wasn't as close to Kace.

"Here." Kace moved his knees again, but not so far this time, reaching for me to help me pass.

"No, no, I'm good, honest." I tried to twist away from his fingertips. "It's fine."

He nodded, and I'd almost made it past him when he placed his hand on the small of my back, the feel of his touch all wrong. The pressure, the size of his hand, the warmth.

It was at that moment that I realized two things. The first was that I'd grown so accustomed to Austin's touch that I knew it by feel. I knew when it wasn't his, and it felt wrong.

The second was a lot more jarring.

CHAPTER 18

RAGE BLED THROUGH me, but it wasn't *my* rage.
Movement made me jerk my head up before I could fully lower into my seat.

Austin reached us in a few steps, his face still hard but his eyes burning.

He grabbed Kace by the back of the shirt and ripped him upward. Kace's butt caught the back of the chair, and it toppled over. His shirt ripped up the back and he dropped, struggling to get his bearings.

"Crap." I hurried forward, knowing this had happened because Austin had sensed my discomfort through the link. He didn't have all the information and was just trying to protect me.

Austin let go of Kace's shirt, letting him fall to the ground, then grabbed his arm and swung him toward the back of the bar.

Just like last time, I magically sent people running from the bar, closing them off from the action. Only Niamh and one other person remained, Sir Stares-a-

238

Lot. Niamh wasn't bothered by my spell, but he clearly felt my shove and was pushing back.

I didn't have the time to make a point.

I slapped an inverted shield around him to keep him from seeing what went down. Austin was ashamed of his darkness, and if he let it leak out again, he wouldn't want everyone to know. The spell was crude but serviceable. And although the big shifter got to work fighting it immediately (he couldn't see me, but I could still see him), it was a powerful spell. Not even Austin would have been able to break out of it. Probably.

Austin pinned one of Kace's arms with one hand and grabbed his throat with the other. I grimaced, knowing Kace could easily land a punch on Austin's exposed face. If he still had that knife, he could stick it into Austin's exposed neck.

"Hey, hey." I paused with my hand on Austin's shoulder, only then registering that Kace's eyes were downcast, his body relaxed. He was yielding to Austin's rage. To his dominance.

Austin leaned over him, face inches away, aggression plain but fingers not squeezing Kace's windpipe. This wasn't like last time at all. Austin wasn't out of control, lost to the blackness. He was letting his rage send a message, but he wasn't succumbing to it. He was proving the status quo, like Ulric had said.

I took my hand away and stepped back, thinking maybe I'd acted prematurely with the magical screen.

"Niamh, do I let people see this?" I shouted.

"Let the angry one by the door see it," she replied. "Leave the rest out. They're wreckin' me head."

Fair enough.

I ripped Sir-Stares-a-Lot's inverted shield away, and he stepped forward, his own rage consuming him. He roared, not entirely human, and surged toward me.

A blistering spell was at my disposal immediately, muscle memory, ready to be unleashed.

Austin got there first, so fast that I startled. Pinning Kace one moment, he was in front of me the next, tucking me behind him and putting himself between me and the charge.

"Don't release that, whatever it is, Jess," Austin snarled, though his anger was not directed at me.

The other man slowed, perhaps sensing the change in the tide, or maybe he realized I had some ammo he didn't want to mess with. Still, he was bristling with anger, power surging from him.

But Austin's power was mightier. I could feel it vibrating through me, singing through my blood and electrifying my body. I touched his back, unable to help it, and leaned into his warmth, needing more. Lost to it and not sure why. Drowning in it but not wanting to come up for air.

"It's done," Austin said to the man savagely, reaching back and bracing me against him. "It's done. Back down."

"Are you in control?" the other man asked, and I wondered the same thing about him.

"Yes. Unless she's harmed. Then it'll be a problem."

I took two fistfuls of Austin's shirt and leaned against his strong back, feeling the play of muscle as he braced and altered his weight, not at all worried about what would happen, even though logic dictated that I *should* be worried.

"What is happening to me?" I asked myself, pushing away from Austin, struggling out from under his arm.

I stepped out from behind him, but his arm flared, creating a divider between me and Sir Stares-a-Lot, who did not tear his focus away from Austin.

"It's fine." I pushed at his arm. It didn't budge.

Sir Stares-a-Lot nodded curtly, and his muscles relaxed little by little. Austin followed suit, as though they were doing the shifter equivalent of putting down their swords. Kace had stayed where Austin had left him, hunched a little, his eyes downcast.

"You can let everyone back in, Jess," Austin said, and his arm loosened, dropping to his side.

"Wait." Sir Stares-a-Lot's focus was on me again. "What happened here?"

"Sit." Austin jerked his head toward Niamh. "I'll join you. There's something I haven't told you."

Sir Stares-a-Lot nodded again, his gaze shrewd, and made his way toward Niamh.

"Me too, or…" I pointed at my chest.

Austin turned to face me, deliciously close. "Of course you. I don't see any blood. Did you finally do it?"

My mood fell.

"Oops." His smile was a welcome sight after all the hard faces. "I struck a nerve. Go sit. I'll be right there."

I made my way over, moving very slowly because I wasn't in a hurry to sit so close to Sir Stares-a-Lot. One wrong word and I might incite some sort of riot. I glanced back, feeling Austin move toward Kace.

Austin stopped just in front of him, hands at his sides, giving the other man some breathing room this time.

"I apologize, alpha. I didn't know," Kace said.

"Neither does she," Austin said. "For a long while, neither did I. You're blameless. I should've gone about this differently, but…"

"I would've reacted the same way you did, alpha. Probably worse. Bad timing. It's good to see you, sir." Kace stuck out his hand.

Austin took it, and he pulled the other man in for a bro hug, with a chest bump and much beating each other on the backs.

"Do you eavesdrop on private moments often?" Sir Stares-a-Lot asked, and I realized I'd wandered a bit too close without realizing it. He was leaning away from me on his chair to avoid touching me.

I jerked my arm the other way, happy to follow suit. "Yeah, when it's juicy stuff. Don't you?"

I wrestled Faith's chair away, then pulled mine out a little so I had more space. Once sitting, I picked up my drink.

"Today has been a shitshow. What did he mean, Niamh, 'neither did she'? What don't I know?"

"How much time have ye got?" she replied.

"Right. Great. You're in one of those moods, are you?"

"Yes, I am. Go around the bar and get me a drink, won't ya? I'd do it, but I don't want to set that eejit off again."

"I got it." Austin sauntered around the bar, his T-shirt showing off his perfect upper body, his hair messy, like he'd just gotten out of bed. I soaked in his easy grace, the power in each movement.

"What don't I know?" I asked him.

"As it concerns the magical world, I think it would

take every night for the better part of a month to tackle that," he teased, and though part of me was annoyed, a larger part welcomed his light tone. "No wine?"

"She's going to get langers tonight, just ye wait," Niamh said. "If she doesn't have to be carried home, I haven't done my job."

"No." I pointed at her. "No. A lovely buzz, then home."

"Sure, yeah." Niamh nodded dutifully.

Sir Stares-a-Lot studied each of us in turn, his eyes coming back to me the most, sticking for way too long. If he kept it up, I would either start squirming, or lose it and blast him off his stool.

Austin handed a Bud across the bar, and Sir Stares-a-Lot leaned forward to grab it. Next up, he finished pouring what was left in my bottle of beer, and backed me up with another. Niamh got two bottles of cider. For himself he poured a whiskey.

Austin came back around the bar, stopping behind me and reaching over me to put his drink next to mine. His smell stole over me—clean cotton, sweet spice, and a little sweat mixed in. Masculine. He pulled a chair over and settled onto it, his knee rubbing against mine. "Let them in, Jess."

I tugged away the spells and opened the bar door. "I didn't know it would've been okay to let them stay."

"No, you did good. Kace submitted quickly. It calmed things down."

Speaking of whom, Kace didn't leave the bar. He took a seat at the other end, ripped shirt and all, quickly joined by two others. I hoped he wasn't embarrassed.

"He's fine," Austin said softly, pushing my hair off my shoulder before grabbing his drink. "This isn't like the Dick and Jane world. We're all good now."

"Hey, Miss Jessie, are you okay?" Ulric hustled over to us, his eyes lingering on Sir Stares-a-Lot for a moment before landing on Austin. "Alpha, everything okay?"

"Yes. Just a misunderstanding," Austin said, transferring his glass to the other hand and resting his arm over the back of my chair.

Ulric pointed at me, needing the final say-so, and I gave him a thumbs-up. "You guys can go, if you want. Or…whatever you want to do."

Ulric swung the finger to Sir Stares-a-Lot, a silent question for Austin, wondering about the danger level.

"Jess, Ulric, Niamh," Austin said, "meet Kingsley, my brother."

CHAPTER 19

"ANY FOOL COULD'VE seen that coming," Niamh said, her ice cubes chasing each other around the glass.

I raised my hand. "Not this fool."

Ulric stepped back, behind Sir Brother-Who-Stares-a-Lot, and gave me a sympathetic grimace before heading off to talk to the woman he'd called dibs on earlier.

"Kingsley, this is Jess, a good friend of mine," Austin said. "And Niamh, part of the Ivy House crew."

"Good to meet you both," Kingsley said, but instead of shaking my hand, he kept up that unwavering stare. "This Ivy House—you mentioned it on the phone. We are helping you defend the heir. That is…"

I raised my hand.

"And you were…a Jane before all this, is that right? But somehow you're now a female gargoyle?"

His expression didn't change, but his tone conveyed his utter confusion.

Fair enough.

"Where did Ulric go? He likes telling stories," I said.

Austin pulled his arm away from my chair and stood. "I'll send him over. There's some stuff I need to take care of, but I'll head back in time to answer questions. Yes?"

"I can't say this isn't going to end badly for you," I told him.

His smile was slight, but it was there. That was twice tonight. Maybe he'd bought another bit of time with his last outburst.

"Hey, real quick..." I hopped up and put a hand on his hard bicep, directing him away a little and reducing my voice. Shifters had excellent hearing, but he dipped his head closer anyway. "The flying-off-the-handle thing... How can we compromise on that? I don't like when you lose yourself to the shadows. I also don't like trying to come up with ways to let guys down gently. So maybe you can lean on them a little, use just a smidge of rage, I don't have to be the bad guy, and we all win. Doesn't that sound nice?"

He ran his thumb across the edge of my lower lip, over my chin, and down the front of my throat. Something about that touch, and his liquid cobalt eyes, made me shiver, and also turned my body to flame.

"We'll talk about it, okay? I promise you. Now's not

the time, though."

"Totally. I'm good with using a place marker."

He nodded and dropped his hand. "Talk to you soon. Don't stress my brother out too much."

"Stress him out?" I murmured, making my way back to my seat. "*He* stresses *me* out."

"You don't like when he opens up to his beast?" Kingsley asked me after I'd sat down.

"Now who is eavesdropping on private conversations?"

"It isn't so private when it's in a bar."

"So then why'd you say it in the first place?"

He studied me for a while, and I knew his visit was going to feel really long. Then it occurred to me that he was still waiting for an answer.

"Oh, uh…" I shrugged. "You know his past, so I don't have to tell you about that. Not that I would—it's not my place. He doesn't want any recurrences, and I don't like seeing him…out of sorts."

"Troubled," Niamh said.

"Right. I didn't know if I could describe a shifter as troubled." I took another sip of my beer.

"You know nothing about shifters?" Kingsley asked.

"I only learned shifters existed less than a year ago." I paused for a moment. "I sure wish you'd allow in some emotion. It's like speaking to a cyborg."

Niamh laughed. "He is practically yelling his confusion at you right now. He does it in body positioning. Don't tell the mage, though. He's much too interested in shifters, if you ask me."

"Yes, the mage. I'd like to hear why you have one hanging around," Kingsley said, crossing his arms over his chest.

"Ah." I nodded and pointed. "An action. That's better. I can work with that."

"She still doesn't know what it means." Niamh laughed harder, bending over her cider. I figured she wasn't talking about the crossed arms—*that* message seemed obvious—but about whatever Austin had mentioned to Kace.

"What a stupid end to a crappy day," I mumbled. "Anyway, it's very helpful when Austin gets super violent in a battle, but when it happens in the bar, because someone has disrespected me or whatever, then no, I don't like it. The mage is here to help train me. I'm new to everything, including my magic."

"That maggot the other day had it coming." Niamh shook her head. "Talking about that sorry excuse for an alpha taking you and being quick about knocking you up? You should've let Austin finish him."

Kingsley stiffened. "Tell the story."

"Say please," Niamh replied.

He didn't, and she didn't push.

After she was done, he reverted to staring at me. "You pulled him back?"

"Yes," I said. "He doesn't want to go to that place. I caused it, so I figured I should fix it."

"But you did. *You* did."

"Well, yeah. I made everyone else leave the bar."

"You forced everyone out like you did today?" Kingsley asked.

I nodded.

"And you were obviously the one who trapped me in." The growl riding his words was evident. He was not amused.

"Yes. I didn't know whether it was okay for everyone to see Austin...do his thing. The last time he was glad people hadn't witnessed him lose control."

"Tell me about Ivy House," Kingsley said, and I didn't even mind that it was a command. I was not an accomplished storyteller, which meant I had a ready excuse to get up and grab Ulric, since Austin hadn't made it to him yet. Within seconds, Ulric had Kingsley captivated with what hopefully would be a long and drawn-out version of Ivy House history.

I turned back toward the bar, hoping to catch Austin as he walked past, but he was already down at the opposite end, speaking to Kace and the others.

"Is this how it's going to be going forward?" I asked Niamh, doing a quick check of all the magical links, re-muting all of them but my connection to Austin. "All this drama?"

"Nah." Niamh poured cider into her glass, the sparkling liquid rushing through the ice. "After the territory is in full swing, it'll be mostly like before, just with more powerful people who hopefully talk a little less."

"Kingsley originally said mage magic wasn't allowed in here."

Just for kicks, I tried to completely cut off the link between Austin and me, both the input and output.

His head snapped toward me, his eyes hard. Reinstating the link, I felt his confusion and wariness.

"Ack." Niamh leaned her elbow against the bar. "He was trying to get a rise outta ya. See what you'd do. Yer not supposed to use magic in a social place like this, where people are trying to let off a little steam, but it doesn't need to be said. He was just throwing his weight around to see if you'd push back."

"I did. I threatened him."

"Good girl, yerself. Right bold of 'im to walk into someone else's home and start barking orders."

"That's what I was thinking. Also, I'm just in a piss-poor mood."

"Yeah. These shifters are laying it on a little thick, so

they are, with all the brooding and strutting around. Bunch o' donkeys."

I amplified the sensitivity of my link with Austin now, experimenting with him because I could see him, and also because he wouldn't get annoyed and give me a box, as Niamh would say (and do). It wasn't just his emotions I could feel now, but his senses—the whiffs of identifying scents, the cool glass under his fingers, the dried sweat clinging to his body from hard work earlier.

His eyes drifted back toward me, having looked away after I'd reinstated the link. Arousal licked up my middle, and I couldn't tell if that was from him or me. Memories of our late-night activities crowded my mind. We still hadn't talked about our new...pastime, but we also hadn't stopped it. I wondered if he'd be around tonight, or if he'd be too busy with pack business.

He braced his hands against the bar, ignoring those in front of him. I felt a little bad about that. He clearly knew Kace and the others. He obviously wanted to catch up.

Just one more experiment, and I'd let him get back to his night. Maybe it would encourage him to take a much-needed break later.

Breath coming a little heavier, the arousal fanning higher, I ran my fingertips up the inside of my thigh, spreading my legs a little as I did so.

His eyes were cobalt fire. His fingertips dug into the wood. I slipped my other hand under my shirt and felt along my stomach, focusing on my soft skin, drifting upward...

"That's goin'ta get awkward real fast," Niamh drawled.

A zing of embarrassment and I pulled my hands away and clasped them primly in my lap. I yanked my focus away from Austin. "You didn't feel that, did you?"

"Through the link? No. You're starting to be very handy with muffling it. Earl won't like that one bit. But Austin Steele is about to combust, and I can see that yer the reason. Unless ye want to get nailed in the bar's office, I'd stop."

Heat such as I'd never known washed through me, burning me alive.

"Now, *that* I felt," she said. "Maybe just keep going, then."

I clasped my hands more tightly in my lap, barely able to breathe. "I should probably head home."

"Nah." Niamh lifted her hand. "Donna, get Jessie another one."

"No, no, I have one—"

Donna wasted no time in plopping one down in front of me. I sighed.

"There. Now. Enjoy yerself until he has a spare

moment, and then I'm sure he'd be happy to clean yer pipes. Lord knows you need it. Yer too wound up, girl."

"Please stop."

"You need a good rogering."

"Seriously, stop."

"Ye'll be glad ya did."

I took a long sip of my drink and tried not to agree with everything Niamh had said. Tried not to wonder when I'd get Austin alone again. Tried not to make a plan for how I could kill this desperate itch he'd put inside me.

CHAPTER 20

"**H**EY, YOU—"

I jumped and swung out my hand, just barely stopping from saying, "Hah!" with my lame karate chop.

Austin ran his hand down my back, releasing pleasant tingles throughout my body.

"It's just me. I was about to ask if you were good, but I guess I somehow snuck up on you even though you have the link wide open and should be able to feel my every move." He didn't smile, but I felt it in every fiber of his being.

I blew out a breath, which would've probably caught fire if a candle were close by. Ulric had wandered away a while ago, but Kingsley had stuck around, getting rid of the extra seat and pulling up closer, still staring. Always staring. I'd mostly ignored it, chatting to Niamh and watching Austin either work the bar or step away to talk with someone or other. His mood had become darker, likely as a result of more bad news. I'd have to ask him about that.

Tomorrow. Everything could wait until tomorrow. Especially now that I was neck-deep in suds and wouldn't be able to keep my eyes open much longer.

"Yep." I wobbled a thumbs-up at him. "I miss my son, though. I think he had a really good time, don't you?"

Austin pushed in closer, his side pressing against mine. I leaned into his comforting warmth.

"Need this seat?" Kingsley half rose, his hand on the back of his chair.

"No, it's fine. I'll stand." Austin swished my hair over my shoulder, seemingly in a playful mood despite whatever he'd learned. Or maybe he was just laughing at me. I hadn't been this tipsy in a while. "Yes, I do think he had a good time. A great time. He took all of this in…well, almost in stride."

"I wish he could've stayed."

"He's becoming a man. He can't have his mother's butler coddle him all the time."

I spat out a laugh.

"What are ye at?" Niamh leaned away, yanking her arm up to ward off my flying saliva.

"Sorry." I wiped my mouth, leaning harder into Austin because that was the way my body decided to head. I tried to push off with my head, super ladylike, but he curled a hand around my ribcage.

"Those beers are strong," I murmured, straightening up and trying to get back on track. I rolled my shoulders, shrugging Austin away. He wanted to laugh—I could feel it—but his expression didn't show the slightest glimmer of humor.

"I thought, with advanced healing, ye'd eventually grow a tolerance." Niamh rattled the ice in her glass. "Wrong."

I grimaced. "So it seems."

"We're about to do last call," Austin said. He'd slung a hand over my chair's back but respected my desire to sway on my own. "Do you want something else, or should I walk you home?"

"She's no quitter, boy!" Niamh threw back a shot of Jameson. "May as well just finish'r up."

"Hear, hear." I leaned heavily against the bar, sagging. Then groaned.

"You should take her home," Kingsley said.

"It would be a mistake to listen to someone who barely knows me but thinks he should tell me what to do." I straightened up and reached for the full beer that had magically appeared in front of me. Niamh was good. Or Austin was. I'd stopped paying attention to who was ordering them.

"Ah, but he wasn't telling you what to do," Austin

said, the humor bleeding into his voice this time. "He was telling *me* what to do. He thinks he has that right, being my big brother and having done it all of our lives."

"Sometimes you even listened," Kingsley replied.

"Not this time, though." I took another sip. It tasted like water. I was going to regret all of this tomorrow. Maybe not the hangover, since I could probably heal that, but you couldn't heal regret over acting like a fool. "He would get an awful surprise if he listened to you this time." I leveled a finger at Kingsley, then drew a circle in the air. When I'd done that earlier, he'd leaned back and crossed his arms, as though greatly debating grabbing my finger and yanking it off. Now he just sat placidly, one hand curled around a bottle of Bud, and the other splayed in his lap. He'd *finally* realized I was not the threat he'd imagined. "You killed my game earlier today. Or your man did, anyway. I might've gotten stabbed this time, okay, fine. But I was nearly there. I would've definitely gotten him next time." I made a stabbing gesture. "I would've gotten him right in the back."

"What's this now?" Austin asked.

"This is the fifth time she's berated me for Kace stopping her...game." Kingsley's displeasure was evident. "She was about to be stabbed, apparently by design."

"Ah." Austin's gaze roamed the bar, ever watchful.

"You let those sorts of...games happen in the territory?" Kingsley asked.

"That, my dude, is the shifter version of talking trash." I put my finger to my nose. "I've learned a thing or two."

I chuckled under Kingsley's hard stare. Niamh outright laughed.

"No," Austin answered, running his palm across my shoulders gently and down my other arm. "Only Jess gets that privilege."

"Does that not...cause problems?" Kingsley asked. "Tension? People don't like to see a favorite get privileges others do not."

"First of all, not many people, even shifters, would be jealous of a game that always ends in a stab wound. Second, the game was offered to any who wanted to play. Everyone knows how unpredictable she is. How powerful..." Austin paused when Kingsley moved his hand. "You know it's true, brother. She locked you in a spell, right?" Kingsley moved again, almost imperceptibly. Austin inclined his head, some sort of affirmation. I wasn't drunk enough to miss that they were conducting a second conversation in gestures. "You might not be able to feel or smell her power while she is swaying in place right now, but you felt it when she used it. That was no mistake. Right now she is learning, and so she gets passes any trainee would. She doesn't mean anyone harm, and this territory knows that. They are content to allow her these rare...privileges because they like watching when it blows up her in face."

"Well, that is new information," I muttered.

"Only to ye." Niamh chuckled.

"And outsiders?" Kingsley asked.

"Outsiders typically challenge me." Austin ran his fingertips along the back of my neck.

"Wait." I swatted his hand away. I couldn't think when he was doing that. It was turning me into a puddle of goo. "People are challenging you because of me?"

Austin's eyes were soft. "They would've anyway."

"No." I took another sip of beer. It dribbled down the side of my face. "Damn it."

"Ye've got a hole in yer lip," Niamh said.

"Yeah. Awesome." I wiped it away with the back of my hand, swayed toward Austin, was gently nudged back, and clunked my glass down on the bar. "That's probably a good cue to stop."

"Sure, ye've just gotten goin'. Only good things will happen from here on out."

"You just want to see me fall on my face. Little do

you know that I am a professional. I do not fall on my face. Down a flight of stairs, sure, nobody's perfect…"

"The video feature on my phone is already cued up," she replied.

I waved a hand at her image—one of them, at least—and turned in my seat to glare at Austin, closing one eye to keep his image from multiplying. "The stabbing game has them challenging me? I mean you? Because just send them to me. I will rock their world."

"The stabbing game, your random seeping power that I don't control, a mage that I don't cast out…"

I leaned back against the bar, the motion nearly jostling me out of my chair, but whatever. "Because you allow Sebastian in the bar?" I narrowed my eyes at Kingsley. "You were being serious earlier. You really didn't want a mage in here."

"He didn't know who you were," Austin said.

A flash of anger tore through me. Power followed, ballooning around me.

"My kind has been hunted by mages for a decade now," Kingsley said, a growl riding his words. I felt the sweet rush of his answering power. "My pack is too big, too well established, too prosperous for the mages to go after, but if we continue to pretend it isn't happening, it'll only be a matter of time. Meanwhile, entire packs are being wiped out for frivolous reasons. For spite disguised as genuine offense."

It was the same thing Sebastian had said to Niamh. She'd told us about Momar and the threat he posed.

"He would know," Kingsley replied, and I realized I'd said that thought out loud.

"Not all mages are against you," I said. "A blanket generalization will only hurt you in the end, because you'll alienate the mages in the middle—or worse, the ones who support you. Then it'll really be war. If you want to fight Momar, the best approach would be to recruit some mages of your own. He must have a crapload of enemies. Powerful people always do. Find some of those and push back."

"Things are a lot more complicated than that," he replied after a silent beat.

I'd felt a surge of energy, of motivation, but something about his tone took the wind out of my sails. My heart dropped, and I sagged against the bar. "I'm making everything harder on you," I said to Austin, my eyes filling with tears. One got loose and shimmied down my cheek. I quickly wiped it away. Liquid courage had turned into liquid emotion. I needed to get out of here, and I needed some chocolate. "Your pack is in chaos because of me, isn't it? You have people coming to challenge you because they hate that you're working with a mage."

He rubbed my back, humor in his eyes. "They aren't coming because of you. They don't know anything about you until they get here and see you…working on your magic."

"Bumbling around with yer magic, more like," Niamh said.

"God you're surly," I told her.

"Well, aren't ye slow on the uptake tonight?" she replied with a grin.

"Jess, you'll make this territory stronger," Austin said. "And I will make that house stronger. Together, we'll create something that hasn't been accomplished before, and we'll both be stronger for it. And if it doesn't work out that way, Kingsley will get to say, 'I told you so,' for the rest of my life."

Kingsley just grunted and averted his gaze.

"Okay, well…" I pushed the half-filled glass away.

"Here, wait, get one for the road," Niamh said, raising her hand.

"No. No!" I pointed at her and pushed to my feet. She leaned away from my jutting finger. "No more. I am an ab…sol*ute* mess." I hiccupped. "That was timely."

"I'll walk you home." Austin waited by the chair.

"Ulric and Jasper are out there. One of them can walk me home while the other keeps their dates warm. They apparently don't mind sharing. Or you could just set me free, and I'll blast anyone who tries to bother me."

"Ye'd probably accidentally blow up someone friendly and mistakenly get captured by Elliot Graves," Niamh said. "Or whoever's using his name, if that's what's going on."

"Well…" I shrugged. "That might be true."

"Alpha." Donna leaned over the bar. "There's a problem to the south. They need some direction."

Austin paused, frustration and urgency roiling within him. He looked at Kingsley, who nodded.

"Sorry, Jess, I have to go," Austin said. "I'll call you tomorrow, okay? We need to do more planning for the mage visitor."

"Sure, yeah." I clung to his arm for a moment before peeling myself off again. "Sorry. I am not exactly all hands on deck right now." I grimaced.

"Kingsley will take you home. I'll text you later."

"Oh no, I don't need him—" His fingertips on my jaw stopped my breath. I parted my lips, wondering if he would kiss me. Wondering if I'd be able to peel myself away a second time if he did. Instead, he ran his fingers down my throat, and the heat in his eyes made me shiver.

"Let him take you home. I want to make sure you get there safely," he whispered.

"Okay," I heard myself say, as meek as a lamb.

It wasn't until he was striding away that I came out of the heat-induced coma.

"Ye sure told him," Niamh said.

"Shut it," I replied, staring at Kingsley as he rose.

"Ready?" he asked, putting out his hand, offering to help me. Clearly he thought I was a risk to myself.

"I'm good." I waved him away and picked my way through the chairs, bumping into someone once I was free.

Kingsley pushed the person away.

"Sorry, alph—sir," the man said, edging farther away, a bubble opening up around me.

"That's embarrassing," I murmured, eyeing the bathroom. "I'm just going to hit the loo."

And then give him the slip. I got why Austin was worried: I was not thinking rationally. But seriously, I had the guys to watch me and my magic to protect me. Kingsley would just turn a pleasant drunken walk into an uncomfortable slog.

"Ye are saying out loud every single thought that is in yer head," Niamh said, then stood and gulped the last of her drink. "I'll take her home. I'm going that way anyway. I live right next to her."

"Use the restroom. I'll be waiting outside." Kingsley walked from the room, commanding a wide berth from everyone as he did so.

"Ah well, it was worth a try." Niamh sat back down.

"Wait, what?" I grabbed the chair back to steady myself. "You're going home anyway."

"They'll give me one more if I ask real nicely." She gave Paul a bulldog stare. He flinched, pausing in taking a glass off the bar.

Knowing I wouldn't be able to convince her, I didn't bother with the restroom (I hadn't actually needed to go) and met Kingsley on the sidewalk. He was waiting on the curb, watching everyone meander away, but he stepped closer as soon as he saw me.

Without a word, we started walking down the sidewalk toward home.

"So." I swerved a little his way, and it was the first time I saw him tense. He put out a hand but didn't actually touch me, as though he didn't want to make contact unless I was actually falling. "You shifters aren't really touchy-feely types, huh?"

"Touching means something different in our world, especially when it concerns someone Austin...cares about."

"Oh. That. With the past and everything." I paused on the corner, looking down the main drag, seeing broad bodies walking with purpose. Patrolling, probably. "He only got upset earlier because I was uncomfortable."

Kingsley reached out again as I stepped off the curb. "It's shocking how easily you get intoxicated."

"Apparently. Niamh finds it endlessly entertaining."

"Austin has calmed down since I saw him last."

"He's been trying, I think, to get over that."

"Yet he didn't step up to claim his position as alpha until you."

"Yeah." I ran my fingers through my hair. My toe hit a crack and my body weight shifted forward. "Bugger." I staggered to a stop, Kingsley's hand gentle around my arm, stabilizing me. "It's fine, seriously. I fall a lot. It's really not a big deal. I have this sleek, athletic body again. I don't care. I can heal myself really quickly. I can heal you, too, if you want. You tired? I can fix that up really quick."

"No."

"Okay. Just say the word and..." I snapped my fingers, only no sound came out. "You get it."

"No one has spoken to me like this in..." He peered down the next street we reached, only one person down the way, the hourglass figure indicating she was female, the powerful frame saying I didn't want to fight her. "It's a lesson in control, one I haven't had to wrestle in—"

"You should get out more. It's good for you."

"My brother has never lost his temper with you? He's never lost his temper with others because of you, other than earlier tonight and the instance you spoke of earlier?"

"Well there was one time at Ivy House. This other alpha didn't like Austin, and Austin didn't like him, and they almost went at each other. I kept Austin from blowing up, and I shut the door on the other dude. They had a bit of a scuff-up another time, too, when Dam— the other alpha—was a douche in Austin's bar. But honestly, Austin is really worried about losing control, but he doesn't do it much. He really doesn't."

"And you don't want him to."

It wasn't a question this time.

I paused at the next corner, looking both ways, feeling a little strange. I put a hand to my stomach, wondering if it was the beginning of the end. I didn't think I was going to hug a toilet, but sometimes it snuck up on me.

"I should be able to heal an upset stomach, though," I said to myself, looking back the way we had come. My senses were swimming in alcohol, but I knew that danger lurked that way. Something was amiss.

I put my hand out, meaning to touch Kingsley's shoulder, a silent command to stop. Only that was a Jane sort of gesture, and he moved out of the way, trying to keep contact to a minimum.

I pitched forward like a puppet with broken strings, my limbs flailing and my balance obliterated. My knee gave out and I staggered off the curb, not adjusting for the sudden change in altitude, and dove forward. My hip hit first and I rolled, my arms slapping cement, my legs askew.

"You moved," I bleated, knowing when I was sunk. I went limp, lying on the street, now huffing out laughter. "You moved!"

"I apologize. I wasn't thinking about—" He bent to me, his arms out, looking utterly lost and disheveled. This man who'd shown no outward emotion all night clearly had no idea what to do. Where to grab. "Can I— How can I—"

"It's fine." I lay there for a moment. "I'm good." The night sky looked down on me, floating softly, pricks of light swimming in the black. "It's a lovely night, though, isn't it?"

"Can I help you up?"

"Nah. I got it." I pushed myself to sitting, only because he was clearly uncomfortable.

"Are you hurt? Do you need to be carried?"

My laugh was soft at first, but soon I was guffawing again. "I'm sorry. I'm just a little emotional because my son came to visit, and he had to go home yesterday. It's hard when they leave. This is the first time I've lived away from him. I've been so busy with this new life, but seeing him again…" Tears filled my eyes and dribbled down my cheeks. "Sorry." I wiped them away, trying to stifle sobs. "I'm a little more broken up than I'd expected to be."

"Ah." Surprisingly, Kingsley sat down next to me, legs crisscrossed. "I didn't realize. I'm sorry. My kids are getting to about that age now." He paused for a moment. "Since you are not a shifter, or in the pack, or even part of this territory, I wonder if I might be frank with you?"

"Ugh. I'm not sure I'm up for your criticism right now. Can't it wait until tomorrow?"

"No, I meant…can I be open about my own situation?"

"Oh sure, yeah. I didn't realize you shouldn't be. I don't know the shifter rules."

"Yes. That is apparent." He glanced away, watching the quiet town. "I have a boy and a girl. They both have the makings of a good alpha, but my girl is…cutthroat. She's a handful. She'll leave first, I know she will. She is eager to start her life away from her parents' guidance. I just want to hold on with everything I have. To keep her home, safe. Every time she takes my hand, I worry it will be the last."

Tears rolled down my cheeks again, but this time I didn't stop them. I nodded and clasped my hands so that I wouldn't give in to the urge to pat his knee or shoulder and send him scurrying away. "It is hard, but as parents, that means we've done a good job. We've prepared them for the world and empowered them to find their own path."

Five animals ran into the back woods of Ivy House. They were moving fast.

"Do you know what animal they are?" I asked Ivy House, only not really, because I'd just said it out loud, and she couldn't hear me when I talked to her like that unless I was on the property.

"What?" Kingsley asked, sensing my change in mood immediately.

"*Do you know what animals they are?*" I asked Ivy House properly this time, using our connection.

"*Wolves. Shifters. Friend or foe?*" she answered, keyed up, I could tell.

"Crap." I wobbled up onto my feet. "Crap, I'm drunk. I need to figure out how to heal drunk." I staggered forward, wondering if drunk flying would be as dangerous as it sounded. "Five wolf shifters just ran onto Ivy House property." I upped my speed, feeling like I was running a million miles an hour. Kingsley was barely jogging beside me. "I need to heal drunk. Get

Niamh."

"I'm not leaving you. Are they with Austin's pack?"

"I wasn't talking to you..." I tapped into my connection with Ivy House again. *"Bring in Niamh and the others. What is Mr. Tom doing?"*

"Preparing to call you."

Austin was away to the south dealing with his own problems. I didn't need him for anything other than identifying the pack members.

"Are they with Austin's pack?" Kingsley asked again, a growl riding his words.

"I don't know." My phone rang, and I answered it on the run, the world jiggling around me. "Mr. Tom, hi, ask Niamh to bring in someone that can identify..." More shifters blipped onto my radar, behind the others, spreading out within the woods and coming our way. The intruders weren't attacking Ivy House: they were cutting through the property to get into town.

There was not one person familiar with this town that would do something like that. Everyone knew better.

"They aren't friendlies," I said into the phone. "They can't be. Mr. Tom, hang tight. Ivy House will bring in the others."

CHAPTER 21

I HANDED THE phone off to Kingsley. "Find Sebastian's name and push it. I can't look for it, run, and try to cure alcohol poisoning all at the same time."

He did as he was tasked, and I focused on going faster, feeling those shifters eating up ground. I wanted to be on Ivy House soil before I had to use her defenses. Or offenses.

The phone was handed back.

"Hello?" Sebastian said, his voice crisp. Alert.

"Were you awake?"

"Yes. Are you drunk?"

"Very. Do you have something to help with that?"

"Yes. How quickly do you need it?"

"Now-ish."

"Then no. What's going on?"

"Someone is using Ivy House as a... Oh crap—" Something else burst onto my radar: the basajaun was following the shifters, and given his size and my current lack of speed, he'd get to them sooner than I would. I pulled the phone away from my face. "Kingsley, can you run faster than this while carrying me?"

"Yes."

"Do it." I staggered to a stop and put up my hands like a child. "Do it now! Head toward Ivy House." I directed him down the correct street, just up ahead.

He scooped me up and threw me over his shoulder, not the most comfortable of holds, especially since his hard-as-rocks shoulder was digging into my full and fragile stomach. I tried to perch on his back to no avail, and then just worked on not throwing up.

"*Ivy House, how do you heal drunk?*" I asked, Sebastian still on the phone. I lifted it to my ear.

"Jessie? Jacinta!"

He actually sounded worried.

"*Are you sure? I can't make you drunk again—you'd have to start all over.*"

"*Just do it.*"

"I'm fine," I said between wheezes, my stomach rolling. If Ivy House really did have a cure, it wasn't helping fast enough. To be fair, its power was much stronger on the actual property. "Shifters are…running through my property…followed by the basajaun. I don't know…what they did, but if I don't get to them before…he does, there won't be…anything—ow—left to question."

"The basajaun from the mountain?" Kingsley asked, not even out of breath. He'd been drinking all night as well, beer for beer with me. It hadn't affected him even a little, just like his brother.

"I'll be right there," Sebastian said, and the line went dead.

He'd be too late. We might all be too late.

"Ivy House, slow that basajaun down, but—"

"You're talking to me again," Kingsley said.

"Damn it!" I switched gears. "*Ivy House, slow that basajaun down, but don't hurt him. I want him to stay on my side.*"

The house glowed like a beacon in the shadows ahead, all the lights on. A lone figure waited out front, and I could feel that it was Edgar. Swooping down from above came the nightmare alicorn with wings of inky darkness. I felt Ulric and Jasper on their way.

Those shifters were halfway through the woods now, coming fast. They were cutting through the property at a diagonal, which would dump them out to the left of the house.

It might not be an attack on me, specifically, but they'd clearly planned to crash into Austin's territory. I knew that wasn't how things were done around here. They'd snuck over the mountain, aggravating the basajaun in the process, and instead of making amends, they'd continued their preplanned journey with a lot more haste. These fellers were in a no-win situation.

"Put me down." I tapped Kingsley's shoulder. A moment later, half sober, I touched down on the sidewalk before Ivy House. "Thank you."

I ran onto the property, the alcohol in my blood draining quickly now. My mind raced for a strategy.

"Jacinta."

Sebastian's voice was magically amplified. A beat-up old VW Beetle rolled down the street, silent as the grave. I couldn't tell if he was propelling it by magic or if he'd magically cut out the sound. No lights announced its entrance.

"Can you trust him?" Kingsley asked. He stood beside me, loose and ready for battle, power pumping out of him.

"Doesn't matter either way. Not on Ivy House soil." I turned to Mr. Tom, coming out of the house, as Niamh touched down. "Get into the air with the other fliers so you can help Ivy House *respectfully* slow the basajaun down. Treat him with kid gloves. If he kills a few of the shifters, fine, but try to keep him from killing everyone."

Mr. Tom nodded and immediately started to change. Niamh lifted into the sky again, Ulric and Jasper showing up. I gestured for them to join the others.

"What do you need?" Sebastian jogged over from his car, his shirt and pants rumpled and his hair mostly standing on end.

"I need to make a wall to keep those shifters from getting out."

"You know how to do that."

"Yeah. Right, yes I do. I also need to keep the basajaun from gruesomely killing everyone."

"I sure hope you know how to do that, too, because I'm at a loss. I've only heard disturbing things about those creatures."

"Yeah. Dang. The things you've heard are mostly true, I'd bet." I ran toward the spot where the shifters would intersect, magically draping a wall over the property line.

"They might scatter once they hit the wall. Our best bet is to keep them contained. What if you magically redirect them?" Sebastian said, running beside me. Kingsley followed us, and Edgar puffed into insects, zooming ahead. "Create a mind confusion spell, or maybe an illusion to make them go where you want them."

"Yeah. Genius. I don't know how."

"Okay. I'll walk you through it. We'll do it together."

It wasn't easy to learn on the run, but with Sebastian teaching me, it was manageable. Kinda. By the time those shifters hit my magical wall—literally slammed into it (oops)—running for all they were worth, a dizzying mind spell picked up from there and directed them back toward the front of the house. I ran to meet them, not good enough to keep the spell turning like Sebastian had suggested.

Which basically put us back where we'd started. Huge gray wolves raced toward us, their growls fierce and saliva dripping from their mouths.

Kingsley yanked me behind him. He quickly started shedding clothes.

"No, no, no!" I shouted, fear gripping me for the first time. "Do not change right now, Kingsley, whatever you do. If the basajaun thinks you're challenging him, he might lose his mind. Just get out of the way."

I tried the dizzying spell again as those wolves bore down on us, intent on chewing their way through us if need be. The basajaun wasn't far behind, swatting at Ulric, who kept diving in front of him and then rolling away, his antics barely slowing the enormous creature. He was pissed and would not be easily distracted.

"Jessie," Sebastian said, his tone wary. "Jessie…"

"Yeah, yeah." I worked at the redirection spell, trying to get it to flow.

"I got it." Sebastian stepped in front of me. Usually he gave a little hand wiggle when he set a spell, nothing more, but this time he moved his body, too, gyrating like a stream through rocks. The spell sparkled into the air in front of us and then pushed out about ten feet.

The wolves hit that, lips pulled back and teeth gnashing, expecting to barrel into us. Instead they curved into a soft turn, running along the front of the yard. I couldn't tell whether they were confused.

"Trap them and stop that basajaun," Sebastian shouted, and I had the feeling he was about to be afraid of one more creature. Mages clearly didn't get out much.

The basajaun was hot on their tail, running toward the front lawn.

Ivy House was already on the bars for the wolves. Steel bars pushed up out of the grass on the other side of the lawn. The wolves ran into them, making *bong* sounds as their heads glanced off the unforgiving material. More bars sprang up on their right and then left, three sides of a cell I hadn't realized were there. The last wolf wasn't in, though, before the leaders realized what was happening.

I sent a shock wave of magic, forcing them forward. The final bars slid up, clipping the tail of one of the wolves and bumping him or her in.

Kingsley had his pants off, about to ignore me and change.

"No, damn it." I ran in front of him, heading off the basajaun with my body.

"No, Jess!" Kingsley shouted, but I blocked him off with a spell.

"Wait, wait, wait." I braced, my hands out, Kingsley still yelling for me to get out of the way. "Basajaun, wait, wait!"

The basajaun's legs churned, his strides long, almost on me.

"Wait!" I shouted, amplifying my voice, sending a shock of manufactured fear through the property. Heavy sheets of fog drifted in, quickly cutting down visibility. Stars blinked out of sight.

The basajaun slowed, eyeing Ivy House's fog warily. He probably remembered the last battle he'd taken part in here, when a poisoned fog had descended. This was just a trick of the air, though. It was my doing, not hers.

"It would be a grave insult to deny my right to punish trespassers," the basajaun said, and his tone raised the small hairs all over my body.

Sebastian stepped in closer to me, and Kingsley thrashed against my magical hold, wanting to do the same. The fliers dipped down, ready to fight. Ivy House braced herself.

"I'm not going to deny you anything," I said quickly, taking a step forward. Sebastian shadowed me. "I just need to talk to those wolves. They're sneaking into Austin's territory. He'll want to know why."

The basajaun's bristled hair sent nervous tremors racing through my body. Austin was on the move, way late to the party.

"I just wanted to slow you down enough to ask if I might trade for a little time with them," I said, remembering his preferred lingo. Everything was a trade with him. "They are on my territory, after all. I do have some say in their fate."

After a tense beat, the hair on the basajaun's body flattened. "Yes, of course. Where are my manners?" He smiled, his large teeth on display.

"Jess," Kingsley growled.

"Oops." The basajaun closed his mouth. "It is hard to know when to smile and when not. Shifters think it means I am about to attack. And you think it is pleasant."

"I don't know about pleasant…" I murmured.

"That is the tiger, is that correct? I remember his scent," the basajaun said. "Austin's brother."

"Oh." I tore down the magic keeping him put. "Yes. He was worried about my safety. I'm sure you understand."

"Yes, of course. My family is the same way. There's no one you can trust with your mate more than your sibling."

"No, it's not that, it's just that I was drunk—"

"He has done no wrong here. Unless he charges now, and then I will have to tear off his limbs. That would hardly be my fault—"

"No!" I put out my hands. "All is well. Let's not use language that might…cause issues."

The wolves circled in the cage, not much room in there to move around, their hackles raised and teeth bared. I cocked my head, aware again of the feeling of approaching danger, but it wasn't from them. It never had been. Something else lurked in the dark.

The woods were clear, though. Not even animals lurked in it tonight. The wolves and the basajaun must've scared everything off.

"Okay, let's see… How will we divide them up?" the basajaun said as the fliers started to land.

I held up a hand, feeling that strange, pulsing sense of danger. It was getting closer.

"Get back in the air," I whispered. "Push out into the woods. Stay out of sight."

I pointed at Kingsley, his stare now on the basajaun, who'd surpassed me as the most dangerous thing around. My gesture grabbed his attention. "Now you can change." His glance back at the basajaun had me shaking my head. "Not because of him—"

Thunder rolled across the darkened sky. I released the fog, letting the stars twinkle down at us, not one cloud hindering their glow.

A flash of heat and light assailed me, Kingsley now a huge tiger, larger than his natural counterpart, his shoulder up to nearly my neck.

"Gracious," Sebastian said softly.

Spiderwebs of lightning crackled through the air as another peal of thunder rolled, this one coming from the west. Beside it glowed a ball of fire; jets of flame dripped down from the sky.

"What is it?" Sebastian asked, turning to look up.

We waited in silence, the danger pulsing in my chest.

"The answer to my summons."

CHAPTER 22

A BIG, DARK blot on the night sky ate the starlight as it passed. Another peal of thunder, closer this time, boomed through the air, chased by zips of electricity around what I realized were huge wings, beating in a steady drum. A different beast trailed the first, its wings leaving curls of flame in their wake.

"There are two," I said, moving without meaning to, walking toward the porch of Ivy House.

"*Prepare*," Ivy House said, as if I needed the warning.

"Blend into the shrubbery, basajaun," I commanded. "I'm not sure how this is going to go. Edgar…keep to the shadows for now. Let's see what happens."

Even the wolves had stopped snarling, now all looking up at the sky.

"Shall I…create some sound and visibility barriers so the non-magical residents in town don't call the police?" Sebastian asked.

"Yes, please, though I think Austin has someone on

the police force." I watched those enormous wings beat at the sky. They had to be twenty or thirty feet wide, the wingspan incredible. Closer still, and I realized the beast actually had two sets of wings, the second and smaller set at the back of its almost serpentine body. I couldn't make out the coloring, but the body was lighter than the wings, which appeared to have a pattern, different areas catching and throwing the light.

It beat at the air, overhead now, before it opened its great beak and blistered more thunder across the sky. Lightning zipped around its wings and snaked out. The power concussed the air as the beast lowered to the ground, lightning still rolling across its feathers.

"Thunderbird," Sebastian said, in awe. "I've never seen one. They are incredibly rare. Your magic called this?"

"Yes. I feel the danger of it."

A phoenix soared above it, wings and tail dripping fire, doing lazy circles as the other landed.

"It called that, too?" Sebastian asked.

"Yes," I said, keeping the "Mr. Obvious" to myself.

The thunderbird pulled in its mighty wings, standing on a pair of legs equipped with three vicious talons each. Lightning climbed from its head like hair before settling down.

The phoenix flapped its wings, and fire blew out in

all directions. It lowered, landing next to the thunderbird in swirls of heated air and flame.

My stomach turned over with nervousness and a little fear, that danger pulsing hot, more so than calling the gargoyles. Much more so, because now that they were here, the feeling didn't abate. If anything, it strengthened.

On the ground, a whirlwind of oranges and reds and ambers flurried around the phoenix, reducing into a petite Asian woman fully dressed in black pants and a shirt, with black-rimmed glasses and a black bob, a light bluish sheen to her midnight hair. Her age was hard to pinpoint; she could have been twenty or fifty—while her spry body and fresh skin indicated the former, she had the canny gaze of someone much older.

The thunderbird did not change, just waited patiently as the woman stepped forward, stopping at the edge of the property.

"You dare call us?" Her high voice, like she'd just sucked down some helium, caught me off guard.

"Uhhm. Yes?" I walked forward slowly, hoping it looked like I was standing on ceremony rather than hesitating. Kingsley followed me on one side, and Sebastian stayed close on the other.

"We answer to no mere mortal," she said. "Our allegiance must be earned."

"Right." I stopped about three-quarters to the sidewalk. "And how do I do that?"

Kingsley growled softly.

She tilted her hand. "Only a master may know." She waved her hand. A rush of blistering fire swept from her like a rogue wave, building higher as it moved, surging toward us.

Kingsley snarled and moved in front of me. Sebastian threw out an arm, smacking me in the chest to keep me back. I couldn't think beyond grabbing it, my eyes widening, watching that flame.

Using his other hand, Sebastian made circles in front of us, his fingers moving quickly. A glittering red shield arched in front of us and then around, cocooning us, a spell I could do, but not with this much power. He needn't have bothered. The fire fizzled and sputtered five feet into Ivy House's territory. Not even the fire of a phoenix could breach her borders for long.

Silence filled the wake, interrupted by Kingsley's soft growl and Sebastian's heavy breathing.

"I have to dominate them," I said, my heart banging against my ribs. "I called them with the understanding that Austin could dominate anyone powerful enough."

"Austin isn't here," Sebastian said.

"Yes, I am well aware of that. That leaves me."

"You don't have the power to handle them," Sebastian said. "Maybe the thunderbird, but I don't think I can take that phoenix."

"What about both of us? Can we do it together?" I asked as the woman eyed the property line. I wondered if she could find a way around Ivy House's magic. She seemed incredibly confident. And competent.

"We don't know each other well enough for that. You have to work with another mage for longer than a few hours a day for a week in order to form a magical union with them, and even then, the mages are usually sleeping together."

"No. Long story short, no. Got it." I gritted my teeth. "I can do it."

"Jacinta." Sebastian grabbed my arm and pulled me, forcing me to look at his worried eyes, the streetlights almost turning them pale blue. "Listen to me. You do not have enough power. Neither does Austin. Not for both of those creatures. Send them back. Or turn them loose. Or…whatever you have to do to make them leave. You're not ready."

"*Yes you are,*" Ivy House said. "*But only if you accept the rest of your magic. It is time to claim what is yours.*"

The woman smiled, as though she could hear everyone speaking, bowed, and retreated back to the thunderbird. "Let us begin."

"No, no, wait—" Sebastian said.

It was then that I felt Ivy House's magic flicker and fail.

"*She has accepted your challenge,*" Ivy House said. "*She has deadened my magic. I cannot help.*"

"But I didn't say anything," I said.

"Send them away," Sebastian cried.

"I don't think I can," I choked out.

The woman smiled. "Until the death."

CHAPTER 23

"WHAT DOES SHE mean, 'until the death'?" I cried, wanting to run but knowing there was nowhere to go. I didn't have Ivy House this time. I didn't have any other artillery. I just had my crew.

"What's happening?" Sebastian asked, his arm still held out in front of me like he was a mother trying to keep her child from hitting the dash.

"It's too late. It's a challenge," I said, swallowing hard.

He swore. "Okay, well, let's see what we can do. We have to kill the phoenix."

"Because they are then reborn," I said, piecing it together.

"They are reborn, yes. But if *you* die, it's forever." Sebastian dragged me a little closer, Kingsley pacing in front of us, his tail twitching at the end as he watched the phoenix.

Edgar ran in from the side in his purple sweats, wielding a long metal stake that was almost certainly more fatal to him than it would be to anyone else. The others flew in from overhead. They must've felt Ivy House's defenses go down.

"Here we go!" Sebastian shouted.

Another burst of fire rose and surged forward, larger than the first, a great blast of heat and flame. Sebastian threw up the same shield, covering Kingsley, himself, and me. Heat bled through, and it felt like it was melting my face off. My clothes were hot against my skin. My eyes burned.

Sebastian swore again. "Think it through," he muttered to himself. "Think it through. It's fire. It is magical fire. It's a natural spell created within the beast. Figure out a way to combat it."

I nodded in encouragement. But the fire died and the thunderbird stepped forward, shaking out its mighty wings. It spread them wide, nearly taking up the whole bulbous end of the street, before flapping them forward and down. A great gust of wind slammed into us, and Sebastian's shield did virtually nothing. The wind ripped us off our feet and flung us backward, slamming us into the house.

"Think it through," I heard Sebastian muttering again, jumping up and running forward. He belted out a spell that twisted and curled into the air, sending the great thunderbird back a step. But the phoenix was ready for Sebastian. She sent off a jet of fire this time, like liquid magma, blistering in intensity, directed at his magical shield.

It would not hold. Not for this. The heat had almost made it through last time, and this attack was much more intense.

I flung out my hand, layering my own shield over his, pouring power into it.

The lava stream slammed against it. My shield held. At first.

Smoke billowed from my magic, melting down to nothing. The stream hit his shield next, blasting around the arch, sinking into the magic.

Yelling wordlessly, knowing that I couldn't heal him if that lava made it through—it would kill him too quickly—I yanked Cheryl from my back pocket and ran forward, snapping it open as I did so.

A roar came from the other side of the attack, but not from a creature. From a Jeep.

Rubber screeched and the back end of the Jeep slid around as it stopped. The door opened and Austin jumped out, naked one minute and a flash of light the next. When it faded, he stood on his hind legs in polar bear form. His roar shook the earth. Shook my bones. Made the wolves in the cage cower and the phoenix and thunderbird shut down their magic (if only for a moment) and turn around.

The basajaun stepped forward now, opening his arms wide. He added his own bellow, the urge to fight singing through me, too.

A neigh from Niamh in the sky and then the roars of gargoyles added to the chorus, the Ivy House team ready to fight. Ready to die, if need be. Kingsley lifted his roar to the heavens last, a great cat ready to support his brother's bad decisions.

"*You have earned the trust of those sworn to you,*" Ivy House said as Austin lowered back down and rushed forward, "*and your allies. They will protect you with their lives. Will you do the same for them?*"

I neared the sidewalk, but Kingsley leapt forward, knocking me out of the way. Cheryl flew. He didn't want me in the fight, probably because he thought I was useless in combat. Or else he thought Austin wouldn't want me in danger. But Austin knew better.

The phoenix sprayed Austin with fire, a preliminary blast, like she'd first tried with us. The basajaun ran at her and swiped, but the moment his palm touched her skin, it burst into flame. He howled, shrinking back. The thunderbird flapped its great wings and lightning flickered. Edgar jolted, on its back. I hadn't realized he'd jumped up there, but he didn't stay there for long. He convulsed and fell, cracking his head on the ground.

The thunderbird launched into the air, each movement showcasing its incredible strength. The gargoyles rolled out of its way, but they immediately turned around and flew after it. Its lightning crawled out around it, giving it a natural shield. Niamh rammed it with her horn, showing no fear. The thunderbird roared as the crystalline horn pierced its side, the sound turning to thunder. Niamh convulsed and fell.

"No!" I threw out a net to catch her, suspending her in the air.

"*Will you protect them with your life? Will you end this?*"

"*Of course I will end this,*" I mentally shouted. "*Send the others away. Let me handle this myself.*"

"*Will you protect your team with your life? Decide now. It will be your lifelong duty.*"

It was already my lifelong duty. We'd become a unit in that first battle, and every battle thereafter had drawn us closer together. There was no way I would walk away when my friends were in danger. There was no way I wouldn't sacrifice myself if it saved all of them, just as they would do for me.

"*Take the oath,*" Ivy House said. "*Take the oath and I can help you save them.*"

A roar of anguish froze my blood. I spun. Austin was on the ground, struggling with the phoenix, everywhere she touched burning.

I crawled through the grass for Cheryl, desperate, hearing another howl of pain from the basajaun, who was probably trying to help Austin. He couldn't handle the burns, though. Another cry from above.

I looked up as Sebastian caught Mr. Tom in a magical net, suspending his fall.

I curled my fingers around Cheryl's hilt.

"What do I say?" I yelled, tears in my eyes. Austin's agonized howls tormented me. I doubted anyone in the world had ever heard them before. He never admitted to being in pain. A grunt was all he'd vocalize, even when a normal person would black out. He was beyond agony right now. Probably beyond what most could tolerate. And still he fought.

I couldn't bear to peek through the link.

"*What do I say?*"

"'*I swear to protect Ivy House and my circle until the day I die. I will uphold the honor that is due my role and the legacy that is Ivy House.*'"

I repeated the words quickly, with trembling lips.

"*Shed blood onto the soil.*"

Sebastian put up another net to catch Ulric.

Austin ripped the petite woman off him and sent her flying. He struggled to stand, burned and bloodied and shaky. I'd never seen him like this. His rage pushed through the muted link, hotter and fiercer than the pain. He was bringing forth the beast. He was shrouding himself in darkness so he could give everything to this fight. I doubted he'd regret it.

"*Shed blood onto the soil,*" Ivy House repeated.

With shaking hands, I sliced my finger; deep crimson welled up. I shoved it into the ground, wincing at the searing pain.

Thunder rolled above. Great wings beat. Our other friend was back. I'd have to beat that bastard in the sky. But first I needed to take out the phoenix.

"*With great power comes great responsibility,*" Ivy House said.

The petite woman pushed up from the ground, facing Austin. She knew which of us was her greatest competition.

Kingsley paced in front of me, watching his brother, keeping me from the fight.

Austin stood on his hind legs, bent over a little toward her, and roared.

They ran at each other.

"*With great responsibility, you must have great courage. The courage to do what is right, and not what is easy. The courage to protect those sworn to you. The courage to wield the power without blinking.*"

Before the woman could reach Austin, he swiped,

his great paw hitting her shoulder. I could hear the crack from here. She rolled across the ground like a tumbleweed. Down on all fours, he ran after her, but this time he knew better than to pounce. She was good on the ground. Her body was a weapon, and she used it to her advantage.

"*Use it wisely.*"

A tidal wave of power welled up inside me, pumping through my blood. Stretching my skin to cracking. Dizzying my mind.

Through it, I could see the woman charging Austin, her injured arm tucked close to her body, flames rising from her skin. Austin swiped again, but she ducked under the strike and kept going. He lowered quickly, mouth open, and clamped on to her other shoulder, ignoring the pain I could feel blistering through the link. He wrapped his arms around her, a bear hug, the pain now agonizing, tearing him apart, no beginning and no end.

He tore with his teeth, ripping out her shoulder. Still squeezing, ignoring the misery it was causing him. Ignoring her screams. Trapped, she had one power, the pain she bestowed, but he was pushing past it. He opened his great jaw wide and clamped down on her head, his teeth digging into bone, and then he wrenched. The victor.

I turned from the grisly aftermath and magically cut off his pain. He didn't need it anymore. He didn't need to know when he was nearing the edge of never coming back. Now he just needed to heal. Something I would help him with after I dealt with the thunderbird.

He'd taken down one of the pair, and I fully intended to handle the other. But I'd have to fly to do it.

I shed my clothes and shifted, wasting no time. Color swirled from my tiny little wings, nothing compared to that mammoth in the sky.

Sebastian jogged toward me, looking up as I thrummed my wings, calling to me. I didn't know what he was saying.

That big beast soared above the woods effortlessly, born to fly.

I labored after it, definitely not.

Frustration and fear bled through the now unmuted link. Austin didn't want me to go. He'd done his part, though, and Ivy House had given me the power to do mine.

Jasper still flew around the thunderbird, and as I neared, I could see him dipping in and coming away, making small attacks. He was still getting shocked, but not badly enough for it to take him down. He couldn't hope to take this creature on his own, but he hadn't given up. He hadn't relented.

My heart surged. He'd been a good choice.

Another shape caught my notice. Another gargoyle flew toward us, moonlight shimmering off its silvery hide.

The last part of the summons. Just one gargoyle this time. No team to sort through or try out. One gargoyle to help me do the impossible.

Nearer still, he carved through the sky with a dexterity that not even Damarion had been able to achieve. The thunderbird rolled, tucking in its wings and diving, nearly smashing Jasper out of the sky. But Jasper pulled back at the last moment, careening and then correcting his course.

The newcomer moved with great speed, silvery light slicing through the dark night. When he neared, he snapped his wings out, the effect thunderous, and hung stationary in the sky. His wings thrummed like a hummingbird's, although the motion was barely noticeable, creating a low-pitched sound that pulled at the center of me.

Jasper rose higher. Then, across the town, I saw other fliers lift above the trees and buildings, rising like balloons after a parade. Most of the gargoyles that hadn't made the cut at Ivy House had stayed in the area, and I knew—without quite understanding *how* I knew—that they'd heard this newcomer's call to arms.

Heard the distinct sound that brought their kind together.

Mr. Tom and Ulric tried to rise as well, clearly knowing what it meant.

Without specifically knowing how, but feeling the rightness in my blood, I cut out the sound to them. Just to them. Like snipping the strings of an instrument.

The thunderbird regained height and then banked lazily, heading back in my direction.

"Here we go," I said, the actual sound like a jumbled mess around my enlarged teeth.

The lesser-statured gargoyles filed in, flocking to this newcomer like they had Damarion back in the day. This time, Austin could pull rank if he needed to. I wouldn't stand in his way. The newcomer had a good trick, and I wanted it at my disposal.

The newcomer darted forward, flying toward me. I gestured like an idiot, not sure how to communicate. It turned out I didn't need to.

Jasper soared to my left and flew at my speed. The larger new guy took my right. All the others spread out around us, some above, some below, some behind.

The thunderbird shot straight for us. To touch it in any meaningful way would send a shock of electricity through us.

Think it through.

I had to cut out that electricity. Or shield the gargoyles from it.

The gargoyles flew steadily around me. The one at my side thrummed and then snapped his wings, like a battle commander barking commands.

Think it through.

It occurred to me that I really didn't know what that meant, and repeating it over and over wouldn't help anything.

Charge that sonuvabitch and think on the fly.

That had always been more my speed, anyway.

The speed with which the thunderbird flew frazzled my brain, though, and it wasn't even trying! It was just gliding, as handy as it liked.

The gargoyles around me shot upward, and New Guy dove in to attack just behind the thunderbird's head. I slapped up a protective barrier for him, and the lightning zipped around him, leaving him unharmed. Another went in, following New Guy's lead. And another. I covered for them, fast as I could, missing one and throwing up a net to catch him down toward the trees.

The thunderbird was right on me.

I flapped harder to dart upward, but it was coming too fast for me to gain enough altitude. I thought about dropping, but it pumped its wings and shot forward. I wrapped myself in an energy-absorbing shield as the newcomer rose and turned my way. He would never get there in time.

The lightning hit my shield first, soaking in. The beak hit next, trying to pierce me through the middle. It hit off my shield, and the shock turned to a violent explosive. The great bird's head shot backward and its wings pumped helplessly at the sky, offering me a killing shot.

But I was sailing away end over end, rocketed just as hard by the blast but much, *much* lighter.

I was spinning so fast that I couldn't even figure out where I should throw a net. I flared my wings, but the wind caught them and tweaked one, wrenching it painfully. I cried out, pulling it in, spinning. The trees reached up to break my fall and probably crack my limbs.

A body hit me from the side. Strong arms wrapped around me and held me close while large wings snapped open and stopped our fall. The newcomer grunted as he took to the sky.

The thunderbird had regained control, and it was flying faster now, angry. It went after the other gargoyles, trying to peck at their wings, beating its hind wings quickly to send out flurries of electricity. A great, thunderous roar scattered everyone close to it.

I pointed. *Get me closer.*

New Guy flew at incredible speed, pulling up behind it. Apparently he thought I was going to do something.

He was right.

That thing wasn't impervious to blasts, and I was really good at blowing things up.

Right on its tail, I sent off an explosive spell. I immediately pointed away, and New Guy banked, so smooth and natural, so much less jarring than flying with Damarion had been. Or maybe I was just used to it, although I could never fly like this on my own. My wings simply weren't made for it.

The explosive hit and the bird squealed, flapping and trying to turn. Its wings weren't as dexterous as gargoyle's, though. We banked and dove, getting under it.

"Waaai-t," the new guy said in my ear.

A gargoyle dove in from the side, and I threw up a barrier for him. It occurred to me that the blows they were landing probably wouldn't even leave bruises. They certainly weren't doing any real damage. I had to cut out that electricity or they could just go home.

What was the nemesis of electricity?

"No-ow," the gargoyle said, the word surprisingly clear. Male gargoyles had bigger fangs than I did and struggled more to communicate in their shifted forms.

I blasted the thunderbird in the neck this time. It squawked, knocked off-kilter, flapping its wings.

Ground. Lightning was extinguished when it hit the ground.

The next time New Guy swooped around, I hit the bird with a different spell, covering it with a fine layer of rock. Skin like a gargoyle's.

The bird's flapping increased, laborious now. Thunder still rolled from each of its wingbeats, but no one was in front of it to get hit by the sonic waves. Gargoyles dove in, punching at it like they'd been doing, then realized they could dig in.

New Guy tossed me up into the air and banked, heading for the bird.

"Oh shii—" I flapped my arms for some insane reason, caught off guard.

A moment later, coming to my senses, I switched to flapping my wings and quickly climbed in altitude. Turning, I found two gargoyles had stationed themselves between me and the thunderbird, clearly guarding me in case it managed to shake off the stone skin. But the thunderbird flailed, one set of wings wounded, the gargoyles working on the other. In a matter of moments, the bird tucked its wings in and fell like a stone, crashing through the trees and into the ground.

I followed it down, the others allowing me to go first. I stuck my landing, meaning that I hit it wrong, staggered, and then fell flat on my face. The snap of wings announced the arrival of New Guy, who held out a firm but gentle helping hand. Lord only knew what he thought of the illustrious female gargoyle.

Pushing that thought aside, I stepped forward and found a tall, well-muscled man lying on his stomach in his birthday suit, his dark skin glistening with sweat and his head turned to the side. Both arms were tucked under him in a defensive position and his back rose and fell with breath. Not dead.

I changed into my skin, trying not to show how uncomfortable I was being naked in front of a stranger.

"Hey." I wrapped bands of magic around him to keep him put before edging closer. "Do you die and come back? Should I kill you to win, like the phoenix? I don't know anything about thunderbirds."

"All you had to do was kill the phoenix. I wasn't part of the trial. I left that battle out front to get out of the way. I'm just the other guy."

I lifted my eyebrows as I felt Austin draw closer. "Oh? But you were just…attacking us."

"Are you stupid or something?" He tried to reposition and groaned. "You all attacked me first! What am I supposed to do, just take it? The phoenix is more dominant. Like I said, I'm just the other guy. I got the summons. I met her along the way."

I grimaced as Austin ran into the trees, his fur restored to snowy white, the burned patches gone. He changed into his skin, his gaze devouring every inch of me, making sure I was all right.

"This guy says he's not part of the trial?" I said to Austin.

Kingsley paced within the trees, still in his tiger form, his eyes on the new gargoyle standing just beside me. Austin didn't pay him any notice.

"The phoenix was the more dominant of the pair," he said, turning to look at the downed man now that my safety was accounted for. "Is he bound?"

"Yeah. Should I undo that?" I asked hesitantly.

"What kind of clown show is this?" said the man on the ground.

"She's new to magic," Austin said.

"So…we didn't have to go after him?" I asked hesitantly.

"No…" the man on the ground said, and it sounded more like a long groan. "Why did you call us if you didn't know what you were doing?"

"I didn't call you specifically," I said, kneeling beside him, hunching so most of my body was covered. His face was angled in the opposite direction. "I basically made a list and called whoever fit it."

"Some list," he murmured. "Did he say you're new to magic?"

"Yeah."

He flinched when I laid my palm on his back, closing my eyes and feeling around his body, like a magical X-ray. Austin stood beside me, probably in case this guy tried to pull a fast one.

"Broken arms, bruised ribs, and your neck hurts," I said, leaving my hand where it was. "It must hurt to lie on them."

"It does."

"O-kay. Well, I can heal you if you're telling the truth about your role here."

"I hate my life," he muttered.

"Go ahead," Austin said.

I started the process and then stood. I didn't need to keep touching him for it to work.

"You're a female gargoyle, aren't you?" the man asked, still not moving.

"Yeah. Your arms aren't going to heal properly if you keep lying on them."

"I don't want you savages to damage them further."

"Right, but…right now, *you* are damaging them further."

He flopped over onto his back, a leaf stuck to his privates, reminding me of those statues that had fig leaves carved onto them after the fact. His body was perfectly sculpted, his muscles shining with sweat in the moonlight. He had tight black curls, a handsome face with a wide nose, and a scowl meant for me.

"None of this makes sense," he said, still holding his arms to his chest. "I haven't heard of a living female gargoyle. Someone would've said."

"Do you want help up?" I asked.

"Not really."

"I'm new to magic. I'm the heir of Ivy House."

"So?"

"So she imparts magic to the person of her choice. She chose me. The magic she imparts is that of a female gargoyle. Hence, I am a female gargoyle and am new to magic."

"You have a crapload of power."

"I just got a bunch of it tonight."

He rolled his eyes to the sky. "I've never been very lucky. Now what?"

I looked at Austin. "They have to stay in Ivy House, right? There are no hotels close by with vacancies?"

He nodded slowly. "The danger should be squared away."

Ivy House magic was back online, I could feel it.

She'd make sure they stayed in line while they were in residence.

As one, we both realized the piece we'd forgotten.

There was a new gargoyle on the scene, and his compliance wasn't connected to the phoenix. I hoped he wouldn't pose as many problems for Austin as the last alpha gargoyle.

CHAPTER 24

T HE NEXT DAY, midafternoon, Austin pulled out of his garage. He and Kingsley were heading to Ivy House for a strategy meeting. They had just under a month before the mage's visit. The territory was still in chaos, but Jess had gained three important advantages the previous night.

"I don't get you, Austin." Kingsley clicked his seatbelt into place. He shook his head, looking out of the window, allowing himself freedom of expression, since Austin was family. "You left her alone overnight, sleeping and vulnerable, with three powerful strangers. You could've returned to Ivy House after you took care of the shifters who'd snuck into town."

"You don't understand. When she's in that house, she's safe."

"But they were in there with her. A door is an easy thing to get through. You've been away from pack life for too long. You need to protect your own."

Austin tightened his fingers on the steering wheel.

"I can't protect her like Ivy House can. It's a magical Fort Knox, Kingsley. You have no idea."

Kingsley pulled the seatbelt away, holding it out so it didn't press into him. "Maybe so, but you're holding back. I'm not trying to tell you your business, but...Jess is nothing like Destiny. *Nothing* like her. Destiny twisted your head all around. On purpose. She saw potential, young and dumb potential, and she manipulated you. But you've come a long way since then, even before you left the pack. Giving in and officially committing to Miss Ivy House isn't going to turn you into the guy you once were. Nothing will, at this point."

"Destiny did nothing more than highlight what I'm capable of. Who I am."

"Your bullheadedness in the face of opposition, your ability to cut out everything but winning, your unbridled determination to claim dominance... Those are all highly prized qualities in a shifter. She just coaxed them out before you had the ability to control them."

Austin shook his head. "I think time has glossed over what went down."

"It wasn't time that gave me a new perspective," Kingsley said. "She moved on to another pack, picked out another young alpha, and finally got her way."

That was news to Austin. Although he had heard

she'd moved on, he'd never asked for details.

"The next guy was strong and fierce, but he couldn't see his way through the rage she'd wound up in him," Kingsley said. "Strong of body but not of mind. He killed the pack alpha and replaced her. Killed the beta, too, giving that role to Destiny. Then the kid killed his own father for trying to do right by the pack and take him down. Killed his nephew for getting in the way. He ran that pack into the ground. The alpha of one of the neighboring packs, who'd tried to help but wasn't strong enough, contacted me five years or so ago, and I traveled there to take him down. I tried to help his people pick up the pieces, but they were in poverty by then. Those who could afford to get out had already left. I accepted any willing shifters into my pack and paid for the rest to be reunited with family or head out on their own. It was not a pretty sight. Destiny had long since left."

Austin wound the Jeep through the hillside, dense trees shutting out his view of what lay beyond. "How can you be sure she's the one who drove him to it? Maybe she just has a type. I would've run the pack into the ground, too."

"The shifters in that pack said otherwise." Kingsley paused for a moment. "And you're wrong. You wouldn't have driven the pack into the ground. You were ready to take over when you left. Half of the pack was calling for you to replace me."

Austin pulled into an outlet and stopped. Here it came.

He looked straight ahead, waiting, bracing himself.

Kingsley watched him for a long time before speaking.

"You left my pack in pieces when you walked away," he finally said.

Austin nodded. "Yes, I did. I apologize for that. I have apologized for that. But I told you that I would leave when the pack's allegiance shifted, and I meant it. You're the best alpha I've ever known, Kingsley."

"I've thought about this for years. No other alpha of your stature would've left. It must have torn you apart to go, knowing what it would do to the pack."

"I made a promise. It was my fault for staying too long."

His brother gave him one of those long, assessing looks again. "If you'd stayed, I have no doubt it would've boosted the pack to the next level. You've always worried you're like our father because you inherited his animal, his darkness, but you got our mother's tenacity, too, and you tempered that darkness into unbreakable steel. The name this place gave you is incredibly fitting, and they gave it before you ever thought you'd be their alpha, right?"

Austin tightened his lips, and Kingsley nodded. "I've talked to many of the people here. You might not have been crowned, but you ran this place like a territory. You looked after it and protected it. The people here are fiercely loyal to you. They let you have your eccentrics, allowing your pet to—"

Austin shot his hand out and gripped Kingsley's throat before he'd even thought about it. Once he did, though, he squeezed. "If you call her a pet again, I will make your wife a widow."

Kingsley gave him a humorless smile. He'd baited Austin on purpose.

"That's not a spot to poke," Austin growled. He released his grip.

Kingsley didn't even reach up to rub his neck. He'd expected the reaction.

"Here's what I think," he said. "You left Gossamer Falls because you were scared. You wanted to learn how to control yourself, what it meant to be a good alpha, but you didn't trust yourself to be one. You slunk away instead."

"Maybe," Austin said. It would do no good to lie to his brother. It had certainly never helped when he'd lied to himself. "But it was still the right thing to do. I wouldn't have taken the pack from you, Kingsley. I wouldn't have taken it from your family."

"Yes. I can see that. But I'm not wrong, either. You were afraid. You came here, you did what you were bred and trained to do, but you wouldn't accept a title for it. Until Jacinta."

Austin nearly held his breath.

"I stayed up most of the night looking into the folklore and the myths of Ivy House," his brother went on. "Obviously the internet only has so much information about a magical house that old, but with what I found and the explanation of that pink gargoyle, I got what I needed. That woman just inherited more power than I've probably ever encountered. She called in two legendary creatures."

Did Austin hear a little excitement in Kingsley's voice?

"She was handed a golden ticket," Kingsley said, "and that ticket is going to paint a very large target on her back."

"I know. Why do you think I came to you for help after what I did to your pack?"

Kingsley continued on as though he hadn't heard Austin. "I think Fate had a hand in this. You are exactly where you need to be. She needs someone loyal—someone who can't be swayed from the moral high ground—to guard her back. And you need her unwavering trust. You need a reason to face down your past and rise to your mantle."

"When did you turn into a life coach?" Austin asked dryly.

"Earnessa would be proud. She always says I have the emotional range of a rock and I can't see what's going on right in front of my face. But this is just too obvious."

"I won't deny it. Jess needs help, more so than I think you understand, and I will do everything in my power to protect her."

"Like claiming her for all to see without her knowledge, but still keeping her at arm's length? You're taking advantage of her ignorance of the shifter world."

Austin lost his breath, looking out the window. He'd lied to himself a million different ways. Told himself she'd be safer if everyone thought she was his. That he was just showing friendship and support in a way a Jane would understand, and he'd step out of the way if need be. And his personal favorite—she didn't know what it meant, and didn't mind the attention, so what was the big deal?

But that wasn't why he'd claimed her. Nor was it why he kept claiming her.

He wanted her.

He wanted the honor of everyone knowing she was

his. The very thought of another male approaching her with intentions made his blood pressure soar and rage seep through him.

He rubbed his hand down his face. "In the shifter world, yes, you're right. But she has dated. I haven't stood in her way. If she chose someone new tomorrow, I'd accept that. Someone outside of the pack," he growled. "There is only so much I can bear. I *will* step out of the way if she doesn't want me—I will make myself—but…"

"I don't think she's the problem here. I think it's you."

Austin took a deep breath and pulled back out onto the street. "I have to say, you really took the long road to lecture me about my dating life."

"We needed to clear the air about how you left the pack."

"Were you worried that I'd come back one day?"

"When I didn't hear you'd started a place of your own? Yes."

Austin glanced over. "Truly?"

"It was always in the back of my head. You're better than me. I knew that when you left. I see it now, as you piece together this territory."

"You must have a poor impression of me if you thought I'd come back for your territory."

"I run one of the largest, most profitable territories in the country. Like I said, most alphas of your stature never would've left. But this is better." Kingsley gestured around him. "It'll be bigger. With Jacinta Ironheart and all her power at the center, you'll create something no one can penetrate. Or duplicate. You have the power without the drama." He smiled a little. "You've always been lucky."

Austin had heard people start to call her that. Apparently it had caught on if Kingsley was using it. Austin's territory had given her a name, like they had him. Like they would an alpha.

"Lucky, sure." Austin huffed before regaining his seriousness. "A territory no one can penetrate is the goal."

"But first you need to tell her you're interested. She is incredibly clueless about body language. Kace thought she was being coy. Turned out, she was completely uninterested in him." Kingsley paused, grinning. "Too soon?"

Austin shook his head, wondering why the rage didn't come. "I'm surprised she didn't have to talk me down from that. She did the last time. I wasn't in control."

"When it comes to our mates, none of us are. If someone had said that to Earnessa, I would have killed him, and she wouldn't have stopped me."

"She's not my mate."

"That's only because you're too chickenshit to start the ball rolling."

Austin turned toward town. "I was waiting to see…" He pressed his lips together. He hated the need he felt for his brother's approval. "I wasn't sure whether I was a danger to her. To this territory. When I lost control last week, it didn't take long to figure out why. But…our father…"

"Our father was a miserable excuse for a shifter. Mother was young and dumb once, too. You know what that's like. She chased the bad boy—the wild one who would never be tamed. Well, she got him. She may have kicked him out, but she loved him, Austin. Of course, she also hated him. It's a tricky business, love and hate. Two sides of the same coin.

"But she saw her family in danger, her pack in danger, and she did what any great alpha would: she took action. You did the same thing. You reached a limit, and backed off to protect our family. I was never prouder than when you came to me the day after pulling back from killing me, and asked to learn. You're nothing like Dad, Austin. I've known that ever since that day. So has Mom."

Austin shook his head, looking out the windshield,

his eyes glassy. He didn't know what to say. It was the best string of words he'd probably ever heard in his life, and it meant *everything* coming from his brother.

"We thought you'd realize some sort of potential long before now, though," Kingsley added softly.

Austin laughed, raw inside. He was quiet for a beat. "I wouldn't be able to stand myself if I ever lifted a hand to Jess, not for any reason. Despite what you say, I'm still terrified I'll lose my temper and turn into our father."

"You've risen above him in all things, Austin. *All* things. You've tamed yourself, whereas he never tried. Besides, that woman would blast a hole in your head if you lifted a finger to her."

"She's too good for me. Too kind."

"You've got that right. You've leveled up with her. I've read up on female gargoyles. It's one of the rarest magics in the world. You'll have a target on your back, too, you know. People will be jealous of you. They'll try to cut you out of the picture and take her for themselves."

"If I win her."

"Even if you decided not to try. Any suitor will see it as a threat."

"Good," Austin growled before he could stop himself. He hated talking about suitors for Jess. Hated thinking about anyone else seeing her sleepy smile, or getting to kiss those incredible lips.

It was time he found his courage and put himself out there. Past time.

"I'd planned to invite her for dinner in a couple days so you could properly meet her," he said.

"She shows every single thought she has on her face, and if that weren't enough, she tells them to you when she gets drunk."

He turned onto Ivy House's street. "Still, I'd like you to properly meet her."

"Is this you asking for my blessing?"

Austin didn't speak for a moment. "Yeah, I guess it is."

Kingsley inclined his head. Approval granted.

A surge of emotion ripped through Austin. Relief, joy, nervousness. Fear.

"I don't know if she is ready to… What she is ready for," he said quietly as he parked. "I'm not sure what I'm ready for."

"You don't need to plan your life, brother. Just plan dinner. See where it goes from there. Let your animals decide. They already *have* decided, I think. Her animal seems volatile, though. Might be fun; might be a nightmare. I'd watch it. Female gargoyles are said to be temperamental."

"Yeah." Austin looked up at the house. He waited for a moment, but ultimately, he couldn't help himself. "It's a helluva thing, seeing a female gargoyle, isn't it? I'd thought they'd be as ugly as the males, but it's hard to tear my eyes away."

"It literally stopped my heart when she took off into the sky. I wasn't expecting the light show. That isn't sexual or anything, so don't come after me, but…"

Austin couldn't contain a surge of pride. "I know. I was in a cage with her when she first learned how to change. I nearly fell backward, which would've been messy because of the long drop ending in six-foot-high spikes…"

Kingsley just gave him a look.

"Long story," Austin said, unperturbed. "There's a lot I haven't told you."

"Well, that's going to have to change, because I plan on shamelessly using both of you to up my status."

"You might want to wait awhile. I still have a mess of a territory to sort through, or didn't you forget I had to call you, crying for help?"

Kingsley gave him a hard stare. "You can be modest with everyone else, brother, but don't try that crap with me. You took down a *phoenix*."

Austin blew out a breath, trying not to preen. "I had help."

"Bull. It was just you against the phoenix, and you *won*. I've never heard of a shifter bringing one down. She was no joke, either. The females are more powerful than the males. This is going to elevate our whole family line."

He leaned over and mock-punched Austin before climbing out of the Jeep. "And then that crazy woman of yours went after the thunderbird! When she didn't have to! This territory has taken down a phoenix and a thunderbird, and a basajaun fights beside you. Welcome to the big leagues of status, brother." He laughed. "I'm not sure I could be more jealous."

But it was pure pride in his voice. It felt beyond good to hear it—it felt vindicating.

Austin got out of the car and took a long look at his brother, seeing the years he'd missed in Kingsley's graying hair and the deep lines creasing his face. They'd lost so much time. Austin hadn't realized how much he'd missed his family. How much it meant to him that his brother had come the moment he'd called. "Thanks, bro. For turning up."

"It's good to see you. We've all missed you. We purposely gave you space, but we've missed the contact, Mom most of all."

Austin nodded. He needed to call her. To apologize. To explain.

Kingsley put his hands in his pockets, a sign of respect and trust. "Mom is going to want to visit once it's all set up. Meeting a basajaun would've been enough of a draw, but if that phoenix and thunderbird are still here... I think I'm going to lose 'favorite' status."

"It's about time," Austin said with a smile. "Let me have a turn."

They reached the door, but Kingsley turned his back to it, looking out over the grounds and street. "Tell her how you feel," he said after a moment. "She needs to know. Hell, she's obviously on board—she must've instinctively known you were claiming her, and if she didn't approve, I think the whole bar would've known."

They turned to face the door, which opened of its own volition. An army of dolls waited inside, sad baby faces or manic Halloween green faces with black stitches, many of them holding real knives.

"What in the..." Kingsley stepped backward.

Austin could barely keep from laughing. Time for a little Ivy House initiation.

"You didn't think the house could protect Jess. It took offense. Looks like it's going to show you what's what. You'll probably need to submit, or leave the property. I'll let you decide. Good luck."

Austin laughed at Kingsley's bewildered expression and made his way through the dolls. Poor Kingsley would have to learn about Ivy House the hard way.

CHAPTER 25

A WEEK AFTER meeting with everyone to discuss plans, I walked down the hall toward the stairs, a million things on my mind. We'd decided to mostly host the coming mages in restaurants or a banquet hall in town, which would make things easier, but a dinner or two might take place in Ivy House, which meant I needed to update the furniture in at least a few of the rooms and hallways. I'd always thought of it as stately and homely, but Niamh had pointed out that I was crazy, and the furniture was actually gaudy and severely outdated. I'd never claimed to be good at interior design.

I could pick a few pieces of furniture, but I didn't have a clue on how to bring a look together. The whole situation was a nightmare, not to mention I was constantly training with Sebastian, trying to learn all I could in the few short weeks to come.

Information Niamh had been gathering wasn't easing my mind. Sebastian had been right—it seemed this mage had a reputation for cunning, cutthroat deals and behavior. Lesser mages disappeared after meetings with him, but he was never investigated by the Mages' Guild. Alliances ended abruptly, usually with an "unexplained" death, and often leaving him the better for it. He seemed underhanded and downright slimy.

To make matters worse, Sebastian said he'd always heard this mage had a fragile ego. The smallest slight would create big issues, and since the mage did have some wealth, he could hire mercenaries if he had to, intent on using force to look like the bigger man.

Bottom line, he didn't seem like someone I wanted a connection with, but he was certainly someone I didn't want on my bad side. I'd need to really watch myself in the dinners and meetings, showing him my best face, and aiming to end the week as neutrally as possible. That was the best way.

"Miss, Austin Steele will pick you up in…" Mr. Tom checked his Spider-Man watch. Jimmy had accidentally left it behind and said Mr. Tom could keep it. It was cheap and silly, and I had no idea why my son had had it in the first place, but now Mr. Tom wore it as though it were a priceless relic. "Fifteen minutes. Is that what you're going to wear?"

I looked down at my jeans and pastel pink blouse. "Yes?"

"Oh no, miss, no. You're going to dinner with two alphas. You need to dress nicely."

"I know, but Austin said this was just an informal dinner with his brother."

"Dinner, though." Mr. Tom put his hands behind his back and lifted his eyebrows. "With two alphas."

I sighed. "Fine, what should I wear?"

"How nice of you to ask. Since I am clearly a master on the latest trends for ladies, let me just select something for you."

The amazing thing was that he wasn't joking.

Austin had originally asked for me to come over a few days ago, but shifters kept trying to sneak into the territory and cause a ruckus. I didn't understand the point or the politics—maybe they were trying to see how well the borders were locked down?—but it was keeping Austin incredibly busy.

Mr. Tom picked out a little black dress, simple but elegant, and not at all what I would wear over to someone's house for a casual dinner.

"Is this a 'dress for the job you want' situation?" I asked, changing in my closet while he waited at the little table near the window.

"Yes." When I came out, he stood and looked me over. "A touch of makeup, a tighter curl, and then we'll see about some jewels."

I frowned at him before heading back to the bathroom. Dinner with two alphas was clearly a much bigger deal than I'd thought.

Or maybe Mr. Tom knew something I didn't. Were Austin and Kingsley having doubts that I could pull off a façade of refined elegance for the visiting mage? Was this dinner a trial run, of sorts, to see what they were working with?

If so, they clearly didn't know about my past. After attending hundreds of work parties and boring, WASP-y functions with my ex and his parents, I knew how to pull off regal, self-important, and stuffy. Conversation might pose more difficulties, of course.

A little while later, Mr. Tom came back with a stack of long, flat black boxes. He set them on the table and began arranging them.

"How about this?" I emerged from the threshold to the bathroom. "I don't want to go too formal with makeup and hair because it'll look out of whack with the dress. I've had extensive training on how those things go together. My ex-mother-in-law criticized me every time she saw me for the first five years of my marriage."

Mr. Tom straightened and turned, scanning me from head to toe. "You are a vision, miss. Perfect."

I beamed. My ex's mother had never said anything

like that, that was for sure.

"Now. All you need are some finishing touches." Mr. Tom stepped to the side as he partially turned, looking down at the boxes, then back at me. "Which do you think?"

Stepping closer, I nearly choked on my spit. My ex had been in the habit of buying me nice jewelry—expensive jewelry—which I had always liked. Sometimes a lady needed a little bling. But *this*!

Four boxes in total, each containing a necklace, earrings, and a bracelet, except for the last one, which didn't have a bracelet. The first set was a tasteful and elegant design of pearls separated with diamonds. My ex's mother would highly approve. Those were out.

The next box held a simple strand of diamonds, all the same size on the necklace, studs for earrings, and a tennis bracelet. The third set incorporated rubies, the teardrop necklace ending in a large crimson stone, the earrings a similar design, and the bracelet switching off diamonds and rubies. But it was the last set that stole my ability to speak. The earrings were elegant strands of diamonds, but the real beauty was the necklace: a sort of webbing of black and white diamonds that would drape down the neck, almost to the cleavage. The crisscrossed strands were dainty, the glitter elegant but not overbearing, and the wow factor off the charts. That one would make my ex-mother-in-law green with envy, and if I ever met her again, I'd wear it.

Might as well practice now, just in case.

I pointed, half wondering if I'd wake up to Mr. Tom's face and a cup of coffee.

"Excellent choice, miss. I nearly didn't bring that one. It almost seemed too flashy for your attire, but I think you can pull it off. We'll need to shop for some simple pieces. Everything else is much too formal for a light affair such as this."

"Where..." I gulped as he gingerly lifted the necklace and unhooked the clasp, walking around me. I carefully swept my hair out of the way. "Where did you get these?"

"I keep a selection of jewelry in my closet. Most pieces are old and were kept with the house. I updated their boxes or containers." He fastened the necklace and stepped around to look at it, nodding. "Keeping them in my room stops that insufferable Irishwoman from playing dress-up and heading to the bar. She used to hope someone would try to mug her. Well, someone eventually did, and it created an awful problem with the local Dick law enforcement. She broke five of the mugger's bones and was in the process of trying to crack his neck—she was clearly out of practice—when the Dick policeman showed up to help. Only, the policeman didn't know who to help at that point. There was a lot of explaining to do. Old Jane women do not usually assault their attackers in that way. She broke the necklace, and we had to get it mended." He tsked and shook his head, handing me an earring and waiting for me to fasten it before he handed over the next. "I keep them hidden around my room now. She can't get in."

Checking the additions in the full-length mirror, I couldn't believe how much they elevated my simple black dress. I looked like some cartoon princess, ready to go to her less-than-formal ball.

"If nothing else, I look the part," I murmured.

"You always did, miss." He checked his watch. "He'll be early. Too anxious, I think."

Mr. Tom was right—Austin was nearly here, although a couple minutes didn't really count as early.

A flutter of nervousness rolled through my belly, and I frowned when I realized it wasn't mine. Looking myself over in the mirror, mostly just staring at the necklace, I felt Austin walking toward the door. Ivy House didn't open it this time, waiting for Mr. Tom to launch into his formal butler shtick.

"*Grab some condoms,*" Ivy House said.

This surge of nervousness was all my own, my stomach flipping and then dropping, like I was in a free fall. I stood, frozen, feeling the front door open and knowing Mr. Tom was inviting Austin in, offering him a place in the sitting room and a beverage while he waited.

I would've usually ignored Ivy House. Rolled my eyes, even.

Tingles covered my body, my limbs shaking, and this time...

This time...

Hastening into the bathroom, I did just as she'd said, grabbing a couple, just in case, then stuffed them into my clutch and snapped it shut. He was a friend. He didn't want to get involved. He wanted to keep his distance.

We'd made mistakes before...

Dabbing the sudden sheen of sweat from my forehead, I slipped the tissue into my clutch as well and slowly walked out of the room, composing myself. Mr. Tom was just leaving the front sitting room when I reached the bottom of the stairs.

"Would you like a drink here before you go?" he asked me. "Mr. Steele said it was your choice."

"No, thanks." I passed him, my back a little too stiff, and paused awkwardly at the door.

Nathanial, the new gargoyle, whose warm brown eyes were undermined by his near-permanent scowl, sat in the far corner, his ankle crossed over his knee and fingers clasped in his lap. He stared at Austin while Austin leafed through a furniture magazine, not bothered.

Austin looked up, eyes appreciative. He put the magazine aside and stood, his movements rippling with lethal grace. A black dress shirt with blue pinstripes hugged his muscular torso, showing off his girth and outlining his pecs. His biceps strained his sleeves and a black belt cinched around his trim hips. Dark blue jeans hugged his thighs, and his black shoes shone in the light. His rich cobalt eyes accented his rugged, incredibly handsome face.

"You look beautiful, Jacinta," he said, his move toward me more of a swagger.

"Thanks," I said, both hands on my clutch, held in front of me like a shield. "You do too."

"Ready?"

"Yes. Yup." I stepped toward the door and turned to the side, ready for him to lead the way.

Instead, he stopped right beside me, standing close, almost predatory in his intensity. A shiver ran over me, my body suddenly tight and loose all at the same time.

"I didn't bring flowers this time," he said, and I glanced at the blue orchid still standing proudly next to the front door, the gift he'd given me before our friend date.

"It is too early to be slipping, Mr. Steele," Mr. Tom said, standing by the door.

A smile curled Austin's lips. "But I did think of it. I'll ask that you have patience."

I frowned at him. "Sure, but I don't need flowers."

"Of course you do." He nodded and turned, touching the small of my back. "Shall we?"

"Who did you want on detail, miss?" Mr. Tom asked.

"I will be accompanying you, miss, if acceptable." Nathanial appeared in the sitting room doorway, in house sweats with his wings dusting his ankles, no small feat for a guy who was six-four.

"Yeah, sure," I replied, knowing there was no point in telling them they didn't need to come with two alpha shifters on scene. "Maybe Jasper, too, so there's someone I'm connected with."

"I'd like to go." Hollace, the thunderbird, leaned against the wall at the top of the stairs, holding a book that rested against his thigh. "My liver is broken from trying to keep up with that Irishwoman at the bar last night. I need something peaceful to do, and this house keeps making the dolls knock on my door. It's creepy." He started down the stairs.

It turned out that as soon as I healed him (after I'd taken him down), and he got a little information about why I didn't know his role, he lightened up significantly. He'd answered my summons, and that to him was a willingness to sign on, as weird as the situation might be.

I smiled. "Grab Jasper, would you?"

Hollace stopped and then retreated. "Yup."

I nodded at Austin to get going.

"If it pleases milady," he said softly, then led me to the Jeep and opened the passenger door for me.

"When do you plan on putting a bag over my head?" I asked while strapping myself in.

He climbed in the other side and started the Jeep up. "I didn't know you were into that."

"I've never seen where you live. I figured you were keeping it a secret."

"Ah." He clicked in his seatbelt and away we went. "No, it's just that your house is safer. Well, safer for everyone except for Kingsley. I think those dolls have been giving him nightmares."

"That guy doesn't seem like he'd be scared of anything."

We turned onto a small road that led away from town, barely two lanes and with trees pressing in on both sides.

"He's not scared of much, that's for sure. But Ivy House has a strange way of inducing fear."

We wound around up the mountain, no shortage of them in the Sierras, the headlights clicking on as the sunlight dimmed, the day giving way to night.

"How are the new people coming along?" he asked, hitting a fork in the road and going left, winding higher still.

I thought back on the past week.

"Hollace and Nathanial are incredibly chill. Always very helpful. The phoenix just chirps because she's too young to take human form, but she follows us around from room to room, or flies around the house. She has set fire to a few things, but the dolls run around with glasses of water to put them out, so that's fine. They finally have a good purpose, but now we randomly have puddles, dribbles, and half-burned items littering the place."

"Sounds like a good time."

"Definitely not. Nathanial thanked me for summoning him, told me what an honor it was, and then basically just drifted into the background."

"If he works out, he could be incredibly useful. I think we need to bring in more gargoyles so you can have an extended pack. You should have an army of them."

"I would never be able to handle that many people answering to me," I said, shuddering at the thought.

"They'd answer to Nathanial, and he would answer to you or me, depending on the circumstances. Chain of command. You handle him. He handles them."

"And if he rises up against me?"

"He won't. He has fully submitted to you. But if he tries anything, you could have Ivy House kill him in his sleep so you don't have to do the dirty work."

I smirked and looked out the window, at the dying light dancing through the pine needles.

"Hollace and the phoenix are mythical beings," he said. "They're magical creatures with human forms. Their souls live forever, born into new bodies. I don't know the exact details, but creatures like them only join forces once in a great while, every few lifetimes. You clearly got a couple that were ready to shed their vacation clothes and get to work. Cyra made us work for it, but she wouldn't have answered the summons if she wasn't intrigued."

"That makes me a little nervous."

"It makes me a little giddy. Kingsley is as jealous as they come."

The road opened up into a wide driveway leading to a two-story house. A huge, well-lit window looked out on an expanse of grass, pushed up against the woods at the back. Stone pillars bracketed the front porch, and the white door was flanked with colorful stained glass glinting in the porch lights. A wood deck hugged the second story and wrapped around the side. From my vantage point, I could see part of the house stepped up into the mountain, worked into the terrain. Its rustic look, all stone and wood and glass, fit in perfectly with the environment.

"Wow, Austin, this place is gorgeous. I love the stone around the base. That's a nice touch."

He exited his side and came around, opening my door and helping me out. "Thank you. I had it custom built."

"I thought you didn't dip into your inheritance until you became alpha?"

He didn't release my hand as we walked toward the welcoming porch, a rocking chair to either side.

"I didn't. The bar doesn't look like much, but it has always been busy."

Impressed, I waited until he opened the door. He stepped back, motioning for me to enter before him.

The inside was even nicer than the outside, and I stopped and gaped at the stairwell on the left, which gracefully curved to the right and then kind of swooped over the hall beyond the entranceway, giving an open, cavernous feeling to the foyer and providing space for a gorgeous iron and crystal chandelier. A sliding glass door at the far side of the space shined light onto a deck.

"You designed this?" I asked in awe.

He threaded his fingers through mine, close enough for his warmth to soak into me. "Yes. Would you like a tour?"

"I'll probably want to switch houses. Do you have a doll room?"

"Sadly, no."

"Huh. Strike against you."

He chuckled and led me straight back, past the archway into a large living room, showing me the spacious laundry room, the guest bath with rough gray stone underfoot and muted earthy accents. The wooden furniture, mostly rich mahogany and hazelnut, worked seamlessly with the glossy wooden floors, and modern accents gave the place a rustic *chic* vibe.

Kingsley sat on the leather sofa in the large living room, great windows overlooking the valley below, spiked with treetops. Stone framed the fireplace and crawled up to the ceiling, and I smiled at a family picture of Kingsley and his wife and kids, framed on one side, and one of an older woman I figured was their mom next to it. Candleholders held unused cream and burgundy candles.

"Did an interior decorator come through?" I asked.

"No. Why, does it need help?"

I laughed and released his hand, nudging his big

arm out of the way and leaning into him. He draped an arm around me.

"No. It's…" I shook my head, looking at Kingsley, his legs crossed at the ankles on the ottoman, a black remote gripped in one hand and his other arm thrown over the leather back. He looked how I felt, and I blurted out without thinking, "I feel like I've come home."

No one had been moving, but even so, the room stilled. For an incredible beat, my only awareness was of the man pressed against my side, his arm draped around my back, his spicy and clean cotton scent comforting me as his heart beat alongside mine. I found myself leaning into him and clutching the side of his shirt, like I might get ripped away if I didn't hold on tightly enough.

"I want to show you something, and then how about some appetizers?" Austin's voice rumbled in his chest.

"I don't…"

I didn't want to move. For reasons I didn't understand, I was afraid to shatter this moment. Afraid to physically let go of him.

"Good." Kingsley clicked off the stupidly big TV across the room before tossing the remote onto the couch beside him. "I'm starving."

He stood and passed by, nodding hello to me, and then did a double take. A wrinkle formed between his eyebrows.

"Hi," he said.

"Hey," I replied, still frozen, feeling a little foolish now, wanting to release the death grip I had on Austin's shirt and step away like a normal person. "You good?" I asked, trying to cover the moment, wondering why Austin hadn't asked me what was wrong.

"Yep. You?"

"Hard to tell just now."

His gaze flicked to Austin and then away. "Like a snowball rolling downhill," he murmured.

I wasn't sure what he meant by that.

"You need any help with prep, Austin?" Kingsley called back from the archway separating the kitchen from the living room.

"No. It's all done." He turned to me, taking a step closer, and I relished the proximity.

"I am having a very strange reaction just now," I whispered, his heart still beating with mine. His scent washed over me in heady waves, making me dizzy.

"Oh yeah?" He trailed his fingertips along my jaw. I loved when he did that, and the way he looked at me when he then dragged them down my neck. "What's it like?"

I stared into his eyes, lost. Confused. I should be terrified. My body was practically frozen, unable to move. His touch thrummed through me, seeping down deep, but the craving to have his body wrapped around mine didn't just stem from lust, or even love. I was in the grips of some sort of primal need I didn't understand.

Mine.

I shook my head and pushed away. The world tilted for a moment. The instinct to lurch forward and grab on to him again nearly overtook me.

"It's nothing." I sucked air into my lungs and forced a smile, nearly falling into his gaze again, nearly stepping forward and melting into his arms. "Dang it." I about-faced, ignoring the small smile pulling at his lips. "What's for dinner? Can I help? Have any wine?"

Laughter rolled out of him, rich and deep, but he didn't answer.

The kitchen was just as perfect as the rest of the house, with new appliances, mahogany-stained cabinets, and even a cappuccino maker tucked into the side. Kingsley stood in front of the wine rack in the corner, pulling a cork out of a bottle of red.

"You gave me a facial expression. You feeling okay?" I asked him, coming to a stop at the corner of the island.

Austin passed around me, his hand sliding along my lower back. I could barely keep myself from closing my eyes and purring in delight as he did so.

Maybe Mr. Tom had been right and I needed to get laid. Clearly all of those late-night exchanges with Austin had gotten to me.

Kingsley's voice was so low that I barely heard what he said—something along the lines of: "Gargoyles definitely mate."

Heat warmed my cheeks, and I looked down at my empty hands, remembering what I had put into my clutch…and also realizing I no longer held it.

"I left my clutch in the car, I think," I said.

The cork popped and Kingsley set the bottle down on the counter. "I'm with friends and family, so yes, I allow myself more freedom of expression, especially since I have to be pret-ty obvious in order for you to get what I'm saying." He twisted the cork off the bottle opener. "I can grab your purse."

"No smiling, though?" I asked him. "You're still in the camp that smiling is for chumps?"

"No," he said. "Your jokes are just that bad."

I laughed as Austin pulled a brick-red apron over his head. It boasted a white silhouette of a hen on the front above the words "Baking Is Gangsta." He tied the strings around his waist and rolled his shirt sleeves past his forearms.

The domestic quality of the apron teamed with such a strong, fierce man was so cute and so hot and so sexy, all at once. My core pounded and my heart felt like it was melting all over the floor.

"Can I help?" I asked as Kingsley walked past.

He paused to point at the bottle. "That's breathing. Don't touch."

Austin huffed out a laugh before washing his hands in the sink, right below a window boasting another great view.

"Nope. Just sit down and relax." Austin pointed at a high-backed chair next to the island, and I lowered onto it. "Kingsley wants meat, always. I'd planned to make rib-eyes for us and filet mignon for you. I can pair that with a baked potato, twice-baked potato, freshly made pasta with some store-bought tomatoes and basil, or a little blue cheese risotto—Oh no, you don't like blue cheese, do you? Some risotto or other, I'll figure it out, and asparagus."

He stared at me expectantly. I stared back, still trying to unpack all of that while fighting the suddenly uncontrollable urge to rip through his clothes and lick his fantastic body from head to toe.

"Store-bought tomato and basil?" It was all I could grab on to.

"My garden isn't ready yet. I had to settle for buying tomatoes."

"And you garden."

"That's how you get fresh vegetables."

"Indeed." I leaned against the island as Kingsley reentered carrying my clutch. "Fresh pasta?"

"From scratch. It's the only way to go."

"Only way to go," Kingsley said, putting my clutch next to me and then grabbing wine glasses from the cupboard.

"Sure. And different meat for me—you can make all of that?"

"Food is a big deal for a shifter," Kingsley said, pouring the wine. "Our family functions all revolve around food. Often we'll hunt first, those of us who take the form of predators, and then we'll cook it up and share it with our loved ones. Dating starts with sharing food, usually. A new alpha honors his pack with a feast. And so on. It's part of our culture."

"And you all cook like this? Pasta from scratch and gardening and everything?" I asked, seriously impressed.

Kingsley laughed, setting the wine bottle and two empty glasses on the counter near Austin. "Not even remotely. Austin has really upped his game. He could barely make mac and cheese back in the day."

"That's what happens when you don't have a pack or a girlfriend and live alone." Austin picked up the bottle and poured the two glasses. "I have many hobbies, and given how much time I've dedicated to them over the years, I am great at them all. It cures the boredom. Mostly."

"Buying drinks"—I pointed at Austin holding the bottle—"that means something, right? Niamh wouldn't let me buy a beer for Kace, or vice versa. Actually, she wouldn't even let me buy one for myself. She never does."

"*I* never do, actually," Austin said, handing me one of the glasses across the island. "I put your drinks on my tab. Because yes, buying drinks for a shifter is more than just buying drinks. It's a declaration of *interest*. Kind of like when a Dick offers to buy a strange lady a drink. We don't go in rounds like you try to do, Jess."

Heat burned through my body. It felt like I couldn't breathe. "You always buy my drinks?"

"Yes."

"Oh. I've always said thank you to Niamh. I assumed she just had Ivy House pay her back."

"And I'm sure she thought it was hilarious to take credit for something I was doing." Austin grinned and opened the fridge.

I narrowed my eyes at him. "So you've been silently

telling me you want to bang me this whole time?"

Kingsley choked into his wine and bent forward so as not to spill it down his crisp beige button-up.

Austin turned back from the fridge with a plate of scallops and a long dish with covered compartments that probably contained his prepped ingredients. He pulled the plastic off the scallops and set the plate on the island. "No. With you…it's complicated."

"You bought me a bottle of wine my first night. Or…gave it to me, I guess."

"Yeah…" He drew out the word. Kingsley sat down beside me, and Austin sprinkled some salt and pepper over the scallops. "You frazzled me that first night. I couldn't make you out, and then you were politely calling me out for my wine selection and blindsiding me with knowledge about women. I didn't know up from down. I didn't know *what* I was doing. I gave you that first bottle without thinking about it, then bought you another because you were so funny and unique that I wanted to keep you from leaving."

He pulled out a pan and set it on the burner, located on the island. It was a perfect design for cooking while still chatting with guests. Given the house was custom built, he must've planned it that way.

Kingsley swirled his wine in his glass, giving it air to open up the flavor. "I can sympathize," he said. "She rammed into me, challenged me, and then mocked me, all within the space of five minutes. It took everything I had not to burst out laughing. Like a little fly buzzing around, talking tough."

"Little did you know," Austin said, setting the flame before pouring olive oil into the pan.

He placed the scallops on the hot pan, searing them. Steam rose toward the hood above the stove, and he flicked on the fan, a soft whirring now accompanying his words. "Anyway, Jess, after that, it was like a snowball effect. It felt normal buying you drinks, and because you thought nothing of it, it seemed harmless."

"Unless her intention was to move on another shifter," Kingsley said, setting his glass down. He grunted at the wine. "Good. Much better than the wineries around me."

"The winemaker is a contender for our new winery." Austin pointed a spatula at the bottle before carefully but expertly flipping the first scallop. The cooked side was perfectly golden brown. "I tried to make it known that I was her protector but didn't have a claim on her."

Another flip of the spatula.

Kingsley huffed. "I bet that came across loud and clear."

Austin tensed but didn't comment.

My heart beat strong and sure. My core pounded. Both were a response to hearing that Austin had essentially claimed me so long ago. He may not have meant to or tried to, but he'd done it all the same.

"Thanks." I took a sip of my wine, the flavors of chocolate and spice exploding on my palate. "I'm sure it kept a lot of unwanted attention away."

"It was probably Niamh who kept a lot of the unwanted attention away." Austin grinned, flipping the last two scallops and then taking plates out of the cupboard.

"That too."

"You still haven't told me what you want for dinner." Austin removed the scallops and slid them onto a waiting plate.

"Oh…um…whatever. I'm happy not to decide, actually. I always hated choosing what was for dinner. Even takeout. I always had to decide literally every meal. I'd ask the ex, he'd defer to me, I'd choose something, and he'd argue about the choice. It drove me nuts. Now I'm just happy I don't have to cook. I'll eat whatever, even if I don't really like it. Mr. Tom makes eggplant every so often, and I can't stand it. But whatever. He goes to all the trouble."

"Wow. So that's a bonus," Kingsley said. "Easy to please with food."

Austin glanced at Kingsley. "Do you care what I make?"

"Baked potato. I'm a simple man."

"In the head, yeah," I said, because honestly, the setup was too good.

Austin dropped butter into the pan and swirled it around the bottom before adding garlic, moving it around with a wooden spoon. He grabbed a bottle of white wine from behind him and poured in a big splash, a plume of smoke heading for the fan, liquid jumping and spitting.

I leaned back, feasting my eyes on him while he worked, now stirring to reduce it down, his biceps and shoulder muscles popping and rolling, his movements so graceful, even here. A sheen of sweat covered his face from the heat, and an image of his glistening body in low light crowded my mind.

He looked up through his lashes at me, as though he knew what I was thinking.

Who was I kidding? He could *feel* my thoughts. I hadn't muted the link.

I didn't now, either.

"How do you feel about that mage coming to meet you?" Kingsley asked me, leaning forward on his elbows. "Nervous?"

I pulled my lips down at the corners. "Not really. I'll

probably get nervous right before he arrives, but right now there's too much to do. I need to completely overhaul Ivy House, at least the rooms we'll be using. I'm starting to think it'll take much longer than a few weeks to get it right, though. I want it to look like this, like what Austin has done with his place. But I haven't even ordered anything yet."

"Stage it." Austin turned, and I marveled at his big, broad, muscular back. He resumed his place at the pan and splashed lemon into it before adding more butter and stirring again. "Get all the unwanted furniture out and hire a company to rent you something. We'll only be there for a dinner or two. Maybe even one dinner and a garden party. That was nice, a couple weeks ago. We should do that more often."

"You missed the basajaun freaking out and fighting his way through the hedge to get out of the maze." I laughed, lifting my glass for a sip.

"Think we can get him to make an appearance?" Kingsley asked, his focus suddenly razor sharp. He could peel back the fun and games at a moment's notice.

Austin pointed a spoon at me before lifting the pan and placing it on a cold burner. He turned the flame off before replacing the scallops into the pan.

"She's your go-to with the basajaun," he said, turning back to the side of the island with the plates, taking the pan with him.

"I probably could." I shrugged. "I don't think he'd hang out for a meal or anything. But he would most likely be happy to stalk them through the woods and scare the life out of them."

"Yes." Kingsley nodded. "Scare them, look wild, speak to Jess, and then take off. That's a good intimidation tactic."

"The only problem is, what I'd have to trade for it would probably give Edgar a heart attack." I chewed my lip, then tried to discreetly rub my teeth, hoping I didn't have lipstick on them.

Austin placed a plate in front of me, two caramelized scallops sprinkled with parsley, sitting atop a bright butter-yellow sauce. He set a plate down for his brother and put one at the end of the island on my side for himself before handing out forks and walking to his plate.

The slight crunch at the beginning, followed by the easy slide of my fork through the scallop, made my mouth water. It was glistening inside, perfectly cooked, and the flavor exploded on my tongue. I moaned softly, closing my eyes, chewing in delight. I rolled the next bite around in that butter sauce, wanting to weep from the heavenly flavors.

"These are the best scallops I've ever had."

I barely opened my eyes through the whole experience, focusing on those flavors, lost in how good it was. After coming to the surface, I was sad to see the plate empty, then mortified to see the guys staring at me.

"Sorry, those were really good." I laid the fork down on the plate, just barely stopping myself from running my finger through the remaining sauce. Then deciding to hell with it and doing it anyway. "We're among friends here, right?"

I sucked my finger, swirling my tongue around it, eyes closed. The flavor gone, I pushed the plate away lest I do it again, and noticed Kingsley had left and Austin was staring at me with barely contained hunger.

My face flamed. "Sorry again, but you're a really good cook. I am never, at my best, close to that good. Mr. Tom isn't either. It caught me by surprise. Did I scare Kingsley away?"

"No." His voice was gruff. "He's checking on the barbecue. You are so incredibly sexy, Jacinta, when you let yourself go like that. So incredibly sexy."

My body burned to match the heat in his eyes, and in that moment, all the months and months of push and pull between us fell away.

"Kiss me, Austin," I whispered.

He moved around the corner of the island as if in

slow motion, then leaned down and touched his lips to mine. His tongue brushed against my lips, and I opened my mouth, quickly filled with his taste. His kiss was languid, as if he was in no hurry, but he pulled away too soon.

"Would you like to move outside?" he asked, his eyes soft. "I need to barbecue."

"Sure."

He put out a hand to help me up, and I moved beside him as if on a cloud.

"We should've started earlier in the afternoon so we could've enjoyed the view." He led me to the sliding glass door at the side of the kitchen and stepped out onto a large deck.

"Weren't you busy earlier?"

He closed the door behind me and pulled a couple of chairs from the edge of the deck toward the barbecue. Kingsley finished spreading out the coals, then put the grate back on the grill and sat.

"Oops, forgot the steaks." Austin brushed his fingers across my cheek before heading back into the house.

I gasped when I saw the ground beyond the deck, sloping downward before the tree line. The last shards of light fell across small blue flowers speckled with buttercups, swaying softly in the breeze, just like in the meadow we'd overlooked on our first date.

These were the flowers he'd referred to earlier, when he picked me up. They weren't native to this mountain-side, as this small area was the only one covered in them. I knew without asking that he'd put them here to remind me of that perfect outing. He was so dang romantic that it almost hurt my heart.

I stood in silence for a moment, my mind a little dizzied again, my body humming, desperate to be touched. My heart beat harder but not faster, and I put my hand to my chest, not sure if I should be alarmed. Wanting to go after Austin. Wanting him to come back out here.

Wanting to know what was happening to me, and wanting it to keep happening.

CHAPTER 26

KINGSLEY WATCHED JESS'S face go through a gamut of emotions, ending on confusion. She'd already entered the mating slide. The effect was plainer than in any shifter he'd ever known, and not because she relayed everything she felt on her face. He'd bet female gargoyles mated explosively, territorially. Permanently. She'd be a handful when the mating link settled. Volatile and extremely dangerous. Austin would be in for a wild ride.

One thing was clear: Jess had absolutely no idea what was happening. She was the driver of the mating bond, she was choosing the speed (and wasting no time), but she didn't realize it.

Given she still thought like a Jane, Kingsley couldn't fault Austin for not explaining any of this to her. She'd probably spook and go running. She was fighting the bond even now, which meant she had a stubborn streak a mile wide.

"How much do you know about gargoyles?" Kingsley asked her.

"Some."

"Are they territorial?"

She thought about it, those thoughts sitting on her face and in her body movements for all to see. Thankfully, mages couldn't read people any better than she could, or the upcoming meeting with the mage probably wouldn't go well.

"I've only seen them in my territory, so I don't know," she finally answered.

"You're not territorial over your...property?" But he already knew the answer.

"No," she said. "I mean, I don't like Peeping Toms, obviously, but I don't really think of it as my territory. It's Ivy House's territory. She handles most things."

He sat and then leaned back and crossed an ankle over his knee. Austin stepped out with three potatoes wrapped in foil, placed them on the grill, and closed the lid. A glance at Kingsley let him know to get lost. It was interrogation time, and Austin would just get in the way.

The warning in Austin's posture was clear. *Take it easy on her. Don't hurt her.* He winked at Jess before ducking back into the house.

"Thanks for the flow—" The door closed before she could get all the words out. "I feel like I should be helping," she murmured.

"He's cooking for you. Let him."

A thoughtful expression stole over her face. Her eyes wandered; she was probably calling up memories of what Kingsley had said earlier about shifters cooking for their women. She crossed her legs, her discomfort incredibly plain, the reasons equally so.

His wife, Earnessa, should be having this talk with Jess, not him. It was borderline unacceptable for a male to talk this through with a female, at least when the female was this expressive, not to mention she'd been claimed by the strongest alpha in the world (or near enough).

Into the silence, he asked, "Are gargoyles protective of their females?"

She bit her lip. "The guys aren't protective of their…of the women they meet in the bar. But I doubt that counts."

"No, that doesn't count."

"Then I don't know."

"You?"

She shrugged. "I don't think so. I've only been on a couple of dates since inheriting the magic."

"So you know very little about gargoyle culture."

"It certainly seems like it."

Kingsley lazily swirled the wine in his glass, watching it in the glow of the deck light, the darkness having finally swallowed the last rays of the sun. "Shifters are territorial."

"That's pretty obvious."

"Not just of property. In love, we are territorial of our partners, females as well as males."

She sipped her wine, then said, "I've realized that."

"Austin is an alpha, and that means his reactions are stronger in comparison to other shifters. You've seen what happens. It can get worse, if the offense is worse. It's not his past that drives it. It's his emotion fueling his animal, do you understand? It's a primal reaction."

"I understand what you're saying, but I don't necessarily understand what you're driving at."

"His intense reaction to someone touching you, or inappropriately flirting with you, will never go away. In possibly the very near future, it might get infinitely worse, at least for a time." Until the mating bond was firmly established.

"Define 'inappropriately flirting.'"

"If they're too close, too aggressive in their flirting, we'll say, and it's making you uncomfortable. I've seen shifters flirt with you in a friendly way, and that doesn't concern him. He has more control than he'll ever give himself credit for. But the second you get uncomfortable, for any reason, it'll flip his switch, do you get me?"

"Yes. Why are you telling me all this?"

"Because if you can't handle that side of him, you need to leave now. Or maybe after dinner, because I agree, he is one helluva cook. But if you can't handle that side of him, then you should not stay the night."

Nervousness filled her expression this time. She shifted uncomfortably, squeezing her crossed legs, and Kingsley looked away.

"He has to ask me to stay over first…" she said quietly, and it dragged his gaze back.

She was such a riddle, this woman. Very intelligent, fast on her feet, but wow, did the obvious just fly right past her sometimes. That was probably the only way she could stay in that deathtrap of a house with those intensely weird caretakers.

Determination infused her bearing. "I can handle that side of him. News flash: women don't like inappropriate flirting. Using him as a scapegoat will be good stuff."

"You took down a thunderbird. You don't need a scapegoat."

"I mean, sure, I could handle it myself, but a lot of guys who get turned down, even respectfully, fly off the handle. They make a scene. It's nicer to just avoid it."

Kingsley was glad he didn't have to hide his look of utter bewilderment and disgust. "Does that go on in the

Jane and Dick world?"

"Doesn't it go on here?"

He shook his head in disbelief, the situation with Kace making a lot more sense. "Listen, if someone makes you uncomfortable in the magical world, you tell them to piss off. If they don't, you make them, or you'll look weak. Don't wait for Austin next time. Do it yourself."

"I would've felt bad telling Kace to piss off. He was being respectful about the whole thing."

"Did you feel bad when Austin ripped Kace out of his chair and made him submit in front of the whole bar?"

A grimace creased her face. "Yes? I honestly hardly remember. I just remember this weird need to clutch on to Austin's back like a mountain climber afraid of falling off. Which is embarrassing to admit, but…"

Oh yeah, she was definitely in the mating slide. That was behavior similar to a powerful female shifter entering the mating bond. Earnessa had once nearly killed a female who'd rubbed Kingsley's shoulder. He'd never been so turned on in his life, watching his girlfriend at the time defend her claim on him. Jess had only just started the slide. For her to act like this already…

"Man, I wish I lived around here," he said, then

sipped his wine. "You are going to be fireworks when things start rolling. I'd ask your gargoyle buddies about being territorial, if I were you. If gargoyles are more territorial over their mates than shifters are, and some lady drapes herself over Austin, you will burn this town to the ground."

CHAPTER 27

I SAT AT the island, stuffed and happy, watching Austin bent over a handmade crème brûlée with a cooking blowtorch, finishing up the crust on top. I was content in a way I'd never been, utterly peaceful. Full, fulfilled, relaxed…

Except one idea kept circling through my mind.

Mate.

Cold shivers worked through me as I watched Austin's bicep pop when he leaned down to finish the last crème brûlée.

Female gargoyles mated. I'd heard that in the beginning of this magical journey. They banged everyone in sight and then settled on one mate. Permanently. I wasn't a total fool—I knew what Kingsley had been telling me.

Austin glanced over at me, lifting the blowtorch a little. I muted the link between us so he couldn't feel my mild freak-out.

It suddenly felt like my life was hurtling forward at a

million miles an hour. I'd done the blood oath with Ivy House, signing on for life, which played hell on my nerves when I really let myself think about it. I'd launched into this new life less than a year ago, and here I was making life decisions again. Only this one was permanent.

And now...

"With shifters, when you mate...that's like marriage, right?" I asked.

Austin looked back at Kingsley, as if tapping him to answer, before bending over the last dessert again.

"No," Kingsley answered, tracing the stem of his wine glass with his fingers. "Marriage is a legal contract establishing joint assets. Mating is a physical bond between two people. A chemical bond, I guess, that forges within the hearts of shifters." He touched the center of his chest.

"And you establish it with a ritual?" I asked. "A ritual around food?"

"No. There is a ritual, but it's mostly a celebration. When the bond is locking into place, it is at its most intense. The shifters involved become unfit for society, to put it mildly. They become much too possessive. They'll violently defend their mate over the smallest of grievances. So we have a celebration when the shifters are entering this final phase, and then we send them into the woods on their own. They get to celebrate their bond, reveling in each other, and everyone else gets some peace."

"So then, how do you…establish a bond? Magic? A spell?"

"I've never had to explain this to an outsider," Kingsley told Austin. "It's surprisingly difficult." He poured himself more wine and took a deep breath. "First, you don't choose a mate. Not the kind of mate we're talking about. Shifters can get married without ever experiencing the mating bond. Or you can start dating someone, and *bam*, you slip into the mating bond and forever knocks on your door before you really even know the person. Usually, though, it's somewhere in the middle. You meet someone, you get to know them, and you gradually slip into this long slide of mating. It's basically falling in love."

"It *is* falling in love," Austin said, delivering the white porcelain dish in front of me, the sugary top browned to perfection. He laid down a cloth napkin and placed a spoon on top. "Sometimes you fall in love gradually, and sometimes all at once. The mating bond happens when two souls unite, and there can be no other."

"But you choose who you fall in love with," I said, cracking into the surface of the crème brûlée. I loved that sound.

"Do you?" Kingsley asked, picking up his newly delivered spoon.

"Well, you choose to date them, then like them, and then it grows from there."

"Which is usually how mating works. For shifters, at any rate. I have no idea what it's like for gargoyles."

I told them what little I knew from Mr. Tom.

"Probably a very similar setup to shifters." Kingsley scooped up some of his dessert. "But you don't choose. You don't *will* the bond to come. It's a natural process your animal mostly decides. It happens or it doesn't. You feel it, and give in to it, or you don't."

"What if you don't give in to it?" I asked, then slid a spoon of custard into my mouth. As with everything Austin had made, the flavors exploded on my tongue. I moaned and put my hand on his arm. When we'd moved inside so he could finish preparing dessert, I'd claimed the middle seat so I could sit next to him.

"Damn, brother, I might have to start moaning too." Kingsley scooped up more custard. "This is good." He swallowed before he continued. "Sometimes you do get a bullheaded shifter, usually female—"

Austin laughed. "He just says that because he was the one who tried to dig in his heels."

"If *she* digs in her heels," Kingsley went on with a

smile, "then it might never happen. But I've never heard of anyone strong enough to resist forever. Still, nothing can force one person to stay with another. If two people are bonded and one of them leaves, they'll feel each other, always, but some people don't want the settled life. They prefer to stay solo."

I stopped with the spoon nearly to my mouth and looked at Austin. "Is that what happened with you and Destiny? You told me you thought she'd be your mate."

"I thought it would happen between us, yes"—his lush lips closed over the spoon, and I couldn't help but watch—"but now I realize it was never going to happen."

"How do you know?" I asked.

He shrugged, daintily loading the end of his spoon. A big, strong man, still in his apron, dainty with his dessert. It stoked my desire to impossible levels.

"Because I'm older now," he said. "Wiser. If I found my mate, I would never leave her. I would always protect her. Nothing would tear me away from her."

The pressure on my chest made it hard to breathe. Hard to even think. His cobalt eyes burned with fire and determination, and my heart and core had started to throb in tandem.

"The good news, for those that are a lee-tle wary about commitment, is that it usually doesn't happen all at once. It *is* a slide," Kingsley said, tilting his dish and scraping it clean with his spoon. "You'll feel it happening, and everything might seem a little topsy-turvy, but you'll have time to get used to it. As someone who got used to it *very* slowly, I know this is true."

I finished off my crème brûlée and immediately looked over at Austin's to see if I could steal a little more. Finding half a dish, I smiled and leaned over with my spoon out.

"Are you going to eat all of that?" I asked.

"Take whatever you want, milady," he answered softly.

Smiling, I tried to take a dainty spoonful, but I scooped up more than I'd planned and couldn't find it in me to feel guilty. It was simply that good.

"Before you ask," Kingsley said, standing with his dish and walking around to the sink, "I don't know if there is one special mate for everyone, decided by Fate, or a few for everyone and you just go with the first one you find."

"I'd like to think there's only one." Austin's deep voice rumbled, and shivers skated down my body. "I'd like to think Fate plays a hand in bringing us to our perfect mate, even if the road to finding her is long and lonely."

The moment reduced down to him and me, and I

felt the power of it beating in my chest. The need to clutch on to him and never let go.

I wondered if the situation was the same for female gargoyles. Was there one possible mate or more?

Was this slide Kingsley had described what was happening to me?

✧　✧　✧

"YOU NEVER GOT a look at the upstairs." Austin led me away from the kitchen and Kingsley, who was doing dishes. "Would you like to? Or maybe we can sit out on the deck with a glass of wine. Of course, I can take you home if you'd prefer."

I slipped my arm around his middle, sighing when he pulled me into his arms. "You have a deck upstairs, don't you? I thought I saw a wraparound one up there."

"I do, yes. Would you like to sit up there?"

"Yes, please."

Austin nodded and opened a fresh bottle of wine. Apparently Kingsley would be drinking the rest of the other one. Grabbing two glasses, Austin guided me upstairs.

"There is a second living room up here, for overflow or if people want to get away from each other. Then a few guestrooms." Austin stopped next to the living room, similar to the one downstairs but without a fireplace.

"Your room?"

A wave of heat and nervousness washed back and forth across the link, both of us feeling the same heady combination.

"This way, please, milady." He gestured me down the hall.

I started forward with a dopey grin. "It's so corny when you call me milady, and I love it so much."

I chuckled as we reached a flat storm-gray wall with a plant standing in front of it and a large painting of the deep woods, with moss-covered rocks and swooping branches. He looked down at me, as though waiting for me to comment on it.

"Really lovely. It reminds me of Ivy House."

With a smile, he stepped around the plant and disappeared behind the wall.

"What the…" I put out my hands and stepped forward, draping the wall with magic to see if I could decipher the spell. Upon closer inspection, though, there wasn't a spell. It was a trick of the eye. The oversized painting clung to the edge of a wall that ended, the plant positioned in such a way that it further masked the opening. A small hallway beyond it led to a door, which opened into a spacious room at the back of the house. The setup was very similar to my bedroom in

Ivy House. Instead of a table by the window, though, he had a love seat and a table set off to the side around the fireplace.

"No TV?" I followed him to the veranda, where a table was set up to look out over the darkness. The sky stretched out above us, the sea of stars infinite and breathtaking.

"I don't actually watch much TV."

"Hence why you are so good at your hobbies."

He set the glasses and bottle onto the table and pulled out a chair for me. He pulled a wine opener from his pocket and sat before opening the bottle.

"Is the hidden doorway in case someone tries to at-tack?" I asked, leaning back and sighing.

"Yes. The wraparound porch gives me a range of places to jump down if I need to escape. I never trust wards. Mages put them up—they can pull them down."

"Too bad you don't have a magical house to protect you."

"Yes. Too bad."

He poured our wine and then held his glass up. "To you finally getting to know my brother. I hope you don't ghost me."

I laughed and clinked my glass with his. "I like Kingsley, actually. I don't think he's as chill and bal-anced as you always said, but he's good people."

"He is chill and balanced for an alpha, trust me."

"Not as much as you."

He frowned at me. "That's probably because I've always allowed myself to smile with you. To laugh. I'm only newly an alpha."

"Yeah, why is that? You never gave me that hard alpha shtick—even the hard shifter shtick—like Kingsley and all his people do. Like *you* do to most of the people in your bar."

He was quiet for a long while. "Probably because I knew, even then."

"Knew what?"

His gaze was heavy on me. "I haven't wanted to smile and laugh for…so long. Since I met Destiny, but before that, too. The stigma of my father has always hung over me. The bad apple. The black sheep. I've always feared that I'd become the thing my mother dreaded. Even when I was a kid, I was too rough with play, too aggressive. At one point, I thought power was the only answer for taming my beast. After I left home, I decided it was solitude.

"Then you walked in the door that day, a Jane in a magical world, starting over and facing an uncertain future with a broken smile… It touched me. It blew something sweet and soft into a hard, desolate place. Your fresh take on the world, your courage, your insight—it revived me. I think I knew then that I'd care for you more than I've ever cared for anyone. That I'd want to protect you in a way that felt wholesome and good. That felt—*feels*—like what I'm designed for. You make my world make sense. I never knew what peace and happiness would feel like, until you."

I blinked away tears, not trusting myself to speak, my middle throbbing.

Silence passed between us and we sipped our wine. Through the link he was peaceful, content in the moment.

"Having a man cook for me has always been a dream of mine," I murmured. "You pulled it off to perfection."

"Thank you. And I knew that, about it being your dream."

"Oh? I don't recall mentioning it."

"You didn't. Jimmy did, before he left."

Jimmy approved of Austin. He must've, if he'd told him that. He'd wanted to help Austin woo me.

My heart warmed in an unexpected way, as if it beat in tandem with another. With Austin's. I blinked away tears. Suddenly, all I wanted to do was express myself to him. With him. I didn't want words. I wanted action.

"What does this view look like in the morning?" I asked quietly.

"Would you like to stay and see?"

"Yes, please."

He set his glass down and rose. I expected another flurry of nerves, but deep, throbbing desire pooled inside me instead. He put out a hand, and I took it, letting him pull me to him. We left our glasses and entered the room, Austin closing the glass door behind us.

I reached up for him, unable to wait any longer. His lips found mine, and he backed me toward the bed.

I worked at his first button and he pulled back, his hands on my shoulders, watching me as I tugged the button free. The moment slowed, the tone turning languid instead of urgent.

I pulled the second button free, and our gazes locked, my heart throbbing with his.

"We've started the slide, haven't we?" I whispered, pulling the third button free, spreading his shirt and revealing his delicious, muscled chest. "That's what your brother was getting at."

"Yes," Austin said softly, running his thumb across my bottom lip. I leaned forward and took it into my mouth, sucking on it. "It started a while ago for me, I think. It's been so slow, so gradual that I didn't notice at first. I thought it was attraction and deepening feelings, not *this*. Not when I'd sworn myself to solitude."

"I'm just starting to feel…weird, though," I said, the last button opened. I pulled his shirt out of his pants and gently pushed it off his large shoulders. "The thing with Kace was the first time I really noticed."

"It is not unusual for one to feel it before the other. Usually that halts things. Or slows it. Maybe that's why it was so gradual for me, I don't know. I don't think anyone really knows until it happens to them."

He closed his eyes and breathed out when I ran my palms over his pecs and then his shoulders, leaning forward to kiss his skin.

"It worries me, Austin. I've just promised the rest of my life to Ivy House. I'm not ready for…a mate. For mating…"

"We'll take it slow."

My hand on the back of his neck, I pushed his lips down to mine, saying one thing, desperate for another.

He sucked in my bottom lip before opening his mouth, eliciting the same response from me. He swirled his tongue with mine before pulling back to suck on my lips again.

I let my fingertips glide down between us and circle his belt and buckle. Desperation overcame me, hard and heavy, yanking a moan from my lips. I pulled at his belt, fevered, incensed.

Mine.

I ripped open the button and pushed his jeans away, his boxers with them. I'd seen his hard length many times by now, but this was the first time I'd gripped it. One stroke, and the wildness in me calmed down. Looking into his heavily lidded eyes, with his hands squeezing my shoulders and his precious commodity in my hands, I felt…settled.

"I'll probably dig in my heels," I said, lowering onto my knees, burning alive. "I'll probably freak out and push back."

"That's okay," he whispered, watching my progress. "I'll wait as long as you need. Forever."

When he couldn't keep his hands on my shoulders anymore, he roughly grabbed my hair. The middle dropped out of me in excitement, and right then I knew I was in good hands. He could do anything—I knew he'd never hurt me. I trusted him with everything that I was, a trust we'd been building since we'd first met. A trust I knew we each held sacred.

"Sometimes I might tease you." My voice belonged to a stranger, husky and wanton. Desperate. I licked the end of his shaft. "I might ignore you to try to get a handle on my feelings."

His breathing hitched as I sucked in his length.

My lips moved against the tip. "I might not give in…"

I held his eyes as I took him in again, his hand tangled in my hair.

In a rush of strength and power, he reached down under my arms and ripped me up to standing.

"You'll give in to me eventually." He ripped my dress away in one harsh movement. My body both tightened up and loosened, and I hooked my hands around his neck. Wanting him hard. Wanting him *now*. "You're *mine*," he growled. "You will come to me eventually."

The alpha had taken over.

He ripped away my panties and sank down in front of me, stopping to suck in a budded nipple on his way down. I hooked a knee over his shoulder and feathered my eyes shut. He licked up my middle before feasting on the collection of nerves at the top. His fingers entered me, one at a time, before working a fast rhythm.

An orgasm shattered me as I moved against his mouth, shuddering. I moaned, rolling my hips in little circles as the waves of pleasure washed through my body.

He stood, his touch against my fevered skin, cupping a breast as he kissed me on the lips. He backed me over the bed and lay with me, spreading my legs around him, my thighs over his hips.

He bent to flick a nipple with his tongue. I moaned,

rubbing my hand over his back. He moved to the other nipple, his fingers working me again, knowing exactly where to touch and how hard—or softly in this case, because he was deliciously teasing me.

I'd meant to say I'd definitely—probably?—need time, and would definitely—maybe?—push back against any permanent kind of commitment, but words escaped me. He kissed up the center of my chest and lightly dragged his teeth over my throat. I shivered.

His kiss increased in urgency, his tongue plunging in and retreating, his body hard against me. Breathing faster, he reached down between us and massaged me while his tip kissed my opening.

He nipped my neck with his teeth. His thrust stole my breath.

I arched and squeezed his body with my legs, filled to bursting, my heart still throbbing in time with his, my body rising and falling, banging against him with each thrust, retreating in delicious sensation.

"Take as long as you need," he growled. "But when you come to me, I *will* claim you, body and soul."

His final thrust sent me over the edge. I cried out, clutching him, squeezing my eyes shut against the tidal wave of pleasure. He shuddered over me, groaning, holding me tight.

As an aftershock rolled through me, he kissed me

languidly, not taking himself out. In a moment, I realized why. He was starting again.

I slid my knees up his sides with an appreciative mew when reality struck.

I froze, pushing at his shoulders.

"Oh God, Austin, we didn't use protection. I have it in my clutch—I don't know if I can still get pregnant, but I might be able to, and—"

"*Shh*, it's okay," he said, no longer moving but still inside me. "I took care of that shortly after the fight with my brother. After my niece stopped me from killing him. I got a vasectomy so I wouldn't pass on what I was to anyone else. The madness ends with me."

My heart broke into a million pieces for the self-loathing he must've felt to do that as a young man. For the crushing judgment he'd levied on himself.

Austin was truly the best man I'd ever known, something I'd seen evidence of from the day we met. He'd never let me down. He'd always built me up. He had always been there for me, and given himself for me, even when he didn't want anything in return. *Especially* when he didn't want anything in return. All the men in the world, and I had lucked out by finding him. What kind of an idiot would push that away?

I placed my palm against his cheek and kissed him again, circling my hips and delighting in his growl of pleasure. "I will come around eventually," I murmured, getting lost in his body. In the feel of him. "After you work for it."

CHAPTER 28

THE NEXT THREE weeks passed in a blur.

With the new direction for Ivy House, using staging furniture, which was much faster than choosing a household full of new stuff, I was able to get the house ready in a couple weeks (the old stuff was in storage). The representative from the company had helped me pick out the latest looks. It didn't look as good as Austin's place, but it would work. When this all settled down, I'd force Austin to help me redecorate. I would never admit it to Ivy House, but I liked his house better. It really did look and feel like home. I loved watching the sunset with him from the deck, soaking in the sweeping views of the valley.

I'd stayed there a few nights, drooling over him while he cooked, letting Kingsley spoil me by doing the dishes, and ending the night by twisting in the sheets with Austin. The man was an absolute legend. He could evoke sensations in me that I hadn't even known were possible. He was relentless, fully ensuring my satisfaction over and over. With some guys, "all night" could be tedious. Not with him. I couldn't get enough. I'd become insatiable.

But I had a duty to the people of Ivy House (literally). They were counting on me. I had to remain focused on the possible magical threat posed by the visiting mage. I had to keep focused on the politics I would need to play. I had to be lucid! Whatever was happening between Austin and me (I still hadn't looked into what that meant for a female gargoyle—I was kind of afraid to find out), it had to wait until the danger passed. Until I wasn't practicing magic constantly, constructing wards and creating potions, trying to anticipate which talents I'd need to match wits and skills with our visitor. Right now the pressure was too high for me to figure us out—I needed some room to breathe, and so did he.

His territory was coming together with Kingsley's help, but it was clearly taxing. Kingsley said he'd never seen such a rush to join a pack, and the resulting chaos was a real thing. People were coming in droves now, having completely overrun the few towns Austin had claimed for his territory, forcing him to expand to a few more. Realtors were having a field day. Hotels, restaurants, and bars were rolling in cash. It had taken an insane amount of work in a very short time, but finally Austin said things were getting in line, just in time. His defense and the structure of his territory would somewhat be in place.

"Miss." Mr. Tom stuck his head into my room. I sat at the table in front of the windows, the midmorning sun falling over my empty breakfast plate and bone-dry coffee mug. My stomach was tied in knots.

Today was the day. The visiting mage and his people would be arriving and settling in. It was time to be on my best behavior, and to put my best foot forward. I was representing my people and Ivy House, and I would do them proud.

We'd decided to meet him and his people at the swankiest restaurant in the county, two towns over, which Austin just happened to own, a recent acquisition. That gave us control—he'd closed it down for the night and set up his people within the grounds.

"Yes." I stood and picked up the plate.

Mr. Tom bustled in and took it from me. "Sebastian needs you in his makeshift lab. He says it's urgent."

I slowly let out a breath to keep from shaking. Sebastian had been working overtime these last couple weeks, helping me prepare for what he called *nice-nice warfare*—everyone acting pleasant to your face, only to gouge you in the back the moment you turned around. Having played a part in previous such occasions, he had a good idea of what spells and potions they might use against me—and he'd been training me in their use and applications. It was a different kind of battle than I was used to, but he'd made it clear it was a battle all the same.

Sebastian was convinced this visiting mage was no more than training wheels. That I'd have no trouble dealing with him, what with my power, growing knowledge base, and magical crew.

He didn't seem to understand that I had absolutely no experience when it came to mages beyond my close brushes with Elliot Graves's people, and none of them had sat down with me for tea. I wasn't magical at heart, and I didn't know anything about the politics of the magical world.

"Of course." I smoothed my sweats down my legs.

"Miss." Mr. Tom paused in picking up the plain white mug.

"Yes?"

"You have no reason to be nervous. By allowing these miscreants into your territory, you are essentially stooping to their level. It has to be done, as these things often do, but they are lucky to bask in your presence. You are the heir of Ivy House. You are the queen of the gargoyles. You are majestic. If anyone should be nervous, it's the mage and his ragtag crew."

I released a smile. He always built me up too high,

and this was no exception, but right now I needed it.

"Thanks, Mr. Tom," I said, stepping away from the chair.

"There is nothing to thank me for. Now, go down and help Sebastian before he pops a blood vessel. He is very worked up about something."

I took the secret hallways to the heart of the house, Sebastian's voice floating out to me as I approached the cavern holding the crystals. "I don't have enough power for this spell. Ain't that a bitch? When was the last time that happened? A long while, I can tell you."

I stepped into the room. Sebastian was bent over the bookstand holding the second magical spell book, facing the pulsing crystals in the center of the rough-hewn rock and stone room. No one else stood with him.

"Who were you talking to?" I stepped around a robust camping stove set up to the right, army green and with a large cast-iron pot sitting on the burner.

Sebastian glanced back before returning to the book, his hands braced on his hips. "Ivy House. It's much more rewarding than talking to a plant because I know Ivy House can actually hear me."

"Can't answer you, though."

"Neither can a plant."

I stopped beside him. "This is true. Edgar let you look through the book?"

Edgar usually kept it in a hiding place in his cottage for safekeeping.

"No. Ivy House arranged it. I assume so, at any rate, because it was waiting for me on the stand this morning. If Edgar had wanted to show me something, he would have watched me the whole time to make sure I didn't write anything down. He's been suspicious of me ever since I leaned over his shoulder and commented on how useful one of the spells would be in my new life. It was the spell that turns people mute. Obviously, he didn't get the joke."

I laughed. "And after you guys got so chummy over the new growth elixir."

"I feel bad about that." He wiped his eyes. "I was just trying to correct the one he had. I didn't think it through. The original serum worked just badly enough not to totally count as cheating. This one... He'll inevitably win more gardening competitions, and I'll be an accomplice. Soil will be on my hands."

I laughed again. Sebastian was not usually this light and humorous. I wondered if it was his way of releasing his nerves about the week to come.

"It was always cheating," I said, patting him on the back. He tensed but then relaxed into the touch. "Think of it this way: you'll make the flowers taste better for the basajaun. Can't hurt having that kind of friend."

"That is true." He checked his watch. "I can only assume that we'll hear screeches come training time, and Edgar will run out yelling that I've stolen this book."

"Probably."

"The book was open to this page when I came in." He pointed down at a spell, the title not in English and therefore incomprehensible to me. "An invisibility spell. I've done some similar things, as you know, but nothing this powerful. This spell calls up ancient magic, I'll bet you anything. It's a doozy. Why teach you mine when we can learn this one, am I right?"

"Isn't that the kind of magic I have, ancient? Passed down through the years, stored within this house for safekeeping?"

He twisted to smile at me. "Yes. Your magic is stolen out of time. All magic stems from the same place, the same time, but yours is closer to the root. You could make this potion, but I'm certain I can't. For once, I am not the most powerful mage in the room. It's strangely…refreshing. Like the pressure has been taken off."

Sebastian's ego was as tame as Austin's—he cared more about getting the job done than letting everyone know he'd done the legwork.

A rush of urgency rolled through me. I wanted time to speed up so I could see Austin sooner. He'd been too busy to stay over the night before, but he'd called before bed to say goodnight. We ended up chatting for an hour while he ate and then got ready to supervise various challenges for pack placement and hierarchy. Sleeping on my own was great, but sleeping in the same bed with him was infinitely better. His warm body curled around mine, his sweet breath dusting my face, his heart beating inside of my chest...

"Let me know when you're done," Sebastian said, tracing a line in the book with his finger.

"What?" I glanced around. "Me? Done with what?"

He glanced at me, pale eyes assessing. "You're back. Great. I never know how long you'll spend thinking about him. It's fun to fall in love. I try not to interrupt."

My face flamed and I didn't know what to say.

"Now, I know Edgar usually reads these to you," he continued, "but since the house showed the book to me, I assume it'll be okay if I read them. You'll have to let me know what she says. I don't want to step on any toes."

"*He has been approved,*" Ivy House said.

I relayed the message.

"Oh. Great." He ran his fingers through his hair. "I thought maybe she'd strike me dead."

"*He is watched, always, and if he steps wrong, I will ensure the fear he feels during his slow death will cure him of chasing his next adrenaline high.*"

"Good grief." I scrunched my nose but relayed the message.

"That's fair," he murmured.

"What do you say to her?"

"Oh, just odds and ends, truths and horrors of my past. My plant is surely happy to be rid of me. It's probably less depressed on its own."

I couldn't decide if I should give him a comforting word or two, or just blink at his oddness. He certainly fit into my crew.

"Must be hard working for powerful people, huh?" I finally said.

"In my world, yes. In your world, it seems not. Now, this passage is entirely written in Latin. It is incredibly advanced, but since you have a knack for potions—or following directions, as you say—and enough power, I think you'll be fine to learn it now."

"*Right* now?" I checked the time again.

"*Yes, right now,*" Ivy House said.

I rolled my eyes. "Fine," I said, and Sebastian gave me that deadpan stare of his before glancing around. He clearly knew Ivy House had answered.

"You're not weirded out by the magical house, huh?" I rolled up my sleeves and then looked at the stainless-steel pot on the camping stove. "Did you remember to turn on the gas?" I checked the propane tank on the side of the setup without waiting for an answer.

"Do you know what's funny?" Sebastian tapped the page and then took two sideways steps over to a clunky green card table with stains in deep red, black, royal blue, and one rusty orange. Little dishes sat on it containing herbs or leaves, one holding tiny eyeballs and another containing a black talon. Sebastian prepped for potions like Austin did for cooking.

I pushed the rush of heat away.

"No," I said, pulling a blue rubber apron over my clothes. I'd learned to keep it down here for this purpose. "What spell are we doing again?"

"Using a camping stove to create potions is considered incredibly gauche. If I weren't so powerful, everyone in the mage community would look down on me. They'd ridicule me. But since I am powerful, with a good and respected position, they call me eccentric."

I frowned at the equipment. "This is a high-dollar camping stove. My ex used to take a similar one for camping trips."

Sebastian laughed. "Yes, see? That is what I mean. Because of my power and placement, magical people think I'm making a statement of some sort. You just take it for what it is—a good-quality contraption that gets the job done."

"You're in a part of the house that has no electricity. How else would you cook the potions?"

"Crisscrossed logs and magical fire."

"This is a way easier setup. You can just fold it up and put it away when you're done. It has a handle and everything."

He laughed again. "The cooking pot is another item I'm side-eyed for using. My kind use cauldrons, like in the stories."

"Oh. Well, yeah, I can see how that would be more fun."

"But not as practical."

"No. You can wash this in the dishwasher. I doubt a cauldron would fit in there. We never make that much potion, anyway."

He bent with his hands on his knees, laughter ripping through him. He was shaking with it. "Yes." He wiped his eyes when he straightened up. "Yes, exactly. You don't think I am eccentric—you think I am practical."

"I just thought you were normal"—or normal for this house—"but yeah, I'll go with practical."

"I *am* normal, actually. Far too normal for the life I lead." He took a deep breath, and a few more chuckles escaped. "To answer your question, Miss Jacinta, I *do* like this magical house. I like it very much. I like that it has a personality, that it values people on their merits, and that it will kill me if I step out of line. Its rules make sense. Now, let's get to work. We'll be making a kind of invisibility potion that will trump all the others I've ever heard of. I highly doubt anyone will be able to create a counter-spell to this, which means you can truly be invisible in a way few can."

"Or...*you* can, right? Since we've agreed to go with Niamh's strategy?"

Niamh had suggested we keep Sebastian as the silent partner for as long as possible. Keep him in the shadows. That way, I'd still seem inexperienced and naïve, which would make Kinsella think he had the upper hand, while still having Sebastian close at hand for backup. It was a good plan.

He offered me a slight bow. "If you wish."

"So why won't other revealing spells—antidotes—work on this one?"

"This spell has a few steps I've never considered adding. Given no one else knows about it, the mage's people won't be able to create an antidote or spying serum capable of seeing through it."

"Only two people know about it?"

"Yes. And I am very good at keeping secrets. Let's begin."

CHAPTER 29

"MISS, IT'S TIME."

I turned in the mirror in the bathroom, looking at my dress's deep, plunging back, ending in a V above my waist.

"Okay," I called to Mr. Tom.

Turning back, I smoothed the front down my stomach, the neckline cutting across the base of my throat, ending in a design of white lace flower petals at my shoulders that flowed down the side of my body to the floor, revealing a thin slice of skin. The skirt, fitted at the waist, pooled when it reached the floor, the back creating a train.

Mr. Tom had picked it out, and it was as elegant as it was beautiful. He'd insisted I go without jewelry. Not even earrings. I had no idea why, but given he was two for two on dresses, I'd decided to just go with it. He did seem to know his fashion, something he didn't apply to himself, because when I found him waiting by my bedroom door, he had on the same tux he always wore, freshly pressed with tails down the back, a little too formal for the dinner we were going to and a lot too formal for being my butler.

"Miss, you look lovely, I must say. That dress is absolutely divine."

I lightly ran my hands over my hips, feeling the soft, intricate lace. "Thank you. It's gorgeous."

"*You* are gorgeous. The dress is just fabric."

I felt Austin walking up to the porch, his steps unhurried. He'd be escorting me tonight, and Sebastian seemed to think that made a very loud statement. When I pressed him about it, he'd said, "You have shifters on your side. I think it's wise that you are using them."

Mr. Tom followed me downstairs, where the rest of my crew awaited us, each dressed to the nines. Cyra, the phoenix, who'd finally regained the ability to assume a human form, stood at the front in a deep red satin dress flowing over a slightly pudgy body that caught the fabric in some of her belly folds. She was clearly not interested in Spanx. I was glad for it. She was a badass who'd nearly taken Austin down. I was glad she wasn't forcing herself to be uncomfortable in order to fit a certain body mold. I'd always hated Spanx.

I was also glad she held no ill feelings toward Austin or me for being killed. She was like a shifter after a challenge—the more dominant creature was decided.

That was that.

Hollace stood behind her, his white suit offsetting his dark skin. He'd paired the suit with a white shirt and cream tie, and looked swank and fantastic. I smiled at him and received a nod. Niamh leaned against the wall behind him, holding a can of beer. She wore a long-sleeved, glittery black dress, her white hair lightly tufted and gelled into place. I was impressed she'd actually tried. Nathanial stood in a plain black suit and tie, the shirt and jacket elegantly tailored to fit around his wings, his hands at his sides and his "cape" draping down his back. His wide shoulders and robust body carried off the look. Ulric waited behind him, his fuchsia suit and blue tie matching his two-tone hair. The only muted parts of the look were his black shirt and shiny black shoes.

"Wow," I said. "The eighties called; they want their suit back."

"He looks like a clown show. Kingsley will get a fright," Mr. Tom drawled. "Why doesn't Ulric carry a doll around with him, too? Maybe a puppet. They'll think he's your jester."

"I'm in if you are." Ulric laughed.

Jasper's look was similar to Nathanial's, but he'd gone with a cream tie and a matching pocket square. Edgar skulked last, his suit, shirt, and tie all black.

Someone had clearly helped him, because the clothes were expertly made and fitted. If he weren't hunching, he'd look almost normal.

"Okay. Just need one more."

The door opened as if on cue. Austin waited there with one hand tucked into his trouser pocket and the other down at his side with a glittering silver watch on his wrist, accented with diamonds. He had on a black suit with a white shirt, accented with a ruby-red bow tie and matching pocket square. It fit him perfectly, and he had the ease and confidence of a lord, full of swagger and zero concern. He looked like the owner of this world, just renting it out to those who'd come to visit.

I let out a shaky breath, feasting my eyes on him, letting my gaze trail down that fitted suit.

"Hey, baby, you look lovely," he said softly. "I brought something over for you earlier, if you'll honor me and wear it."

Mr. Tom picked up a long package off the table by the wall, wrapped in white with a red bow. He brought it to me on two flat palms, his nose up, his demeanor at its stuffiest. That meant this was an occasion.

I flashed Austin a smile before gingerly taking the gift and peeling off the paper to reveal a black velvet box. I opened the lid slowly, gasping when I saw the necklace nestled within it: an intricate design of rubies, diamonds, and pearls, the stones smaller on the outside and bigger in the middle, which would hang against my chest. There were earrings and a bracelet to match.

I pushed it at Mr. Tom, thinking about dropping it and backing away.

"No, Austin." I shook my head, unable to take my eyes off the set. "I can't accept this."

"Of course you can." He stepped into the house and took the box. "It'll go perfectly with your dress."

I shot a suspicious look at Mr. Tom. He'd told me not to wear any jewelry because he'd known this was coming. The sneaky dog. Austin had even matched the crimson with his tie and pocket square.

Austin extracted the necklace. "An alpha's lady must look the part." He laid the necklace against my chest and hooked it in the back. "Every time you wear a nice set of jewelry, you can't stop touching it to make sure it's still there. I figured this was better than flowers."

"It's too much," I whispered. "This is way too much."

Austin fastened the bracelet before handing me one earring at a time. "Nothing is too much for you. I will give you the world if it will make you smile."

Tears clouded my vision. My lower lip trembled.

He softly brushed his thumb across my throat. "It

suits you."

I threw my arms around his neck and kissed him, knowing I'd get lipstick on him but not able to help it. Instead of backing away, like my ex might have, he deepened the kiss. By the time he backed off, I was breathless and my heart ached with wanting.

"Thank you," I murmured.

"It is my infinite pleasure, milady," he responded, his eyes so deep and blue.

"Mr. Steele, let me just allow you to..." Mr. Tom stepped forward with a tub of baby wipes he'd retrieved from God only knew where. He opened the flap for Austin to grab one out.

"Thanks." He wiped the lipstick from his lips and asked me, "Good?"

A tear slipped down my cheek. My ex had liked seeing my face done up, but he'd always refused to kiss me when it was. And if I forgot and kissed him anyway, he'd get cold. This easy, no-big-deal approach nearly undid me.

"You okay?" Austin asked. Time was ticking, but you wouldn't know it from looking at him. He was in no hurry.

"Yes. Sorry, I'm good." I beamed at him and gave him a tight hug. "Really good."

Austin turned and cocked an elbow, and I slipped

my hand through his arm.

"Miss, we'll refresh your lipstick when you get there," Mr. Tom said, grabbing my clutch.

"Thank you, Mr. Tom." I laughed for no reason.

With a stupid smile, walking on air, I headed for the door. Mr. Tom fell back, taking his place between Jasper and Edgar. Sebastian would meet us there, hanging around the edges, hopefully invisible. Only my crew and Austin's crew should be able to see him. I'd made plenty of potion to go around. It had taken most of the day.

"You're going to knock 'em dead," Austin said as we slowly sauntered down the walkway.

Parked at the curb was an incredibly sleek sports car in metallic midnight blue, low to the ground, the tires large and wide, the price tag probably enormous. Behind it waited a black stretch limo, and another sat at the curb in front of Niamh's house.

"What's…" My eyes followed the smooth curves of the sports car. "Is that…?"

"It's a McLaren. I just got it. It goes very fast."

"What happened to the Jeep?"

He stopped by the passenger door. "It's at the house. If I'll be escorting you to fancy parties, I better look and drive the part, right?" He opened the door for me and held out his hand.

"Or I could drive? I have a beat-up old Honda that

kind of matches the speck of dirt on your shoe."

"I have no dirt on these shoes." He winked and handed me into the car.

After he closed the door he crossed to the other side, his hand still in his pocket, his shoulders swaying, his vibe smooth and debonair. I just stared in mute fascination for a moment. I knew he was playing a part, but holy crap, he was playing it well. That raw, primal quality of his was still there, but the rough edges had been smoothed away into a glossy exterior. His power pulsed in waves, heady and tantalizing, and his swagger mixed with his rock-solid confidence nearly caused me to combust.

He got into the car, which molded to him like that suit, an extension of the persona he'd created. He pushed the button to start it and threw it into gear, the car chirping as it jumped forward.

"Jacinta, your beauty has me entranced," he said, speeding to the end of the street. "You are perfection."

"Thank you," I whispered, my heart expanding until it didn't feel like my body could contain it anymore.

"May I please ask that you be careful about touching other males tonight, and allowing them to touch you? I know I sound like a jealous—"

"No, I get it. I understand that shifters are weird about that. Kingsley makes it awkward."

"If you knew Earnessa, you'd know why. She's as possessive as any alpha. Kingsley loves that about her." He took a deep breath, whipping the car around the corner. Unlike with Damarion, his speed didn't bother me at all, probably because I knew he was in complete control. He was always in complete control, unless someone was threatening me. Or when we were twisted in each other's bodies, not knowing where he ended and I began.

"I will control myself to the best of my ability. I trust you implicitly…I hope you know that. Logic fights my beast most of the time, but at a certain point, my animal takes over. Especially now, since we've made love…"

"Austin, trust me, I do not want random guys touching me. You're not asking much, and I understand why you're asking at all."

He jammed the gear stick up and stepped on the gas, the car shooting forward as it climbed the onramp to the highway.

My lips pulled to the side of their own accord, half a smile. "But I hope you know this goes both ways—you can't ask me to follow a rule you won't follow. That's not how I roll."

Shadows passed through his eyes. "I remember my mom and dad fighting about that when I was a kid. He'd fly off the handle when she so much as smiled at a male, but he used to cheat on her left and right." He shook his head. "It was a messed-up situation."

"I won't let you turn into your father. Not only out of duty to you, but mostly because no one has time for that. I will be treated well, or I will leave."

"If I ever act out of turn, do as any alpha female would. Make me submit to you. You have the power to do it." He rolled his shoulders, the dash lights highlighting his handsome face. "I will do anything for you, Jacinta. And that includes fighting my animal to do right by you, at every turn if I need to."

I placed my hand on his thigh. He pulled his hand from the shifter and covered mine.

"You still don't give yourself enough credit, but okay," I said. "I'll keep you in line if things ever go topsy-turvy."

A smirk played on his lips, his dark mood lifting a little. "And if you get out of line, I promise to throw chocolate at you and run."

I laughed. "Yes, good thinking."

The closer we got to the restaurant, the more my stomach twisted.

"Have any of your people seen them yet?" I asked, leaving my hand on his thigh when he changed gears and slowed the car, pulling into a long driveway with dense trees to either side. I knew he had shifters patrolling the area in animal form, watching in case anything went wrong.

"Yes. We've been monitoring their team closely. It looks like they brought about a hundred people, though we're not yet sure what they're capable of, magically speaking."

"A hundred people?" I cried out. "Is that normal?"

"Kingsley doesn't think so. I wanted to ask Sebastian about it."

That didn't bode well for our "friendly" meetup.

I blew out a breath. "We definitely needed your brother's help."

The trees opened up and the restaurant glowed and twinkled ahead, pixie lights on poles lining a red carpet leading into the establishment. A perfect line of muscle-bound people waited on one side, hands clasped in front of them. The men wore black suits with red ties and matching pocket squares, and the women wore red dresses with loose bodices and long slits in the skirts. They'd be easy to get off in a hurry. Kace stood in the second position of the line, and Kingsley waited at the front, looking straight ahead, the broadest of them, his very stance and posture easily communicating that he'd give someone real trouble in a fight.

A line of limos waited in the parking lot beyond them, the first half-dozen long and black, just like those used by the Ivy House crew. Huge SUV limos took up residence on the other side of the parking lot, dwarfing the others, their number identical.

"Which limos did your people take?" I asked.

Austin pulled into a spot directly in front, next to the sign reading "owner." "The larger ones. Kingsley and Sebastian both said mages often think shifters are the animals they turn into. That we live in filth, don't have money, don't have a sense of status or the ability to play politics, don't have class…"

"You're going to rub their faces in it."

"Yes, I am." He grinned at me before grabbing the door handle. "And I'm going to scare the ever-loving shit out of them while I'm at it."

I pulled a vial of pink revealing potion from my clutch and drank it. "Do you want one?"

"Not at the moment. I'll let you know if I think I need it."

"Did the other shifters take it?"

"Those who've already shifted have, but Kingsley wanted to see if his people that are out in plain view could sense the lurkers. They all have a vial on their person, though, so if they need it, they have it."

In the weeks leading up to this visit, Sebastian had been testing the shifters in every way he could think of. His findings had made him even warier of shifters, something that, conversely, increased his delight in them. With a superior ability to hear and smell, and sometimes even a preternatural sense for foreign presences, the shifters weren't hindered by most concealing spells. Not all shifters were created equal, of course, but Kingsley's team and those Austin had selected to help with this endeavor were better than most. Still, shifters already in their animal form would have a hard time taking a potion without hands. Better to be safe than sorry.

Austin exited the car and adjusted his suit jacket before sauntering around to my door. After opening it, he bent to help me out of the car. He shut the door behind me and slipped his hand into his pocket, bending his other arm for me. His face was stern as his gaze zipped around the edges of the parking lot.

Figures stood near the trees, still as statues, silent as the grave. I couldn't see their faces within the shadow.

"Vampires," Austin murmured, escorting me to the top of the red carpet and stopping. Kingsley's eyes darted over. His very slight movements communicated something. Austin made no movements to answer that I saw or felt. "Younger ones, by the smell of it. Cheap labor. Not as dangerous."

The limos transporting my team stopped in front of the walkway, one at a time. The driver of the first opened the door, and Cyra climbed out, stumbling a little. The driver held out his hand, but she waved him away. She stepped to the side, sucked in a breath, and then sneezed, throwing her hands wide as she did so. Fire blew out of her mouth and nose. A shock wave of heat shed from her skin, not bothering her dress.

"Cover your mouth," Hollace said, standing beside and a little behind her, clasping his hands in front of him like the shifters were doing.

"I don't spread germs."

"Fire snot is still gross."

Niamh took her place beside and a little behind Hollace, forming the beginnings of a diagonal line. She was uncharacteristically quiet, staring straight ahead with her hands at her sides. She didn't have a quip for her neighbors or even seem to notice the lurkers around the area. I'd given the revealing potions to everyone, so she'd see them all, but she didn't appear to notice or care.

"What's wrong with Niamh?" I asked, feeling anticipation through the link.

My vision wobbled and hazed over, the potion taking effect, and a few more figures popped into the area, one out near the limos, a couple milling around in the open spaces between the building and the trees, and a few waiting off to the left, on the other side of the walkway from the shifters, giving Austin and me a wide berth. Only one invisible mage waited near the line of shifters, near the front corner of the building. He shifted and fidgeted often, and I wondered if he'd managed to deaden his noise and smell as well as his visual footprint. If not, he was not even close to invisible to that line of lethal shifters. Nor could he run fast enough if they decided to attack.

"Niamh's playing a role, like all of us." Austin continued to wait patiently, no longer looking around the area. "Well…" He looked down at me, smiling. "Maybe not like you."

"You're going to allow yourself to smile?" I whispered.

"To you? Yes. To this visiting party? Only if I am silently promising to kill them."

Edgar was the last out of the second limo, and upon seeing the vampires waiting around the restaurant at the tree line, he puffed into a swarm of insects and zipped to his position behind them.

"Even Edgar has a role to play, and he just showed that he is the most lethal vampire on these grounds," Austin murmured, his voice so low that I barely made out the words. "Hopefully he remembers not to speak and ruin the illusion."

Only powerful vampires could change into a swarm

of insects. In his prime, Edgar had been an extremely powerful vampire, but vampires could get too old, just like everyone else. Although old age wouldn't kill them, it did steal some of their facilities—their minds went fuzzy, they became weaker, and they lost the ability to stalk prey as effectively. Ivy House had restored Edgar's abilities, if not his mind. Which was why we'd told him to remain the silent menace and, for the love of God, stand up straight and try not to run. He looked ridiculous when he ran.

Movement caught my eye to the left.

"Don't look," Austin murmured.

In a moment, I saw why.

Sebastian wandered out of the trees. Austin must've smelled him. He was completely at ease, his poise more confident than I could remember, shoulders back and spine straight. It struck me that he always cowered around the shifters, showing his submission to their more dominant personas, but now, around other mages and on the offensive (even if invisible to them), he was clearly in his element.

He strolled through the space seemingly without a care in the world, like he could wipe the floor with every person he saw, vampires included. He walked right past them, lingering briefly, sometimes so close that he could lean over and blow into their faces. If they'd reached out, they could have pulled him into a hug. The Ivy

House potion was clearly beyond any revealing potion these people possessed. Sebastian had been right. Good news.

He met us at the beginning of the walkway as Austin looked back at our line of people.

"Thanks for waiting, alpha," he said, stepping behind me. Austin wouldn't be able to hear him, though, not with that potion. I relayed what was said in as low of an undertone as I could muster.

"He didn't take the potion?" Sebastian asked me.

I barely shook my head, not wanting to draw attention to the fact that I was talking to someone.

"Then tell him, when you can, that those vampires will be easy prey for his shifters. Their power scale is nothing. The mage must have brought in this many people because he's wary of the shifters. He has people hiding in the trees, but they're not bothering to mask their smell." He laughed. "He has no idea what he is walking into. Absolutely no idea."

"Shall we?" Austin asked me.

"Of course," I said.

"Use your magic inside, miss," Sebastian said, following close behind us. "You will be safe here tonight. The shifters have the outside covered, and your alpha and I will protect you inside, but you need to practice. Keep your wits. Just like any meeting with an established mage, you're entering the snake pit."

CHAPTER 30

J ESS TENSED BESIDE Austin as they entered the restaurant. The only renovations Austin had been able to pull off were freshening up the paint and decor. There was a lot more work planned, but hopefully it would serve its purpose for the first meeting.

Janet stood at a small podium in the waiting area, a fresh-faced twenty-something who'd been in the area for a while but had rarely visited O'Briens. She was a raccoon shifter, but she seemed to have very little interest in a magical life and zero interest in joining a pack. She hadn't been thrilled to learn Austin had taken over the restaurant. It was a shame—a raccoon would be a good spy, able to get out of tight corners with ease. Mean little buggers, raccoons. Were-raccoons were ten times worse when cornered.

"Mr. Steele, good evening." Her smile was entirely forced. It could've been a reaction to him, or perhaps to the invisible presence standing off to her right. This mage's invisibility potion wasn't nearly as good as

Sebastian's—it didn't even mask scent. He'd thought smell and sight went hand in hand with those potions, but clearly they came in all sizes.

Why bother at all? They had to know every shifter and probably gargoyle in this place would be able to pinpoint their silent watchers. Were they shortsighted, stupid, or simply ignorant of what shifters could do? This night would be telling.

Janet's gaze slid to Jess. "Miss Ironheart, welcome."

"Who?" Jess looked behind her.

"That's the name they've given you," Austin murmured as a line formed between Janet's brows.

"Oh, really? Who did?"

"I'm not sure who started it, but my territory all seems to agree." He slid his arm around Jess's waist and let his hand rest on her hip.

"Janet, show us to our guest—"

But Jess wiggled her fingers and swept her arm toward the dining area. "There's some kind of ward up," she murmured. Then she cocked her head as if listening to something. Sebastian.

Rage boiled through the link from Jess, and her hands balled into fists. She closed her eyes and took a deep breath.

"They created a ward in the dining room to keep shifters out," she said in a tight but even tone. "You are apparently not welcome in your own restaurant, Austin. What do you think of that? This mage has zero respect for me and my crew, because he and his friends aren't asking me to come without my shifter date—they are trying to *tell* me, like I'm a child. They are trying to force me to do what they want." She paused for a moment. "Be calm. Yeah, right," she murmured. "Austin, if you want, you can tear down that ward yourself. Sebastian seems to think you can do it. There is a woman standing on your left trying to break out of the binding and gagging spell I currently have on her. Sebastian says I shouldn't show my power level yet, but I'm having a slight rage problem, and I'm not exactly in control."

Desire pooled hot at his future mate's protectiveness of him, and he constricted his arm, pulling her tightly against him. Her soft moan nearly undid him.

"No problem," he said, walking forward with her.

"He's in the center of the room, Mr. Steele," Janet said. "He chose the table. It seems like..." Her brow wrinkled. "This is just a hunch, but there's more than meets the eye in that room. I wouldn't be surprised if there's danger in there I can't actually see. Mages are underhanded like that. They put up that ward right after I seated him, so they might've changed the seating arrangement."

"You'd be a damn fine asset to my pack, Janet," Austin said, reaching what felt like an elastic wall. He didn't see her reaction as he swelled his power and forced another step, then another, the wall trying to keep him put as he continued to push it back. If he was in his animal form, he could tear through this thing no problem. Trying to be civilized about it took a little more effort.

With a last push forward, it felt like the resistance snapped, falling away.

"Sebastian is asking how easy that was," Jess whispered. The woman she'd magically subdued couldn't be the only watcher, but he couldn't feel the others at present. Maybe they weren't close.

"No sweat," he said as they walked past a potted plant and then the bar on their left, a lone bartender waiting behind it.

"Just follow the alpha back," he heard Janet say, and felt the rest of the Ivy House crew following them in.

"I agree," Jess murmured, her fingers moving, her body close to him.

"What's that?" he asked.

"They clearly don't know how adept shifters are with scent," she replied, barely a whisper as they entered the main floor of the restaurant, the lights turned low and candles glittering in crystal holders on each of the square tables swathed in white tablecloths. "They might be trying to intimidate you. They spared some time and power by using potions that only cut out sight. If they ever battle a shifter, they'll get a rude awakening."

"More than one," Austin said.

Their man sat at one of the center tables, his bald head reflecting the light and his black suit a tad big in the shoulders. A beautiful brunette sat on his right, less than half his age, in a dress barely containing her chest. From the way she smiled at him and batted her lashes, she wasn't a constant in his life and clearly wanted to be. She'd be in it for the money or the power—or both. It couldn't be about his looks, with his pointed face and big nose.

The tables directly around him sat empty, but clusters of his people were dotted throughout the rest of the space.

"The back wall is lined with invisible mages, and a bunch of people are on the side and at the entrance to the other dining area," Jess said softly. "The back corner table of six is full."

Austin glanced there and then away, the chairs pulled out enough to fit a person, whereas the rest of the empty chairs were pressed up close. Pretty obvious, that, if someone knew what they were looking for.

Did they think Jess and her people were stupid, or

just incredibly naive?

She gave the mage a tight smile after stopping behind the open chairs opposite him. "Mr. Kinsella, lovely to meet you."

His shrewd brown-eyed gaze took in her face and then dress, lingering on the necklace. He waved the woman at his side away like a fly. She stood without a word and slunk to one of the back tables. No one joined her.

"Yes. Ms. Evans." He gestured at the chair in front of him, not bothering to stand for her or show common courtesy. He clearly thought she was well beneath him.

Anger simmered deep within Austin's gut, but he pushed it down. This was not the time or place to let his feelings for Jess provoke his animal. She could use this contact in the magical world. He wouldn't get in her way.

He pulled the chair out for her.

"I see you let him through." The mage didn't look at Austin. "I didn't think you'd even know what the ward was, new as you are to magic."

Jess's rage boiled again and her hands tightened at her sides. The mage noticed, and a tiny grin played on his colorless lips. He liked that he was getting to her.

"I've heard of him," Kinsella said. "The bear who killed the phoenix, right? Tall tales, of course, but I like fables as much as the next mage." That watery-eyed stare slid to Austin. Kinsella flinched when he met Austin's gaze and pulled back into himself, his shoulders rolling forward, compressing his chest. A primal defensive technique to protect the vitals.

Jess slowly lowered into the chair. She didn't comment.

Her people filed into the room, spreading out, choosing tables alone or in pairs. Niamh sat across from one of Kinsella's people, and his brow lowered in annoyance. She winked at him. Only two tables were left vacant.

Kinsella observed them as they came in and sat, his eyes narrowing at Cyra. Fire puffed in her wake.

"Is that actually a phoenix?" he asked. "Wow. What do they cost? I don't know anyone else who has one."

"She is actually a phoenix, yes." Jess clasped her fingers in her lap. "They're free, if you believe in fables."

Kinsella watched her for a beat, and Austin pulled out the chair next to her, half wondering if maybe he should find somewhere else to be. This mage would make an issue of having Austin so close. Kinsella's body language indicated he was trying to ignore the fear racing through him at Austin's power and proximity. Trying to assure himself that his magic and/or his people would—*could*—subdue Austin if anything went wrong. He was desperately trying to put on a brave face.

The foolishness of it made Austin appreciate Sebastian, who'd never tried to conceal his fear. Somewhere along the way, he'd stopped being wary of Sebastian, and clearly for good reason. He didn't seem to be like this mage at all.

Pretend all you want, but we both know the status quo, and we both know I am no fable.

"Peculiar, your situation, isn't it?" Kinsella rested his forearm on the table.

Jess cocked her head, listening. If these mages could see Sebastian, they gave no sign of it.

"If you plan on breaking custom, so will I." Jess put a hand on the table as well.

Kinsella's eyes twinkled, but he kept his hand where it was. He thought he was the bigger player here, and the hand thing was an intimidation tactic if Austin had ever seen one. He thought he could get a spell off before Jess could counter. He was an utter fool.

"You were a Jane, and a magical house gave you a little power." His smile was insulting. "Lucky you. But you'll always be a Jane at heart."

Anger throbbed within Austin as he sat down. He pushed it away. Forced it back. He needed to let Jess handle this.

"Clearly you don't think much of Janes," Jess said as

the waitress approached.

The woman handed out menus and asked, "May I get you something to drink?"

After they ordered, Kinsella said, "Dicks and Janes are inferior. It's nothing personal."

"Ah, but I did get a little magic, so…"

Kinsella narrowed his eyes, looking at her as though he wanted to tilt back her cranium and get a peek at her brain.

"Yes, you did. I looked the house up. Back in the day, it had much status. Its mistresses have always had large quantities of power. How far it has fallen now, hmm? It had to elevate a Jane so that it could be said to have elevated someone at all. When you start below nothing, rising up is not hard."

"This is true," she said, and Austin's anger throbbed. He wanted to reach over the table, rip this fool out of his chair, and tear him apart.

"Tell me, why is Elliot Graves interested in you?" Kinsella asked. "Don't get me wrong, the joke was a nice touch, sending a team of animals at you when you employ animals. He's always had a strange sense of humor."

"Do you know him, then?"

"I've met him a time or two. If he didn't have so much magic, he'd be a laughingstock. He might have had high status for a while, but he fell into obscurity. He's a has-been."

"Then why do you care that he's interested in me?"

Kinsella shrugged. "Curiosity. He has never been interested in anyone. Why you? What am I missing?"

"Fashion sense. Tact. Manners. A good barber..." she murmured, so softly that Austin could barely hear. Given a mage's hearing was nothing compared to a shifter, Kinsella wouldn't be the wiser.

It took everything Austin had not to bark out a laugh.

"Is it the money?" Kinsella wondered aloud. "That house had wealth back in the day, correct? It's been a long time. Does it still have holdings?" His gaze dipped to the necklace adorning her neck.

"Austin Steele gave me this, actually." Jess touched his shoulder as she said it.

Kinsella laughed. "Sure, sure. Why not, huh?"

Jess frowned, not understanding the joke. Austin didn't require clarification: Kinsella thought the notion of a shifter with money preposterous.

He leaned forward a little, as though getting intimate. "Why don't you send away your lap dog? You're perfectly safe."

Austin didn't need the link to know the rage Jess had barely been keeping at bay was finally crashing over her and dragging her under. It rolled across her face and screamed through every line in her suddenly tense body. Her beast was emerging. The female gargoyle was indeed a violent species where it concerned her intended mate.

He thought about touching her arm to reassure her it was fine—that he could change tables—but Niamh's movement at the edge of his vision caught his notice. She was looking directly at him and shaking her head. *Don't interfere.*

"If you disrespect him like that again," Jess said in a deathly quiet voice, "I will kill you where you sit, do you understand me?"

Kinsella's eyebrows lowered and a spark of anger lit his eyes. Cunning took its place.

"Oh, now I see," he said, leaning back and placing his other hand on the table. Austin felt a hand press down on his shoulder and squeeze twice, reassuringly. Sebastian. Like Niamh, he was telling Austin to stay put, to leave this to Jess. "You like to bed filthy, dimwitted *animals.*"

A jet of red zipped from Kinsella's fingers, and Austin couldn't stop himself from jumping up and reaching for Jess. Only he didn't get his butt far off the seat before a hard rush of magic slammed him back down. A comforting feeling came through the link with Jess. She was the one who'd held him in place.

The red jet of magic hit the air right in front of her chest and dissolved. She shoved out her hands, and tables skidded across the floor, chairs toppling over. Some were empty—belonging to the invisible people, Austin felt sure—and others contained Kinsella's associates, who were then shoved against the far wall. They cried out as they were magically pinned.

Jess's people still sat calmly in their places, untouched.

Kinsella's eyes widened. He shook in his place, trying to get up and unable to move.

"I did warn you," Jess said with a little smile. "Apparently I shouldn't kill you, though. Something to do with the Mages' Guild? I didn't even know there was such a thing before you sent the invite. Doesn't matter. I don't need to kill you to make an example of you."

Kinsella screamed before his feet were ripped out from under him. They saw the sky as his body was dragged off his chair and hoisted up into the middle of the room.

"Austin did force the phoenix to submit." Jess clasped her hands in her lap. "He owns this restaurant and bought the jewels I'm wearing. And no, I didn't know what that ward was out front. My associate had to tell me. He then told Austin he could break it by walking through it. Which Austin did. No problem.

You don't even have half the power my boyfriend has." She put her hand on Austin's arm. "My boyfriend, the animal, in case that wasn't clear. I turn into a gargoyle, did anyone tell you that? I'm an animal, too, I suppose. And you are a clown." She stood. "Oh, and my associate has been here the whole time. I'm sure you took a revealing potion, but you couldn't reveal my invisibility potion, could you? Your people are disguised very poorly."

Her chair moved backward, seemingly by itself, before it pulled to the side and out of the way.

Kinsella's eyes widened further. Apparently the invisibility potion he couldn't detect was more surprising to him than anything else that had happened.

"Sorry you had to come all this way." She took a step back, and the invisible hold she'd had on Austin released, allowing him to stand. She took his hand. "But it's pretty clear we can't be friends." She turned to go, but stopped. "Oh, and I saw your fear when you looked at Austin Steele earlier. The only reason he didn't tear you apart was out of respect for me. Next time, he can do as he pleases. Trust me, you'd rather deal with me."

As she turned, Kinsella fell from the sky, landing on the chair and crashing to the ground.

"That sounded like it hurt," she said, holding Austin's hand on the way out. Her people stood and followed without a word.

Outside, Kingsley lifted his eyebrows.

"Make sure they leave without destroying anything," Austin told him.

"Sebastian—stop laughing—you stay too." Jess looked behind her. "Make sure none of ours get hurt."

"What about us?" Niamh called as Austin pulled the door open for Jess.

"We should go." Cyra pushed her glasses farther up her nose with her pointer finger. "That man's ego was very fragile. Jessie made him feel small—rightly so—and he will seek revenge. He seemed clueless. It would be best to surprise him with our—all of our—talents."

"She has a valid point," Austin said. Then he waited for Jess's response, making sure Cyra saw that Jess had the final word in this crew. If there'd been a question on leadership, he'd just helped Cyra answer it.

"They have a lot of people, though," she said, and concern bled through the link. "They have a lot of mages and who knows what else. Kingsley's people are outnumbered."

Austin huffed out a laugh. "But not even close to outmatched. We have a lot of shifters in the woods. He'll be fine."

She shrugged. "Okay, then. Let's go back to Ivy House. I'm starving. I would've liked to try the food there. It's a nice restaurant."

"We'll come back when the company is better." He

closed the door, and Sebastian appeared five feet away, putting an empty vial into his pocket.

"Any intelligent mage would pack it in and head out after that scene inside," Sebastian said. "She gave him a show of her true power, and a smart mage would know when he was beaten. This mage is a moron, and Cyra is right: he has a fragile ego and will not think kindly on Jessie's"—he shook with laughter, having a hard time getting the words out—"response." He laughed harder and wiped his eyes. "Her response was so brazen it was comical. Mages and power players are usually subtle and sly to their enemy's faces and then cunning and lethal behind their backs. Jessie just made him look like a chump!" He held his stomach and guffawed. "In front of all his people!"

"Is there a point?" Austin asked.

"Yes, sorry." Sebastian wiped his eyes again. "Sorry! Yes. The point is…" He straightened up. "The point is that this mage will want to get even. You haven't seen the last of him. If—when—they engage, make sure your shifters make your response a spectacle. The more brutal, the better. Most mages I know think like he does. Even I had no idea of your power. Of your types of power. To best protect Miss Ironheart, you should make a display my kind will think twice about before deciding to engage."

CHAPTER 31

"**W**HAT AN ABSOLUTE…" I huffed out a breath, trying to think of a swear big enough for Kinsella, and pushed back in my seat as Austin hit the gas and the car lurched forward. "Drive fast. I'm still really angry about the things that mage said about you. Lap dog…" My jaw ached from clenching it so hard. "He was clearly afraid of you. Who was he trying to fool? He was spitting in my eye, that's what he was doing."

Lust filtered through the link. Delight. Austin was responding to my possessiveness. He probably thought it was funny, like Sebastian did, but my God, when that idiot mage was so dismissive of Austin, it had set something off in me that I couldn't hope to control. It was like a tidal wave of black rage had wiped out all my logical thinking and ability to reason. All I'd wanted to do was kill. If Sebastian hadn't talked me around, I would've. It had been a very close call.

I looked at my incredibly handsome boyfriend in

his slick suit, the red dash lights highlighting his cheekbones and shapely lips. Maybe it was time to ask the guys about mating as a female gargoyle. Ulric would know the scoop, and if he didn't, he'd find out. I needed to know what was coming my way. This thing between Austin and me might blow over in a couple of days maybe, but...

I stopped that thought even as my heart surged, expanding until it filled my whole chest. My whole being. No one had ever supported me like Austin did. He'd always bent over backwards to accommodate me, to change his life to make mine easier, and he'd ignored that awful man's slights tonight so I could keep the meeting peaceful if I wanted to. At one point, he would've even allowed that disgusting human being to wave him away from the table like he had that woman. Austin would've endured the treatment...for me.

The feeling swelled until I could barely stand it. Until I had to reach out and touch him, placing my hand on his thigh, the urge to straddle his lap overwhelming.

"Thank you," I said softly. "For everything."

He sped onto the highway before covering my hand with his. "I'm at your service."

This wasn't going to blow over. Maybe some would call this a rebound—the divorce had only gone down a year ago—but it felt like I'd finally found my home.

Finally found the person who both grounded me and lifted me up. There weren't one in a million guys like Austin Steele, and having met his brother, I knew he came from a family of good, solid people. This wasn't an act. Why keep looking when I'd found someone who was perfect for me?

I let my head fall back against the headrest and looked out the window, taking a deep breath.

"I really like you," I whispered.

"I really like you too," he replied, just as quietly, his words almost inaudible over the roar of the engine. "I've always really liked you, since the first moment you walked into my bar."

I felt the warmth of his thigh through my palm, and I increased the sensitivity of the link so he could feel the aching for him in my core. He sucked in a breath, and I smiled.

"Ironheart," I said. "Do the people of this town think I'm a jerk, or something?" I asked as he slowed for a turn. "Why else would they give me a name like that? Iron is worse than a heart of stone."

Austin chuckled. "I think the iron alludes to your strength. It's one of the hardest metals on earth, and it's been a go-to metal for tool and weapons makers throughout the ages. It's also one of the components in steel. I think the whole town knows the pack wouldn't exist without you. They know that I do all this for you. To protect you."

I wiped a tear away. "Stop being so sweet. It's ruining my makeup."

He smiled and squeezed my hand. "Heart refers to your generous heart. Your empathy. Your mercy. You always think of the safety of those around you. Everyone in this town knows they can count on you clearing them out and keeping them safe whenever anything dangerous happens in a crowded place. You are strong and your heart is pure. Ironheart."

"Wow." I didn't know what else to say. That was incredibly touching. It was better than any name I could have chosen for myself.

"Haven't you ever wondered why Ryan sits near you?"

I frowned at his mention of Sasquatch, but I had to admit, yes I did. He got so much abuse from Niamh, and he couldn't stand me. Yet he always seemed to sit near us.

"He isn't much of a shifter, but he knows how to survive," Austin said. "He chooses the safest place in the bar. When you're there, it is near you."

Now I *really* didn't know what to say.

"Kingsley told me that I'd leveled up with you." He slowed as he approached Ivy House. "I agree with him."

"I think you guys have that backwards."

"Agree to disagree. Do you mind if I stay tonight? I'd take you to my house, but under the circumstances, I think Ivy House is safer."

"You never have to ask. The answer is always yes."

"You say that now. Wait until I piss you off." He turned off the car and got out. He opened my door a moment later and reached down to help me out.

"I don't think it's me you have to worry about when it comes to that." I stepped close, pressing my body firmly against his. "It's pissing off Ivy House that you should be wary of."

"Until you get rid of those dolls, I'd have to agree." He leaned down and met my lips with his, his kiss deep and sensual. He shut the car door before swooping me up into his arms and holding me to his chest. "It was hot when you defended my honor." He started walking to the house. "No wonder Kingsley never checks Earnessa when she violently reacts to other women flirting with him."

"Shifters are nuts."

"Apparently so are female gargoyles."

"Did you hear what that guy said about Elliot Graves? He confirmed what Sebastian said. He's a has-been."

"Yes. In all of this, it has become increasingly apparent how ignorant we are of the larger world of magic. You're not to blame, obviously, but the rest of us have practically been hibernating from the rest of the world. My brother has not been subtle in his disapproval. When this is over, we'll need to remedy that."

"But why is Elliot so obsessed with me and Ivy House?"

"A comeback, maybe? Wanting to use your magic to be relevant again? It's clear he's still being heavily watched. He might not be a player right now, but he's not obscure."

Ivy House opened the front door for us. Once inside, Austin didn't set me down. He carried me up the stairs and into my bedroom, closing the door with a sweep of his foot. He gently lowered me to the ground and sucked in my bottom lip, his hands on my hips and then my breasts.

I moaned into his mouth, hurrying to undo his buttons and push the jacket off those large shoulders. He slipped my necklace beneath the neck of my dress before bending and grabbing the bottom. He pulled the dress up and off, flinging it onto the bed. I untied the bow tie, finished the buttons on his dress shirt, and slipped my hands down to his pants as he pulled the tails of the shirt from the base of his trousers and dropped it to the ground.

One warm hand on my shoulder, he held me put while pressing his palm against the necklace lying against my bare skin. I hadn't worn a bra with the dress, since the straps would have shown and I no longer needed one for support (thank you, Ivy House), so now he let his fingers trail over my budded nipples.

"Your boyfriend?" His voice was deep and thick.

I slipped out of his grip so as to push his pants and boxers to the ground. As he slipped out of his shoes and then the fabric, I hooked my thumbs into the straps of my lacy little thong.

"Leave that," he said, walking me to the edge of the bed, his large erection trapped between our bodies. "The heels, too."

Excitement and anticipation bit through me.

"I didn't know what else to call you." I ran my hands up his chest, my fingers outlining his cut muscles. "Sorry if I overstepped, but I wanted—"

His mouth on mine cut off my words. His tongue swept through my mouth and then plunged in deep. His fingers encircled my nipples before he reached down low and traced the edges of lace between my thighs.

"I'd like to retain that title, if you don't mind." He picked me up and then gently lowered me onto the bed before crawling over me, hands on my knees spreading me wide. He sat back, his length standing large and proud; I salivated for the taste and feel of him.

His gaze roamed my body slowly. He was not touching, just looking.

"There is only one, Jacinta." He curled his fingers around my ankle before lifting it to his shoulder. "When it comes to mating, I am firmly convinced that there is only one for each of us." My other ankle followed the first, on his other shoulder. My hair was splayed across the pillow and my necklace rested just above my exposed breasts. "I am equally convinced that I have found that one for me. There could be no other. Not for me."

He traced down the outsides of my legs and stopped on my hips. He bent forward, his shoulders lowering until they fit into the crease of my knees. One hand traced the edges of the lace panties again, and I arched back, needing that touch to drift toward the center. Needing it deeper.

"For me, there is only you." He moved the slip of fabric to the side, trailing his tongue up the middle of me.

I pulled in a deep breath, soaking in that feeling, focusing on that tricky tongue, the fingers plunging deep. I let out a breath slowly, my legs falling from him and spreading even wider, wanting to give him all the access I hoped he'd use.

He lifted and slipped my panties off, his mouth on me again, drawing out my moans. Winding me tighter. His tongue doing dizzying circles.

I threaded my fingers through his hair, cried his name, and shuddered with a violent climax.

He kissed up my stomach before sucking in a nipple. He massaged me down low again, readying me for the next dizzying orgasm.

His body pushed me into the soft mattress, and I wrapped my legs around him, the pounding in my middle harder than that in my core. I kissed him with all the passion and desperation I felt.

"I don't remember how I felt first with the ex," I said softly, needing to say my piece, needing him to know where I stood. "I remember being in love, but I was so young. I didn't really understand what I was getting myself into. Love changes as you get older. It isn't just about that initial rush of feeling; it's about the capacity for mutual respect and compromise. It's about how two people take care of each other, honor each other, and trust each other. I wasn't mature enough to recognize that. I've never experienced all of that with someone. But I feel all of that with you. I only want to take it slow so I can be sure. So I can avoid repeating my mistakes. I already trust you implicitly—I just want to trust myself too."

His eyes were so deep and blue. He kissed me softly. "I meant what I said. I won't rush you. Take your time figuring it all out. I'll be here when you inevitably come begging." His smile was smug.

I laughed and slid my hands up his arms and around his neck. He kissed me, pressing himself against me, and just like that, my anticipation was building again.

"In the meantime, I'll revel in your body." He ran his lips down my throat and growled softly.

"Why does that turn me on so much?" I asked, breathless.

"Because you sense the danger of a predator at your neck." He ran his lips down and across my collarbone. "You submit to me every time you feel it, trusting me with your life. You didn't always get off on it. You do now because of what I do to you after."

He enclosed a budded nipple in his mouth and softly ran his teeth over it. I shivered with the feeling, eyes closed, and arched up to meet him.

"What about if I did that to you?" I asked, guiding his hand down between my legs.

He pushed two fingers into me, his pace slow and deep, his thumb massaging on top.

"I'd get turned on too, especially if you sat on me while you did it."

It took no time at all for me to flip him onto his back and lower myself onto him, trapping his hard length between our bodies. I unhooked the necklace, and as I leaned over to place it on a side table, the tips of his fingers glanced off my core. I moaned softly, taking off the earrings and bracelet before moving back over him. I kissed up his chest and along the side of his neck.

He breathed softly, and a glance revealed his eyes were closed and his mouth had dropped open. He lightly cupped my breasts, stroking my nipples. It was an amazing sort of distraction.

I kissed his lips, and he slid his hands from my breasts up around my neck and shoulders. I trailed kisses down slowly, from his chin with the light stubble to the underside of his jaw and then the top of his throat. His breathing quickened, and I couldn't help a smile. I moved a little slower and a little lower, feeling each hollow between bones. I reached his Adam's apple and scraped my teeth along it. He shivered under me.

"I've never let anyone do that," he said, spreading his hands down my back.

"What about Destiny?"

"No. She tried, but I never allowed her. I didn't think I was capable of allowing myself to be so vulnerable."

"I've kissed your neck before." I lifted up a little and

leaned forward, his tip dragging against me and then finding my entrance. I only sat enough to keep it put.

"You didn't notice, but I moved just enough to keep you to the sides. Not directly down my throat."

I kissed lower still, at the base of his neck before starting back up. "I couldn't kill you like this."

"No, but it's… It's hard to explain." He squeezed my arms as I made another pass, applying a little more pressure this time, feeling his heart thump under my palm. "It's a vulnerable place. A shifter won't heal in time from a wound like a slit throat, or someone ripping our throats out. We'd bleed out too fast. Allowing someone access, even like this, is…a feat of trust."

"You wouldn't bleed out too fast." I kissed his lips and circled my hips, toying with pressure, his hard length slipping in just a bit before I moved away.

"Damn it, Jacinta," he growled, pushing upward. I evaded, not letting him find purchase.

"I'd heal you before you died," I said against his lips, kissing him hard, moving my body around him. Anticipation built.

"My shield," he said, pushing his chin up, inviting me in again.

I raked my teeth along his throat as I sat down hard, moaning with the sensation. He crushed me to his chest, control fleeing in an instant. He pumped upward, spearing me deliciously, and I pushed against him, getting him deep.

He sat up, his arms around me, helping me bob atop him, kissing my neck and my lips. And again I was lost to it, unable to think beyond the feel of our bodies intertwined, the heat within me, the feel of him.

I groaned, gyrating, winding tighter, pleasure bearing down on me from all sides, almost unbearable in its intensity.

An orgasm ripped his name from my lips, filling the room. Sensation filled my world. He shuddered below me, and I clung to him, breathing heavily. But he kept moving, going for one more and getting it a moment later. He pulled my hair with his release, and I smiled harder than I ever had as yet another wave of bliss washed through me, cracking me apart and piecing me together again.

I wilted over him in the aftermath, completely spent. So full of warmth and light.

Still holding me to him, he lay back, cradling me above him.

"Sex has never felt this good before," he said, his breathing starting to even out. "It's so easy with you. I barely have to try, and I'm always ready. Always. I'm never sated. I'm almost at the point of asking my brother if it's a medical condition, or part of the mating, or what."

"If it's a medical condition, I hope there is no cure," I said, my eyelids drooping. I felt the rest of the team in the house, having come back sometime during our lovemaking.

He stroked my hair. "We should probably go down to them and discuss what happened."

"We should. Sebastian doesn't think that mage is going anywhere."

Austin was silent for a moment, softly stroking my hair. "Do you think he has access to better forces?"

"Sebastian has reason to believe that he could, and would, buy mercenaries."

He nodded but didn't say anything. Instead, he pressed his hands against my lower back and swung upward, hard again.

I put my worries out of my mind and lost myself again in Austin. There'd be plenty of time to worry tomorrow.

CHAPTER 32

TWO DAYS LATER, we all sat or stood around a circular white table in the backyard, the sun bright, the grass green, and the apology invitation open on the table, completely unbelievable.

Kinsella was sorry. He hadn't meant to offend me. He wanted to make it up to me with dinner and dancing at the banquet hall in O'Briens. I could bring my "friends."

He'd probably sneered as he wrote that word.

My rage was a hurricane inside of me.

"Why are we doing this outside?" Hollace asked, his glass of champagne almost empty.

"Because it's a nice day." Cyra's champagne was boiling, steam rising from the glass. She could transfer heat to anything with a simple touch. She apparently didn't much care for champagne.

"Yes." Mr. Tom slid a plate of melon slices wrapped in prosciutto onto the table. "Easter was so nice, I thought we might do something similar. I did not hide any eggs, though. I didn't want to offend God."

"That's not..." I shook my head, letting it go.

"This is a trap," Austin said, in jeans and a T-shirt, his hair rumpled and a spot of blood on his neck. A grizzly bear shifter had challenged him earlier in the day. He was happy to have acquired the shifter for his pack, but the sight of his gashes and seeping wounds had not made *me* happy. In the future, I intended to be at hand for challenges like that. I didn't give a crap how shifters did things—I would not allow someone to kill Austin.

"Traps are good. We get to flex our muscles," Cyra said.

"It takes a lot of the risk out of it when you come back from the dead." Ulric scanned the ground even though Mr. Tom had said he hadn't hidden any eggs.

"Yes, but dying still hurts," she replied. Little flames replaced the steam at the top of her glass. "Dying at the hand of the alpha was not pleasant."

Sebastian stood a few feet away in the sun, watching the basajaun eat flowers near the tree line. He'd come to check on me. The mage had foolishly sent the vampires after the shifters following our dinner, something that hadn't ended well for the vampires, and the basajaun had heard the fighting through the trees.

"I called the closest office of magical mercenaries,"

Sebastian said. "They're sold out. They had access to fifty contractors, but they wouldn't tell me if the same person took them all."

"There's an office for that stuff?" I asked, leaning my elbows on the table.

"Of course," he replied. "How else would you hire them?"

"That seems awfully civilized," I murmured.

"Tell me about the banquet hall," Kingsley said, sitting beside his brother.

Austin leaned back and rubbed his fingers through his hair. "It's a large facility used for weddings or special events, able to house...three hundred, probably. The inside is mostly open—there are four rooms: a main room, an entrance area, and a kitchen and dining room grouped together. Very few places to hide. The grounds are geared toward pictures and parking, mostly. There's a large lot with plenty of space for us to maneuver the limos. The trick is that the place is on a rolling hill leading up a mountain. Great views, but the only way in and out for a car is a narrow two-lane road with very few pullouts. Block that road, and you block road transportation."

"What do we care about road transportation?" Kingsley asked.

"Why do *we* care about road transportation?" Ulric

asked with a laugh. "That sounds like the perfect setup for fliers."

"If you go in," Kingsley told Austin, "you cannot leave until the battle is done. If you go running, it'll undermine Ivy House *and* your territory. Mercenaries for hire can be strong contenders. They have advanced weapons and are capable of handling all manner of magical creatures. Fifty or so of those plus whomever he's called in from home, plus the people we didn't take out the other night…"

"Failing to show won't look any better," Austin said. "Though we could just refuse his—"

"We're not going to fail to show, and we're not going to go running," I said. "I gave him an opportunity to leave. He chose to double down on being a dick. So now we'll send a message."

Sebastian nodded, still watching the basajaun. So was Edgar, quietly sitting at the table, his champagne untouched. Why anyone had poured him any, I had no clue.

"Kingsley, can I have a word?" Austin said before glancing back at me. "Jess?"

We walked a few paces away from the others, and I wrapped us in a soundproof bubble.

Austin's voice was low despite the spell protection. "I've dealt with mercenaries around here before. They are unnecessarily vicious and they don't fight fair. They aim to kill, and they can do it from a distance. They'll go for the most powerful first."

"Mercenaries are the same everywhere." Kingsley's hands stayed at his sides, but he somehow gave the illusion of flaring them wide, bracing for a fight. "His people were nothing. Those mercenaries will be our real adversaries."

"His people can be used to create chaos." Austin squared off with his brother, and I realized there was something behind the scenes here that I didn't understand. "Sheer numbers can dominate in something like this, and he'll have those numbers, I can feel it. They're going to try to trap us."

"Let them," Sebastian said, stepping toward us. Austin and his brother shot him fearsome looks, and he grimaced. "No one else can hear you, just me. Jess's spells are really coming along, but she hasn't fixed this one. It's pretty easy to circumvent. If I may…" He sidled closer, hunched a little and with his hands up—a defensive posture—and I expanded the bubble to include him. "They're trying to trap you. Let them. We have two powerful mages and the most fearsome alpha in the world, whose rage is tethered by a deteriorating leash. That's all we need to win."

"*Two* of the most fearsome alphas," Kingsley

growled.

"You have a family at home, Kingsley Barazza," Austin replied, his eyes hard. "This isn't your fight. You've been an incredible help to me, but my little niece needs a father. I nearly took you from her once. I will not do it again."

"Your little niece isn't so little anymore, and she would scold me if I walked away from Uncle Auzzie at a time like this." Kingsley leaned in a little, and my small hairs stood on end. "We're brothers. I've got your back, no matter what. I'm in this."

They stared at each other for a tense moment. Sebastian scooted away again, hunching even more now.

As though a bubble burst, both men breathed out and their postures relaxed. Austin held out his hand, and Kingsley grabbed it, pulling him into a bro hug.

"Don't think I won't call you if someone tries to steamroll my pack," Kingsley told Austin.

"I'd expect nothing less."

They stepped back, and I popped the bubble of silence, making a mental note to ask Sebastian how to make a better one.

"Now that *that's* settled, whatever it was"—Mr. Tom walked over with a silver tray laden with champagne—"care for another drink, anyone?"

"Do you have any beer?" Kingsley asked.

"At a garden party?" Mr. Tom put up his nose and pushed the tray forward. "I most certainly do not."

Kingsley took the champagne, staring Mr. Tom down all the while.

"Go ahead, do your worst," Mr. Tom responded. "I'm used to it."

Austin turned to Sebastian. "You said two powerful mages. Do you plan to do more than lurk this time?"

Sebastian gave a humorless grin. "I most certainly do. And I can't wait to see their faces when I let the magic fly."

✧   ✧   ✧

I'D ACCEPTED THE invitation shortly after receiving it, and now, two days later, we were preparing to walk into the belly of the beast.

Austin sat at the table by my bedroom window, waiting for me to finish getting ready. He had on jeans and a T-shirt (we'd decided there was no point in being uncomfortable for what was surely going to be a battle). His people were assembled and ready, along with Kingsley and his people, all waiting at the base of the mountain in animal form. They would scale the mountain with Edgar, and Austin, Sebastian, and I would drive up. The basajaun, who'd offered to help because he'd overindulged in flowers at the forced garden party

(Niamh maintained that he'd done it on purpose because he wanted to come all along), would ride with us. Sebastian was the one who'd made the suggestion about the ride-along—he wanted to see the mages' face when they caught sight of our fearsome friend. Given the basajaun's great love was causing horrible surprises, he'd been tickled by the idea. The rest of my people would fly in as we drove, swooping down when the action started.

Speaking of my team…

"I want to give Cyra, Hollace, and Nathanial more time," I called to Austin, "because I haven't gotten to properly interact with them, but it seems like the right time to ask Sebastian to join the team. What do you think?"

"I'd say it's a good bet. He's done nothing but help you, and he gets along with everyone."

I nodded. "Good. I mean, we'll see how he does with the…possibly very awkward and embarrassing dinner and dancing coming up."

"Fat chance."

"We'll see how he does in the battle, then."

"I think the team is shaping up to be really strong, babe," he said, standing when I exited the bathroom.

I walked into his arms, needing a moment to lean on him, to soak in his strength. It still felt surreal that we were together, that someone as hot as him was calling me babe. The most desirable bachelor in the area, for Janes and magical people alike, had said he'd wait for me to come around and be his mate.

"Good," I said, "but I'm still not looking forward to this." I huffed out a shaky laugh. "You'd think I'd be used to fighting by now."

"I don't think you'll ever get used to bloodshed, but you, Jacinta Ironheart, are strong enough to bear anything."

"Let's hope." I pushed away from him lest I lose my nerve. "Showtime."

My people were waiting in the front, all in human form, all seemingly calm and ready. Austin's Jeep waited by the curb, the top off.

Ulric reached out and squeezed my arm supportively. "We've got this, Miss Jessie."

I smiled, nodding to Mr. Tom and the others as I passed them.

"No fancy car today?" I asked, turning to Austin.

"Nope." He stopped by the passenger door, in case I needed a hand in. "They get plain old me today. No bells and whistles."

"I don't think they are going to like plain old you. I have a feeling they will rethink their treatment of the bells-and-whistles you."

"I think you're right."

Sebastian and the basajaun climbed in after us, the basajaun completely scrunched in the smallish back seat with his legs half hanging over the side, and Sebastian sitting as far to the right as possible, squished against the roll bar.

"I'm now starting to rethink this driving idea," Sebastian murmured.

Austin started the Jeep, and my people shed their clothes, Niamh giving me a thumbs-up before changing into her nightmare alicorn form.

"You'll do great, miss," Mr. Tom yelled after me as Austin made his way down the street.

I felt Sebastian touch my arm from the back seat. "It'll be okay. You have a lot of people around you who will make sure nothing happens to you."

I took a deep breath. "I'm not concerned about me. I don't want anyone else to get hurt."

I thought I heard him mutter, "Ironheart," before he squeezed my arm and pulled back.

The banquet hall was on the outskirts of town. As Austin maneuvered the Jeep down the narrow road, I felt my people on their way, high in the sky. I couldn't see any shifters, but they'd never required invisibility spells to blend into the woods. The saffron-yellow sunlight was starting to fade by the time we reached the top of the hill, the mountain at our backs and the valley spanning out in front of us. This time, large passenger vans filled the lot instead of limos. It was obvious they weren't here to square-dance, and judging by the quantity, nearly a dozen, it was equally as clear that they had a great many people.

Nervousness tightened my gut. The sound of the Jeep's engine vibrated through the silence as Austin slowed down. Sebastian tapped my arm and passed up a vial, the revealing serum. Since we'd already discussed the likelihood that Kinsella would take a sneakier approach this time, hiding the mages' scents too, Austin also downed one of the vials. Bodies started popping into view.

Austin stopped at the beginning of the long driveway, the expansive lawn off to the left showcasing a picturesque white gazebo nestled into bright pink and blue flowers. The hill dropped away just beneath it, probably a steep slope to the valley below. A lone figure waited within the gazebo wearing a long black robe. He hadn't taken an invisibility potion, but everyone else around him had—mages clustered around the gazebo, lined up on either side, and loitered around the trees on my side of the car, too, at the base of the mountain.

"What a showboat," Sebastian said, clearly talking about Kinsella waiting for me in the gazebo.

"I don't understand why he went to the trouble of dosing them all with invisibility potion, knowing I can just create a revealing serum." Part of me wanted to sit on my shaking hands. I'd come to realize that the calm leading up to the battle greatly tested my courage. "Or did he think I'd keep it from the shifters?"

Sebastian chuckled low. "He has clearly spent the last two days making or procuring the very best he can get. He probably doesn't think your revealing spell is powerful enough to show his people. He's a fool who didn't pay attention the other night. And no, he surely doesn't think you gave all the shifters the revealing potion. Or that you could make so much in such a short time. Of course, he also doesn't know you had help." Out of the corner of my eye, I caught a vial being passed. "Here, basajaun. So you can see the surprise on their faces when you charge them away from the gazebo."

"Jess." Austin turned to me, a bleak look in his eyes. "This mage came to our territory, insulted us, and now plans to attack us on our own ground. That has to be grounds for an excusal from the Mages' Guild. We have to end this brutally. We have to make a statement. This isn't the time to show mercy. Make sure mercenaries everywhere use you—us—as a cautionary tale. Do you understand?"

"Yes," I said, sensing the truth in that. People would continue coming if they thought we were weak or lenient. "I just wish we were fighting Elliot Graves so we could end this once and for all."

"If this goes how I think it'll go," Sebastian said, "Domino Kinsella won't be the only one who hears the message. We ready?"

Austin turned off the engine and swung his legs out the open door. Apparently we'd be walking a ways.

As if hearing my thought, Austin said, "I want them to see what the big, hairy beast in the back is as he is running at them."

"Yes. That will be a better approach." The basajaun's hair bristled, making him look just that much bigger. He crawled out over the back of the car. "Should I go now?"

"No." Austin stripped off his shirt. "Jess and I will make the first approach. When they attack, we counter."

"Miss Jessie," Sebastian said, grabbing my arm. "Remember that shield spell we went over. Use it. Keep it around you at all times. It'll keep his spells off you."

I nodded and pulled it around me right then. Austin slipped out of his pants and immediately changed into his polar bear form. He started forward, and I kept pace, walking with my head held high, my body brimming with magic. Time to show Kinsella the goods. Maybe he'd be smart, apologize, and leave.

Fat chance.

Kinsella's people watched us approach, having created a funnel for us to walk down—a funnel that closed in behind us as we passed them, separating us from the basajaun. My heart beat faster, the pulse joined by Austin's. Our link was not just from Ivy House now, but from the strengthening bond growing between us. It comforted me. Energized me. Gave me just a bit more courage.

"He isn't even trying to hide that he's an animal anymore, hmm?" Kinsella gave Austin a look of pure disgust as we approached.

"Just like you aren't trying to hide your ridiculous taste in clothing. What is that, a nightshirt?" I stopped just before the gazebo. My people weren't far away, having stopped at the base of the hill to keep out of sight. I looked around. "No champagne? When I show up to dinner and dancing, I typically expect some sort of libation."

"I likely won't get any sort of status boost when I kill you and all your animals, but at least I will let Elliot Graves know that he is nothing. There is some consolation in that."

"You sure do know how to make a woman feel

treasured. Speaking of, where's your date? Or have you put away the Viagra for the night?"

His eyes narrowed slightly, and I actually found myself laughing.

"Struck a nerve with that one, did I?" I laughed harder.

"I will enjoy killing you," he spat.

"Actually, you won't even enjoy trying."

He threw out his hands, a zip of light speeding through the air at me. I braced myself, but the shield took it easily, the spell like one I've used before, but with more bells and whistles.

His spell bounced off, fractured, then enhanced, increasing in power as it sprayed back at him. He screeched and dove out of the back of the gazebo. Two of his people, waiting behind him, threw up their hands as the spell sliced right through them. He'd shot a nasty spell at me, and an even nastier one had been sent back.

Austin stood up on his hind legs and roared, the sound rumbling through the ground and crowding the air. Everyone in the area flinched and then cowered, unable to help themselves. A loud bang came from the banquet door. It flew off its hinges and tumbled onto the walkway. Men and women in black poured out of the door, all dressed the same, holding weapons and moving with lethal economy. Magical mercenaries.

An answering roar rode the tail of Austin's call, and then the basajaun launched himself into the fray, his long legs and hairy body quickly eating the distance between him and the enemy. He was at the gazebo in no time, his large teeth flashing, his arms swinging, and the enemies' eyes rounded comically.

"It's Bigfoot!" someone shouted, the pitch much too high for a man but coming from one all the same. "It's Bigfoot, save yourselves!"

Kinsella swallowed down a potion as the invisible people around me rushed forward, firing spells at us. Austin lowered and rushed right, out of my protective bubble and not worried about it. He swiped a woman with his great paw, smashing her to the side, before lunging forward and biting through a man's face.

My belly rolled and I turned away, my defensive spell doing my work for me. Even still, I zipped off a few more spells as the basajaun scooped someone up, bashed their head on the ground, and then threw them over the lip of the hill. He charged someone else, who immediately reduced down into a little ball of person, his arms over his head, shaking. He wasn't going to try to defend himself, too scared of the giant beast charging him. The basajaun's laughter at what he perceived a great joke made his incredible violence that much more gruesome.

"Jessie, Kinsella!" Sebastian stood in the center of the driveway, his own shield up and taking fire. He had just enough time to fling up a hand.

Kinsella had slipped out of the melee, coward that he was, and was now sprinting for the banquet hall.

But Austin and I were surrounded, under constant firepower, and their sheer numbers were doing the work for them.

Shifters exploded out of the trees at the base of the mountain. Wolves, big cats, a couple of bears, and one hippopotamus, of all things. Another group charged over the edge of the hill and onto the grass, a great Siberian tiger, Kingsley, leading the charge.

The mercenaries spread out in front of the banquet hall, movements unhurried, weapons at the ready. They would be the real danger.

I blasted someone with a spell. He fell away, revealing another enemy mage ready to fire at me. A snow leopard, Layan, flew through the air, tackling the mage and knocking him out of the way. I ran forward, just seeing Kinsella slip past his line of paid fighters. More people poured out of the banquet hall, the building clearly storing everyone who hadn't gotten potion.

My swear was drowned out by the cacophonous beating of the thunderbird's wings as Hollace rose into the sky. Cyra came next, then Ivy House's gargoyle crew, followed by the gargoyles from town, organized and ready for battle.

Niamh jetted out from behind and didn't waste any time. She pulled in her wings, tucked up her feet, and dove horn first. It hit a woman in the back and punched through. Her scream was short-lived, and Niamh tossed the woman over her back so she could move on to the next enemy.

The first line of mercenaries, nearly to Sebastian, took a knee and brought up their guns.

"Oh no." I ran harder, straight for him, not knowing what I'd do against actual bullets but not wanting him to take the brunt of this by himself. Kinsella would have to wait.

"No, Jessie." Sebastian flung out his hand to stop me. A wave of magic materialized in my path. I slammed into it and bounced off, knocked onto my butt. I brushed it off and sprang up as the mercenaries fired, some aiming for Sebastian, some aiming for shifters.

They weren't actual bullets. Zips of color, like lasers, shot out. Yelps blared through the space. A bear roared, a sound that was half pain, half anger. Sebastian threw up his hands, probably to fortify his shield.

Cyra swooped down out of nowhere in phoenix form. Mouth open, she ingested the zip of color meant for Sebastian. Fire flew out of her rear before she turned, flapping her wings for speed, and dive-bombed the mercenaries, blasting them with fire. Thunder rolled across the plane, and Hollace dove as well.

The mercenaries didn't so much as flinch. Those who were standing tilted up their guns to aim at him. They fired, but before the light could pierce Hollace, he let out another thunderous roar. Lightning charged the air around him, eating away whatever magic was fired from those guns.

Vampires rushed out from behind the mercenaries, lunging for the shifters. Gargoyles dove out of the sky, grabbing them and pulling them up, digging their claws in before dropping them. A fall like that wouldn't kill them, but Edgar was waiting down below. He turned from swarm to himself, grabbed a newly splatted vampire, and ripped off its head.

The kneeling mercenaries continued to fire, hitting vampires and shifters, not at all caring who was friendly and who was the enemy. More agonized howls and yelps filled the air as the colorful blasts found their marks.

A few wolves reached the mercenaries, lunging into the crowd. Two of the mercs, a man and a woman, stood and slung their guns over their backs. Knives came out of nowhere, and then they were all action, grappling with the large wolf bodies, their movements lightning fast. The woman plunged a knife into a furry belly, then dragged it across the wolf's throat.

"No!" I shed my clothes and changed, taking to the sky to get there faster. A zip of magic came for me, one of those lasers. It hit my shield and tried to bleed my magic away, but power boiled in my blood, fueled by the agonized wails all around me. By the vampires reaching the shifters, by Sebastian barely able to fight mages back while defending whomever he could against the mercenaries, by all of this unnecessary violence that Kinsella had forced on us.

I pumped my wings as hard as I could, pushing for speed. Cyra dive-bombed the line again, taking fire and giving it back. Hollace dove, snatching up a person in black in each taloned foot before swooping up, his electric energy taking them out instantly. I was there a moment later, scraping across someone's face and sending a blast of magic through their line. It exploded, tossing people into the air. But not before two of them got off shots. Their blasts hit Sebastian's shield and bled through it, striking his body.

A cry of fury shot out of me, slightly garbled by my fangs. Dark rage rose through me. I ripped out a throat with my claws and sent a magical kill shot of a spell, ripping someone apart, before covering the short distance to Sebastian. I grabbed him around the chest and hips, using my clawed feet as another way to hold him, and soared into the sky. I used my healing magic on him right away, cutting out his pain. Anguish in my heart, I lowered him onto the roof of the banquet hall, figuring it was the safest place for him. I set him down gently, splaying my clawed hand over the bleeding wound in his side and taking in his leg. Blood soaked through his shirt and pants. Those wounds would be closed shortly, hopefully before he bled out.

"Mu-scht halllllp odders," I said, hoping he understood.

He nodded, and a little smile tickled his lips. "Iron-heart. You have my allegiance...forever."

That answered the question of whether he would take the job.

I patted his shoulder and took to the sky. If Austin wanted brutal, I'd give these people brutal.

CHAPTER 33

S EBASTIAN WAITED FOR the angel of a woman to fly
away, vengeance on her mind. He watched her
descend on the mercenaries a moment later, swirls of
pink and purple magic trailing her, wondrous and
beautiful. She was everything his research had said she'd
be and then some. Beautiful of mind and body, majestic,
and so insanely powerful that he was giddy just thinking
about it. She had absolutely no idea the kinds of things
she could do with that power. How unstoppable she'd
be.

Assuming she didn't go the way of the others and
fall for the wrong man.

The magic could be transferred between Jessie and
her mate, when she chose one. From what Sebastian
had read, the ability was meant to help the mate protect
her. Unfortunately, in the past, the heirs had chosen
handsome young douches who'd wanted the power for
themselves. They always died, of course, but they
usually brought the heir down with them. By then, it

was too late to alter the way the magic worked.

This time, though…

The powerhouse of a polar bear shifter crossed the distance to Jessie in a rush of his own power, his ferocity and prowess unmatched. Not even a mythical phoenix could tear him down. The alpha wouldn't want to try to steal the Ivy House magic. He probably wouldn't even accept a gift like that from Jessie unless there was no other way.

Ivy House had chosen well in its heir, and the heir had chosen well in her mate. Or soon would. It seemed like they were still dancing around each other, each afraid to fall into the void of hearts and flowers and forever.

Sebastian groaned as he rolled onto his side, not feeling the pain but all too conscious that it was there. He'd let too much of the spear gun leak through, a magical gun intended specifically for harming mages. The guns weren't powerful enough to pierce his shield unless he was struck by seven at the same time. Or unless he allowed it to happen. He'd hoped someone would remove him from battle, or that he'd get the green light to crawl away.

Being put on the roof hadn't entered into his plans, though.

On his hands and knees, he crawled toward the back

of the building until his wounds had healed enough for him to stand and walk. Jessie's healing magic was on the case, plus his own fast healing patched him up. Moving so soon probably wasn't the greatest of ideas, but he couldn't wait. Very soon, Domino Kinsella would realize he had greatly underestimated the up-and-coming mage, and he'd get out of town. He was a fool, but he knew how to survive. Sebastian had to find him before he snuck away.

At the edge of the roof, Sebastian found a tree close enough to jump to, but that was more of a plan B. If he took the tree route, he'd probably miss the branch, fall, and break his neck. Jessie's magic wouldn't be able to save him from that. A couple of moments later, he spotted a trellis with ivy.

After slipping twice, knocking his knee and skinning his ankle, he finally managed to descend onto flat ground. His magical tracker spell pulsed in his middle. Somewhere right. His target was somewhere right.

He'd known it would go down like this the second he'd heard Domino issue that invitation to Jessie. Domino was a useless and disgusting mage who hated shifters more than most. Any idiot could have predicted he would not want to work with Jessie, and sure enough, he'd given offense at every turn. Sebastian had thought the alpha would crack Kinsella's neck in that first meeting, but it was Jessie who'd reacted, defending her mate. Very cute. Sebastian had put a tracker spell on Kinsella before he'd left the restaurant. Nothing to it.

The pulse grew stronger. The shouts and roars of the battle floated on the light breeze around the side of the building where Domino hid in a cluster of bushes. A peal of thunder drowned out the lessening blasts of the guns. The mercenaries were almost done, and they were the only ones capable of putting up a real fight.

"What kind of an idiot would pick a fight—" Sebastian began, cutting himself off to deflect a spell that burst from the bushes. He tsked. "That won't work on me, Domino, you should know that. As I was saying, what kind of an idiot would pick a fight with a mage who has a thunderbird and a phoenix at her disposal? Are you that dumb, or just suicidal?"

Another blast of magic erupted from the bushes, the power nothing. He waved it away, and then let the illusion dissolve to reveal his true appearance.

"Is that how you treat an old friend, Domino?"

Domino's face appeared against the leaves, his eyes rounded, his expression one of utter disbelief.

"Elliot Graves," he whispered.

Sebastian gave a little bow, acknowledging the name he'd chosen for himself in the magical world. Birth names, Sebastian in this case, were only for friends and family. And for new potential allies, Jessie wasn't ready to find out that he was Elliot Graves, not after all the hell he'd put her through, but hopefully she'd come around. He was well aware he'd have to eat crow.

He'd come clean to Ivy House, however. He'd visited the room of crystals and offered himself up to it. It could've killed him right then, or at any time thereafter. Instead, it had offered him more resources with which to train Jessie. The house had clearly agreed with him— his actions might not be conventional, but they *were* necessary. His master plan was coming along.

Sebastian just had to convince Jessie of that, preferably without the big alpha ripping his throat out before he could finish. But before that could happen, there was one more trick he had to pull off. One more little fib he would need to tell.

He knew Jessie was about to offer him a role on her team. If the circumstances had been different, he'd have taken it in a heartbeat, but the time wasn't right. The alpha had a bit more work to do on his territory, and Jessie needed to get those others on her crew, and *then* all could be revealed, and Sebastian could grovel for the first and only ally he ever planned to take. His late sister's *Sight*, the *Seeing* that had killed her, would not go ignored.

"In the flesh," Sebastian said. "Pray tell, what are you doing here?"

"What are *you* doing here?" Domino stepped out of the bushes.

"I'm protecting my interests, obviously. I thought it was quite clear to anyone listening that Jacinta of Ivy House was mine?"

Domino sneered. "All due respect, you always were a disgrace. You'd work with her...*team*?"

"Oops, your ignorance is showing." Sebastian lifted his eyebrows. "Her team is incredible. Even you should see that. It is so confusing to me—she's a female gargoyle, with a thunderbird, a phoenix, a puca, and other gargoyles on her team. Every one of them turns from human into something else, yet you're so fixated on the shifters." He put out his finger, and Domino flinched. "It's fear, isn't it? Shifters are terrifying. They are a force all their own, especially the alpha ones. Watch out for those, by the way." He rolled his eyes. "Oh, what am I saying? You won't need to watch out for them. You'll be dead."

Domino's sneer was a defense mechanism. "What do you think you'll do? I'm protected by the Mages' Guild. They will claim vengeance for my death."

Sebastian laughed. "The Mages' Guild would surely go after Jacinta Ironheart, this is true, but we both know they won't dare come after me. Which is why I will spare her the hardship and kill you myself."

A peal of thunder rolled through the sky, temporarily drowning out a few remaining gun blasts. It was almost over. Sebastian had to hurry this up.

"What do you want?" Domino straightened up. "Money? Meetings with my connections to get back into the magical elite? Done. If you want the halfwit mage, have her. She's nothing. I was simply curious."

"I have all the money I could ever want, actually. And no, I don't need your paltry connections. I need a body. My plans won't work without one. You'll do nicely. Your ugly mug doesn't matter much, because I'll give you a new one. Mine, if you must know. Well, not mine exactly, but the one I've been wearing." He let himself grin. "Around the shifters, she never worried about its expressionlessness. That was a stroke of luck."

Fear crept into Kinsella's eyes and his brow lowered. "You're nothing. Momar owns the magical world now, not you. He pushed you aside. You're lucky he didn't kill you."

"He certainly tried." Sebastian took a step forward. "There is a difference between stepping back from the magical world...and being pushed aside. I wanted to see about some predictions made by my late sister. My situation these past years was entirely voluntary, and entirely temporary. Soon I will reemerge. Hopefully I will do it with the only female gargoyle in existence, and the most powerful shifter alive. Soon I will take Momar's nightmares directly to him, and watch him dance."

CHAPTER 34

S ILENCE DESCENDED AROUND us. Movement slowed and then stopped, my team looking around for anyone still standing. None of our enemies were—those who hadn't fallen had fled.

Sucking in deep breaths, I changed back into my human form. "Check our people," I called out. "Make sure no one is too badly hurt. Call me if someone needs healing." I looked around the ground for my clothes, trying to stand straight and tall like the nakedness wasn't bothering me.

Shifters started moving immediately, some changing into human form and others staying furry. Cyra changed into human as well, her clothes magically still on. Totally unfair. She didn't check on our side, though—she checked on theirs. If she found someone moving around, she fixed the glitch.

"No, no, let them—"

"It has to be done," Kingsley said, also naked and giving me plenty of space. It shocked me mute, and I stared really hard at his face so I didn't give in to curiosity and accidentally check if he was blessed with size like his brother. "You have to send a message that you will not tolerate attacks."

Other shifters changed, Austin being one of them, and he immediately started looking after his people. He glanced my way but didn't say anything. He was leaving the call up to me.

I bit my lip as Cyra moved on to someone else. She pointed, and Hollace swooped down to blast the man with electricity. They were dividing up the gore for sport, it seemed like. For fun.

My stomach turned. My jaw hurt from clenching my teeth.

Sebastian limped out from around the side of the banquet hall, holding his side. The sight of his wounds tore at me.

"No." I continued to stare at Kingsley. I saw the spark of violence in his eyes, the evidence that he was not used to having his authority challenged.

But he had no authority here.

"No," I repeated. I threw bands around Cyra to keep her from cracking a wounded woman's neck. She struggled, trying to burn through my magic. I wouldn't allow it. "I can't do this. We will not continue to assassinate the wounded. That is not what I stand for.

They will be given a chance to reform." I raised my voice and backed it by magic. "If you are still alive, you will remain so. I'll do everything I can to make sure of that. But if you ever come back here, intending to do me or mine harm, I'll kill you myself. Is that clear?"

I didn't wait for them to respond. I assumed they wouldn't. Nor did I need Kingsley's curt nod. I would not compromise my own principles because things were done differently in the magical world. My people would have to live with that, or they could leave.

"Jessie, how can I help?" Sebastian asked as he neared me.

"Can you heal?"

"No. Not without a camping stove, pot, and potion ingredients."

"Then just rest. I'll handle it."

A roar ripped through the battlefield, and the basajaun literally drop-kicked someone over the edge of the hill, their body somersaulting through the air before it landed awkwardly and rolled away.

He stuck up his hand, not turning. "Last one, Miss Jessie. He tried to stab me. Vengeance was necessary. It is done."

I just blinked at him for a second. I didn't miss Kingsley's tiny smile before it morphed back into his hard alpha frown. Shaking my head, I got to work.

✧   ✧   ✧

A FEW HOURS later, Austin pulled up to Ivy House and I just sat in the passenger seat, exhausted in a way I hadn't known I could be. There had been a lot of people to heal. A *lot*. Each took energy. Some had required a lot of energy.

"I'm pissed Kinsella took off," I said, not lifting my head off the headrest. "He left all his people to fight and die for him, and he just left? What kind of a coward is that?"

"Mages aren't usually on the front line," Sebastian said from the back seat. The basajaun hadn't come back with us. He'd decided to head back to his mountain through the trees. I suspected he wanted to see if he could track down any escapees and deal with them how he saw fit.

Gargoyles landed on the front grass, the night cloaking them. Cyra and Hollace followed, the night showing off their respective flames and lightning. The police would probably get a few calls of unidentified animals flying through the night sky, but Austin's inside guy would hopefully handle it. The rest of my people had already landed, Edgar having been carried (it would be an incredibly long flight as a swarm of insects).

"You were," I commented as Austin got out of the

Jeep.

"I wasn't doing it for myself," Sebastian said. "I was doing it for you. Difference. I'm a peon, and you're a gargoyle, so we aren't breaking any stereotypes. In case that might bother you."

I smiled, happy he was okay. "Can you stay a little while? For tea or a beer or something?"

"Sure. I'm too tired to walk home right now, anyway."

Austin stopped next to me and, before I realized what he was doing, lifted me into his arms.

"I'm not hurt," I told him, though I didn't try to escape his arms. I didn't want to.

"You're more powerful than those spear guns," he murmured, his voice low and still full of pride.

I leaned my head against his shoulder. "I guess so."

"Are we thinking dinner or a snack?" Mr. Tom asked as Austin walked me to the door, having just shifted back to human.

"We're thinking ye need to cover yer bollocks," Niamh said. "They're down around yer ankles."

"It is an awful burden to have your company always forced upon us." Mr. Tom sniffed as he followed Austin and me indoors.

"I'm starving," I told Mr. Tom.

"Perfect. I shall prepare something and alert you

when it's ready. Austin Steele, will your brother be joining us?"

"No. He's going straight back to my house. Sebastian, follow us."

Austin took me back to my smaller, mostly private sitting room and situated me on his lap. It wasn't strictly the most professional setup, but I didn't care to fix it.

"You were magnificent today," he said as Sebastian detoured through the kitchen, apparently thinking he needed to take the long way and give us a moment. "I'm glad you stood up to my brother. I would have done things differently, but you need to stick up for what you believe in. I respect that."

"You *did* do things differently. I saw your guys help a few of the wounded into that good night."

Austin trailed his lips along my jaw. "It was your fight, but it happened in my territory, so…bygones? They were calling us filthy names."

I closed my eyes, soaking in the feel of his lips against my skin. "That's what I figured. I didn't try very hard to save the surly ones."

"You saved a good few mercenaries."

"Yeah, well, they were just doing a job. Niamh said that if I saved their lives, they wouldn't ever take a job against me again."

"They won't, especially since a good few of them want to join our territory."

"*Our* territory?"

He touched my chin and gently applied pressure until my lips were close to his. "Yes. Some called it yours. Some called it mine. Some called it ours. I think 'ours' makes the most sense. Your interactions with the magical world will always spill out of this property. You need to have a say in how things are handled." He kissed me softly.

"Is that allowed, though? Won't your people be confused?"

"Nothing about our setup is normal. They won't be any more confused than they are now." He kissed me again as Sebastian approached the door. Then Austin rose, lifting me with him, and deposited me onto the couch. "I know you want to ask him about joining the council, so I'll let you talk to him alone. When you're done, I'll meet you in your bedroom?"

A rush of heat stole through me and I nodded. Sebastian, just about to enter, hunched down and backed up, letting Austin pass.

"Hey," Sebastian said, straightening up as he came in. He stalled by the door. "Open or closed?"

"Closed, please."

He shut the door, and I closed my eyes and leaned

back.

"Tired?" he asked. "I mean, I know you're tired, but…"

"I am, yes. I've never done so much healing. Fighting with magic didn't actually tire me out like it has in the past. Like…" I frowned. "Kind of at all. It felt…so much easier."

"They were all so far below you. If we were to battle, it would be a different story. Or another mage of my caliber."

"You'd kill me pretty easily."

"In a one-on-one fight away from Ivy House, yes, I probably would. But only because I have more experience. Add in your alpha and his shifters, and I wouldn't give myself great odds, even with a team. I might run, like Kinsella did."

I frowned as my eyes met his pale gray gaze. "What do I do about that? Do I hunt him down, or assume he's learned his lesson?"

"In the magical world, normally I'd say you'd have to hunt him down, but you'd need to take him out in a cunning way, in cold blood, and I don't know that you are capable of that. Plus, your territory is not entirely established yet. Let him run in disgrace. If he resurfaces in any meaningful way, and he is a thorn in your side, then you take him out."

I nodded, taking a deep breath. "Listen, I wondered... First, do you know how the setup works here? The link with the Ivy House crew?"

"Yes," he said, and his eye color almost seemed to shift to the palest shade of blue, excitement sparking deep inside of them. In a moment, though, the effect was gone. My fatigue was getting to me. My desire to go upstairs and cuddle Austin was almost overwhelming.

"I wondered, would you like to join my crew? You'd get a room here and youthful vigor, though maybe you don't need it, plus the other perks Ivy House has to offer."

"I would, yes. But maybe..." He looked down at himself. "If I could shower..."

"Oh, totally." I held up my hand. "Sorry, yes, we can do it some other time once we've all recovered."

He nodded, and one of his weird, crooked smiles worked up his face. He looked out the window. "It feels good...to be asked."

"You're a valuable member of the team. It's a no-brainer."

His smile broadened. "Still feels good. That you think I'm good enough to join your team. That you don't look down on me for my oddities or my flaws."

I huffed out a laugh. "That would be something, wouldn't it? If I looked down on someone else for being odd and having flaws?" I raised my hand. "Hello? Pot calling the kettle black. Besides, everyone in this house is unpardonably odd and has more flaws than normal qualities. You fit in just fine."

Still smiling, still looking away from me, he nodded slowly. "I do fit in here. And maybe that's why she believed in me."

"Who?"

His eyebrows went up. "Oh. You. Sorry, I was lost in my thoughts. Well...if that's all?" He partially stood. "I don't want to keep you from your alpha. I might go home and shower now after all. I suddenly feel invigorated."

I laughed and stood, wobbling a little. He stepped forward to steady me, backing off when I gave a thumbs-up. "Welcome, in advance. To the team."

"Thank you."

I trudged up to my bedroom, not sure how much fun I'd be with Austin, since I could barely lug myself around. He'd have to do all the work, not that he'd mind.

Soft candlelight greeted me when I opened the door, flickering in the dimly lit room. Fresh roses in a vase sat on my little table by the window, which also held a bottle of wine and two glasses. Austin sat on the edge of my bed, bare-chested and godly, the top button on his jeans undone and his feet bare. His smile dwindled and his eyes took on a focused look to match the pulsing warmth radiating through the link.

Something about the way he was sitting there, dressed down and gorgeous, weakened my knees and made my heart swoon. This powerful, fearsome alpha had always let me see his softer side, the easygoing part of him with a little smile around his full lips. Both sides appealed to me—his power and strength, and his smiles and laughter. I'd been lucky to have him as a friend for all these months, and I was luckier still to have this new intimacy I couldn't seem to get enough of. I hadn't even totally given in to it yet, and it had still consumed part of my soul.

I'd need to figure all that out, eventually. Today, though, I just needed to chill. It had been a long day.

"Hey," I said, closing the door after me.

"Hey." He held out his arms, and I walked into them, dropping my hand to his shoulder, feeling the electricity zing between us.

He sat me down on his knee and ran his palm under my shirt and across my stomach.

"What do you think about a relaxing bath?" he asked. "You haven't felt one of my massages."

"Oh? Are they famous or something?"

"Probably not. I don't give them often, but I'm pretty sure they help pass the time."

I smiled and kissed his lips. "Sounds good."

He waited for me to stand before joining me, grabbing the bottom of my shirt and readying to pull it off.

A foot I didn't recognize stepped onto Ivy House soil. Austin paused. The intruder continued up the walk, the steps slow and clumsy, not in a straight line. A moment later, the person turned and ran off.

Mr. Tom approached the front door, and I waited to see what would happen, dread filtering through my middle. After every battle or magical hurdle, there was one person who'd always made his presence known. One person who'd always turned up.

The front door opened. Mr. Tom stepped out. Shock blasted through the link, and then sorrow, and then rage.

I was running before I'd made a conscious effort.

"Go get the miss," Mr. Tom shouted, perhaps to Ivy House, because no one else was there.

"I'm here." I took the stairs down two at a time, Austin right behind me. "I'm here. What is it?"

But he didn't need to answer me. As soon as I reached the threshold, I saw.

Sebastian lay sprawled out on the grass, a knife in his heart pinning a note to his chest. His face was so bloody that it was almost hard to tell who he was, but those sightless gray eyes were looking up at the sky. I recognized the shape of his face, too, and the clothes he'd been wearing when he'd left. I hadn't felt him on the grounds, so he must've been force-fed the potion to hide him from Ivy House. I'd put up a spell to unmask that potion, but it hadn't bothered Sebastian, it seemed.

"Because he's dead," I breathed, anger and sadness welling up through me. "My spell to unmask people seeks out pent-up energy and danger. He no longer has either."

The note read, *This was my employee. Then he was your employee. Now he is no one's employee. Want to come over for a drink next month? I'll send a jet. Check yes or no.*

Two square boxes were under that. He literally wanted me to check a box. He'd likely magically receive the answer. His name was at the bottom, no PS this time.

Tears clouded my vision. My hands balled at my sides. My gut twisted with guilt. I was the reason Sebastian was dead. He'd helped me, and I'd gotten him killed.

I couldn't do this anymore. I couldn't live with that nutcase dogging my every step, watching me from the shadows.

"Yes, I will meet him," I said through clenched

teeth. "I will meet him face to face, and I will kill him for everything he's done to me. Someone get me a pen."

"*I have a confession*," Ivy House said.

I waited for more bad news, and for a pen, and for the sobs to come. There had been too much death today. Austin had lost a few of his people, we'd taken the lives of more people than I cared to admit, and now Sebastian was gone, the guy who was supposed to join my team. My house. My life.

"*I deadened my magic with the phoenix so you'd fight,*" she said. "*You needed them on your side, and you also needed a little shove to give the blood oath. By putting you in a dangerous situation, I nudged you into it.*"

I closed my eyes, breathing through my nose. "*I don't care about that. I would've done it eventually anyway.*"

"*Just remember, I nudge because I love, and because sometimes you need it to reach your true potential.*"

"*This is not the time!*"

"*Good call. Chat later. Bye.*"

What'd she think, we were on a call?

Mr. Tom handed me a pen. I reached down and checked "yes."

The body disappeared.

Elliot Graves was ten times more advanced than I

was. More experienced. If he'd employed Sebastian as a peon, then he was probably leagues above him in terms of magical ability.

I gritted my teeth. I didn't care. I would take him on, and I would end his meddling in my life.

EPILOGUE

"IT'S BEEN AN enlightening visit, to say the least," Kingsley said, standing with Austin and me in the front yard of Ivy House. The rest of my people were in the house, flying around the woods, or tending to the flowers. Hollace had a green thumb, it turned out, and an eye for how a garden should look. He was quickly becoming Edgar's best friend. He didn't seem excited about that prospect.

It was a week after we'd ended the threat of Kinsella, although we still had no idea what had happened to the mage. Austin's territory was as buttoned up as it needed to be, and Kingsley was anxious to get back to his family and his own territory.

"I haven't taken orders from anyone but my wife in a long time," Kingsley said, his eyes twinkling and a grin on his lips. He was usually only this free with facial expressions at Austin's house, but clearly he was making an exception. "Not to mention I got to see some fabled creatures, including a female gargoyle and a freaking basajaun." He shook his head. "That thing was ruthless. I'm glad I got off his mountain alive. I would rather not tango with one of those."

"I hear that," Austin said.

"Can you handle it if I hug her?" Kingsley asked Austin.

"Yeah."

They weren't teasing.

Kingsley stepped closer and wrapped me in a bear hug, lifting me up and shaking me a little. I groaned as the air was squeezed out of me. He set me down and backed away, laughing.

"It was good meeting you, Jessie Ironheart," he said. "Thank you for pushing my brother back to his family. We've missed him. Maybe now he'll visit once in a while. And sorry about..." He pointed at the grass. "I don't tend to like mages, but he was all right."

I nodded, my guilt over Sebastian's death still fresh. "Thanks for coming," I said. "We couldn't have done it without you."

He clapped Austin on the back. "I figured I'd tell you here, in front of Jess. The people I brought knew going in that they'd have a choice to stay here and join your pack at the end of all this. I brought the guys and gals who never wanted you to leave in the first place, plus some newbies who need more room to advance than is available right now in my pack. All but a couple of them are going to stay."

Austin's eyes widened. "I can't let you do that."

"It's done. Consider it a territory-warming present. Once you get everything official, throw a huge feast for everyone."

"You're too good to me, brother." Austin put out his hand to shake.

Kingsley grabbed it and pulled him in closer, bumping chests and patting him on the back. "We're family, and families stick together. We want to hear from you. Aurora especially wants to hear from her Uncle Auzzie."

Austin nodded, his heart warm, his face unreadable. Kingsley nodded as though he knew how much his words meant to Austin, how much Austin had needed to hear them.

Kingsley gave me one last nod. "Take care of him, because he won't take care of himself. And let him take care of you. It's his job, and he won't want to do anything else."

"Okay."

To Austin he said, "Don't let her get into any trouble."

"Yeah, right, as though I could stop her," Austin replied with a laugh.

Kingsley looked at Ivy House one last time and then turned toward Austin's waiting Jeep. Austin gave me a quick kiss.

"Will you be around later?" he asked.

"Of course. I just have to finally sign the papers to make everything official with Ivy House, and then I'm free to leave."

"My house, then?" He chuckled softly and kissed me again. "I love you. See you tonight."

He was striding away before I could respond. Which was maybe for the best. My heart fluttered with joy to hear it, but I was still afraid to say it. To feel it. It seemed too soon. It seemed not soon enough.

Shaking my head, I headed into the house, up the stairs, and into the office, the furniture still the same as it had been on my last visit. I sat in the creaking leather chair and took a deep breath, placing my hands on the desk.

"Mr. Tom?"

"You *rang*?" He stepped into the room.

I rolled my eyes. "The ledger, if you please."

"Yes, miss," he said, and I could tell he was almost giddy with excitement and trying not to show it.

He laid a large tome on the desk in front of me, years and years of markings contained within its pages. He opened to the last used pages, the neat scrawl only reaching halfway down the second page. The total number in all the combined accounts stared back at me.

"This is after the winery expenses, right?" I asked.

"Yes, as you will see here." He traced a line farther up the page. "The cash has been sent to the escrow account. Tomorrow you go in to sign a few more documents and then it is all done."

"Right." I blew out a breath. "The blood oath is done, but I have to sign something, right?"

"Yes, for legal purposes." He brought over a rolled-up parchment, flattening it out in front of me. He held out a fountain pen. "Make your mark at the bottom."

A large X waited in front of a long line at the bottom of a document that was written in Latin or some other language I couldn't read. The text was dirty red and looked suspiciously like dried blood.

"It isn't blood, though, right?" I asked Mr. Tom.

"*It is blood,*" Ivy House said. "*It is your blood, collected from the soil and transferred here after you assumed your power. You have but to sign, and it is done.*"

I hadn't put that much blood in the soil, but I didn't see the point in saying so. They'd just tell me this could all easily be explained by magic.

I scribbled my name down.

Mr. Tom nodded, collected the paper, and rolled it

back up. "Fantastic, miss. You are now officially the rightful heir to Ivy House. Congratulations. The Havercamps no longer have a claim to this house, not that Peggy wanted it anyway after she was denied."

"Okay, then." I stared at the ledger. "We're going to automate this, I hope you know. Get a proper bookkeeping system up and running. Pay things online."

Mr. Tom pursed his lips. "If you say so."

"And this money..." I tapped the last number on the right. "I get that I can't pass it down or anything, but are there rules on what I can spend it on? Can I, like, buy a vacation house?"

"Yes, and Ivy House has several vacation houses and castles already. I haven't been to any of them, but the documents and details are in the filing cabinet. They probably all need work. Otherwise, you can do anything you like with it, miss, within reason. You can't give it all away to Austin Steele, or anything like that, for example. You may donate to a reputable charity up to a certain percentage per year. And no, you cannot take it with you when you die. It stays with the house, and will be transferred to the next heir. But you can pay off Jimmy's school tuition and your debts, and maybe buy yourself a nicer car and better clothes and fix up the furnishings."

"Yes, yes, I get it."

"Maybe a haircut and something besides sweats and jeans might be nice—"

"I got it. Fix myself up. Loud and clear." I shook my head, letting it sink in. "I'm a billionaire."

"As long as you are living, yes, you are a billionaire. One hundred and sixty times over. Not all liquid, though, let's be realistic."

I felt faint. "I might be the richest person in the world."

"Those things always change, but you'll certainly be one of them."

"What a crazy life."

"Yes, miss, I believe we covered that when you were trying to wrap your head around magic. Now, would you like to make any changes?"

I rubbed my eyes. "Give me some time to look through everything, Mr. Tom. I'm a whiz with a budget, not that I expressly need that skill now, but I need some time to sort through all this handwritten...stuff."

"Yes, miss. I'll bring up some coffee and snacks. Anything else?"

My head slid to what happened a week ago. To what would happen next month.

"No, thanks," I said, because money could fix many things, but it couldn't help me prepare for what I would be facing. I wasn't sure anything could. I'd need to learn attack and kill spells, and if I didn't basically use them before Elliot Graves could open his mouth, I'd be beaten before the duel started.

Because it would be a duel—of that I was certain—and I did not intend to lose.

THE END

About the Author

K.F. Breene is a Wall Street Journal, USA Today, Washington Post, Amazon Most Sold Charts and #1 Kindle Store bestselling author of paranormal romance, urban fantasy and fantasy novels. With over four million books sold, when she's not penning stories about magic and what goes bump in the night, she's sipping wine and planning shenanigans. She lives in Northern California with her husband, two children, and out of work treadmill.

Sign up for her newsletter to hear about the latest news and receive free bonus content.

www.kfbreene.com

CPSIA information can be obtained
at www.ICGtesting.com
Printed in the USA
LVHW030856110721
692343LV00001B/7